An Unattainable Stronghold

Book 8 of the Peninsular War Saga

by

Lynn Bryant

In loving memory of my uncle, William 'Bill' Bryant

And to my aunt, Joan Bryant, with much love

About the Author

Lynn Bryant was born and raised in London's East End. She studied History at Loughborough University and had dreams of being a writer from a young age. Since this was clearly not something a working-class-girl-made-good could aspire to, she had a variety of careers including a librarian, NHS administrator, relationship counsellor, manager of an art gallery and running an Irish dance school before she realised that most of these were just as unlikely as being a writer and took the step of publishing her first book.

She now lives in the Isle of Man and is married to a man who understands technology, which saves her a job, and has two grown-up children and two Labradors. History is still a passion, with a particular enthusiasm for the Napoleonic era and the sixteenth century. When not writing, she walks her dogs, reads anything that's put in front of her and makes periodic and unsuccessful attempts to keep a tidy house.

Acknowledgements

Research is a huge part of the writing I do, and I'd like to thank various historians and writers who have helped me with the maddest questions, especially Jacqueline Reiter, Gareth Glover, Rob Griffith, Rory Muir, Andrew Bamford, Zack White and Carole Divall, along with many others on social media and in person. Twitter is the best research tool. Thank you all.

Thanks to my fabulous editor, Heather Paisley. We've been friends for more than thirty years and it's insane I didn't think to ask her about editing services sooner. It turns out we work very well together and I'm looking forward to many more joint projects.

Thanks to Richard Dawson, my husband, for another amazing cover, for technical help and for endless support and patience during the writing of this book.

Thanks to my son Jon, for loving me, ignoring my historical ramblings and feeding me when I forget about dinner. Thanks to my daughter Anya for invading my study to play the piano and forgetting about dinner alongside me.

Finally, thanks to the stars of *Writing With Labradors* who share my study and bring me joy every day. Oscar, my big black Labrador is five now, a gentle giant and a very patient big brother. Alfie, the fox-red Labrador has just turned two and has brought new happiness and a whole new level of chaos to my daily life.

And in loving memory of Toby and Joey, the original stars of *Writing With Labradors*. You will both always be with me in spirit.

Chapter One

The far pickets caught sight of a small party of horsemen in the early afternoon. By chance there was an officer with them, a young ensign making an unscheduled inspection to check that the men were doing their job properly. Ensign Mortimer had found nothing wrong and had not expected to, but with no other duties he lingered for a while, talking to Corporal Kirk and his men.

Mortimer had joined the army just over a year ago and had been slightly shocked, during his first weeks with his new regiment, to discover that the rigid boundaries between officers and men were distinctly blurred in the 110th Light Infantry. He spent the first month feeling constantly worried that he was either too familiar with the men of his company or not familiar enough, but long hours on the march followed by his first experience of bloody battle had swept away his anxiety. The 110th held excellent discipline and Mortimer thought he was just beginning to understand how it worked. His commanding officer seemed perfectly happy with him and he had made some good friends. He had also lost one, along with several of his men, on the field of Vitoria. Shared sadness, Mortimer discovered, was a great leveller.

He was checking the girth on his horse in preparation for the ride back down to his billet when Corporal Kirk called to him.

"Riders coming up, sir."

Mortimer spun around, his heart beating more quickly. The Light Division had been enjoying a week's respite in the little mountain village of San Estevan with no sign of the French, but Mortimer had no idea how far away they were.

"Ours, Corporal?"

"Yes, sir. Only four of them. Not sure, but I think it might be Lord Wellington."

Mortimer swung himself into the saddle and reached for his small field telescope. He opened it and put it to his eye, looking out over the valley which was shimmering peacefully in the afternoon heat. It had rained during the night and the meadows were just beginning to dry out, with small clouds of steam above some of the puddles. The four horsemen were still some way off; three redcoats and a man in a blue jacket wearing a simple bicorn hat. He was mounted on a dark-chestnut horse with a slightly unusual gait and Mortimer had no difficulty in recognising the Commander-in-Chief, riding Copenhagen, his favourite mount. He snapped his glass shut.

"I think you're right, Corporal. Better make sure you're all properly turned out. I don't give a damn about open buttons and that bottle Stephens is trying to hide in his pocket, but his Lordship won't be amused."

Kirk saluted, grinning. "Yes, sir. Sorry, sir, should have offered you some."

"How could you, when I can't even see it? I'll take the message down to the General."

"Reckon we'll be on the move, sir?"

"Yes, tonight or tomorrow. It's a shame, I'll miss this place."

Kirk gave a crack of laughter. "Aye, I reckon most of the young officers will miss the sight of the local girls doing their laundry in the stream each morning, with their skirts hitched above their knees. It's been a rare entertainment watching you all jostling for the best viewpoint, sir."

Mortimer felt himself flush a little but grinned, knowing himself guilty. "No harm in looking, Kirk."

"That there isn't, sir. Best get going. His Lordship doesn't hang about."

Mortimer acknowledged Kirk's salute and took the steep track down into San Estevan at a brisk canter. He passed his own billet and took the road on the far side of the village which led up to a substantial farmhouse, framed against a glorious backdrop of flower-strewn hillsides and soaring mountains. It rained a lot in this upland country but the sunny days were so perfect that they seemed to make up for it. Mortimer looked around him a little sadly. After the relentless pace of marching and fighting which had given Wellington's army only a few days respite in three months, it had been wonderful to have a week to rest and recover in such a beautiful place.

Mortimer slowed his pace as he approached the farmhouse. The weather had brought a number of the officers of the Light Division out of doors. Several of them had carried a wooden table outside and were playing cards, while others sprawled on blankets or on the damp grass reading or writing letters. Mortimer scanned the various groupings and spotted his company officer, Captain Fenwick. He was seated on a stool with a portable writing desk balanced on his knee, frowning hideously at a ledger. Mortimer dismounted and looped his reins around the wooden fence, then went through the gate. Fenwick looked up as he approached and closed the ledger with an expression of relief.

"Thank God: an interruption. I'm beginning to adjust to most of my duties as temporary brigade-major, including being the first in the firing line when he's pissed off. But Manson needs to get back here soon or I'll die of administrative duties. What is it, Mortimer? Anything wrong with the sentries?"

"No sir, but while I was up there I could see Lord Wellington approaching."

2

Fenwick gave a sigh and got up, setting the ledger down on the stool. "Damn it, I was hoping he wouldn't turn up until tomorrow. All right, Ensign, I'll tell the General. Will you ride down to General Alten's headquarters and give him the joyous news?"

"Yes, sir."

Fenwick looked around, then raised his voice. "Colonel Wheeler, any idea where General van Daan is?"

Colonel Johnny Wheeler looked up from his hand of cards. "Inside the house, I think. Is there a message, Mr Mortimer?"

"Lord Wellington is on his way, sir, I saw him riding in from the top picket station."

"Ah, I see." Wheeler rose, putting down his cards. "It seems we'll need to finish this another time, gentlemen. Best get back to your men and make sure they're ready to march if we have to. I'll go and find…"

"There is no need to institute a search, Colonel Wheeler," another voice said. Mortimer looked around him in surprise and then up at the house. An open window on the first floor had been raised further and a fair head appeared. Mortimer stared up and managed an awkward salute.

"Sorry, sir, I didn't know…"

"Nor were you supposed to, Ensign, I was congratulating myself on having sneaked off very successfully. What's going on?"

"Lord Wellington is on his way down, sir. Thought you'd want to know."

There was a brief silence and then the man above spoke again.

"Well I didn't. But I suppose I know now so I can't pretend ignorance. All right, gentlemen, let's get moving. Whether tonight or tomorrow, the holiday is over. But given the frequent inefficiency of the commissariat, we are not going anywhere until we've eaten dinner and if Lord Wellington tries to make us, I'm going to shoot him in the head. Captain Fenwick, get messages sent out to Alten, Kempt and Skerrett. Ask them to dine with us, will you? I'll let Sergeant Kelly know. His Lordship is going to want some time to yell at me before we march out. We might as well make it easy for him. Get moving all of you."

Mortimer saluted again although it felt ridiculous. He thought that Major-General Paul van Daan, who was in shirt sleeves with tousled hair, looked as though he had been taking an afternoon nap. His commander returned the salute with a grin and began to withdraw back into the room, but misjudged the space and hit the back of his head on the window frame with a sharp crack which made Mortimer wince.

"Are you all right, sir?" Wheeler called up.

"No, I am not all right, Colonel, thank you for asking," Van Daan bellowed. "Although maybe I should have tried a bit harder to knock myself out and then you could take over command of the brigade and I could go back to bed. O'Reilly, fuck off and do your job, I can see you laughing."

There was another sound of laughter, a woman's voice floating from the General's room. "Oh dear, that sounded painful. Come inside, Paul and let

3

me check you've not injured yourself. After that, I'll go and speak to George about dinner."

There was another muttered curse and the window slammed shut. Around the garden, the officers were moving, rolling up blankets and going back to their billets, where hopefully they would have time to dine before Lord Wellington's orders sent them on the march again. Mortimer suspected that his face had turned pink. He wondered if he was the only man present who had not realised that General van Daan's decision to take a siesta had nothing to do with sleep. He caught Colonel Wheeler's eye. Wheeler smiled sympathetically.

"Get yourself down to General Alten, Ensign and then go and find some food. Depending on Lord Wellington's mood, this could be a very long day."

***

Having soothed her husband, helped him dress and sent him on his way, Anne van Daan called for her Spanish maid to bring more water to wash with, still smiling at Paul's show of bad temper. She was not fooled. After almost a week living in idyllic conditions in San Estevan, he had already been showing signs of restlessness and she recognised that he was ready to resume the march. Privately, Anne thought that they could all have done with a little longer, given the relentless pace of this campaign, but four years of army life had accustomed her to sudden changes and she had done most of her packing two days ago when Lord Wellington had written to warn them of his arrival.

She sat before her portable mirror as her maid did her hair and thought how quick and deft Ariana had become. Anne was good at managing without a maid but she was beginning to appreciate the Spanish girl's single-minded determination to be good at her job. She also enjoyed her company. She had employed Ariana, whom most of the brigade still referred to by her nickname of Brat, so that the girl could accompany the army on campaign and not be separated from Captain Michael O'Reilly, with whom she was conducting a surprisingly decorous courtship. Anne had intended it as a good deed but she had come to the conclusion that she had done very well out of the bargain.

When she was ready, Anne rose and looked around for her shawl, then smiled to see that Brat was already holding it for her.

"Thank you, Ariana. Have you finished packing?"

"Almost, Señora. Do you think we will leave today?"

"If not, it will be early tomorrow. Make sure you remember to eat something, it never pays to forget about food at the beginning of a march."

"I will eat in the kitchen, Señora. You should go, it sounds as though Lord Wellington has arrived."

His Lordship was just entering the big farmhouse living area as Anne arrived down the stairs. Paul went to greet him, saluting, and Anne moved forward to join her husband, glancing around the room to make sure that her large dog was not present. She did not think Lord Wellington would be keen to meet Craufurd at the moment.

4

"It is very good to see you, my Lord. Would you like some wine? I've asked Jenson to serve it in the garden, it's such a lovely day. I hope you will stay to dine with us."

Wellington snorted but he took Anne's hand and bowed over it. "I thank you, ma'am, but this is not a social visit. I have orders and the Light Division must be on the road at dawn."

"Of course," Anne said smoothly, treading on Paul's foot as he opened his mouth. "That is why General van Daan has asked Generals Alten, Kempt and Skerrett to join us. That way, you may give your orders over dinner."

Wellington's expression of baffled exasperation caused Anne to bite the inside of her lip to avoid laughing. He stood looking down at her for a long moment then seemed to realise he was still holding her hand. He released it hastily and glared at Paul, who was not even attempting to hide his amusement. Anne flashed both of them a smile and took Paul's arm, steering him firmly in the direction of the garden where Jenson, Paul's orderly, was setting wine and glasses out on the table which was now covered with a white cloth. Anne wondered where he had found the cloth.

"Wipe that smirk off your face, Van Daan, or I will remove you from command," Wellington said.

"Sorry, sir. I wasn't laughing at you, it's just the sight of my wife managing the army always brings joy to my heart. Thank you, Jenson, we'll pour for ourselves. Can you bring the others through when they arrive please?"

"Yes, sir."

When Jenson had gone, Wellington accepted a wooden chair and a glass of wine and sipped it. "The best wine, General? Are you hoping to ingratiate yourself with me?"

"No sir, I just like good wine and this one probably won't travel well. How are you?"

"Irritated," Wellington said. "And keen to progress with the campaign. Have you really invited Alten and the others to dinner?"

"They'll be here soon, sir."

Wellington grunted. "Well. Yes, I suppose that was a good idea. I will remain here tonight and return to Lesaca tomorrow. Are your men ready?"

"Yes, sir, we did final kit inspections yesterday and the baggage wagons are loaded up apart from the usual last minute essentials. Which in our case appears to include a rather fine linen table cloth. Any idea, Nan?"

"None at all. Perhaps it belongs to the farmer. It can't be ours, it would be covered in stains by now."

"It would have been ripped up for bandages by now," Paul said. "What are our orders, sir? Or do you want to wait until the others arrive?"

"I will wait, I believe. In the meantime, I wish to speak to you about another matter. My hunting bitch, in fact."

Anne's foot hovered above Paul's under the table but he managed to maintain a grave expression. "Yes, sir, you mentioned the problem in your letter.

5

I understand she's due a happy event. Any idea when? Has the veterinary surgeon seen her?"

Wellington almost growled. "Do not provoke me, General. I am confident that I can predict to within a day or two when those puppies will be born. All I have to do is count from the occasion when your mongrel escaped from the stables at headquarters. I am furious. She is a well-bred hunting greyhound and if I decided to breed from her, I had intended to choose her mate very carefully with an eye to his pedigree. Instead, I am faced with the prospect of a litter of oversized shaggy animals of uncertain ancestry."

"I wonder what the puppies will look like?" Paul said with sudden interest. "Rather like very fast hearthrugs, I should think."

Anne managed not to laugh. Wellington shot him a look of pure loathing. "Pearl is far too young to breed," he snapped. "If anything happens to her I shall be seriously displeased."

Paul opened his mouth to speak and closed it again as Anne gave a little warning shake of her head. She enjoyed his sense of humour but she did not think this was the right time for it. Behind his assumed anger she could sense that Wellington was genuinely upset.

"I'm so sorry, sir," she said quickly. "Please don't blame Paul, it was my fault. I asked him to take Craufurd with him that day, he needed a run and I was busy. I should have thought about Pearl. He's my dog and I take full responsibility for what has happened. You must be very worried."

Wellington flushed a little and Anne saw Paul sit back with an expression of enjoyment which she considered extremely ill-timed. "I do not blame you, ma'am, you could not have known. And I have no time to worry over a dog; it is a trivial matter compared to the running of this campaign. I have so much on my mind, I cannot afford this distraction. Only..."

He broke off as though changing his mind about what he had been about to say. Anne studied the tired face and felt a rush of compassion. "Only you are very fond of her."

Wellington looked up quickly, as though startled. "Fond...oh, yes. Yes, I suppose I am. She has become my constant companion. It must sound foolish."

"If it is foolish, then it's a folly I share, my Lord. I'm devoted to Craufurd with all his faults. He saved my life in that river last year. And like Pearl, he's still young. We really are sorry, but you don't have to manage Pearl. If you're right about when it happened, and I'm sure you are, it will only be another few weeks. I'll give you all the help I can. If necessary, you can leave Pearl with us, she can travel in my carriage..."

"No," Wellington said quickly. "She can remain...she will be safe with my grooms, they take good care of her. But at the birth, ma'am, if you could see your way to helping..."

"I promise I will."

Wellington gave a small smile. "Thank you." He shifted his gaze to Paul and managed another glare although Anne could see that he was feeling happier. "As for you, General, since it was your carelessness that brought about

6

this unfortunate event, bend your mind to finding homes for these puppies once they are weaned. And you will not bring that hound to headquarters again."

Paul smiled and Anne observed that his amusement had softened into sympathy. "I promise, sir. As for the puppies, I'm sure I can find owners for them. Andrew Barnard sounds like a good candidate, he can talk to the dog instead of himself when he's inebriated. And perhaps Harry Smith would like one, to keep that pug of his wife's company."

Anne decided it was time to intervene. Paul loved a problem to solve and she could see by the faraway look in his blue eyes that finding homes for puppies had temporarily driven all thought of the continuing campaign from his mind. She rose.

"If you will excuse me, my Lord, I think I see my remaining guests approaching. I will leave you to discuss your orders while I check on the kitchen. Paul, if you're about to start compiling a list of suitable dog owners, stop it. We've plenty of time."

Her husband looked surprised, as if he had temporarily forgotten the real purpose of this meeting, then grinned.

"Sorry, sir. I got carried away. Thank you, girl of my heart. Will you find Johnny and Philip Norton and ask them if they'll join us for dinner as well? Sir, how is Sir Thomas Graham getting on at San Sebastian? I feel as though I've not seen you for months, it's been like living in another world out here. I'd almost forgotten there was a war on."

Wellington took another sip of wine and gave a small grim smile. "Allow me to remind you, General," he said. "I should have asked, ma'am, if your table can accommodate my companions. I brought Somerset, Gordon and March with me though I've no idea where they went."

"They're hiding in the dining room with Giles Fenwick until you've finished yelling at me," Paul said helpfully. "Send them out for some wine, would you, Nan? I think the worst is over."

***

Lord Wellington had set up his headquarters in the village of Lesaca, which was fifteen miles to the north of San Estevan. He rode at the head of the Light Division beside Lieutenant-General Charles Alten, the Hanoverian commander. Wellington had requested the attendance of Paul on the first part of the march and then as an afterthought suggested that Major-General Kempt and Major-General Skerrett should join the party as well. Paul thought it an improvement on the recent Vitoria campaign where Wellington had appeared to forget for whole periods of the battle who was actually in command of Kempt's brigade. He wondered if Alten had found a way to tactfully remind him. Alten was an excellent general and a skilled diplomat and managed Wellington very well.

The division marched along a winding mountain track which followed the course of the river. At times the height above the water was dizzying and

Paul thought, not for the first time, that getting artillery over some of these mountains was going to be a nightmare for those responsible. He was glad it was not him. After two years in command of his brigade, he was very comfortable in his position and had no desire to change it. Occasionally in the past, Wellington had hinted at a staff post, but he had never attempted to push the idea beyond Paul's firm refusal. Paul's friendship with Wellington allowed him to get away with more than most other officers but he did not think it would survive daily life at headquarters.

There had been some changes to both the division and Paul's brigade in the aftermath of Wellington's defeat of the French at Vitoria. At brigade level, Paul had said a regretful farewell to the battalion of the King's German Legion which had served under him since just before Fuentes de Oñoro and had now been transferred to another division. He had liked the Germans, but he had to admit that with the addition of five companies of the 115th, his brigade had become unwieldy. He had wondered if Wellington might decide to move Lieutenant-Colonel Norton and his battalion elsewhere but so far there had been no mention of it. They were not formally designated as light infantry but had fought well at Vitoria. Paul was developing a good relationship with Norton and hoped that they remained with him for a while.

At divisional level, Paul regretted the loss of General Vandeleur who had been transferred to the cavalry. He had not really had much opportunity yet to get to know his replacement at the head of the second brigade. John Byrne Skerrett had served widely in the West Indies, India and at the Cape of Good Hope before arriving in Spain. Initially he had been in Cadiz then had moved to the Fourth Division under Wellington for a short time. Paul had met him socially and found him pleasant but somewhat distant. He was only a few years older than Paul, a dark intense man who did not seem to find it easy to join in with the cheerful banter between the other Light Division officers. Paul hoped he would settle down once he got used to it, though he wondered if Skerrett was ever going to get accustomed to the exuberant good humour of Captain Harry Smith, his brigade-major, whom he had inherited from Vandeleur. Paul had known Smith for years and even he found him exhausting at times.

The small town of Lesaca sat astride the River Onin, a tributary of the Bidassoa. It was a charming town of cobbled streets and graceful houses, with a selection of defensive towers and small palaces which testified to its prosperity. Wellington had acquired a Basque guide called Xavier; a slight man in his twenties who clearly understood Spanish perfectly but spoke it with such a heavy accent that only Anne seemed able to make out most of what he said. Paul wondered how useful it was to have a guide that was impossible to understand but he did not mention that to Wellington who seemed unusually cheerful after a good meal and a night's sleep.

Xavier was visibly dazzled by Anne and finding her full of questions about the town and the surrounding area, drew his hardy mountain pony alongside her black mare and prepared to enjoy himself. Paul rode beside Kempt, glancing behind him occasionally with a smile. During Anne's early days in

Portugal when she was still married to her brutal first husband, Paul could remember being fascinated by both her language skills and her ability to talk easily to everybody from Lord Wellington down to the camp followers. Paul was no longer surprised by either and used her talents shamelessly when diplomacy was required. He knew that Wellington often did the same and as the thought came into his head, he glanced behind again and then over at Wellington, more sharply. Wellington was also looking round, watching Anne and his new guide and Paul moved Rufus, his roan gelding, closer to the Commander-in-Chief saying softly:

"If you're recruiting my wife into the ranks of your exploring officers, sir, it would have been polite to mention it."

"To you or to her?"

"Either. Both. What's going on?"

"This man, along with a number of others, was released from a French prison in the town after their troops fled and we moved in. I am told that he is a pedlar by trade and knows these mountain villages and passes extremely well. The French attempted to obtain his services and he was un-cooperative which is why he was imprisoned. I want to use him, but although it's clear he understands me very well, his speech is almost unintelligible. We need a fluent translator and my agents are searching for one but it suddenly occurred to me that your wife has an unusually good ear for languages and might have some success with his accent. It sounds as though I was right. Don't worry, General, I was not intending to ask her to ride off into the hills with him. But I would like to borrow her while I interview him. It will only take an hour or two and I'll send her on with an escort…"

"In these mountains, with very little idea of the terrain and the presence of the French? I don't think so, sir, do you? She'll remain with the brigade until we've seen the situation at Vera. Once we're properly encamped, I'll bring her myself if you need her. I don't send her off with an escort these days."

Wellington's austere expression softened slightly. "Of course. I'm sorry, I did not think. Whenever it is convenient to you, General."

Paul nodded, but did not reply. He knew his tone had been sharp and he appreciated Wellington's understanding. It had been eighteen months since Anne's capture by the French had led to a horrific ordeal. Anne appeared to have made a remarkable recovery, apart from an occasional nightmare, but it left Paul permanently on edge about her safety.

The brigade halted on the edge of Lesaca with permission to cook their meal and Wellington extended an invitation to Alten and his brigade commanders to dine with him before resuming their march. Paul suspected it would be nothing more than cold meat and bread and if Wellington were not so keen to foster Anne's conversation with his maddeningly elusive guide he would have not have invited them at all.

The town was attractive, despite the air of bewildered chaos caused by dozens of red-coated officers and staff members milling about trying to find billets and stabling for their horses. Lord Wellington had taken possession of a

9

surprisingly comfortable house which stood in the shadow of an imposing tower beside the river. The tower had already been commandeered for those members of headquarters who could not be accommodated in the main house. The river stretched between two cobbled streets through the centre of the town, and a myriad of tiny canals ran off it reminding Paul of a miniature version of Venice, which he had visited many years ago.

Paul moved away from the chaos to give orders about the disposition of his troops and the behaviour expected of them during their brief stop. He was exasperated by the delay and would have preferred to march on immediately towards the town of Vera, where the Light Division had orders to evict the French pickets and take possession of the town and the heights of Santa Barbara.

"Lord Wellington seems surprisingly hospitable today, General."

Paul glanced around to see that he had been joined by General Alten. The Hanoverian was at his most bland. Paul grinned.

"Isn't he? He's got my wife trying to make sense of his Basque guide for him. God knows why. With a bit of time and patience, probably anybody could understand the man; he's speaking Spanish. Just very, very strangely."

"I think it peculiar that you should use the words time and patience so casually in a sentence about Lord Wellington, General," Alten said in a tone of mild reproof. Paul snorted with laughter so loudly that Wellington turned to glare at him suspiciously.

"If you wish to eat, General van Daan, I suggest you join us," he snapped. "You'll need to be on the road in an hour."

He offered his arm to Anne and disappeared into the house. Paul gave Alten a look. "Don't do that to me, sir, I nearly choked. I appreciate his Lordship's problem, but we could have done without this halt. Don't tell me the French don't have scouts out. They were always going to know we were coming, but now they've an extra hour to prepare."

"They do, General, but we also have our scouts out watching them. If they are making preparations for a stand, there is no sign of it. Come, let us eat in case the supply wagons get lost in the dark again."

They ate dishes of cold meat and salads laid out by Wellington's servants in a long, panelled dining room. The meal was constantly interrupted by the comings and goings of staff members trying to set up headquarters and Paul was entertained by the sight of Lord Fitzroy Somerset, Wellington's young military secretary, who was covertly grabbing slices of chicken and ham to eat on the move as he passed through. Somerset caught his eye and grinned at him and Paul smiled back.

When the meal was over, Wellington remained closeted with Anne and his guide for another half hour while the Light Division commanders returned to their men and gave orders to form up for the march. Paul could feel a rising tension as the long column fell into place and there was still no sign of Anne.

"She'll be here, sir," his second-in-command said reassuringly. "He wants us gone and he must know you well enough to know you won't leave without her."

10

"He bloody ought to. Well if Alten gives the order to march in a minute, you're in command of the brigade, Colonel Wheeler, while I go and retrieve her. I don't know why I'm so edgy about it today, but I am."

"It's new territory, sir. We don't know these mountains the way we got to know the Portuguese border and we're alarmingly close to France here. I'm not surprised you want to be cautious."

Paul looked at his friend and relaxed a little, smiling. "You're remarkably soothing, Johnny, do you know that? You're right of course. It feels a little odd to realise we could actually march into France from here in less than a day. I've spent almost five years trying to imagine what it would feel like to push them back this far. To be this close. Now I'm here it's a bit nerve-wracking."

"You think they're preparing to make a stand?"

"I think they're preparing to make an assault, Johnny. We might have taken them apart at Vitoria, but we did not destroy them and we all know that they have the ability to rebuild a functioning army quicker than we ever can. They've caught us napping far too often because Wellington underestimates that ability. I really hope he gets it right this time."

Johnny was looking over Paul's shoulder. "Well he's got one thing right at least," he said. Paul turned and felt an irrational flood of relief at the sight of his wife cantering over one of the small bridges from the town, her Portuguese groom riding behind her and six cavalry troopers surrounding her. The escort was clearly excessive for such a short ride back to the column and Paul laughed inwardly and mentally chalked up a point to Wellington. He had never understood why so many officers claimed that their commander had no sense of humour. On occasion, his comic timing was perfect.

Anne reined in beside Paul and dismissed her escort with a warm smile of thanks, which Paul thought would probably give the younger men unsuitable dreams for days. When they had cantered back over the bridge into the town, she turned to Paul.

"I'm sorry, General, were you getting anxious?"

"No," Paul said.

"Yes," Johnny interpolated with a grin. "He was just about to come in search of you, ma'am. Were you able to help his Lordship?"

"I believe so, although I'm not sure how much of the information will be useful. I discovered some fascinating facts about the town, which is a centre for iron and metal working. I also know a great deal about the girl Xavier hoped to marry, who chose a blacksmith with a more settled job. I then spent fifteen minutes trying to explain to his Lordship that he does not need a translator because Xavier understands and speaks Spanish very well. He just needs to learn some patience and listen without interrupting. It's a Basque accent not Chinese. Now that I am becoming used to it, I rather like it. Sorry, I'm chattering on and I can see you need to go. Do you want me to go to the rear with the baggage?"

"I think so, girl of my heart. Alten's scouts tell him the French have skirmishers swarming all over the slopes above Vera so we may see some

11

sporadic fighting. Best not take any chances." Paul leaned from the saddle to kiss her. "I don't suppose there's the least chance that Wellington will listen to your advice but thank you for trying. I'll see you soon. Costa, take care of her."

The groom assented enthusiastically and Anne rolled her eyes and pulled a face before turning Bella towards the rear of the long column. Paul had employed Isair Costa in the months after Anne's captivity, more to calm his own ragged nerves than because Anne really needed a groom. For a while Paul had not thought it was going to work. Anne was fiercely independent and loathed feeling coddled or restricted and Costa had been shocked at the range of her activities and unable to hide his disapproval at her freedom to go where she chose without reference to her husband. Time seemed to have improved their relationship, however. Costa was learning, somewhat painfully, not to make lengthy reports to Paul about Anne's lack of propriety and Anne had become used to his constant presence at her heels. She teased him unmercifully and he repaid her with a devotion which reminded Paul of Anne's enormous dog.

Reassured about his wife, Paul turned his attention back to his job. The Light Division marched in brigade order which meant that Paul's job was to protect their rear. He did not expect to see any action today unless Alten's scouts had got it badly wrong, which was unlikely. They marched at a brisk pace towards the village of Vera and Paul was surprised to see signs of enemy activity almost immediately. Wellington had given the impression that the first French troops were a long way off, but they were close by, though not in great numbers, clearly visible on the hills of Santa Barbara which soared above the village.

With the enemy in sight, Alten halted his column and gave his orders, sending Kempt's brigade forward to the lower slopes of Santa Barbara. Paul's brigade, kept well to the rear, had an excellent view of the green-coated riflemen making their way steadily up towards the French, followed by the red jackets of the 43rd. It was steep going and Paul approved the caution of the riflemen as they approached some crumbling stone walls, pushing the French out from behind them and onwards through a series of orchards. The trees were ideal cover for skirmishing but, apart from an occasional flurry of shots when the 95th came too close, the French put up little resistance. Clearly these were outposts, with orders to retreat if pressed. Paul was not surprised. There was no point in trying to defend the village and lower hills when there was an excellent position straddling the Puerto de Vera as it crossed the mountains through a rocky pass into France. There were French reinforcements available across the river but Wellington had sent Spanish troops to keep them occupied and to prevent them going to the aid of the troops in Vera.

As the Rifles cleared the upper slopes, the 43rd drove the French from the town. Paul watched the action from horseback at the edge of the lines, curbing his impatience. He had never been good at inactivity and it was painful to observe from the rear while other men fought, but experience had taught him to manage his irritation. He knew that Alten was right; there was no need to throw three brigades into action where one would do perfectly well and if fresh troops were needed they could be deployed very easily.

By nightfall the Rifles had reached the peak of the Santa Barbara heights. All shooting had died away and the sound of cheering floated down from the top. Paul was in the middle of issuing orders to bivouac his brigade for the night. He paused, listening and grinned at his brigade-major.

"Sounds as though they're there. Noisy bastards. Do you think Colonel Barnard has managed to haul a crate of Spanish wine up there? We should have searched him."

Giles Fenwick laughed. "Too late for that, sir. It's a bit steep for a crate of wine but I'd bet he's got a bottle of French brandy with him."

"Probably a gift from my wife. I don't begrudge it to him though. He's stuck up there in a howling wind all night whereas I intend to find a nice warm spot in that barn and eat my rations along with the smoked ham that Wellington gave to my wife earlier. Get them settled, Captain. We're not getting called out tonight now. If they were going to try an attack on the village they'd have done it by now. Make sure the pickets are wide awake and tell the officers not to let the men drink anything more than their grog ration. I want them ready to fight at dawn, we're going to kick the remaining French out of the churchyard. If they've not already gone by then, which I bet they will have."

"Yes, sir."

"Carry on then, Captain. Oh, Giles?"

"Sir?"

"When you've done, come and join us. Unlike poor Barnard, I do have a couple of bottles of wine and you can share the ham."

The younger man gave a broad smile and saluted. "Thank you, sir. Be with you as soon as I can."

Chapter Two

With the French dislodged from both the village and the hills above it, the Light Division settled down to await further orders. Kempt's first brigade was encamped on the slopes of Santa Barbara while the second brigade under Skerrett, was settled in the valley close to the town of Vera. After some discussion with Wellington, Alten instructed Paul to set up camp two miles further east, towards the French border. The ground was excellent, with gentle rolling pastures where cattle, sheep and goats grazed peacefully beside a bubbling stream, almost big enough to be called a river, which was lined with graceful trees. It was good farmland running crops, fruit trees and livestock.

Captain Simon Carlyon felt sorry for the local farmers. He had accompanied Giles Fenwick and Captain Ross Mackenzie on a tour of the local farmsteads where Paul's brigade-major explained what was about to happen to some of their pastures and made helpful suggestions about removing their livestock to higher ground. Paul never made the mistake of assuming all his men honest and in addition to his outlying pickets who were watching for the French, he had set an inner ring whose job it was to keep an eye on any man straying from the camp. Punishment was swift for a man caught stealing, but that would be no consolation to a farmer who had lost a valuable sheep and half his poultry.

"We got the best of the three camp sites," Simon remarked as they rode between two farmsteads. The buildings were similar to the wooden farmhouses they had stayed in during their brief time in San Estevan. It was a bright morning and Simon shaded his eyes to look up to the mountains, soaring into brilliant blue skies above the foothills. "Luck, do you think, or a gift from Lord Wellington to Mrs van Daan?"

Ross Mackenzie, who was Paul's senior quartermaster laughed aloud. "Well it might be," he admitted. "When I first arrived I thought that was a regimental joke, but now that I've seen what he's like with her, I realise there's something to it."

Giles chuckled. "Not this time," he said. "There are several reasons. We're right in the centre here which means if either of the two brigades gets into trouble, we can get there fast. We're also closer to the border. Not that the French are likely to come this way; there are no proper roads and they'd never get artillery across country. Still, I think Wellington likes the idea of having this route covered. But I think the main reason is that this is the richest part of the countryside here. Look at it. Olives, fruit trees, livestock…there are even some wheat fields. If you need to dump a pack of thieves and looters down in a place like this, you want to know that their officers are right there ready to kick their arses if they take one step out of line. Hence our privileged position."

"Of course there's no objection to us buying from the local farmers," Ross said cheerfully. He had already completed several successful negotiations, including the exclusive use of a bread oven for the duration of their stay, and he looked pleased with himself. "We've done very well; first San Estevan and now this, I'm beginning to feel as though we're still on furlough."

"Sadly, I don't think it's going to last," Giles said regretfully.

"Nor do I, or I'd send for my wife."

Giles shot him a sideways glance. "Missing her, Ross?"

"God, yes. Having her out here through winter quarters was perfect. And made the separation that much worse." Ross paused and Simon suspected he was controlling his voice with an effort. "There was something to be said for wasting my career as barracks-master in Melton Mowbray. At least I was with Katja and the children."

"You're a lucky man, Ross."

"One day, Giles."

Fenwick shook his fair head decidedly. "I don't think I'm husband material. And I'll never be able to afford a wife anyway. Now Simon here is another matter. He won't even have to search for one. He's Mrs van Daan's brother-in-law and neighbour to her family. I'd be willing to bet that she has a list prepared, ready for when he gets back home."

"You're only saying that because you're a senior officer, so I can neither challenge you nor punch you," Simon said. "Don't you dare say that to her, though, Fenwick. She might not have thought of it yet."

"She's thought of it, trust me. Women love to match-make and she's probably got a gaggle of girlhood friends needing husbands."

Simon grinned. "You're forgetting I knew her in her younger days, Fenwick. She got on better with the boys than the girls."

"Nothing's changed there then. Two more farms along this road then I think we'll loop back along by the stream. All these landowners will pass the news along to their neighbours and I don't think we need to worry about the outlying farms anyway. Those greedy bastards won't make it that far before our pickets catch them."

"Shouldn't we be worried about the pickets, though?"

"No, they'll all be accompanied by an NCO. And if you think any of our corporals or sergeants are going to risk getting on the wrong side of him for looting, Ross, you've not been here long enough. They'd be too terrified. Come on, I want to get back. The 95th have challenged us to a cricket match tomorrow, if the French don't attack, and I want to practise my batting. I've not hit anything other than a Frenchman for over a year, I'll be hopeless."

It was close to noon as they rode back into camp. The tents stood in their usual neat lines and there was a familiar hum of noise. An army camp was never silent. Even in the middle of the night, there were the sounds of horses and pack animals from the baggage park, a rumbling of voices from around dying camp fires and an even deeper rumbling of snoring from various tents. The three men walked their horses across springy grass already becoming flattened and muddy, to the headquarters tents of the 110th. As they dismounted, two grooms appeared to take the horses. Simon relinquished his reins with a smile of thanks and dug into his pocket for a horse nut. As he fed his gelding, a voice hailed them.

"Captain Carlyon, the very man I want. This way, I have a job for you."

Simon swore softly under his breath and heard both Ross and Giles laughing. He turned to salute his brigade-commander who had appeared from a large tent on the far side of a cleared area. In the centre of the square, Sergeant George Kelly, Paul's cook, was giving instructions to several servants in the matter of building the big cooking fires. Both Ross and Giles saluted as Paul approached. He returned the salute and fixed ominous blue eyes onto his brigade-major.

"Cricket, Captain? Have I ever given you my opinion of cricket?"

"More than once, sir. I think the last time I made notes."

Paul dissolved into laughter. "You cheeky bastard. You're getting as bad as Manson, I don't know what I do to deserve this in my brigade-majors. Piss off and hit balls, Fenwick. And make sure you win tomorrow, I've got a bet on with Andrew Barnard. Oh and Captain Mackenzie, I've sent a message to Captain White from the Cavalry Staff Corps asking to meet with him while we have a few days rest. I'd like you to be there. You too, Giles. I'll let you know when."

"Me?" Giles said, sounding startled. "What have I done?"

"Paid your last mess bill from the proceeds of a card game against Lord Dalhousie," Paul said smoothly and Fenwick's eyes widened.

"How in God's name did you know that, sir?"

"I didn't, Giles. I just made it up. Was it Dalhousie by the way?"

Fenwick grinned. "He was there," he admitted. "I was invited by Somerset and March. The Prince of Orange was there as well. But it was a fair game, sir, I promise you."

"I'm sure it was, Captain. Even I can beat Slender Billy at cards and I don't even play regularly. He's as easily distracted as my wife's dog. More so, probably. I appreciate your need for funds, but don't do it too often. A reputation as a card sharp isn't going to help your future prospects."

"They could try paying us on time occasionally, sir. Then I wouldn't need to."

Paul gave a wry smile. "There's a lot of truth in that. Come to me if you're stuck, Giles. I know you'll repay me when you can."

16

Fenwick's face softened into a smile. "It's not that bad, sir. But thank you."

The party broke up and Simon followed his commanding officer into his tent. It was spacious inside and very well organised, with an improvised curtain screening off the Van Daans' sleeping area and a number of chests scattered around for storage. A folding table served as Paul's desk and Simon was amused to see that it was already untidy with a scattering of letters and two bound ledgers covering the surface. Paul waved Simon to a canvas chair. A limping step heralded the arrival of Jenson, Paul's orderly.

"Sorry, sir, I've not quite finished the unpacking. Do you want me to find the brandy?"

"No, it's too early for me, I'll doze off before dinner. Do you want one, Simon?"

"Not really, sir."

"I'll get Sergeant Kelly to make some tea."

Paul watched him leave then looked at Simon and gave a somewhat sheepish grin. "I'm getting old," he said. "I can remember serving in India at twenty-two, being astonished at how much the officers drank and at what bizarre times of the day. It creeps up on you over the years. I was at a dinner with Picton recently and I decided to call a halt early. You'd have thought I'd refused an order to go into battle, it was so dramatic."

Simon grinned. "Did you give in, sir?"

"Good God no. It wasn't worth the argument though, so I accepted the port and quietly tipped it into Wellington's glass. I thought he hadn't noticed, but I got a royal earful when we got outside."

"Did he drink it?"

"No, he'd tipped it into March's glass. Poor March couldn't walk straight by the time we left."

Simon was laughing aloud. "I don't know how you get away with it with his Lordship, sir."

"We've been friends for a long time. Don't look so worried, Simon, you're not in trouble. There are a couple of things I wanted to speak to you about and both are confidential at present, though you can speak to Captain Witham about this, because he already knows."

Simon was puzzled. "Yes, sir, of course."

"I've been looking over the returns since Vitoria and have been involved in discussions with Wellington. I've also been corresponding with Horse Guards in London. As you can imagine, that was a real pleasure."

"I know how much you always enjoy it, sir."

Paul grinned. "My wife edits my replies, which is why I've not been cashiered yet. We're struggling for numbers. We still have a lot on the sick list, not just from the battle but because of that fever outbreak while we were pointlessly chasing Soult around the countryside. I'm hoping most of them will make it back eventually, but some won't. It's particularly bad in the 115th."

"I know, sir. Colonel Norton has spoken about it."

"Last month, Lord Wellington received orders from Horse Guards. A contingent of new recruits are on their way and we're expecting them some time during the summer. That will pull the 110th up to strength and there are some for the 112th but you don't seem to have had much luck with the 115th."

Simon felt a sinking sensation in the pit of his stomach. He suspected he knew what was coming. "Are they recalling us, sir?"

"They want to. They're talking of getting you back to barracks and sending out another battalion."

Simon shook his head decidedly. "I'll start looking around me for a transfer then. I don't want to leave your brigade, sir, but I'll take what I can get. I'm not being sent home, not now that we're so close to France. I'm sure Nicholas said the same."

"Captain Witham gave me time to finish my explanation, Simon, so he was better informed than you are right now."

Simon flushed. "Sorry, sir. Carry on."

"Thank you," Paul said with gentle irony. "Wellington is furious and he's having none of it. The 115th might only have half its proper complement of men but they're very experienced. They've come a long way since Badajoz and Philip Norton is an excellent commander. Wellington doesn't want them to be replaced by an inexperienced battalion at this stage in the war."

"Does he have a choice, sir?"

Paul grinned. "Officially, no. However, it's a long way to London and Wellington is already in the middle of this particular argument with the Duke of York. Adding another battalion to the list isn't going to make it any worse."

Simon froze, suddenly understanding. "He wants to form us into a provisional battalion?"

"The fifth provisional battalion, to be precise. The fourth one didn't make it through winter quarters as we know, but he doesn't want to use that title again in case it's seen as unlucky. Ah Jenson, thank you. Put it down on that chest. For some reason there's no room on my desk."

Jenson lowered the tea tray to a wooden campaign chest and cast a disparaging eye over the litter of paperwork. "I don't know how you manage to make so much mess so quickly," he said, pouring the tea. "It looks like you opened up a box of papers and tipped it upside down then gave it a good stir. Milk, Captain Carlyon?"

"The ledgers are out because I wanted to check some figures for Wellington," Paul said, making no reference to the mess of papers. Jenson grinned.

"Were you looking for a particular letter as well, sir?"

Paul accepted his cup, giving his orderly a look. "I was looking for the letter about Ensign Fox as you know perfectly well, you impudent bastard. Don't worry about it, my wife will sort it out when she comes in. She has a mania for filing, you know she does."

"When she sees the mess you've made of her neat files, she's likely to shove that letter where you'll feel it most, sir. Don't spill tea over those, she'll go mad."

Paul grinned and swept some of the papers to one side before setting down his cup. "Get out of here, Jenson. I'm blaming any spills on you."

His orderly departed with an audible snort and Paul turned back to Simon.

"I've already spoken to both Colonel Wheeler and Lieutenant-Colonel Norton about this, Simon. The plan is to combine the 112th and 115th to form a new provisional battalion. Recruitment will continue at home in the hope of bringing both battalions up to full strength again but this will give Wellington a way of keeping you out here."

"Won't Horse Guards be upset? I thought he'd been forbidden to do this again."

"He was forbidden to do it in the first place, but short of turning up with an armed guard and marching the battalions to the coast personally, there's not much York can do apart from howl. And he's been howling." Paul sipped his tea and gave a crooked smile. "To be honest, I put Wellington up to this one. I've seen it coming for a while with the 115th and after the fiasco with Major Vane during winter quarters, I was almost willing to let them go providing I could find places for you and Nick and one or two other good officers. But since Norton and Tyler took over, I've changed my mind."

"But who will command it, sir?"

"Colonel Wheeler of course."

"What about Colonel Norton?"

"He's staying. Since I knew this was coming, I've spoken privately to a number of officers whom I suspected wouldn't be averse to a move. Once again, this is between us, Captain. I'm treating you as family here."

Simon felt a little rush of pleasure. Both Paul and Anne van Daan had been widowed when they married and Anne's first husband had been Simon's elder brother Robert. The marriage had been unhappy and Simon still felt a residual shame at his brother's appalling treatment of Anne. When he joined the brigade the previous year he had been surprised and ridiculously pleased to find that both Anne and her husband treated him as her brother-in-law regardless of Robert's misdeeds.

"George Zouch wants to go home," Paul said. "He mentioned it when I first told him about his promotion. To be honest I was a bit exasperated, he's been wanting that promotion for so long. But his father is very ill and he has a younger brother and sister on his hands as well as his mother. More to the point, he wants to get married. He has a long standing attachment to the daughter of one of our previous regimental colonels. She's been nursing her father who has been ill for years; the combined effects of the Corunna campaign and then Walcheren. Colonel Johnstone has just died."

"I'm sorry to hear that, sir. I've heard him spoken of very fondly."

"Yes, he was a good man, we got on well. Anyway, I wrote to Lieutenant-General Lord Chatham to ask if he would look out for a suitable posting for Zouch and he wrote straight back to offer him a position serving under him in the Eastern District."

"You know the Earl of Chatham, sir?" Simon asked, rather taken aback. He knew that Paul's mother had been a member of the aristocracy but nothing else about his commander led him to suspect that Paul was used to moving in the best society.

"We haven't met for many years, but we're acquainted and we've corresponded occasionally," Paul said. Simon opened his mouth to ask then closed it again. He wondered if he might ask Anne at some point. He was wildly curious. The Earl of Chatham's last overseas command had ended in the expensive debacle of the Scheldt campaign and Simon had heard Paul express his opinion on that very freely.

Paul seemed to guess his thoughts because he grinned. "I've never served under him," he said. "I was a boy when we met and he and his wife were good to me. Anyway, that's ancient history. The point is that with Zouch gone, I can move Gervase Clevedon over to the 110th which is where he belongs, whatever Johnny may say. Johnny won't mind, however, because he gets Philip Norton as his second-in-command. Combining the 112th with the remains of your battalion will work better than any of the other provisional battalions because you're already used to working together."

Simon thought about it for a while, sipping his tea. The General did not interrupt. Finally Simon set down his cup.

"Thank you for telling me ahead of the others, sir. I'm…I don't know what to think about it, to be honest. The 115th is my regiment, but since I've been here I probably feel more loyalty to my brigade and to you. I wouldn't want to see it stood down, though. Is it likely to be?"

"They're not standing anybody down until the end of this war, Captain. They need all the troops they can get. I was more worried they'd get you back home, shovel half a battalion of inexperienced militia men into your ranks and ship you off to America or the West Indies. Wellington has put a stop to that for the time being. But after the war, once we've got rid of Bonaparte, they're going to reduce the size of the army. I don't think they'll be getting rid of the 43rd, the 52nd or the 110th. I think these days even the 112th might make the cut. I'm not so sure about the 115th which is really what I wanted to say to you and Nick. We're not done here yet. We'll lose more officers, to wounds, sickness, death or going home for personal reasons. The minute a vacancy opens up in the 110th or the 112th I'm offering it to you. Then Nick."

Simon felt his spirits life. "Not ahead of their own men, sir?"

"Not at all. But I will bring you in rather than waive the long service rules as I normally would. The others will understand, I promise you. Their turn will come."

"Thank you. That's reassuring. When are you going to announce this?"

"Over the next couple of days. As soon as I have it in writing from Wellington. He'll put it in place before writing to London and then it's up to him to deal with the flood of furious letters."

"Will he do so, sir?"

"Oh he'll ignore them. He's been doing it for several years. He's quite proud of how long he's been able to string out this argument with York. With any luck the war will be over before the Duke manages to work out how to deal with him. I wish him luck with it. I've served under him on and off for ten years now and I still can't always work out how to deal with him. Right, that's the administrative nonsense out of the way. I've got a more personal favour to ask."

"Always glad to help if I can, sir."

Paul finished his tea and set his cup down. "It concerns Ensign Fox."

Simon felt his heart sink. "Fox, sir?"

His General gave an inelegant snort of laughter. "That tone of voice tells me you have encountered Ensign Fox already."

Simon gave a reluctant smile. "We all know each other, sir. And I suppose he's about to become part of my battalion if we're combining with the 112th. We're not friends. Not really my kind of person, sir."

"Ensign Fox isn't anybody's kind of person, the little tick," Paul said with a sigh. "I'm generally against young officers selling out without good reason in wartime but if Fox came to me and asked me to sign his papers I'd knock the inkpot over in my enthusiasm. Sadly he isn't going to do so. How much do you know about Fox?"

"I know he's driving Colonel Wheeler up the wall," Simon said with feeling. "He's spoken about it. I hope you don't mind that, sir?"

"Good God no, I know how close you and Johnny have become. In fact it's the reason I've chosen you for this particularly irritating duty, because I was pretty sure you'd already know about it. Fox is a drunken, insubordinate layabout who will perform the most extraordinary contortions to avoid a day's work. He's rude to his seniors and has been reported several times for brawling with the men. I have it on reliable authority that he gambles above his means and owes money to several of his mess mates. All of those are exasperating but can probably be fixed in time. But I have reason to believe that during the battle at Vitoria he disappeared from sight and only reappeared after the fighting was over. We can't prove it. Who knows what the hell happened in that chaos? But I don't think Fox was there during the battle, which means he wasn't doing his job with his men. If that's because he was afraid, he's a dangerous liability and I need him to sell out."

"You won't cashier him then, sir?"

"I'd rather not, although I'll find an excuse if I have to. I'm really hoping he'll go of his own accord."

"What do you want me to do, sir?"

"I'm transferring him into your company. It's unorthodox and both he and either Worthington or Middleton will have to agree to it, but I'm going to bully him into it. Captain Marshall is a good officer but I don't think he's going

21

to be tough enough on young Fox. He's already covered up for him once. I have complete faith in you not to do that, Simon."

"Not a chance. If he goes absent without leave on my watch, sir, I'll nail his balls to the doorpost. But if he hates it that much, why in God's name doesn't he sell out?"

"Johnny's theory is that he's trying to get himself cashiered. His older brother dumped him into the army as a last chance to sort himself out. If he resigns his commission, he'll be cut off without a penny. If he gets kicked out, perhaps he thinks he can spin Sir Oliver a sob story and get his allowance reinstated. Myself, I think Sir Oliver would have to be an idiot to fall for that but who knows? Anyway, I want you on his back, Simon. I want him to have to work. And for God's sake don't give him any kind of independent command, especially if we're likely to be in combat. Imbeciles like Fox get men killed."

"Yes, sir."

Paul stood up. "Thank you. I'm sorry about all this upheaval, but I know I can rely on you. Come up for dinner tomorrow and we'll feed you by way of an apology. Bring Nicholas. Good luck, Simon."

***

With all three brigades of the Light Division encamped in and around the village of Vera there was a shortage of accommodation for both officers and men and Paul had decided to keep his brigade in tents. He disliked having officers and men scattered between different villages; it made discipline more difficult and looting more likely. The officers grumbled but did so quietly and were mollified when Anne managed to arrange a substantial barn which could be used as an officers' mess.

The weather remained warm and sunny with the occasional heavy shower mostly at night. The men had no orders apart from regular picket duty and Anne thought that some of them looked likely to treat this as a holiday. Many of the local farms made their own wine and spirits and Anne strongly suspected that some of the men and their women-folk were wealthier than usual after the systematic looting of King Joseph Bonaparte's baggage train after the battle of Vitoria.

Paul and Anne had been watching the men with interest to see if any of them showed signs of new prosperity but it was one of the wives who gave the first indication of how well she had done from her looting. Anne had noticed on the march that Hannah Bowlby, the wife of one of the sergeants of the 110th, seemed to have acquired a new mule which was piled high with bags and boxes. Anne kept her husband amused for several days speculating on the contents of Hannah's looted baggage.

It was not until they were settled in camp that the mystery was solved. Captain Michael O'Reilly approached Anne on their second morning in camp as she was giving orders to Sergeant Kelly about dinner.

"Good morning, ma'am. It looks like another fine one."

Anne finished her conversation with Kelly then gave Michael her full attention. "I hope this lasts. I was talking to the farmer yesterday and he was telling me they have very impressive thunderstorms in these mountains. I'd rather not be in a tent with a deluge coming down again. I've never forgotten the night before Salamanca."

"It'll happen at some point. Not today, though."

"Have you time for some coffee, Michael?"

"Thank you, ma'am, I have."

Anne went to the camp fire where the remains of the breakfast coffee was keeping warm. She filled two cups and handed one to Michael. "Come and sit down."

There was an awning set up outside the tent with a collection of folding chairs and stools. Anne took her favourite chair and Michael sat opposite, his hands wrapped around his cup.

"Were you looking for the General? He rode out early with General Alten and I think they'll be a couple of hours at least. They're exploring the local area. You know how he likes to have a good sense of the terrain, wherever he is."

"I do, ma'am. I also know that he's the worst fidget in the army and it's a relief to find him something to do."

Anne gave a gurgle of laughter. "That is also true. Can I help?"

"I'm not in need of anything, ma'am. I wondered if I might be of help to you. Had you heard of Mrs Bowlby's auction today?"

Anne raised her eyebrows. "Mrs Bowlby is going into business?"

Michael grinned. "It would seem so. She sent one of her boys over to inform me that his mother has – quite legitimately of course – acquired a selection of ladies clothing which she considers too fine to sell for twopence to her fellow army wives and any passing camp followers. She is accordingly holding an auction outside her tent before the dinner hour today and invites prospective buyers down at any time before then to inspect the merchandise."

"Really?" Anne said, intrigued. "I wonder why I wasn't invited?"

"Oh you were. He was on his way up to you next, ma'am. I told him I needed to speak to you so I'd take the message. He was very relieved, I think he's in awe of you."

"I think the hefty clip round the ear I gave him for trying to steal Señora Caldera's apples while we were in San Estevan might have something to do with that."

"Ah. Yes, that makes sense."

Anne sipped her coffee and met Michael's ingenuous gaze, trying not to laugh aloud. "The question, of course, is not why young Jem Bowlby didn't manage to invite me, Captain. It's why you were on his invitation list. I wonder if his mother is under the impression that you might have a need to buy elegant female raiment for somebody?"

Michael rolled his dark eyes expressively. "Only the fact that you're a lady prevents me from answering that as you deserve, ma'am."

23

"You mean only the fact that if you use that kind of language to me I'll smack you as hard as I did Jem Bowlby, don't you?"

"Well yes, ma'am. It's not worth the risk."

Anne dissolved into giggles. "I think people are beginning to talk about your relationship with my Spanish maidservant, Michael."

"Is that so? It'll be a nice short conversation then, won't it?"

Anne picked up on his tone and decided that Michael's sense of humour was failing him on this occasion. With an effort she suppressed her laughter.

"I'm sorry, Michael, I'm teasing you and I shouldn't. I know better than most people how it feels to be the target of army gossip. Is everything all right? Ariana hasn't said anything to me, but if anybody is making her feel uncomfortable about this I promise I will deal with them."

Michael's taut expression softened into a smile. "God love you, ma'am, I know you would. It's nothing really. To tell you the truth it's not Brat who's struggling. I'd like to go down to see Hannah and buy half her stock for the girl but I'm not able to do so."

"Money?"

"No, I'm not short of money just now. She won't allow it. The closest thing to a gift she'll accept is a posy of wild flowers and she's probably sick of those because I cleared out every meadow in San Estevan just to give her something."

Anne was touched. "Michael, it has nothing to do with how she feels about you. It's about her self-respect."

"It's about my reputation," Michael said grimly. "They've all made sure she knows that I've stood at other auctions like this buying gifts for other women. She thinks I'm trying to…"

He broke off and Anne was surprised to see that he was blushing. She could not often remember seeing the Irishman blush. Of all her friends in the brigade he was the least likely to moderate his language because of the presence of his commander's wife and he usually spoke to Anne with a frankness which horrified some of his friends. Anne loved it. She studied the thin, attractive face and thought with compassion that she had never before seen Michael O'Reilly so much out of his depth.

She knew that Paul and some of the other officers were following his careful courtship of Ariana Ibanez with great amusement. Michael had never been in the least ashamed of his reputation for finding a pretty mistress in every village and town they stayed in for more than a few days, but it rather looked as though his history was returning to haunt him with a vengeance. Paul was not sympathetic. He had pointed out that during his own younger and much wilder days, Michael had thoroughly enjoyed making the most of his indiscretions and definitely had this coming. Watching the expression on Michael's face now, Anne thought she saw real pain behind the dark eyes.

"Michael, none of this has anything to do with Hannah Bowlby's auction. This is about you and Ariana. What's going on?"

Michael shot her an embarrassed glance. "I probably shouldn't be talking about this to you, ma'am."

"Do you remember a conversation we had in a muddy farmyard in Portugal more than three years ago, Michael? It was the morning after Rowena died. Most of the escort you commanded had been killed in the French attack and Paul and I spent the night trying to help his wife deliver their child then watched her bleed to death in a pile of straw."

"I don't think any of us are ever going to forget that day, ma'am."

"I was numb. I was going through the motions of treating the wounded men and taking care of the baby, though I had no idea what I was doing with her at that point. Dreading what my husband was going to do to me for leaving with Rowena without his permission. And trying so hard not to look at Paul because all I could see was his pain and I couldn't go to him and hold him and comfort him because I felt too guilty about how much I loved my best friend's husband."

Michael did not reply for a moment then she saw the flicker of a smile. "That's funny," he said. "All I remember about you that day was how courageous and how competent you were. Taking care of Carter and young Davison, managing the child, speaking Portuguese to that woman we found who could feed her for a couple of days. To say nothing of the fact that the previous night you'd saved Carter's life by stepping between him and that French bastard's blade. You showed none of what you were feeling, ma'am."

"When you came to speak to me that day, you talked of my relationship with Paul so openly, it was as if a weight lifted from my shoulders. You didn't judge, you didn't criticise and you didn't tell me all the reasons I shouldn't love him. You just accepted the way things were. I've always known from that day to this that you'll be there for me, no matter what happens. After Paul, you are the man in this army I'd trust with anything, Michael."

She watched him assimilate what she had said, giving him plenty of time. There were tears somewhere, held firmly back because he did not need to see them, but she was not surprised when he lifted his dark eyes to hers and she saw that he was crying.

"Thank you. You've no idea what that means to me. I trust you too."

"Then bloody well talk to me."

He laughed as she had known he would and shook his head. "That's very unladylike language, ma'am."

"You drive me to it. A few months ago, Ariana came to me and asked if I would take her on as a maid given that I, once again, was without one. Her stated reason was that she wanted to come with the army because of you."

"She told me the same thing."

"Since then I've been watching both of you. Don't forget, I've previously had the experience of observing my maidservant trying to hide the fact that she is sleeping with a man of the regiment. I'm used to the signs, it's quite entertaining to watch."

"I'm sorry not to have provided you with more entertainment, ma'am."

25

"Well I'm glad you haven't, Michael, but I'm curious. Is that your choice or hers?"

The Irishman gave a crooked smile. "I'm not sure."

"That's confusing."

"It's confusing to me too, ma'am. When she told me she'd taken employment with you, she was very clear. She usually is. It's one of the things I like about Brat."

"I like that about her too. She's rather like me in that way."

Michael laughed aloud. "Yes, she is. I never knew how much I liked plain-spoken women until I met you; it was like a breath of fresh air. But Brat and I had such a strange start. She was a skinny, underfed urchin, dressed as a boy, that I found in an alley in Madrid. I didn't even know how old she was at the start; I thought she was a child. She followed me from one camp to another until it seemed easier to keep her on as a servant than try and get rid of her. There was no possibility of anything else with that girl."

"And then it changed."

"When she followed me on that mission to Castro Urdiales, I was angry. It was different in camp. I could take care of her. But even if I couldn't, somebody else would. Out there in the Cantabrian mountains, there were only four of us and Fenwick was furious that she'd turned up and pushed her way into the expedition. Three weeks later he was asking her advice and giving her picket duties."

"She is an extraordinary girl, Michael."

"I never meant it to change and I don't think she did either. She attached herself to me in sheer desperation at the start because I was kind to her. But it did change, gradually, over those months. It was as if she grew into a woman before my eyes. Giles saw it. So did Antonio. I think I was the last to do so and by the time I did it was very much too late."

"Michael, none of this explains what's happening with you now."

"Yes, it does. I feel responsible for her. I also feel guilty for feeling the way I do. She's fifteen years younger than me and I've not lived as a monk. When we spoke, before the march, she told me that she'd never be just another one of my women. And she isn't. I've not felt this way since I was a stupid boy of nineteen or twenty. In fact I've never felt this way, because what I had then never stood the test of time and understanding. Since then I've had a parade of pretty girls in my life and an unrequited affection…"

He broke off, appalled, and Anne said quickly:

"It's all right, Michael. You can leave it there."

He regarded her steadily. "I was never sure that you knew."

"I didn't for one moment think it would survive meeting the woman you actually loved. Have you told her?"

"No. What in God's name can I say? How do I convince her that this is not just the latest in a series of relationships that went nowhere?"

Anne was silent for a long time. Then she said:

"You could ask her to marry you."

Michael rose and walked a few paces away, keeping his back to her. She could see his anger and tension in the taut line of his body.

"And what then? A few months of happiness until they carry me in bleeding on a stretcher and she's either a widow or a woman in charge of a crippled husband. What kind of life is that for a woman like Brat?"

Anne set down her coffee cup and rose. She went to Michael and put her hand on his shoulder, turning him firmly to face her.

"That is not your decision."

"It should be. She's young. She's a child. She should…"

"She saw her father murdered and she was raped by three French dragoons when she was barely sixteen. How dare you try to tell her what she should and should not feel?"

Her anger seemed to check him and he paused, breathing hard. Eventually he said:

"I'm sorry. That was crass."

"Yes, it was. I will forgive you only because I genuinely think that you care for her. Michael, you have several choices here. You can do your best to seduce her and you'll probably succeed eventually because she loves you. But I'm interested that you've not even considered that option. You can walk away and allow some other man to find her. Somebody will. Ariana is both attractive and intelligent. At some point she is going to meet a man who is not afraid to approach her and even the best of women will grow tired of waiting. Or you can tell her how you feel and ask her to be your wife and take the chance you are terrified of taking. That would be my preference; I care about both of you and I want you to be happy. And I think you would. But whatever you decide, make a decision. Convention dictates she's not allowed to do it for you."

Michael was silent for a long while then raised his head and looked at her. "She doesn't even know my real name."

"Then tell her. And start using hers. Brat was the servant girl dressed as a boy. Why do you think I refuse to use it?"

He did not speak for a moment. Eventually he said:

"I don't know if I'm ready."

"You don't have to be. Just make sure you know where you're going."

He smiled then. It was a little lopsided but it reassured Anne that she had not got this dreadfully wrong. "All right, I'll think about it. Just don't say anything…"

"I will say nothing to Paul or anybody else, Michael. This is your business not theirs. Just don't allow their view of who you are influence who you really want to be."

The Irishman said nothing for a moment. Then he shook his head. "You're so wise. How the hell do you do it?"

"Painful experience, Michael. What is your real name? Does even Paul know?"

"No and he doesn't need to. I could tell you…I might tell you one day. I've been Michael O'Reilly since I joined up after the failed rebellion in 1798. I

27

needed to leave my own name behind, along with everything else I had. But that man…that boy…if anybody deserves to hear that story first, it's Brat."

Anne was content. "I agree," she said serenely. "I don't know if this has helped at all…"

"It has," he said fervently. "Not that I've wholly decided. But at least I know what I need to think about, which is a big help. Thank you, ma'am."

Anne went to kiss him on the cheek. "I'm glad, Michael. Take whatever time you need. But if you're going to let her down, please tell me. I want to be there for her."

"I'm not," Michael said fiercely and Anne managed to hide her smile at his tone. "I'll never hurt her. I just…it seems to be taking some time."

"Take the time. Just include her in the process. And thank you for telling me about the auction. Would you like to be my escort?"

"Of course, if you'd like me to."

"Bring your purse. If you see something she'd like, buy it for her, Michael. You can choose your own time to give it. Now finish your coffee. I want to write a quick note to Juana Smith, I'm inviting them to dinner tomorrow. You're invited as well along with Ariana. Juana loves to be able to speak to somebody close to her age in her own language.

Michael drained his cup and set it down. He reached for her hand and raised it to his lips, holding it there for rather longer than propriety allowed. Anne raised her eyebrows and he grinned and released her.

"Thank you, ma'am. I'd be honoured to join you for dinner along with your Spanish maid and the child-bride of a Rifleman. Have you ever considered how on earth you're going to manage when we finally get back to England and you'll be expected to conform to the normal rules of society again?"

"All the time," Anne said cheerfully. "I expect I'll cope. It's Paul I worry about. I'm not sure he had much idea to begin with to be honest. I'll just write this note and I'll join you in fifteen minutes."

Chapter Three

Mrs Bowlby had set out her wares for inspection with a great deal of care. Most of the clothing was displayed on makeshift hangers, made out of tree branches or draped over a borrowed cart. It was artfully done but Michael thought Hannah might find herself in trouble if the weather suddenly changed as it was apt to do in these mountains.

There was a rough trestle table made from what looked like wagon boards laid across two piles of stone. Smaller items were laid out on it; several glass perfume bottles, a hairbrush and comb, some shoes and boots and a collection of shawls, scarves and ribbons draped in a riot of colour at one end. Anne was inspecting some beautifully embroidered children's clothing. Michael suspected that when Sergeant-Major Carter brought his small daughter back to the lines she was going to be the best-dressed army brat in camp.

He went to rummage through the scarves and hesitated over a brilliant green one which would look lovely against Brat's auburn curls. He picked it up, studying it, wondering why he associated this colour so strongly with her and then dropped it as though it burned his fingers at a sudden memory. Brat had owned a very similar scarf and had given it to Giles Fenwick so that he would have a gift for a pretty Spanish girl with whom he had shared a brief, affectionate connection. Michael did not know if Brat would mind but he suspected that Giles would find the memory painful every time he saw her wearing it.

Beside the heap of fabric was an item he had not noticed before. Michael picked it up. It was a quilted case with a spray of white flowers embroidered across it, fastened with white ribbons. He untied them and took out a pair of soft tan leather riding gloves. They were beautifully made, with exquisite stitching. Michael examined them but could find no flaw. He wondered if they would fit Brat. She seldom wore gloves over her work-roughened hands, though Anne had found her an old pair for riding.

"Those are perfect," Anne said at his elbow. Michael looked around to find her with an armful of white garments. In addition to the baby gowns there were several fine lawn shifts. Michael forced himself not to imagine how Anne might look in them. It was a bad habit and he wanted to break it. They were probably for Teresa Carter anyway.

"Do you think she'd like them? And what about the size? I've no idea…"

"Here, let me try them on. My old gloves fit her very well."

He watched as she drew on the gloves then stretched out her long fingers and flexed them. "Perfect."

"Then I'll bid on them."

"Oh Michael, we're not waiting for the auction. I have three patients to visit and I've promised Lord Wellington I'll ride over to have a look at Pearl. He's like a first-time father; it would be funny if it wasn't so touching. Just wait here, I'll speak to Hannah. She owes me so many favours, I think you'll find she'll be happy to negotiate a price here and now."

Michael watched her go, smiling. He could remember his early acquaintance with the young, headstrong wife of Lieutenant Robert Carlyon when she had arrived in Portugal four years ago. He had found her enchanting, bewildering and rather disturbing and had developed the first serious tendre he had felt for any woman since leaving his first love behind in Ireland. He was not sure when his feelings had changed and deepened into warm and affectionate friendship, but he felt privileged to know her and to be in her confidence. He was also a constant admirer of her determined competence and he had no doubt that he was about to walk away with the fine leather gloves in his pocket at a very reasonable price.

**

Three days after they had set up camp, Paul invited his senior officers to a meeting before dinner. Colonel Johnny Wheeler had been expecting the summons. Sergeant Jenson and his young assistant, Charlie Bannan, set out chairs in front of Paul's tent and distributed drinks. Anne was present, seated on a blanket on the grass close by with her enormous dog stretched out beside her. She was wearing sprigged muslin with a tiny pattern of roses, her hair dressed in a simple arrangement. She was not wearing a hat and Johnny felt a flicker of amusement as his commanding officer emerged from the tent to join the meeting and caught sight of her. He stopped in his tracks, glaring at her. Anne gazed back. Her innocent expression made Johnny laugh aloud. Paul transferred his glare towards him.

"I'm glad you find it amusing, Colonel Wheeler. Wait until you discover that your betrothed has the common sense of a six-year-old when it comes to sunstroke. Where's Brat?"

"She's doing laundry down at the river," Anne said, getting to her feet. "I'll get it myself."

"I'll go, ma'am," Charlie said and shot into the tent. Anne sat down again and reached out to rub Craufurd's tummy. The big dog rolled over onto his back, wriggling in ecstasy. He looked ridiculous.

30

Charlie emerged with a straw bonnet. He took it to Anne, his expression doubtful. "I've found it, ma'am, but I think something's happened to it."

Anne took the hat with a grin. "It's a little battered. Don't worry, Charlie, it will still do the job. Thank you."

She tied the hat over her smooth black hair and Paul made a spluttering sound. "What in God's name happened to that? It looks as though you've taken a bite out of it…oh. That blasted dog."

"It's my fault, I left it on the chest. I'm not sure it can be repaired, but it's an old thing anyway, I only wear it around camp. Don't look at me like that, General, there's nothing I can do. This part of Spain doesn't seem to be packed with fashionable milliners. I'll write to my stepmother. She can send me a new bonnet for my birthday."

"That's months away. We will discuss your hat crisis another time, girl of my heart, but you're not getting away with it." Paul surveyed his officers. "I've spoken to all of you about the proposed changes already. They're coming into force immediately and on Wednesday I'm hosting a dinner in the mess for all the brigade officers to say farewell to Lieutenant-Colonel Zouch before he sets off for England. I've invited Kempt and Skerrett as well as General Alten. I was going to invite Lord Wellington but he's entertaining some Spanish dignitaries on that day. I wanted to meet with you today though to bring you up to date with the latest news and to discuss the next week or two."

"Is that how long we're likely to be here?" Johnny asked.

"Very possibly. I accompanied Charles Alten to headquarters yesterday and although, as we know, things can change at a moment's notice, I don't think we'll be marching immediately."

"I take it we're not required for San Sebastian, then?" Philip Norton asked.

"No, thank God. When he gets time off from being yelled at by me, Captain Fenwick has been drawing maps of the area for his Lordship. He's kindly provided me with a copy as well, probably in an attempt to get into my good books. Bring it up, Giles. Pin it to the tent, there's no breeze so it won't blow away."

Fenwick attached the map and Johnny took a moment to admire it. He was always fascinated by the contrast between Giles Fenwick's apparently chaotic personality in day to day life and the meticulous work he did as an observing officer for Lord Wellington. Johnny had been doubtful when Paul had offered Fenwick command of a company earlier in the year and even more surprised when he had chosen him as temporary brigade-major while Captain Manson was on sick leave, but studying the map he decided that his eccentric commander's instincts had not betrayed him. Fenwick might be incapable of managing his own finances but he was a very good officer.

Paul surveyed the map and Johnny wanted to laugh at the pleased expression on his face.

"It's a work of art, Giles, thank you." Paul pointed to a coastal town. "Welcome to San Sebastian, gentlemen. I've recently received a letter from my

31

good friend, Richard Fletcher, who is in charge of the engineering works at the siege and he tells me that the place is going to be a fucking nightmare to take. Fortunately this time poor Graham's corps has the unenviable task of throwing men at the walls. Our job is to keep the French off his flank while he's doing it."

The officers listened mostly in silence as their General spoke. Paul was a fluent speaker, particularly about military matters and unlike some commanders he preferred his senior officers to have full knowledge of Lord Wellington's plans, as far as Paul knew them himself. He often knew more than most of the army. Wellington's irritability over minor issues did not affect his genuine regard for Paul and he liked to talk his plans through with him. Johnny doubted that either Kempt or Skerrett had been invited to accompany Alten to headquarters.

For the past weeks, Wellington had gradually been moving his army to a line which ran roughly from Irun on the coastline all the way to the high passes across the Pyrenees. Paul pointed out the various locations on the map.

"He's got Longa's Spanish close to San Sebastian so they can link up with Graham at need. The sixth are back at San Estevan in reserve, the lucky bastards, then there's us here at Vera and the Seventh just to the south-east at Echalar. The mongrels are a bit close for comfort but I'm hoping they behave."

There was a roar of laughter. The Seventh was the newest division of Wellington's army, formed two years earlier before Fuentes de Oñoro, and was by far the most cosmopolitan with a colourful variety of uniforms and a polyglot mixture of languages. It had not taken long for the rest of the army to refer to them as the mongrels. Johnny had been present at a lively dinner hosted by Paul when the third brigade had first taken over the estate of Santo Antonio for their winter quarters and he had always suspected that an inebriated Michael O'Reilly had been the originator of the sobriquet. It had quickly spread despite the indignation of the officers of the Seventh who tried hard to convince the rest of the army that they were in fact a newer version of the Light Division. They had not so far succeeded.

The laughter died away and Paul pointed again to the map. "The high passes at Maya and Roncesvalles are the responsibility of the unlucky Second Division with the Portuguese and some Spanish in support. I thought we might get that job and I'm glad we didn't. It's bleak, wet and probably blowing a gale half the time. It's also a challenge to defend because in that countryside…well, I'll let Captain Fenwick explain as he's been up there to have a look. Giles?"

Fenwick stepped up to the map. "It's difficult country. Our front stretches more than sixty miles from the Bidassoa up to Roncesvalles. There are plenty of passes through the mountains into France but very few of them are good enough for large forces dragging artillery and a baggage train. There's the great road which runs by the coast of course. Then there's the road running from Bayonne to Pamplona which goes over the mountains through a little village called Maya. Then there's a third one which goes from St Jean de Pied de Port over a pass at Roncesvalles and down to Pamplona from there."

32

"All roads lead to Pamplona," Colonel Norton said in matter-of-fact tones.

"Which is currently blockaded by the Spanish and which the French would very much like to relieve," Fenwick agreed cordially. "Any attack would need to come along those roads. His Lordship has them all guarded but the high passes are particularly difficult because there are no proper lateral roads between them and it's not possible for the engineers to cut them as they did at places like Bussaco. We're talking mountains here."

"Always assuming we had enough engineers to do so in the first place," Paul said caustically. "I can't remember if I told you, Johnny, but among the imbecilic suggestions coming out of London, is that we try to build the equivalent of the Lines we built to defend Lisbon and then leave the Spanish to defend them."

Johnny stared at him, his mouth open. "Really? Have they actually seen the Pyrenees? And where were they intending to send Wellington and the rest of us? Tell me it's home for a rest. I want to get married."

"No such luck, Colonel. The idea was to send Wellington to Germany, I believe. There are various talks and negotiations going on, trying to bring the Austrians and the Prussians over to our side again. I think the idea is that if there's to be a coalition army, Wellington is the man to lead it, riding high on the glory of kicking Joseph's arse at Vitoria. Which would also leave him in an excellent position to influence any peace settlement."

"There are far too many contingencies in that plan," Gervase Clevedon said. "Starting with the idea we could fortify these mountains with a few redoubts and a line of blockhouses."

"It's politics, Colonel."

"Politics make my head hurt," Johnny complained. "I'm assuming his Lordship has made his position clear?"

"Admirably so, and will continue to do so. Fortunately, after Vitoria they're willing to listen to him. And I think it's very unlikely that the gentleman who came up with that cockeyed scheme has been anywhere near the Pyrenees in his life. Anyway, I'm getting distracted. Carry on, Giles, sorry."

"Yes, sir. I was trying to explain about the lay of the land in those mountains. The bad news is that we have the worst of it on this side. The French will have to advance up some very steep mountains, certainly, but they'll only have to do it once. The plains and the mountains are clearly separated and they've got a good view to the top. They can see where they're going. We, on the other hand, have a series of ridges to get over and they're bloody high. They're also deceptive. You think you're approaching the highest point and will have a pretty view down into France and you suddenly realise that you've got another range in front of you like a brick wall, barring your way. It's hard work and it's going to be tough on morale."

"And is that what Wellington expects us to do?" Clevedon asked.

"Not right now," Paul said, going back to the map. "He's not going anywhere until he's dealt with San Sebastian. Back in 1811 he was held up by the French possession of Badajoz and Ciudad Rodrigo. The following year he got himself stuck at Burgos. Now we have Pamplona and San Sebastian to contend with, since the French blew up Burgos themselves as they scuttled up to Vitoria. I thank them regularly for that in my prayers by the way. Sadly, they're well dug in at the other two places.

"Pamplona is the business of the Spanish. I'm told they've set up an effective blockade and as long as the French don't break through our lines with supplies and reinforcements, we can starve them out. San Sebastian is a different prospect. It's virtually impossible to stop them resupplying it by sea, certainly with the number of ships we have available. Wellington is writing about ten letters a day ranting at the Admiralty to send more. He might get a few, but they're as stretched as we are. All he's going to do is give himself a seizure."

"Who takes over if he does, sir?" Johnny said innocently. Paul gave him a look.

"We are not going to discuss that, Colonel Wheeler, or I'll be the one having a seizure. Anyway, Wellington doesn't intend to make a push for France with two major fortresses in his rear. He's also concerned about what's happening in the East. Some of you will already know this, given that rumours travel faster than the cavalry in this army. I know all about it because I had to endure a twenty minute tirade on the subject over a very bad dinner. He even swore a couple of times which he doesn't usually do with me, since he likes to take the moral high ground on the subject of my language. Sir John Murray decided he didn't like the look of Tarragona and has abandoned his siege operations along with all his guns and stores and his Spanish allies. He's scuttled back aboard the Royal Navy ships, leaving Suchet in control. Wellington is enraged about the loss of the artillery. You know how much he values every single gun. I think it might have something to do with balancing the books. More importantly however, he was relying on Murray to keep Suchet busy so that he wouldn't be able to join up with King Joseph's army if it makes an attempt to attack us."

"Is it even King Joseph's army any more?" Norton asked.

"I've no idea. I imagine neither Joseph or Jourdan should expect a Christmas gift from Bonaparte this year but I don't know exactly how things stand with them. At some point I'm sure we'll find out. What we do know, courtesy of Captain Fenwick's many friends and their habit of stealing French dispatches and correspondence at every opportunity, is that we have a new commander to deal with. Marshal Soult has been sent to pull the army together as fast as he can and to take back Spain."

"Oh Jesus, not Soult again."

"We should probably refer to him as the Duke of Dalmatia," Paul said smoothly. "Especially since it would annoy him as he'd have preferred to be Duke of Austerlitz. We're not doing either however, because I cannot be arsed with anything longer than Soult. The fact that he's been sent back is a sure indication that Joseph's days as King of Spain are over, by the way. He can't stand Soult, he kicked him out of Spain last year and I'm reliably told the bastard needed an extra long baggage train to carry the treasure and artwork he'd been stealing for the previous few years."

"What does Lord Wellington think of this development?" Johnny asked curiously. "He's spent enough time facing Soult over the years. I'm guessing he has an opinion of him."

"His Lordship has an opinion about everything," Paul said grimly. "He told me, in a moment of rare sentimental weakness, that he'd not seen enough of me during this campaign. I was rather touched at the time, but now that I am back in his full confidence my ears are permanently ringing and I'm beginning to miss the quiet. I think he's got the measure of Soult though. He says he's good at both logistics and planning and his troops admire him and will follow him anywhere. However once he's got them into position it often goes to pot. Wellington's opinion is that he puts too much trust in his subordinates and doesn't follow through on his orders. Nobody could ever accuse Wellington of that, I must say."

There was a ripple of laughter and Paul smiled acknowledgement. "I think he's probably right. I don't think Soult is necessarily the man I'd put in charge of what would need to be a complex invasion over difficult country, where good communication and good relationships between the various commanders are of the essence. I suspect he's a difficult bastard to work with. However, what he will do very well is pull that army back together much faster than we'd like."

"Where have I heard that before?" Johnny muttered gloomily.

"Yes, it has a familiar ring, doesn't it? At least Wellington knows it by now, though I'm not sure it helps since the bastard is doing it out of our reach. For now, we hold the line, keep alert; wait for San Sebastian to fall and for news from Germany. Wellington doesn't think there's the slightest chance that any of these talks will result in even a brief peace. The only way we're getting rid of Bonaparte is to kick his arse back to Paris and beyond. Any questions, gentlemen?"

There were a few hands raised. Most of the questions were around supplies and logistics and Paul answered them patiently, referring one or two to his senior quartermaster for further explanation. Major David Cartwright raised his hand.

"What about the cavalry? Is he leaving them behind?"

"Most of them yes. You've heard what Fenwick has said about the country. Once we're over and established on the plains he'll send for them, but this isn't cavalry country. However, some will be needed for communications and escort duty so he's assigning a battalion of cavalry to each infantry division. I know Charles Alten was hoping we'd get the Germans back, they've been with us for so long, but sadly not. For the present, we're getting Colonel Scovell and his brand new Staff Cavalry Corps. That's good news because George is a good friend and won't annoy anybody. However, I did point out to Wellington that their primary responsibility is supposed to be policing and discipline, which might leave us struggling if he suddenly pulls them out on other duties. He agreed surprisingly quickly and has written to Alten to tell him he's getting a battalion of the 9th Dragoon Guards which should be on its way from England as we speak. They might have arrived already."

"I thought the 9th went home?" Clevedon said.

"The 9th Light Dragoons went home. These are heavy cavalry. I'm not sure why we're getting them as opposed to light cavalry. Probably because they've been sent out here and Wellington didn't know what else to do with them. Either that or it's because he is still furious with some of the other cavalry regiments because of the looting of Joseph's baggage train. Anyway, they'll join us shortly. Any more questions?"

There was a silence. Paul waited a moment then looked back at the map and pointed.

"France," he said. "Look at it. It's right there. I don't know how long it's going to take, but we've never been this close before and this time they're on the back foot. We've slogged our way backwards and forwards across Spain and Portugal for the best part of five years. We've stood in line and been mown down by cannon; we've shivered and starved in the pouring rain and waded through snow. We've lost friends and loved ones. And now we're here, standing at the foot of these mountains waiting for the order."

Nobody spoke. The laughter had died away and Johnny suspected that they all shared his sense of tingling anticipation. Often he was able to detach his mind in order to admire Paul van Daan's sheer genius for motivating his officers and men but this time he was caught up in the emotion of the moment. He thought briefly of Lieutenant-Colonel Carl Swanson, invalided out after Vitoria and learning to live with the loss of his left hand. Paul looked over at him and Johnny knew with complete certainty that he was thinking of his missing friend as well. There was a suspicious shine to the blue eyes.

Abruptly Paul slapped his hand on the map, making the tent canvas flap. "The order will come and we'll fight. This is difficult country. It's wooded and steep and rocky. Not the place for neat lines of infantry and a thundering cavalry charge."

He paused for effect and Johnny felt as though the group was collectively holding its breath. He deliberately let his out, waiting.

"This is skirmish territory," Paul said finally. "This is scrambling over stone walls and hiding in farm buildings and scaling slopes that the other buggers don't want to climb. This is our country, gentlemen, and I want them ready. We start training every single day; drill and skirmish. Particularly skirmish. I want my NCOs on their back all the time, checking weapons and equipment. Coates has my orders regarding resupplying those who need it. Wellington tells me he's ordered new uniforms but God knows when they'll arrive. There's also the problem of the men's greatcoats. It was a fucking stupid idea to put them in storage and I told him so. They'll need them in these mountains. Captain Mackenzie, I want them brought up to the lines. I don't care how we do it. Talk to my wife. She'll manage Wellington if he gets difficult."

"Yes, sir."

Paul turned and studied the map again, then carefully unpinned it, rolled it up and handed it back to Fenwick with a little smile.

"Don't lose it, I'm going to need it. And you. You're doing a fine job filling in for Manson, Captain. I might not always appear particularly grateful but I bloody am."

"Thank you, sir."

"Colonel Wheeler, do you have anything to add?"

Johnny's throat was tight. He cleared it and stood up. "I think you've said it all, sir. Maybe a toast?"

"Why don't you do it?"

"Very well. To the third brigade of the Light Division, to Lord Wellington and his army…and to France."

They rose around him, lifting their glasses. Johnny drank and raised his eyebrows at his friend. Paul smiled back and raised his glass again.

"I've another. Two more actually. To Lieutenant-Colonel Carl Swanson who is idling around as a country curate while the rest of us miss him like hell. And to the others from Vitoria. Some will be back soon. Some are at rest there. They'll march into France beside us in spirit, every one of them."

They drank the toast solemnly, then Paul turned to look at Anne. She was on her feet watching him, her dark eyes full of loving concern. She met Paul's gaze and Johnny saw his face soften into a smile. Johnny felt a sharp pang. He thought of Mary, waiting at home in Derbyshire, managing his lands and praying for his safe return and he felt a new bond with his friend. Paul lifted his glass once more.

"To my wife, my lady and my love. You're the heart and soul of this brigade and when I set foot on French soil, I want it to be with you. Thank you, bonny lass. For everything."

She came forward, moving into his arms to kiss him lightly on the lips. Around them the others erupted into laughing cheers. Johnny began to applaud. He appreciated the little byplay on two levels. On the one hand it was a perfect piece of theatre, calculated to tug at the heartstrings of every man present, especially those missing home and family and dreaming of France and an end to the long war. On the other hand it was utterly real. Johnny had shared every painful moment of Paul's love affair and knew that his marriage was based on solid ground and that their shared devotion was unquestionable. He watched them talking and laughing with the officers as the meeting broke up and thought that family was about more than blood and lineage. He had very few living family members, but with the Van Daans and some of the other officers he had served with over the years, he would never feel alone.

As the meeting dispersed Major Cartwright waited behind, clearly wanting to speak to Paul. Anne glanced at him, kissed her husband on the cheek and prepared to depart but Cartwright shook his head.

"No, ma'am, I'd like you to stay. And you too, Colonel Wheeler, if you don't mind. It's a personal matter but you've all been involved to some degree."

Paul studied him for a moment. "Come into the tent, Davy. We'll have another drink and you can talk away."

The men carried several chairs into the tent and Anne poured more wine. Johnny was curious. David Cartwright was one of his favourite officers. He was competent with occasional flashes of brilliance, immensely calm under fire and popular with his junior officers and his men. He was also a thoroughly nice man and Johnny had come to consider him a friend. He could not imagine what this was about.

"What is it, Davy?" Paul asked when they were settled. "Whatever it is, it's between us. You know that."

"Thank you, sir. It's...look, when you mentioned the 9th Dragoon Guards earlier. They've been out here before."

"I know."

Cartwright took a deep painful breath. "This is difficult," he said. "There's an officer who was in Lisbon on sick leave for a time. Two years ago, or more. He is...he was..."

Johnny was bewildered but Anne caught on quickly. "Davy, is he...was he one of Bella's lovers?"

Cartwright's shoulders visibly relaxed with relief. "Yes, ma'am. I've never really known who was the father of her child. I was with the army and you know how rumours spread. Colonel Scovell made the decision to tell me that my wife was pregnant when it couldn't possibly be mine so that I didn't hear it from some drunken idiot at a headquarters party. I've always been grateful to him for that. Afterwards I did hear the rumours of course. There were several lovers I believe. But the one most talked of was an officer of the 9th Dragoon Guards. It was an open scandal in Lisbon."

"Oh Christ, Davy, I'm sorry," Paul said quickly. "As if you've not had enough to put up with."

Cartwright smiled. "Sir, it's all right. I've got over it. Bella is dead and I think that's atonement enough. As for the men involved...I can't really forgive one without forgiving all. I doubt any of them meant to hurt me."

It was a painful admission and Johnny had to restrain himself from embracing Cartwright. Paul van Daan, during the philandering years of his first marriage, had embarked on a brief affair with Arabella Cartwright in Naples. Johnny knew his commander bitterly regretted it. He had been surprised and impressed at Cartwright's ability to forgive and accept a commission under Paul. It had gone very well, helped by Anne van Daan's understanding and remarkable ability to reconcile difficult situations but Johnny thought that Cartwright had suffered enough and did not need this particular wound to be reopened.

"Thank you," Paul said simply. "You know that if I could go back and change what I did, both for your sake and Rowena's, I would do it in a heartbeat. What's his name?"

"I don't think I should tell you, sir. Not right now. I wanted you to know, in case...well in case he proves difficult. But I don't suppose he will. He must know what happened – that Bella and I separated and she went back to

38

England to have the child. He clearly made no effort to contact her or to help in any way. I don't like that about him, but to do the man justice he probably realised that she had more than one lover during that period and there's no certainty that he was the father of her child."

"That's not much of an excuse," Paul said shortly.

"No, sir. And I know that in the same situation, you would have helped her regardless."

"What I know, Davy, is that after she died you went to England, found her child living in appalling poverty and adopted him as your own. There are no words to describe how much I admire you for that."

Cartwright gave a broad, unforced smile. "You don't need to praise me for that, sir. I wanted a family more than anything. She gave me that. I don't give a damn about who fathered him, he's my son. I only wanted you to know in case this man has anything to say about the matter. If he does, I'm going to refer it to you. I am too old to be engaging in pointless squabbles or duels. I have a son to care for. And possibly…"

He broke off and Anne fixed him with an eagle eye. "Possibly? Major Cartwright, is there something about your personal life that I don't know?"

Cartwright laughed aloud. "Ma'am, I don't know it myself yet. When I was on furlough at Christmas I met a lady. The time was too short and it would not have been right. But I do hope that in the future…I have hopes, ma'am."

"Are you corresponding with this lady, Davy?"

"Regularly, ma'am."

"Good. Keep me informed. As for this cavalry officer, it is to be hoped that he has the sense to keep his mouth shut and his head down. I'm sorry you have to deal with this, Davy. But I'm so happy you felt able to share it with us."

"My wife is right as always," Paul said shortly. Johnny could feel his discomfort. Privately he felt that it served Paul right that his early sins came back to bite him occasionally but he appreciated his friend's willingness to admit his faults. "If you don't want to tell me I'll abide by your wishes, Davy. You've earned the right to choose. But if he puts one foot out of place or even looks at you the wrong way, I'm asking you to come straight to me. I will deal with the arsehole, I promise you."

Cartwright stood up, draining his wine glass. He was laughing. "I will, sir. I trust you to do so. Thank you. I'm sorry, I didn't mean to make you feel…"

"It is good for me to feel it occasionally. Your ability to forgive and move forward is astonishing. I'm so grateful to have you in my brigade, Davy. And at some point I require details of this female you've been hiding from us. What's her name?"

"Helen, sir."

"Is she pretty?"

"We are still arguing that point, sir. She thinks not. I think she is beautiful."

"Clearly she needs to bow to your superior knowledge on this matter. I hope it goes well for you."

"So do I, sir. Thank you."

When he had gone, Paul reached for his wine glass and drained it. "Sometimes, I just really want to fight the French," he said in matter of fact tones.

Anne got up and took the glass, setting it down. She was laughing. "I do understand, General. But sometimes, friendship can be painful."

Paul gave her a quick smile. "Worth it though."

He looked over at Johnny who raised his glass and finished his wine. "Very much so, sir. Don't worry about Major Cartwright, I'll keep an eye on him. I'll see you at dinner. Thank you, ma'am."

***

The fine weather broke the following day and the first few days of training were conducted in torrential rain. Living in tents made it difficult to dry out wet clothing as well as managing to get hot food cooked but Paul had learned the hard way to plan for the worst and Anne was an expert in managing a camp. The officers had an area of their big mess barn set aside for drying and several of the men had constructed a covered area just outside for the cooking fires. The heat permeated the barn and every officer smelled faintly of smoke but the system worked. It was more difficult for the men, but the NCOs supervised the building of a selection of makeshift shelters where the men on mess duty could build fires and cook their meals and every one had a variety of garments hung beside it to dry. It was not particularly cold but the damp was miserable and Paul was grateful for the shelter of the barn for eating meals and drying out at the end of the day.

On the fourth day the rain eased and it was warm again, the sun drying out tents and clothing quickly. The camp looked like a second-hand clothes market with jackets and shirts draped everywhere. Paul surveyed it with grim amusement as he walked his horse out to the training ground. His NCOs knew to be tolerant of the chaos after a spell of bad weather. Down at the river he could hear women's voices talking and laughing as they caught up with their laundry, along with the shrieks of children playing. On impulse, Paul changed direction and made his way down to the bank. They were strung out along the river, scrubbing at shirts and linen while their children played in the field behind them.

Paul smiled at the raucous sound of their voices. They spoke a variety of languages. Some of them were army wives who had travelled out with their husbands. Others were local women, picked up in Portugal and Spain, many of them not legally married which meant the men could not draw rations for them or their children. A lot of them earned money by doing laundry and mending for the officers or acting as sutlers, buying food and drink locally and selling it to the men. Some turned to prostitution when times were hard. Many of them stole and looted where they could. If they were caught, they were subject to army discipline like their menfolk but Paul disliked flogging and would certainly not countenance a woman or child being beaten under his command. He had his own methods of keeping order and mostly they worked.

"Look lively, girls, it's the General come down to see if we're behaving ourselves. Let your skirt down, Gisele, you're not decent like that. Morning, sir. And a fine one."

The voice was pure cockney and Paul grinned and touched his hat. The woman was probably in her late thirties, a solidly built Londoner who was currently married to Sergeant Barforth of the 115th but Paul had known her through two previous husbands. She had lost the first at Talavera and the second at Salamanca in a fierce skirmish at Alba de Tormes. Like most of the wives she was pragmatic about the need to find a new protector quickly. Paul understood how vulnerable a woman could be, alone in an army camp, and encouraged his men to marry when there was a chaplain available so that they could draw rations. There was currently no clergyman with the army although Paul had reassured several of the women who were hoping to be married that Wellington's chaplain would shortly be returning from sick leave in England.

"Good morning, Mrs Barforth. Yes, it's a relief to see the sun again. I'm not looking forward to winter out here, the way this weather changes. Hopefully we'll have found decent billets before then."

"You normally manage it, sir. That's why General Picton hates the Light Division so much. His boys need to be a bit quicker to get the best places."

Paul laughed. "Is that what it is, Lucy? I thought he just didn't like me."

"Nah, that can't be it, sir. We all love you, don't we girls? Look at Gisele there with her skirt up round her knees. She wouldn't be flashing her legs about like that to old Picton."

There was a burst of laughter. Gisele, an elegant black woman of around thirty loosed her kilted skirt letting it drop into the shallow water where she was standing barefoot, washing linen. "I am sorry, sir," she said, in heavily accented English. "I did not mean to offend."

"You're not going to offend me, Gisele."

"His wife might not be so impressed mind," another woman said.

Paul swung down from his horse and looped the reins around a branch, letting Rufus graze. He walked down to join the women and paused to speak to Maggie Bennet, the sturdy, sensible wife of a sergeant of the 110th, who often took charge of Anne's household laundry. He had known some of these women for years and objected to the view taken by some of the officers who assumed they were all dishonest and promiscuous. Many of them were respectable women and devoted wives who endured untold hardships to be with their men. Paul had built up a good relationship with most of them over the years.

Gisele was new to the brigade. She had appeared in the ranks of the 110th at the side of Sergeant Ben Cooper of the 110th, two days after the bloody battle at Vitoria. A number of Spanish women had joined Wellington's army after Joseph's defeat and precipitate flight. They had been the mistresses and companions of French officers and men and on the whole had seemed perfectly ready to find new protectors among the Allied army. Paul had asked Anne to check on the women to make sure none felt coerced into staying and after a week of deliberately casual enquiries she had been able to reassure him.

Gisele was like none of the others. She spoke French and some Spanish but no English and she had arrived with nothing but the clothing she wore: a good quality gown which was torn and muddy. She clung to Cooper in the first days with what seemed to be desperate gratitude. The other women regarded her with suspicion at first and Paul understood why. She was so different and her inability to communicate with them set her apart. He knew that his wife was concerned about her and he left it to Anne to find out what she could. It was not part of his job to take care of a casually acquired camp follower but he liked and trusted Cooper and was genuinely curious.

Anne came to him a week later with the story. "She was a slave, Paul. Brought over by a French officer from his family plantation some years ago, ostensibly to work as a servant. In reality, I think she's been his mistress."

Paul understood the quiet anger in Anne's voice. The status of slaves under French law had changed several times during the long years of the revolution but Bonaparte had very firmly reinstated the institution when he came to power. Paul wondered if the young woman had ever been formally freed or if she had travelled through the war with a man who considered her a piece of property.

"How the hell did Cooper take up with her?" he asked.

"I've no idea, Paul, other than that when the French fled from Vitoria she was left behind. I've talked with her. She's painfully shy but she seems adamant that she wants to stay here, with Cooper."

"That's a very odd match," Paul said, shaking his head.

"This is a very odd way of life, love. I'll keep an eye on her. I've offered to help her with her English which will give me an excuse to talk to her, but I don't think you need to worry. Cooper might have been born in an orphanage and dragged up on the streets of Manchester, but he's a good man. He'll look after her."

Paul had to admit that his wife appeared to be right. Gisele's confidence was improving along with her English and he was glad to see that the camp women seemed to be accepting her. He was sure he could have found out more from Cooper but he was reluctant to use his position to pry into his Sergeant's personal life for no better reason than curiosity.

"Any news of RSM Carter, sir?" one of the women called. "When's he coming back?"

"Another month or so I think, Susan. He's pushing to come back sooner but my wife has told him if he turns up here before he's fully recovered, she's going to put him on administrative duties only and confiscate his rifle, so I think he'll behave."

Paul moved along the bank, stopping to talk to the various groupings. The women seemed to form their own version of an army regiment and it could be as hierarchical as any battalion of troops. Wives and girlfriends of the NCOs tended to stick together and held a senior position among the camp followers.

42

They were usually slightly better dressed and many of them had their own baggage mule. They took pride in their appearance, managed their children with a firm hand and were conscious of their husbands' status in the regiment.

The sutlers and tradeswomen formed another group, though there was some overlap between the two. Several of these ran informal grog tents in camp where the men could congregate to drink, gamble and meet women. Paul found this group the most troublesome, simply because their need to acquire stock and attract customers often clashed with army regulations about buying up food ahead of the commissary or providing more drink than was wise during a campaign. Drunkenness was so common in the army that very few officers bothered to complain about it unless it clearly interfered with a man's ability to do his job, but it infuriated Paul and he waged a constant war against one or two of the worst offenders.

The rest of the women were wives or girlfriends of the enlisted men. They were a ragged bunch, often foul-mouthed and poorly-educated, many of them local women picked up on the march during the long years in Portugal and Spain. Paul admired their hardiness under appalling conditions, enjoyed their invariable cheerfulness and was often exasperated by their determination to evade his rules.

Separate to all of these were the prostitutes who had attached themselves to the brigade. They tended to keep themselves apart, though Paul could never tell if that was from choice or because the other women did not welcome them around their menfolk. They were a fluid group, moving between the various sections of the army to pick up trade. Paul suspected that by now all of them had also picked up the pox. He knew that one woman had recently died bearing a child she could not possibly have taken care of. He suspected that they liked to travel with his brigade when they were on the march simply because his iron rules about how women were to be treated meant that they felt safer than with some of the other divisions.

Paul stopped finally beside a slight, dark-haired girl who was loading wet shirts into a battered wicker basket. She looked up at him and gave a quick shy smile.

"That looks heavy. They can't all be Hammond's shirts."

"Oh no, sir. I offered to do Colonel Norton's laundry and mending for him. He's been struggling to find someone since poor Mrs Clay died of the fever and it was painful to watch his servant manage his mending, the man can't sew. Jamie...Sergeant Hammond said I didn't need to take in work but I like to be able to pay my way, since I'm not on strength yet."

"You will be, the minute that blasted chaplain gets back, I promise you, Alison. In the meantime I've told Hammond to come to me if you're finding it difficult."

"We're managing very well, sir. Your wife always asks me to help if she's entertaining and she insists on paying me for it, though she knows I'd do it for nothing. She's been so good to us."

43

"She tells me she couldn't have managed without you back in Vitoria. I'm just grateful for all you did." Paul took out his watch. "I'd better get on, Alison, I'm supposed to be supervising drill and they'll be thinking I overslept this morning."

Alison regarded him gravely. "Sir, nobody is going to think you're late because you were sleeping."

Her delivery was so perfect that, for a moment, Paul was not sure that he had understood her correctly, but the limpid innocence of her gaze told him that he actually had just been teased about his sex life by a seventeen-year-old camp follower. He gave a splutter of laughter.

"You cheeky little baggage. You're getting as bad as Hammond; it must be contagious. I can't even threaten to kick you in the river as I would him."

She laughed, spreading her hands to indicate her damp skirts. "I'm wet enough already, sir."

"Good. You deserve it. In revenge, I'm going to tell Hammond to bring you up for drinks after dinner when I shall bore you senseless by explaining infantry drills. I'll see you later, Alison."

He reined in his horse at the top of the track which led up from the river and looked back at the women. Their noisy chatter and laughter reminded him unaccountably of a flock of geese scattered along a river bank. Paul smiled at the thought then turned and set Rufus at a canter towards the open ground where his officers had already begun to put the men through their first drill manoeuvres.

Chapter Four

After a week of frenzied activity getting the troops clothed, equipped and properly fed, Captain Damien Cavel of the 30th légère was tired of sudden arrivals in camp bringing new orders, which generally meant considerable upheaval. Marshal General Jean-de-Dieu Soult, 1st Duke of Dalmatia, reached his army headquarters in Bayonne on the 12th of July and Cavel did not think he had managed a full night's sleep since. Soult had arrived with orders from Napoleon to reorganise the battered armies which had fled from Vitoria and threw himself into the task with impressive energy.

Colonel Gabriel Bonnet, the recently promoted commander of the 30th, had been heard to voice his opinion that if Soult had spent the past few weeks scrambling over mountain passes with Wellington's army yapping at his heels like a bad-tempered English terrier, he would be less enthusiastic about doing the whole thing again so soon. Cavel had to bite his tongue to stop himself warning Bonnet about his open criticism of his new commander-in-chief. Bonnet was a man willing to speak his mind and a suggestion that he moderate his opinions or at least speak more quietly was only likely to make him worse.

It was just past dawn and the camp was barely stirring when a clatter of horses' hooves brought Cavel from his battered tent. He felt lucky to have a tent at all. The men bivouacked on open ground and in the unpredictable weather of this region of France they had spent several nights huddled under trees or building makeshift shelters from their blankets and whatever material they could scavenge locally. Here in France the supply was limited. If they had still been in Spain, Cavel knew they would have taken what they pleased from the local villages regardless of any official orders about looting. Back in their own country, they were more cautious, correctly assuming that officers would be less likely to turn a blind eye.

Cavel, who had been acting as temporary adjutant during the chaotic final days of the retreat and the current frantic resupplying of the troops, went to meet the horsemen; a group of twelve chasseurs de cheval led by a grim-faced captain who looked as though he was having an even worse day than Cavel. There was no sign of Adjutant Gerard, the non-commissioned officer whom Cavel was training to take over permanently as adjutant. There was also no sign

45

of Colonel Bonnet. Cavel decided that was a good thing. He waited for the officer to dismount and greeted him politely.

"Captain Cavel, 30ᵗʰ légère."

"Dumas, 14ᵗʰ Chasseurs. On special duty at the orders of Marshal Soult."

Cavel hoped he had not rolled his eyes. "How can I help you, Captain Dumas?"

Dumas waved a piece of paper. Cavel took it and moved closer to a lantern which hung on an iron hook. It was not yet fully light and a heavy mist made visibility even more difficult. He peered at the letter, shivering a little in his greatcoat. The handwriting was presumably that of some clerk and Cavel thought that in Soult's shoes he would have sent the man back to the lines and found a replacement who could write legibly.

"Camp followers?" he said finally, looking up at the officer. "He wants to clear out the camp followers?"

"Immediately, if you please, Captain. Your Colonel is requested to muster the battalion for inspection and then my men will go through the camp, assemble the women and march them out."

"March them where?" Cavel enquired sharply. He had no particular interest in the collection of Spanish women who had followed the army out of Spain and into France, but he did not like the idea of abandoning them with no protector and no means of support.

"They will be escorted to a refugee camp on the edge of Bayonne, Captain. Once all regiments have been cleared out they will be marched, under an escort of the local National Guard, down the coast road towards the border near Irun. I'm sure from there they can find their way home. Or if they prefer, I expect Wellington's men will be glad to see them. Let them give the Englishmen the pox for a change."

Cavel sighed. The order was not going to be popular among the troops but there was not a large contingent of Spanish women following the 30ᵗʰ.

"I presume this doesn't apply to wives and cantinieres?"

"Good God, no. Though I'm not sure I'd want to take my wife into these mountains. Where…"

Captain Dumas paused in surprise as a woman emerged from one of the tents nearby. She glanced over at the horsemen and seeing Cavel, gave a little nod of greeting, then went to the smouldering embers of a neatly banked camp fire, reached for a pile of sticks and began to carefully coax the fire back into life.

Cavel watched her. She was in her early thirties, slim and straight with the wiry strength of a woman accustomed to hardship. Her dark hair was pulled up into a knot and she wore a simple blue woollen gown with a dark shawl thrown over it. Her feet were bare and already wet from the dewy grass.

"Is she yours?" Dumas said admiringly.

"No. She's…"

46

"Good. Well we'll start with her, as an example. Plaget, give her time to collect her things if she has any then take her over there. We'll line them up and…"

"Dumas, no," Cavel said quickly but the trooper had already dismounted and was approaching the woman. She looked up in surprise, saw his intent and gave a cry of indignation, backing away from him. Plaget reached for her.

"Come along, Mademoiselle, time to go. Marshal Soult's orders; all Spanish camp followers are to be taken back to…"

The woman struck his hand away so forcefully that Plaget almost fell over backwards in surprise. "Take your hands off me, you imbecile," she said in very good French though with a marked accent. "I am not a camp follower. Gabriel, are you dressed? There is a fool in a cavalry hat wishing to evict me from the camp."

A sound resembling the growling of a wild boar emitted from the tent. Dumas looked at Cavel in surprise. "What in God's name…?"

"I tried to tell you. She's the Colonel's wife."

"Oh shit," Dumas said.

The tent flap flew open and a big man surged out. He went straight to the woman and took her hand, glaring at the trooper who, with great presence of mind, had retreated at speed, putting the fire between them.

"Are you all right, little dove? Did he touch you?"

"No. I was just surprised. He thought I was a camp follower."

Colonel Bonnet regarded her with a long sweeping look. "You look like a camp follower. Where is your pelisse? Where are your shoes? You will catch your death like that."

"Gabriel, I have travelled the length of Spain like this and I am still alive. Stop fussing. Captain Cavel, what is going on?"

"I'm sorry, Madame, I did not have time to explain to this officer who you were."

Cavel was trying not to laugh. He could see the answering sparkle of amusement in her brown eyes. "So I imagined. Why was I to be evicted?"

"Marshal Soult's orders, Madame." Cavel was not sure if Dumas was saluting to Bonnet or his wife but he thought that under the circumstances, both would be a good idea. "My apologies for the misunderstanding. We have been sent to remove any Spanish camp followers before the march."

"This is my wife, not a camp follower," Bonnet growled.

"Of course, Colonel. It is just that she appears to be…that is…she is Spanish. So I thought…"

"There's no evidence that you're capable of thought. Our glorious Emperor is married to an Austrian, but I don't see anybody arresting her because she's not French. Though it might be a relief to her if they sent her back home, now that I come to think of it. What do you want?"

"I bring orders, sir."

Bonnet held out his hand. He put his arm about his wife's shoulders and they read the letter together. Bonnet looked up with a sigh.

"Are you seriously telling me I have to muster my men on parade while your bastard cavalrymen search the camp?"

"Those are my orders, sir."

"For fuck's sake. I thought Joseph was bad enough, but I can see he was just an amateur. All right. Cavel, will you dig out a bugler and get them moving. Dumas, keep your men right here where I can see them. Once they're all here, you can send them to search but I want each one accompanied by one of my NCOs. I'm not having them take the chance to steal what they can under cover of searching for women who aren't here."

Dumas bristled in indignation. "My men are not thieves, sir."

"Then it won't be a problem."

"Are you telling me there are no women in your camp?"

"I'm telling you there are no women who aren't supposed to be here. But you're going to want to look, so let's get on with it. Unless you're going to ask me to find my marriage lines so that you can check I'm not lying to you?"

"No, Colonel." Dumas was visibly sweating despite the chill morning air.

"Good." Bonnet turned to his wife. He bent to kiss her gently. "I'm sorry, sweetheart. This won't take long. Why don't you wait in the tent? It's warmer."

"Of course." Bianca looked over at Dumas. "Good morning, Captain."

"Good day, Madame. Once again, my most sincere apologies."

Cavel summoned the bugler. The high, clear notes rang out and the camp scrambled grudgingly into life. Dumas and his men stood watching as the men of the 30th légère moved into position. They looked sleepy and disgruntled at being called for an early parade when there was no formal inspection and no prospect of a march.

Cavel glanced over at the tents. Beyond them, in the untidy lines of the makeshift camp, he could see the slim form of Bianca Bonnet moving purposefully between the men as they stumbled into bad-tempered lines. He could not have said with any certainty how many Spanish camp followers had crossed the mountains with the men of the 30th, but he was absolutely sure that none of them would be found in camp by the time Dumas sent his men through to search. There were plenty of places to hide in the surrounding woods and plenty of time to rejoin the long column as it ascended up into the Pyrenees when Marshal Soult gave the order. Damien caught his Colonel's eye and almost laughed aloud, as Bonnet gave a slow wink before turning his gaze back onto the assembled ranks of his men with an expression of limpid innocence.

An hour later, Cavel stood beside his Colonel watching as Dumas led his men out of camp. Bianca emerged from the tent and came to stand beside Bonnet. He put his arm about her and gave her an affectionate hug.

"All safely away, ma belle?"

"Yes. There's a wooded area between those hills. It's quite sheltered and there's water. Sergeant-Major Belmas and two of the men escorted them."

"I wondered why I had no sergeant-major in the lines. Will they be all right there?"

"I think so, for now. I talked to them, to explain what was happening. I thought I should give them a choice. One or two of them might prefer an escort to the Spanish border to a difficult march in poor conditions over the mountains. They will talk about it and let me know. Any who wish to leave can be escorted to poor Captain Dumas and his refugee camp. The others will join the battalion when we march."

Bonnet laughed aloud. "You are a good planner, Bianca. I am hoping that you don't want to go with them."

"It would serve you right if I said yes."

Bonnet looked down at her. His expression reminded Cavel of a large, affectionate dog, but he did not find it remotely funny. He had been with the 30th for almost a year now and had plenty of opportunity to observe the fierce mutual devotion between the big, bear-like Bonnet and his Spanish wife. Bianca had travelled with Bonnet since just before the storming of Tarragona two years ago. They had finally managed to marry only a few weeks earlier and Cavel sensed that his commanding officer was thoroughly enjoying the novelty of being able to call her his wife.

Bonnet confirmed it as Bianca went to tend the fire and make coffee. Around the camp, officers and men went to collect rations and cook breakfast. Cavel watched them rather smugly. He had become very close to Bonnet and his wife and some months earlier Bianca had suggested that Cavel join them for meals. She was an excellent cook who took pride in her ability to make a tasty meal out of even the most basic food and Cavel was delighted with the arrangement. He had managed to buy some bacon from a local farm and Bianca had negotiated with one of the cantinieres for some bread. The smell of the bacon frying made Cavel's mouth water. He sat beside Bonnet on folding camp stools sipping black bitter coffee.

"That was so satisfying," Bonnet said.

Cavel gave him a sideways look. "Making fools out of the chasseurs de cheval?"

"Well that too. Though I had little to do with that, it was Bianca's idea. No, I meant being able to tell that officious young bastard to leave my wife alone." Bonnet grinned. "I was almost hoping he'd ask for proof so I could shove my marriage lines in his face before punching it."

"He had more sense. I had a feeling you were enjoying it."

Bonnet sipped his coffee and sighed happily. "I always feel better once I've had coffee," he said. "You can't imagine how many times I have needed to warn some bastard about his manners around Bianca. The first time was three of my men on the day I met her. The second was some cavalry colonel in Tarragona. I knocked him out. Suchet was annoyed. He had some mad idea about a

49

promotion for me back then but he couldn't do it because of that arsehole complaining about me."

Cavel studied him curiously. "You must have been disappointed."

"Not really. I didn't know promotion was even a possibility at that point. I was still recovering from a minor wound during the siege and I was with Bianca. After a lifetime of thinking no woman would ever want to be with me unless money was involved, I was like a child in a toy shop. Nothing could touch me." Bonnet grinned and got up to dip his cup into the coffee pot again. "I was fairly pissed off later though, when they sent the 30th away from the army of Aragon to serve in D'Armagnac's brigade. Suchet liked me. God knows why. I think I made him laugh, which is something the poor bastard didn't get to do that often. But he also liked Bianca's cooking."

"Bianca cooked for Marshal Suchet?" Cavel said in astonishment.

"Marshal Suchet used to spend his free time cadging dinner invitations. I could never work out why he didn't just find himself a decent cook. Occasionally, I worried that he had his eye on mine. But I think he just enjoyed the occasion, to be honest. Excellent food and a bit of normality in the middle of this bloody war. Still, I think I'd have been promoted sooner under his command."

Cavel considered for a moment then decided that his friendship with Bonnet had reached the point where he could ask the question he had been wanting to ask for a while.

"When I first transferred in to the 30th, they told me a story about why the battalion was moved from the east coast to join King Joseph's army," he said cautiously. "I've never known if it was true or not."

Bonnet's responding smile was decidedly evil. "Ah, I see. The tale of the objectionable Captain Vassout and the only time I ever fought a duel. Who told you?"

"Captain Forget."

"At least he wouldn't have embellished it too much. All right, Cavel. As it's you, I'll give you my confession. I did indeed fight a duel."

Cavel could not help smiling. "I expected you to deny it," he said. "Sorry. I just can't imagine you shivering in the dawn mist with a duelling pistol."

"It was fucking freezing and I chose swords. His challenge, so my choice of weapons. Does that make you feel better?"

"I suppose you couldn't refuse a challenge. So was it really over Bianca?"

"It was as far as I was concerned. Vassout would tell you that it was because I humiliated him publicly by tipping him off his fancy horse into a muddy puddle."

"And did you?"

"Of course I did. Stupid arsehole. I'd warned him twice to stop annoying my girl and he laughed in my face and told me that he could say

50

whatever he liked to a Spanish prostitute. The third time he actually put his hands on her."

"Did he hurt her?"

"Not as much as she hurt him. She hit him with a camp kettle and laid him out cold. He was furious and reported her to Lacasse, wanted her kicked out of camp. I responded by reporting him to his commanding officer for assaulting a local woman. He got a formal reprimand and I got an earful from Lacasse about my personal life, which I ignored, like I always did with Lacasse. Vassout was furious. Rode down to our camp and started yelling abuse at me as well as Bianca. I ignored it for a bit then I got bored and tipped him off his horse."

Cavel gave up trying to conceal his laughter. "And what happened?"

"What you'd expect. We fought. I'm not much of a fancy swordsman and if he'd done the intelligent thing and agreed to stop at first blood I'd have let him scratch my arm and be done with it. But he was furious. That type can't stand to be made a fool of and the men had a good laugh at him sprawled in that puddle. He wanted to fight to the death. For me, that means there are no rules. I went for his face. If they're blinded by their own blood it generally stops them. He lost half an ear before Forget and his subalterns turned up and pulled me off him."

"Would you have killed him?"

"Only if I had to. But they didn't know that and it worked very well. From that day to this, not a man of this battalion has so much as looked the wrong way at Bianca." Bonnet drank more coffee, looking over at his wife who was setting out mess tins and breaking up the bread. "Suchet stepped in at that point, which he didn't have to. Told Vassout that it was his fault in the first place for being a twat and that he wanted to hear no more of it. But he'd been asked to send a few battalions over to Joseph to replace troops who'd been sent to Russia and I think he thought it best if I was a long way from Vassout."

"Didn't he trust you?"

"Oh yes. For me, the matter was over. But Vassout was stalking about declaring to the world that this duel would never be over until one of us was dead."

"I see. One of those."

Bonnet grinned. "I see you've heard of the long tale of Pierre Dupont de l'Étang and the arsehole Fournier. I hadn't, until Marshal Suchet told me. Apparently the only reason they're not still fighting duels against one another every ten minutes is because poor Dupont is still locked up for being unable to win with raw levies at Bailén."

"I cannot imagine you fighting repeated duels for almost twenty years, Colonel."

"No, I'd get bored with that very quickly and shoot him in the head when nobody was looking," Bonnet said placidly. "But Suchet didn't want the aggravation and it was easier to get rid of me than Vassout, so we ended up here. Lacasse was furious. He blamed me for the whole thing. Not that it matters now, poor bastard."

51

Cavel said nothing. They had not known the fate of the previous colonel of the 30th until last week when news had come that he had been taken prisoner at Vitoria but died of his wounds shortly afterwards. They sat in silence for a moment until Bianca approached with two mess tins of steaming food.

"Why are you both looking so sad? Gabriel, do not balance your cup there or you will scald yourself. Here, I will take it."

Cavel watched her fussing over her husband and found that his spirits had lifted again. There had been an air of gloom throughout the battalion since Vitoria. They had lost too many officers and men during the battle then in the scrambling retreat over the mountain. Several had made it, only to die of their wounds or of fever in an army hospital. The 30th was not even close to full strength despite receiving several drafts of men from other regiments during Soult's reorganisation of the army and two of Bonnet's companies were now commanded by young officers who were not really ready for the responsibility.

Cavel suspected it must be the same throughout the French army. Since the Emperor's Russian campaign ended in disaster the previous year, Bonaparte had been moving troops around Europe with the panicked speed of a chess master facing a losing game for the first time in his career. He seemed to be hanging on in most of Europe, though he must know that a new coalition, if one could be agreed, would throw his plans into disarray and might force him to fight on several fronts.

Spain had been a disaster for him and rumour suggested that he was unlikely to forgive his brother, the deposed King Joseph, or Marshal Jourdan for the defeat at Vitoria. His response had been swift and decisive and Soult was clearly determined to push Wellington's forces back and re-establish a French foothold in Spain. Cavel had been impressed by the new commander-in-chief's energy and motivation but Bonnet greeted each new order with a derisive snort.

"It'll take more than a scolding from the Emperor, a month's pay and four days rations to dislodge Wellington now he's got this far," he said dismissively. "I think we're about to get another kicking, Cavel, and I hope it's not as bloody as the last one."

"The Emperor has faith in Marshal Soult, Colonel."

Bonnet picked up his tone and grinned. "And you have faith in the Emperor. I think his day is done, Cavel, though I doubt he knows it. And that's what worries me. It's all very fine to believe yourself invincible when you're standing at the top of the pile playing master of all you survey. But that pile is sliding fast now and he's on the way down. I admire your loyalty to him, but I'm afraid mine is a bit frayed round the edges."

"And yet you still fight for him."

"I don't fight for him. I'm not sure I ever have. I fight because I'm a soldier and a bloody good one. I fight for my battalion and my brigade. I'm even prepared to say I fight for my country. But I'm starting to think France could do with a bit less fighting and a bit more peace and stability. And I'm not sure fucking Bonaparte is ever going to be able to provide that."

52

Cavel studied him, troubled. "Does that not make it difficult in battle? If you do not believe…"

"You're not that naïve, Cavel. Look around you. How many of these men believe in anything at all? They're here because they have to be. Some of them joined up because they were starving or wanted adventure and to see the world. Most were conscripted, like you and I. Some of them have nothing to go home to and no idea what they'd do if the war ended. Some of them genuinely believe in the legend he's built up over these years. They think they can carry on fighting and looting and raping the local women forever. But I think even the most stupid of them must be wondering after Vitoria. And you are not one of the stupid ones."

Cavel could not help smiling. "Thank you, Colonel, I am touched."

"I stay because I have to. It's called desertion otherwise. And also because if I were to find a way out of here and go home to introduce my wife to my mother, I'd be leaving this battalion to somebody else. He might be good or he might be a fucking idiot who will get them all killed. I can't do that. They're my men, I've fought with some of them halfway across Europe. I'm in this to the bitter end. I just hope when it does end, I'll still be standing. I hope you are too, by the way. I'd like to meet this Englishwoman of yours."

"I would like that too."

Bonnet finished his bacon and mopped up the grease with the last of his bread. He smiled at Bianca. "Look at us. French, Spanish and English. We have the potential for a European coalition right here. Which is why Soult had better not fuck this up for me or I will be mightily pissed off. Have some more coffee. I've a feeling we'll be on the move tomorrow, we should make the most of this while we can."

***

The recently formed Staff Corps of Cavalry, led by Colonel George Scovell, joined the Light Division at Vera and set up camp just to the north of the third brigade. Scovell was an energetic, intelligent officer approaching forty and a good friend of Paul's. His wife Mary had been in Portugal for a time and got on well with Anne. She had returned to England the previous year but was a regular correspondent.

The Staff Corps of Cavalry was Wellington's first official unit of military police and Paul, who had been pushing for such an initiative for several years, was a firm supporter. Scovell commanded four troops equipped as light dragoons but with their own distinctive red uniform. In addition to their policing duties they were often used for escort duty and sometimes as combat cavalry. Paul had seen little of Scovell since Vitoria. His men had been busy scouring the countryside for deserters or simply men who had wandered off in search of plunder and not yet found their way back to the lines. Wellington had been furious about the break down of discipline after the battle and Paul suspected that Scovell had heard more than enough about it.

53

Anne invited Scovell to dinner shortly after his arrival and he appeared promptly in the barn, brushing raindrops from his cloak and looking around admiringly.

"This is so well-organised. You shouldn't have invited me, ma'am. You're going to find me hovering around your doorstep far too often in the hope of a hot meal in a dry space. How are you? You're looking very well."

Anne gave him her hand with a broad smile. "I am. It's lovely to see you, Colonel and you're always welcome. Come and sit down and have a drink. The furnishings are a little eccentric as you can see; we've borrowed every bench or stool we could from local farmhouses and villages. But you'll get a good dinner, I promise you. How is Mary, have you heard from her?"

The conversation ranged over family and domestic matters for the first part of the meal, but eventually Anne's attention was claimed by Simon Carlyon who was seated on her other side and Paul turned to his friend.

"How's it going?"

"I think it's going well," Scovell said cautiously. "It's always difficult to tell with his Lordship. He's been in a foul temper over the number of men still missing from their battalions but we're still bringing them in. Any of yours still missing, General?"

"A few. Too many, given that I suspect they won't be coming back. One or two of them might be wandering Spain with a pocket full of gold, but honestly, I doubt it. I think they probably died on the battlefield and nobody saw it."

Scovell's expression softened. "How is Sergeant-Major Carter doing?"

"Very well, according to Dr Norris who sends me regular reports. He's taking gentle exercise and has started to help Norris's Commandant of Hospitals with some of his administrative tasks. I've told Norris I don't want him anywhere near the wards though, in case of fever. He was so close to death, I'm worried that an illness now would carry him off. Norris tells me that Carter is itching to come back but I've told Carter he's not stirring an inch until Norris says he's fit enough. I had a letter from Manson yesterday as well. He's a lot better, I suspect he'll be back before Carter, though I've told him not to rush it. He's not had a proper day off since he arrived in Portugal three years ago."

"And Carl?"

Paul felt the accustomed tightening of his throat at the mention of his oldest friend. He was learning to manage it, but he wondered if it would ever go away.

"He's fine. Settling down to life as his father's curate. Learning to ride a horse with only one hand. Happy to be home with his parents. Refusing to admit how much he's missing the army."

Scovell smiled. "He isn't going to tell you that, sir."

"I wish he bloody would, so that I could tell him how much I'm missing him. With all this upheaval and the prospect of crossing into France…I feel as though I've lost my left hand as well, George. But I can't tell him that, it would only make him feel worse."

"You don't think there's any chance he'll change his mind?"

"No. It's one of the many things Carl and I agreed on. We've all watched officers like Edward Paget come back and try to carry on as though nothing had happened. In peacetime it doesn't really matter, but trying to fight with only one hand is madness. For Paget it ended in a French prison. He was lucky. He could have ended up dead."

"I know," Scovell said quietly. "I think Carl made the right decision, sir. But it must be hard for you."

"It is." Paul forced himself to smile. "But sitting crying over my dinner isn't going to help me. Let's talk about something else."

It was full dark when Scovell left and Paul walked him to where Jenson had brought his horse. Charlie Bannan stood holding a lantern as Scovell mounted.

"It's good to see you, Colonel. I hope we'll see a lot more of you. Oh, just one thing. I forgot to mention it at dinner. Do you still have Captain White in the Corps?"

"Yes, of course. We've lost a few officers; this work doesn't suit everybody. And poor Manningham had to go home after Vitoria. But I think White will stay; he's got a feel for this. And he's a damned good soldier."

"Yes, I like him. He was around a lot at one point; he got friendly with Manson. I wanted a word with him about the Rory Stewart case. Can you ask him to ride over when he's free? Sooner rather than later, as we could get orders at any minute."

"I'll send him up tomorrow. Everything all right with Stewart?"

"Yes, he's doing well. Seems like a reformed character. Even I've had to admit his wife was right to give him another chance. Thanks, George. I'll see you soon."

***

Captain Zachariah White appeared the following day, just as Paul was opening a letter from Lord Wellington. He raised a hand in greeting and left Jenson to take White's horse while he skimmed the brief note then swore. Anne looked up from the letter she was writing.

"Is something wrong, Paul?"

"Not exactly wrong. Inconvenient. This is really intended for you, girl of my heart. It seems that Wellington's bitch is about to produce the puppies and his Lordship was wondering if you could assist. Hasn't he got grooms for that? And isn't there a veterinary officer attached to headquarters somewhere?"

Anne set down her pen and capped the ink pot neatly. "No, although I'm sure he could borrow one from the nearest cavalry regiment. He doesn't need to though. I promised I'd go and I will. I won't be away long, Paul, there's no need to worry. Though I suppose I'll need an escort."

"He's sent a cavalry escort. I want you to take Brat with you and I'm sending one of my ADCs. Captain Kuhn will jump at the chance."

55

Anne broke into laughter. "Paul, it's four miles. I can be there and back in..."

"There are currently no females at headquarters, Nan, apart from that terrifyingly bad tempered laundry maid and a couple of kitchen assistants. I know you; if this birth goes on into the night, you won't leave."

"Am I imagining this, or are you actually worried about my reputation?"

He could not help laughing. "No, you impudent baggage, I'm worried about Lord Wellington's. If you don't have a female companion, he'll send you back. You know he will. He adores that blasted dog but he would never let even the faintest whiff of impropriety touch you. Whether that's because he's concerned about you or scared of me, I'm not sure."

Anne's face softened into a smile. She went to kiss him and Paul put his arms about her, prolonging the embrace.

"I know I fuss," he said finally, raising his head. "I know it seems bloody hilarious that I'm preaching propriety given my reputation. I know you're perfectly capable of managing all of this without my interference. I just love you, Nan, and sometimes it's all I can do to let you out of my sight after…well, after some of the things that have happened over the past couple of years."

He saw her expression change and wondered if his oblique reference to the horrors of her two week captivity by the French had upset her. She reached up and caressed his cheek lovingly then stood on tiptoe and kissed him again.

"I know, love. And you're right of course. I will take Ariana, I will take Isair, and I will take Captain Kuhn. I may tease you about it, but I love that you care so much. I'll try to get back tonight if I can, but if it's full dark, I'll stay in Lesaca."

"Make sure you do, bonny lass. These roads are bad enough in daylight."

"I promise. Go and talk to Captain White."

Paul watched her leave in search of her various escorts, smiling a little. When he had first known Anne she had fiercely resisted any attempt on his part to restrict her freedom. What had happened the previous year had affected her confidence but he suspected she had recovered far better than he had. Paul knew perfectly well that his wife accepted his protective measures not because she felt in need of them, but because she understood that he did. During her painful recovery from her ordeal Paul had fretted silently over his failure to keep her safe. He had tried to hide it from Anne but she knew him too well. Her co-operation was a gift to him and Paul was passionately grateful for it.

His reverie was interrupted by his orderly. "Captain White is here, sir. Do you want me to bring him in to your tent?"

"Yes please, Jenson. Oh no wait. I want Colonel Wheeler, Captain Mackenzie and Captain Fenwick to be here for this as well and I don't want to be interrupted."

56

"What about the small surgeon's tent, sir? It only gets used once a day for Mrs van Daan's clinic and it's well away from the officers' tents. I can move some chairs in there."

"As long as I'm not going to find a revolting array of surgical implements used for lancing boils laid out."

Jenson laughed. "If anybody left their instruments lying about she'd skin them alive, sir. I'll get it set up and I'll send Charlie for the others."

"Thank you, Jenson. Oh, take up some of the Portuguese red, will you? I don't think White has the money for good wine and he's going to need a drink for this particular meeting."

"Yes, sir. Want me to wait outside, make sure nobody takes an interest? At a distance, of course."

"Yes, but don't worry about the distance. You know perfectly well what this is about and I trust you implicitly. I don't want Charlie serving the wine though."

"Yes, sir."

By the time Paul reached the tent, the other four men were already seated in camp chairs and Jenson had provided wine and two small folding tables. The men rose to salute him. Captain White looked uncomfortable and Paul did not blame him. His first few meetings with Major-General van Daan earlier in the year had been acrimonious and he was probably wondering what on earth this was about.

"Sit down, gentlemen. Captain White, thank you for coming over so promptly. Did Colonel Scovell give you any idea what this is about?"

"No, sir. He said you would explain it. Have I...am I in trouble?"

Paul smiled. "Good God, no. It wouldn't be any of my business even if you were. I wanted to speak to you because you're familiar with the details of Sergeant Stewart's court martial earlier in the year. Some new information has emerged and I want to discuss it with you."

White looked at him blankly. He was a slender dark-haired man in his late twenties, who had demonstrated remarkable tenacity during the investigations which had let to Sergeant Rory Stewart's conviction for the murder of Major Leonard Vane. Paul knew that he had been warmly commended by Colonel Scovell and received cautious approval from Lord Wellington for the work he had done on the case.

"Of course, sir. I mean...is Stewart in trouble again? Has he done something else?"

"No, he hasn't," Ross Mackenzie said crisply. "Sergeant Stewart is working for me as my quartermaster-sergeant and he hasn't put a foot wrong. He's efficient, reliable and has completely given up strong drink, for which he has my respect. I have no complaints about Sergeant Stewart."

White looked taken aback and Paul was not surprised. He managed not to laugh at the younger man's expression and said soothingly:

"We're very pleased with the Sergeant's progress, Captain White. So far he seems to have learned his lesson very well. I should tell you before I begin that he has no idea this meeting is taking place. I'll decide what to tell him once I've spoken to you."

"Yes, sir."

Paul leaned forward and gently pushed a wine glass towards White. "Drink some wine, Captain. You're going to need it. Captain Mackenzie, will you explain your discovery regarding Sergeant Stewart's bayonet please?"

"Of course." Mackenzie reached inside his jacket and drew out a bound notebook. "I hope you don't mind me referring to my notes, sir. I want to get the dates right."

"Carry on, Captain."

Mackenzie looked at White. "I didn't know Stewart before the court martial; I was new out here and still getting to grips with my job. Naturally I heard about it and I was very surprised, along with the rest of the army, when he was found guilty of murder but not given the death penalty."

"It was a shock to me too," White said with feeling.

"Once I heard that Major Vane had raped Stewart's wife, I felt that the court had made the right decision. All the same, I wasn't enthusiastic when I was asked to give him a try as my assistant quartermaster. He had a reputation as a drunkard and I needed a man I could trust. I've already told you that my views have changed. When he joined me he was still recovering from the flogging. I think he came back too soon but I understood why. He wanted to prove himself, both to the battalion and to his wife. I did a routine kit inspection, mostly because his uniform was a mess. I had to replace pretty much everything. I got him to tally up what was needed and work out what he needed to pay for and what could come out of the new kit allowance that Lord Wellington agreed – shoes and a few other things. As it happened, some of the officers set up a fund to pay for it. But Sergeant Stewart's bayonet was missing."

"His bayonet?" White asked, puzzled. "Should he have had one?"

"Yes, because he'd been broken back to a private because of his drinking and fighting. When he came to me he was made up to sergeant again. He should have traded in his bayonet for a sergeant's sword. He tried avoiding the issue but eventually admitted he'd lost it."

"When?" White asked. Paul could not repress a little smile. He had not underestimated Zachariah White. He had set down his wine glass and was leaning forward, his eyes on Mackenzie. It was clear that he had immediately realised the implications of what had just been said.

"He couldn't tell me; he had no memory of it. I tore him off a strip and told him that as he hadn't lost it in battle, he'd need to pay for it over a period of time. But before we'd even had time to arrange the deductions from his pay, it turned up."

"How?"

"A trooper brought it down. It had been found in a tavern."

"I wasn't told anything about this."

"He might not have been from your troop, Captain and he wouldn't have grasped the significance," Paul said. "Though I can see you have."

"Yes. Do we know when?"

"Yes," Ross said. "The landlord knew Stewart, he drank there regularly. He handed it in to the nearest battalion and forgot about it. Fortunately the quartermaster was a true administrator and wrote up a docket listing where and when it had been found. He added a recommendation that Stewart be disciplined for carelessness. I think the stores held on to it for a while because of the trial. None of us thought he was coming out of that alive. But he did and eventually they sent the bayonet back. It arrived on my desk along with the docket. They got me to sign for it."

"And?" White asked.

"And the whole episode of the loss of that bayonet and its subsequent return was more than two weeks before Major Vane was killed. Stewart had left it in that tavern during a previous drunken stupor. It didn't arrive back here until after the trial."

"That can't be right," White argued. "Somebody would have realised it was missing. Weren't there any inspections or drill? I know it was winter quarters but surely..."

"This is the 110th, Captain White," Giles said gloomily. "There are always inspections. And drills. And training. We don't get time off here."

Johnny gave what Paul strongly suspected was a laugh, hastily disguised as a cough. He gave his friend a look. Johnny attempted to look apologetic.

"Stewart covered it up with the help of some friends," Ross said. "There were several men laid up with fever so they borrowed a bayonet from one of them. But the thing is that the man in the hospital agreed to lend it on the basis that Stewart was only allowed to use it during drills and inspections. At all other times one of the NCOs took care of it. I suppose he didn't want to come out of hospital to find that Stewart had lost his bayonet as well."

White closed his eyes. "It can't be right," he said again. "What does Stewart say?"

"He doesn't realise yet," Ross said. "When I gave him a bollocking for losing it, he admitted that he'd tried asking around but he had no idea where he'd left it. I think he was in a fairly desperate state at that time, White. His wife had left him and he was under the impression that she'd been selling her favours to an officer. He'd been demoted and he was drinking heavily. He told me that there were whole weeks that he just can't remember. When I told him it had been found he was just relieved not to have to pay for it. But I trust the date on that docket and I trust the man who assures me that Stewart had no access to that bayonet on the day of Vane's murder."

"So how did he kill him?" Johnny asked, his tone reasonable.

White did not speak for a long time. Paul watched the mobile intelligent face. He knew how the other man was feeling. He had felt the same way weeks ago when Mackenzie had brought the story to him. Finally White looked up.

"He could have found another weapon. Borrowed someone else's bayonet or stolen a knife."

"That presumes that he went out looking for Vane, but we know he didn't," Johnny said. "He went to find a tavern to get drunk in and he wandered further afield because he'd been thrown out of his usual haunts. And Vane shouldn't have been there. He was absent without leave as well. Neither of them could have expected to run into one another that night. Besides, what did Stewart do with the bayonet or the knife? He didn't make his own way back to barracks. Colonel Swanson and Private Browning brought him back."

"Are you saying he didn't do it?" White said angrily. "He admitted it. He stood up in court and confessed for God's sake. Vane raped his wife, he got drunk and killed the bastard. And knowing what I do about Vane now, I don't blame him. He did it, he confessed and he took his punishment." White looked at Paul. "It's over, sir. Surely there's no sense in dragging this up again?"

"Are you suggesting we suppress it?"

"No. No, of course not. But he did confess."

"No he didn't. I went back and read the trial transcripts again."

"Of course you did," White said bitterly.

"It's my job, Captain. He never actually confessed. He said he couldn't remember. He admitted very freely that he could have done it. He even said he thinks he did it. But he never actually confessed, because he was on oath and he couldn't. He can't remember to this day what happened that night. Don't look so upset. I felt the same way when Captain Mackenzie first landed this little problem on my desk. I've lain awake in the wee small hours worrying at it. But I can't come to any other conclusion. Actually it makes a lot more sense than the version we heard in court. Stewart was a mass of bruises where Vane had given him a kicking. He was known for being an aggressive drunk. If he'd been armed he'd have fought back much sooner and wouldn't have been so badly beaten."

"He might, if Vane was sober."

"In that case he wouldn't have been able to kill Vane at all. How could a man in his condition win a fight against an officer armed with a sword when he didn't even have a bayonet? How did he kill him?"

"Jesus Christ. I can't believe I could have made a mistake like this."

"It wasn't just you. We all did. None of us asked the right questions because Stewart was resigned to his fate. He wasn't even going to mount a defence until my wife got involved."

"We might have hanged an innocent man."

"At least this time we didn't," Johnny said soberly.

White looked genuinely upset. "What in God's name am I going to do? We can't try the man again."

"You're certainly not trying the man again," Paul said grimly. "If we get the wrong officers on the jury they'll probably try to flog him all over again and then it'll be me on trial for murder. I don't know the right thing to do, White. At the moment, I've not even decided what I should say to Stewart. He's settled so well. But I want it on record that I think that verdict might be unsound. Not just because the wrong man was convicted. But because the murderer hasn't been identified."

There was a long, painful silence in the tent. Eventually White picked up his glass and drank deeply. Paul considered another joke about how badly White must need a drink but decided against it. The young Staff Cavalry Corps officer could not express himself freely to a Major-General so it would not be fair.

White set his glass down. "Thank you for drawing this to my attention, sir," he said formally. "With your permission, I'm going to make a report to Colonel Scovell and suggest that we discuss it further with Judge-Advocate-General Larpent. I expect he'll want to speak to you about it and he may want to interview Stewart again."

"I'll make sure Stewart is aware of that possibility. At some point this is going to come to the attention of Lord Wellington. May I suggest that you get me involved at that point? You might as well. The minute he hears about it, he's going to blame me anyway so we can save ourselves some time."

White managed a smile. "Yes, sir. I would like to say this should be kept as quiet as possible, but I suppose there's no chance of that once you've spoken to Stewart."

"I think you'll find that if I ask my Quartermaster-Sergeant to keep his mouth shut, Captain, he'll do just that," Ross said definitely.

White blinked at his tone but said nothing. He rose and saluted. "I'll let you know what happens next, sir. But you do know, I suppose, that there's almost no chance of finding out who really killed Vane? Not after all this time."

Paul returned the salute. "I don't care who killed Vane," he said pleasantly. "Whoever it was, I'll just bet he had a good reason and the women of this army will sleep safer at night knowing that arsehole has gone. What I would like is for that conviction to be quashed and removed from Stewart's record."

"I've no idea if that's even possible, sir."

"Well if it isn't, we're going to set a precedent," Paul said inexorably. "Good luck with Larpent, Captain."

"Of course you know that this whole thing is probably going to be delayed by sudden orders to attack the French, don't you?" Johnny said mildly.

"Very probably, Colonel. But at least I can set it in motion. Good afternoon, Captain White."

They watched as White left the tent. Outside, Paul could hear Jenson speaking briefly as he brought White's horse forward, then there was the muffled sound of hooves as White departed. Nobody spoke for a while, then Giles stirred.

"Thank you for including me, sir. I'm not sure what to say."

"You're my Brigade-Major, Giles. You need to know what's going on."

"I know. But Christ...poor Stewart. I was there that day. For the flogging. I didn't need to be, I was officially on furlough, but I felt as though I should. It was brutal, but at the time I thought he'd got off lightly for killing an officer. To find out that he went through that – and what happened to Sally – for nothing. It's appalling."

"I wonder who did kill Vane," Johnny said. "I don't suppose we'll ever find out."

"I hope we don't," Paul said. "I certainly don't intend to waste any time on it. Vane bloody deserved it and if I'd got my hands on him after I found out what he did to Sally, it would have been me. Jenson, open that second bottle, will you? I need liquid courage and some helpful advice from you lot on the subject of how to tell Rory Stewart about all this."

Chapter Five

By the 24th of July, D'Erlon's brigade had marched into position to scale the pass of Maya. In just over two weeks, Marshal Soult had completely reorganised the army and supplied it to the best of his ability. Gabriel Bonnet approved the man's energy and organisational talent, but was doubtful about his potential for success. He kept his thoughts mostly to himself however, knowing that in difficult conditions, morale was crucial. His men had not had time to recover from the slaughter of Vitoria and he knew there was no possibility of them getting the time they needed. He decided that under these circumstances, revenge would be a better motivator than sympathy and gave a short speech reminding them of the death of their Colonel, their officers and their comrades on the battlefield, before setting off to march to their rallying point.

A longer speech had been sent out with Marshal Soult's final orders, with instructions that it was to be read out to each company. Bonnet sat on horseback, listening to Damien Cavel's impressively literate rendition, and wondered if all the officers were doing as well. Soult's words were cleverly chosen to bolster morale. He expressed disappointment with the failure of the troops to hold Spain but placed the blame squarely on the heads of their former commanders. He assured them that the Emperor had been told of their loyalty and bravery and dismissed the difficulties of the coming campaign with a suggestion that Napoleon's birthday, in August, should be celebrated in the newly regained city of Vitoria. It was a masterly speech, designed to rouse the army to a sense of its place in the Empire and in history. Bonnet personally thought that another two days' rations would have been more useful.

The supply situation worried him. He could remember the barren countryside around Tarragona two years earlier which had meant that Suchet had to be prepared to transport supplies for an army that could not possibly live off the land. The countryside there had been much easier for wheeled transport. Here, food had to be carried in the men's knapsacks. Bonnet had seen what had been issued and he did not think it was the four days' worth that Soult claimed.

Surprise was the key to Soult's plan of attack. The mountainous countryside with its rocky ridges and deep valleys, gave limited visibility to Wellington's men camped up in the high passes. Soult had exchanged letters with the Governor of the besieged city of San Sebastian and been assured that the citadel could hold out for at least another two weeks. He had therefore decided to cross the mountains and relieve Pamplona, sweeping the Allied troops down into the valleys. Bonnet had no idea of the various troop depositions and he worried that Soult might not know either, but the Allies must have exactly the same communication difficulties as the French. This would give the attackers the advantage for a while, until Wellington got news of the assault but Bonnet did not feel complacent. He had seen at Vitoria how fast the Allied troops could move and how quickly Wellington could adapt his plans to changing situations. Bonaparte might sneer at a general who had come to prominence commanding sepoy troops in India but he had not yet faced Wellington across a battlefield and Bonnet thought it was time he did.

Soult had given orders for the French outposts to take hostages from the men of all the frontier villages to prevent information being given to the Allied army. Bonnet considered these terror tactics both unpleasant and ridiculous. The only way Soult could possibly know if information had reached Wellington, would be if his attack encountered much stronger resistance than expected or even a counter-attack. Should that happen, he would presumably be too busy to investigate which Spanish peasant had passed the news to Wellington so the correct hostages could be executed. Perhaps he intended to shoot all of them. Bonnet shuddered a little at the thought. He had never enjoyed the more brutal aspects of occupying foreign territories, but since meeting Bianca, he had a tendency to see such reprisals against her countrymen through her eyes and he hated it.

As with most surprise attacks, things began to go wrong quite quickly. The weather worsened and torrential rain made marching difficult. Soult had sent the guns along with the infantry and this slowed them down even further. Some men collapsed from exhaustion and limited rations before ever reaching the rallying point. The men grumbled and guards were set to protect the transport oxen from hungry men looking for a meal.

The Comte d'Erlon had three divisions under his command, led by Generals D'Armagnac, Abbé and Maransin. The 30th légère had been placed in Chassé's brigade under D'Armagnac They set off from the little village of Espelette at one o'clock in the morning and by the time they reached the meeting point at the northern end of the Mondarrain Mountain, they were exhausted, soaked to the skin and hungry. There was no sign of Abbé's brigade. Bonnet wondered if they had got lost or simply had not bothered to come.

While waiting for orders, he gave permission for his men to eat part of their rations. Peering through the rain, which had subsided to a misty drizzle, he could see the steep slopes rising before him. As dawn gave faint colour to the sky, he could see rocky outcrops jutting out and the path, which seemed barely a goat track in places, looked muddy and difficult. It would be hard enough scrambling up there with weapons and packs without having the men faint from hunger.

General Chassé called his battalion commanders for a final briefing and they huddled under some trees in search of shelter. It was still new to Bonnet to be part of meetings like this. His promotion to command the 30th had been purely accidental. As the most senior captain after the debacle of Vitoria, he had taken command of the battalion on the retreat. He had kept his men together during the long trek over the mountains, had fought brief rear-guard actions against the pursuing Allies and had buried too many of his officers and men along the way. When the various French armies were combined and reorganised, he had vaguely hoped that he would finally be rewarded with his majority. It had not occurred to him that there was nobody else with the experience to take over from Colonel Lacasse. It was a big jump and he was still getting used to it. Having spent the latter years of his army career deliberately not caring about promotion to protect himself from the inevitable disappointment he had temporarily panicked in case he was too old and too set in his ways to do a good job, but he was beginning to settle into the role now.

He did not know Chassé particularly well. The General was Dutch, of a Huguenot family, and had joined the army as a boy; rising to prominence in the forces of the Netherlands. King Louis Bonaparte had given him command of the Dutch brigade when Napoleon demanded troops for the French campaign in Spain in 1808. He had distinguished himself in that brutal war and had been given a baronetcy just before Bonaparte annexed the Kingdom of Holland to the French Empire. Bonnet had heard rumours that Chassé had resented the annexation, so much that he refused to accept a further award from Bonaparte in 1811. Nevertheless he was still here, though in a reduced role as brigade commander.

The plan was for D'Armagnac's division to lead an attack on the Aratesque Hill which was currently occupied by an Allied outpost, before moving on to capture the eastern end of the ridge. General Maransin's brigade would attack the western end once the main assault had started and the columns would push forward to join up as quickly as possible. It was a simple plan, which Bonnet liked but he was still unable to see any sign of Abbé's brigade.

"Any questions, gentlemen?" Chassé said finally.

"What about the other brigade, sir. Do we wait for them?"

"My orders are to prepare to march, then wait. A messenger just rode in; there was some delay in collecting their rations but they're on their way now. General D'Erlon himself will command this wing. The initial attack will consist of eight light companies, led by Commandant Duzer of the 28th. We will follow in immediately afterwards. The companies are as follows."

Bonnet felt his heart sink as Cavel's name was called out. He was not surprised. The 30th had made something of a name for itself at Vitoria and during the retreat, and Cavel was one of the more experienced captains. He would have preferred his friend to go in with the rest of the battalion but he tried to look pleased because he knew Cavel would be. As Chassé gave the order to form up, Bonnet clapped the other man on the shoulder.

"Good luck, Captain Cavel. Don't be a fucking hero today. That's D'Erlon's job, he wants the glory of leading in his division. Let him have it and do the intelligent thing. I need you."

Cavel threw a mocking salute. "As always, Colonel, I shall try to obey your orders."

"Oh piss off. And keep safe. I'll see you up there, we won't be far behind."

"Where is your wife?"

"She's back in Espelette with the baggage wagons. And you wouldn't believe it, but half a dozen of those Spanish women have turned up again. They're getting ready to help with any wounded."

"Unbelievable," Cavel said seriously. "Still, they will be good nurses. How fortunate that they got lost on their way back to Spain and returned to us. I will see you soon, Colonel. Take care of yourself."

It promised to be a fine day as the men formed up with the main column. Bonnet looked up into clear blue skies decorated with drifting clouds, driven by a fresh breeze. After the miserable days of rain it was glorious and he wished he was sitting outside his tent with Cavel, watching Bianca cook dinner. She liked to sing about her work and after two years, the sound of her clear soprano voice still had the power to make him smile. He was smiling now, just thinking about it and he saw Major Faure looking sideways at him. The other officers of the 30th were still getting used to Bonnet's style of command, which was very different to that of Colonel Lacasse, and poor Faure, who was conscientious and brave but very attached to army regulations, looked permanently worried.

"You are smiling, Colonel. Are you so happy to be going into battle?"

Bonnet thought about lying but could not bring himself to do so. "I was thinking about my wife, Major, and wishing I was sitting in the sun with her instead of standing about waiting to risk my neck for fucking Bonaparte again."

Faure looked around quickly. "Colonel, you must not say such things," he said in an agonised whisper. "If General Chassé should hear you…"

"I think General Chassé might agree with me. After all, he lost his country to the bastard." He held up a hand to stop further protests. Faure looked as though he was about to cry. "All right, Major, I will behave. I wonder why we have the honour of leading the column today? Takes me all the way back to Tarragona when we were in the front of every bloody charge."

"I do not know, sir. Perhaps…"

Faure broke off as movement at the front caught his eye. Bonnet reached for his telescope and opened it up, training it on the tirailleurs as they set off and then moving it up the slope to the heights where the enemy were bivouacked. D'Erlon hoped to take the Allies by surprise and it was beginning to look as though, for once, a plan was going to work. There was no sign of increased troop movements and no sounds of marching or shouted orders floating down to the waiting French troops.

In the distance he could see a scattering of white tents on the ridge and some red-coated soldiers occupied a knoll, but the scene was peaceful, as though they had no idea they were about to be attacked. Bonnet studied the slopes and the rocky outcrops and decided that the light companies, now beginning the steep climb, were simply not visible to the sentries yet. He felt a tug of sympathy for the British soldiers. At the same time he was conscious of a sense of grim satisfaction. This army, peacefully encamped under a blue summer sky, had taken his battalion apart only a month earlier at Vitoria. He did not generally hunger for revenge but the memory of their flight from the bloody battlefield and the miserable retreat into France, with Wellington's men snapping at their heels, gave him the desire to demonstrate that the French were not yet cowed and beaten. He did not give a damn for the glory of the Emperor but he would fight for the ghosts of the men he had lost.

The column waited tensely for the order to follow the light companies up the steep track. It came quietly with no blowing of bugles or beating of drums. There was still no sign that the Allied outpost had noticed anything amiss. Bonnet wondered who was in command up there and what the hell they were doing. Troops occupying such a distant outpost in difficult country should have been constantly reconnoitring the area for signs of the enemy. Somebody had blundered badly.

The track from Espelette crossed the border somewhere in the region of the Gorospil peak, then ran along a broad grassy ridge towards the peak of Alcurrunz. As the column climbed higher, Bonnet was becoming breathless. He was sweating with the effort and looked around surreptitiously at his officers and men, relieved to find that most of them were red-faced and breathing hard. He took out his watch. It was almost ten-thirty and the advanced party of light companies could not be more than half a mile from the British pickets.

As he returned the watch to his pocket, there was a sudden flurry of activity ahead of him and the tirailleurs broke into a run. He watched them cover the remaining ground quickly, faintly envious of their energy. Above them, finally, there were shouts of alarm and yelled orders as the British outpost realised that they were under attack. A crackle of musket fire shattered the peaceful morning, drowning out the sounds of birdsong and the distant lowing of cattle.

He called for his men to advance. The bugle sounded and its call was taken up by others, back down the column. Now that the enemy was warned of their approach, they needed to move quickly in support of the light companies. He had no idea how many men defended the pass but he was worried about Cavel. His friend was an intelligent fighter who would not take unnecessary risks but he would be in the thick of any action and Bonnet knew how quickly a screen of skirmishers could get into trouble if the main body of troops dallied too long.

His sudden urgency affected his men and they raced up the slope, ignoring burning muscles and pounding hearts. The musket fire had intensified and it was clear that battle was thoroughly joined. Bonnet reached the final twist in the track, rounded some woodland and found himself at the head of the column with neither D'Erlon or Chassé immediately within sight. For a moment he froze, realising he had outpaced his commanding officers, but it was only a moment's hesitation. He raised his sword and pointed it towards the enemy with a yell and the 30th charged forward.

The knoll was better defended than he would have expected for an outlying picket. He wondered if somebody had finally seen the approaching French and sent in reinforcements. It was impossible to be sure, but he thought there might be three-or-four hundred redcoats. They were falling back quickly into a defensive circle around the upper slopes of the knoll. The ground was dotted with rocky outcrops which provided some rudimentary shelter from musket fire. It also gave the British troops cover to fire their own muskets and he could hear the officers shouting orders, desperately trying to organise their men.

Several horsemen had appeared at the head of the track and Count D'Erlon was giving orders to the rest of D'Armagnac's brigade. It did not concern Bonnet, who knew that his job was to put maximum pressure onto the beleaguered British while his commanders organised an encircling movement. He had no idea how close they were to the rest of the Allied troops but he knew they needed to finish this before reinforcements could arrive.

The 30th were falling back as the British muskets began a steady fire from their rocky fortress. Bonnet called them to order, running an eye over the ground. It was scattered with dead and wounded from both sides, but there were far more redcoats than blue on the ground; a testament to how badly the enemy had been caught unawares by the French light companies. Now that the 30th was in position to lead the main attack, the skirmishers were fanning out on both sides to outflank the British position.

He gave his orders and his men moved quickly into place. This assault was more difficult because the enemy was prepared and could see them coming. His muskets fired a first devastating volley and several men fell, including one of the officers who had found himself in an exposed position while trying to organise his troops. The 30th reloaded quickly but the enemy was quicker and the first row of Bonnet's men were mown down by a well directed response. He swore. The man commanding these troops might have been criminally negligent in matters of reconnaissance and picket duty, but the men themselves knew what they were doing and this promised to be bloody.

He quickly lost track of time and any sense of what was happening elsewhere on the field. Again and again he urged his men forward and seethed with frustration as they were thrown back by a determined defence. The British fought with stubborn courage and he could not decide if they knew reinforcements must be close by or if it was sheer bloody-mindedness. Eventually, Captain Foulon's company forced their way so far up the slope that they reached the first of the defenders and Bonnet could hear the clash of steel as the Allies fought back with bayonets. He gave a bellow of triumph and raced forward, yelling at his men to join him in support, but before he reached Foulon's position there was an enormous crash of musket fire and the French reeled back down the slope, some of them tumbling over in their eagerness to escape the destructive fire. Bonnet's shout turned to one of rage as he realised how many of his men had gone down.

He could not see Foulon in the confused mass of retreating men and he grabbed one of them by the arm. The infantryman was young, barely out of his teens, and his smoke-blackened face was streaked with blood, possibly from whoever had been next to him in the charge. He had been shot, his other arm hanging uselessly, with blood soaking through his jacket.

"Where's Captain Foulon?"

"Down, Colonel. I saw him fall."

"Dead?"

They were both yelling to be heard over the thunder of musket fire. Bonnet's throat was raw and his voice was strained.

"I don't know, sir. I could not see."

Bonnet looked back up the slope. The dead and wounded covered the ground and now many of them were French. It would be impossible to get close enough to search for Foulon without being shot down. He felt a surge of utter fury at the prospect of losing him. He realised he still had no idea what had happened to Cavel either. He released the boy.

"Get yourself back down to the surgeons, boy. You can't fight with that arm."

The thunder of artillery drowned out any reply. Bonnet wheeled around in horror, wondering if the British had guns that he had not seen, but none of his men seemed to have been hit. The top of a nearby knoll was wreathed in smoke but he thought the guns were pointing down the slope. They could not possibly be used in support of the defenders without killing their own men. He suspected he had just heard a warning volley, intended to alert nearby troops of the attack. Given the racket of musket fire, he thought it was superfluous but the gunners probably felt as though they had to do something.

He watched the boy stumbling back towards the path then turned to survey the knoll. Immediately he realised something was different. The musket fire was dying away and in its place was the discordant clash of bayonets which suggested hand to hand fighting. For a moment, he wondered if the British had run out of ammunition then he realised they were fighting on all sides. Somebody, probably the light companies, had encircled the knoll and outflanked the defenders. Looking around him, Bonnet realised that the rest of D'Armagnac's battalions were swarming in over the ridge from all directions, heading for the knoll.

He ran back into the fight, shouting orders to those of his men who could hear him. Halfway up, he encountered a British officer who looked far too young to be wearing the uniform. His white face and terrified eyes almost distracted Bonnet from the swinging sword. He parried it away at the last minute, and the force of his arm combined with the steep slope of the land, caused the younger man to lose his footing. He fell heavily onto his back and Bonnet took a step forward and kicked the sword from his hand. The young officer gave a cry of pain. Bonnet stood over him and placed his sword at the other man's throat.

"Surrender," he said.

Bonnet spoke very little English. During the last campaign, Cavel had discovered this and had spent the retreat trying to teach him, much to Bianca's amusement. He had picked up a little more but there were certain words he had made a point of learning over the years and this was one of them. Silently he pleaded with the young officer to do the intelligent thing. Around him, other men were beginning to drop their weapons and hold up their hands. The knoll was already strewn with bodies and he did not want to kill an unarmed man. There had been enough slaughter here today.

After a long, tense pause the officer nodded cautiously and held up his hands. Bonnet tried not to show his relief too obviously. He bent to clean blood from his sword on the churned up grass then reached out his hand. The British officer looked surprised, but took it and allowed his opponent to help him to his feet. Bonnet ran his eyes over the boy to check for injuries then beckoned to one of his sous-lieutenants.

"Lepattre, escort this officer to the headquarters party; I can see the Comte d'Erlon on that knoll. One of his staff will know where they're taking the prisoners."

"Yes, Colonel."

"What's that noise? Reinforcements?"

"I think they are coming up the ridge, sir."

"I'll be happy to make the bastards' acquaintance, but not until I know about Captain Foulon…"

"He's dead, sir. So are Lieutenant Junot and Sous-Lieutenant Valette. All of them."

Bonnet felt as though he had been punched in the stomach. He stared at Lepattre's bloodshot eyes and realised the younger man had been crying and was trying hard not to show it. He sometimes thought that the long, bloody years of war had hardened him to the loss of friends and comrades but occasionally it hit him anew and all three officers from one company was a shock. He did not speak for a moment and when he did, his voice sounded strange in his own ears.

"Right. Hand this prisoner over the the headquarters staff, Lepattre, then start calling them in. We'll need to combine Foulon's company with another. Allard's, for now." He looked around as the sound of battle grew louder. "I'm glad they've come for another try, I'm in the right fucking mood for these red-coated bastards. Get moving Lepattre."

There was no time for Bonnet to ask about Cavel's light company. D'Armagnac was forming a new line, spread out along the broad saddle between the peaks and Chassé's brigade was lining up at the head of the track which led to the village of Maya. Red-coated soldiers were already arriving at the crest and Bonnet shouted the order to fire. The British fell back but were overtaken by others climbing up. They marched into a solid wall of musketry which made it impossible for them to break through the French advance and Chassé urged his brigade forwards, driving the enemy before him.

70

Glancing around during a brief break in the action, Bonnet was appalled at the reduced numbers in the brigade. He suspected his own battalion had left around a quarter of its men dead and wounded around the peak and he did not think they were the only ones to suffer. The approaching British troops were fresh to the fight but they had been obliged to make the scramble up the steep track at speed and were not in the best condition to deal with the French advance. There were not as many of them as he had expected and he wondered about that. It almost felt as though their commander had been caught napping and was sending troops piecemeal into battle without a proper plan. It meant the French only had to deal with one or two battalions at any given moment and they were slaughtering them.

Bonnet peered through the smoke down the hill. Another battalion was approaching in a two-deep line and the troops ahead of them dropped back and moved behind them. This looked better organised and he watched in growing dismay as the line spread out along the broad track.

French drummers and buglers called a frantic response and Bonnet's men began to move but there was no time and more importantly, no space. Their superior numbers, which had been sweeping the enemy back down the hill with relative ease, were suddenly working against them. To his horror, the British had their muskets at the ready and the French, packed together for the advance, had nowhere to go as the order was called.

A tremendous volley blew the leading ranks of D'Armagnac's division apart. Bonnet's men were in the third rank and only one or two were hit, but the shock of the volley seemed to rock the French backwards and he knew there was more to come. He swore, his voice coming out choked and hoarse with the billowing black smoke. The advantage was that the musket men would not be able to see anything for a while but even with the inaccuracy of their weapons they would not need to aim while the French were advancing in a solid column.

"Faure, Allard, divide the battalion," He yelled, hoping they could hear him. His own ears were ringing from the regular pounding of the guns and he did not really know how loud he was. Beside him, Sergeant-Major Belmas visibly jumped, which he saw as a good sign. "Fan them out on either side as skirmishers. We need to outflank these bastards or we'll be slaughtered."

His men were moving, splitting off from the main column to the right and left under Major Faure and Captain Allard. Bonnet followed Allard's group. Through occasional gaps in the smoke he could see them moving ahead quickly, bounding down the slope at a terrifying speed. Cynically he wondered if his impulsive order had been motivated by shrewd tactical thinking or an instinctive need to get the remainder of his battalion out of the line of fire, but whichever it was, he thought it might work.

As they approached the Allied lines his men searched for cover, finding bushes and rocky outcrops and dropping behind them. It gave them the freedom to advance in pairs without being seen and Bonnet, moving cautiously among them towards the leading skirmishers, realised with considerable satisfaction that the Allied regiment had no idea his men were there.

He had lost all sense of time, but he suspected it had been about twenty minutes since the British line had begun their forward movement and the casualties among the French were appalling. He knew it was only a matter of time before D'Erlon's other divisions arrived to reinforce and he had decided that however the Allied troops were deployed, they were hugely outnumbered by the French. Still, this engagement was going to be bloody on both sides.

With his men in place, Bonnet crouched behind a rock formation beside Faure and was pleased to see the very edge of the thin Allied line. He was close enough to see the yellow facings and silver lace on the flanking troops and he watched them for a moment, admiring the sheer bloody-minded courage with which these men were holding on to an impossible position against overwhelming odds.

"All right Major Faure. Let's get rid of them."

Faure rose, lifting his sword in silent instruction and the men around him stepped into firing position. Bonnet was close enough to hear screams of pain from the British troops as his muskets tore into them. As soon as they had fired, his men fell back into cover to reload, while the second of the skirmishing pair stepped out and fired. This close and with no warning, their volleys were lethal. Men dropped to the ground, dead or wounded and their comrades were beginning to panic, looking around them and peering through the smoke to identify the new threat. He watched them through four more volleys, knowing that on the other side of the line, Allard's men were inflicting similar carnage.

Still the British lines held, though their casualties were horrific. Men were beginning to fall back over the bodies of their comrades but it was a surprisingly orderly retreat. Bonnet could hear approaching drums from the French rear and realised that the inevitable reinforcements were marching up. The Allied troops heard it too. He could only see two officers on their feet, though there might have been others on the far side of the line. Inwardly he pleaded with them to do the right thing. D'Armagnac's men were beginning to fall back to allow the new troops through and Bonnet did not want to watch what was going to happen next. He realised he was holding onto the hilt of his sword so hard that it was hurting his hand and he forced himself to relax his grip.

At that moment, the Allied drums began to call the retreat.

Some of the 30th looked inclined to follow with bayonets and he called them back sharply. He had no wish for them to pursue too far and get themselves cut off. He also did not want to kill any more of these men just now. The smoke began to clear a little, blown away by the brisk mountain breeze, and he looked out over the killing ground and felt sick to his stomach. As far as he could see across the broad ridge, both French and British dead and wounded covered the ground. They had fought and died in their hundreds for this bleak mountain pass and he did not think it was over yet. He stood for a moment and wondered why it was that lately, after every battle, whether he had won or lost, he found himself wishing there was some way he could just walk away and go home.

"Colonel."

He spun around, peering through the smoke and felt sheer happiness at the sight of the tall, spare figure walking towards him. Cavel was limping slightly and there was blood on his left leg but he seemed to be in one piece. Bonnet walked forward and embraced him without hesitation. He had not realised until that moment how much this quiet, self-contained man meant to him. Cavel returned the embrace then stepped back, studying him.

"Was it you who ordered that rather unauthorised flanking movement, sir?"

"Yes. Do they know that?"

Cavel grinned. His smoke-blackened face made him look like a demon. "I think you'll find General Chassé is looking for you."

"Oh fuck. Shall I just desert? I was thinking about it back there but the sight of you distracted me. If they shoot me for this, it's your fault."

"Everything's my fault according to you. I'll come with you."

Bonnet rubbed his hands wearily over his face. They came away black. He thought irrelevantly that his beard needed trimming. The beard was a new acquisition. The repeated loss of various items of baggage over the past month had made it impossible to shave and half the army had sported ragged beards as they crossed the Pyrenees. He had never bothered with the traditional dashing whiskers which were fashionable among officers of light infantry, partly because his scar made it impossible to grow side whiskers properly, but mostly because he could not be bothered to keep them trimmed and waxed. The beard however had proved surprisingly successful and Bianca had announced that it should stay. He had endured some teasing from his fellow officers and one or two pointed looks from his seniors but he was an expert at ignoring those.

He found General Chassé with a group of senior officers huddled around a sketch map which looked as though it had been through a rainstorm. Bonnet wondered how they could possibly work out anything from its blurred lines. He also wondered briefly if that explained some of the more bizarre command decisions he had experienced over the years.

Chassé turned as they approached. He gave a brief order to one of his ADCs then stepped away from the group. Bonnet stood to attention. He had a sudden memory of several of his first meetings with Marshal Suchet during the miserable siege of Tarragona two years earlier and he wondered why a man who had spent so much of his army career trying to keep his head down and not be noticed should be so remarkably bad at it. He could not decide if it was a character flaw or simple bad luck.

"Colonel Bonnet, my aide tells me that you led your battalion in a flank attack on the British column. I saw it happening but I could not see who it was. Your men?"

"Yes, General. My apologies. I was carried away in the heat of battle."

It had always been his standard response to Colonel Lacasse when accused of showing any kind of initiative. He did not really expect it to work but it was the best he could do. Chassé looked at Cavel, standing just behind Bonnet's shoulder.

"And this officer?"

"Captain Damien Cavel, General. His company fought bravely in the first advance…"

"I saw Captain Cavel during the first advance, Colonel. I also observed the damage your battalion did to the flanks of the British line as they were slaughtering the rest of my brigade."

"What was left of my battalion, sir. We suffered greatly up on the knoll."

"I know. The wounded are being taken back down to Espelette. There are wagons to take them back to the hospitals. Captain Cavel, you are hurt?"

"It is not serious, General. A glancing blow from a bayonet, the bleeding has almost stopped. I would like to remain with my company."

"There is a field station at the foot of the hill. Have the wound dressed, if you please, then if the surgeon gives permission you may return. Colonel Bonnet."

"General Chassé."

"My commendation, sir. A brilliant piece of improvisation and a brave charge. I shall remember you and your men. Form them up, sir. General D'Erlon is to reorganise those men still able to fight, but the divisions of Maransin and Abbé will form the first lines. Detach a small party to assist your wounded then join your men."

"Yes, General. My thanks."

As they walked away, Bonnet glanced at Cavel. His friend was looking straight ahead, his gaze fixed on the soaring mountains. Bonnet could sense his amusement.

"Wipe that fucking smile off your face, Cavel and get yourself to the surgeon. I'm putting you in charge of the men detailed to get the wounded out of here. I don't trust these bastards not to make another attack, we don't even know where the fuck half of them are. Your job is to get my men off this mountain as fast as you can. You can pick your own ambulance detail."

"I will, Colonel." Cavel turned to look at Bonnet and his expression was suddenly serious. "I have to tell you that I lost my sous-lieutenant during the attack."

"Young Clement? Christ, I'm sorry."

"I'd like permission to bury him, sir."

"Granted. Providing you then find Foulon and his two officers and bury them as well."

Cavel could not speak for a moment. Eventually he said:

"They're all dead?"

"Yes. Get them off that knoll. I can't bury all my men but I'd like at least one grave to stand for all of them. Get back here as soon as you can. I don't think this is over yet."

Cavel saluted and departed in search of his men. Bonnet watched him go. Then he sighed and turned back towards the rising sounds of battle and went to find his battalion.

Anne had been more concerned than she was prepared to admit about Lord Wellington's prized hunting greyhound. Pearl was young and no experienced breeder would have suggested puppies for at least another year. Wellington, who was often distant and unemotional with people, was an affectionate dog owner and Anne did not blame him for being annoyed at Pearl's unintended encounter with the Van Daans' huge, exuberant dog. She had noticed before that Wellington tended to hide his softer side behind a show of irritability. He greeted Anne on her arrival with visible relief and instructed his servants to show her to a chamber. Anne changed into one of her working gowns and set out for the stable where Wellington's groom had settled Pearl.

Anne was on good terms with many of the headquarters' servants and she found Teddy Brett, one of his Lordship's grooms, in one of the stalls with Pearl. The bitch was warmly settled on a bed of straw and old blankets. Brett looked relieved at the sight of her and made as if to rise, but Anne waved him back down.

"No need for formality today, Brett. How is she?"

"Doing all right I think, ma'am. She's warm enough and seems comfortable. I don't know that he needed to drag you all this way, but Morrison said it would be a good thing because if you're here, he's likely to leave us alone."

Anne laughed aloud. "Is he being difficult?"

"It's his Lordship we're talking about, ma'am. Thank God he's going off to San Sebastian to torment Sir Thomas Graham for a bit. He only waited to be sure you made it here safely."

"Oh dear. I hope this all goes smoothly for him, he has more important things to worry about."

"He can always find room for one extra, ma'am," Brett said placidly. "Spent ten minutes before you arrived writing a long list of everything we should do for her and gave it to Morrison."

Anne studied his grin and made a guess. "Morrison can't read, can he?"

"Not a word, ma'am, though he can write his name. Besides, we'd already got everything set up here. Only thing is, it might get cold if she goes on into the night, but once they're born I've arranged for a room in that tower next door. It's empty but it's got a fireplace. Morrison's getting it set up."

"That's excellent. Do you mind if I take a look at her?"

"She's all yours, ma'am."

Anne knelt in the straw and examined Pearl. The bitch was panting heavily and seemed restless but Anne did not think she was unduly distressed. She was licking repeatedly at her rear end and occasionally made a little moaning sound. Anne examined her carefully and was pleased to realise that the water sac had already ruptured. Hopefully it would not be too long but there was nothing more to do yet. Anne settled herself as comfortably as she could in the straw, with her back against the wooden wall, and stroked Pearl's silky ears soothingly.

"The gunfire seems to have died away," she said. The booming of the guns from San Sebastian had been clearly audible for their entire ride to Lesaca but she realised she could no longer hear them. "I wonder if that means they've breached."

"Hope so, ma'am. His Lordship's valet tells me he's been jumpy for the past day or two. News came in of French movements over by the coast. Smily says he reckons it's just bluffing, to make it look like they're making an advance. But you know how he is when it's not in his control."

"I do, Brett. I bet he's been like a cat on hot tiles all morning. Poor Sir Thomas. I'd hate to be in his shoes, never knowing when his Lordship will turn up without warning to make sure he's doing the right thing."

The day wore on. Anne went outside to stretch her legs several times. Pearl was taking her time, but Anne knew from her experience with the family gun dogs in her younger days that a first litter was often slow to make an appearance. Brat appeared to call her into the house for food and Anne found a selection of cold meats and bread set out. Captain Theo Kuhn, her husband's German ADC, was there in conversation with two of Lord Wellington's aides. He rose immediately to escort her to a chair. Anne looked around the room, aware of a strained atmosphere.

"Captain, is something wrong?"

Lieutenant-Colonel Canning, one of Wellington's ADCs, came forward quickly to draw out the chair for Anne. "Nothing to worry about, ma'am," he said with forced cheer. "Been a bit of a problem over at San Sebastian. Lord Wellington's ridden over there. Let me bring you some food and a glass of wine. Are you sure you're all right spending hours in the stable with the grooms? Lord Wellington said we should take care of you and give you any assistance."

Anne managed not to say the first thing that came into her head, which involved comparing Canning's usefulness unfavourably to the groom's in this instance. She offered him a charming smile and watched as he went to bring food and wine then turned to Kuhn. She knew she could trust him to speak to her as an intelligent adult.

"What's happened, Captain?"

Her husband's ADC looked serious. "The assault on San Sebastian has failed, ma'am. Lord Wellington has ridden to see for himself and to give orders for the further progression of the siege."

"Oh no. I don't suppose we know anything about casualties?"

"We know nothing at all yet, ma'am. His Lordship intends to return tonight, so I expect we will find out more."

Canning returned, setting a plate and a wine glass in front of Anne with a flourish. Anne thanked him warmly then looked back at Kuhn.

"I wonder if this means we'll get orders? Captain, do you think you should ride back to the brigade? I'll be perfectly safe here with Ariana and Isair…where is Ariana by the way?"

Kuhn made a little sound which sounded suspiciously like a laugh, hastily converted into a cough. "She is having her meal in the kitchen, ma'am."

"Oh for..." Anne stopped herself with an effort. "Of course. Anyway, I'll be well taken care of if..."

"No, ma'am. It will not surprise you at all to hear that I have received very specific orders about what I should do if the situation were to change."

"Of course you have," Anne said resignedly. "Very well. There seems no point in worrying about it since I can do nothing to help. Sit down and finish your meal Theo, then I'll get back to my patient. Poor Lord Wellington will be so angry about this. At least I hope to have good news for him about Pearl."

As Anne returned to the stable, Brett looked up with a grin. "Just in time, ma'am. She might need a bit of help with this first one, but she's doing very well. Do you want to do it?"

"Yes. Here let me see...oh goodness, it's almost here."

The first puppy was born with only a little help from Anne, who gently but firmly pulled it out. She held it in one hand, its head down and carefully cleared the tiny mouth of mucus then rubbed its chest with an old towel, watching the tiny face anxiously. The puppy did not let her down and made a spluttering sound then a surprisingly loud squeak. Anne smiled broadly.

"Pass me my scissors, Brett."

She cut the cord neatly then settled the tiny creature against his mother, guiding his mouth to a nipple. Pearl shifted, turning her head to sniff the puppy and Anne sat back, watching. After a moment, the bitch began to lick her puppy enthusiastically.

"Well, will you look at that," Brett said. "She's a natural."

"She's a heroine. He's a good size, look at him."

"Takes after his Da then."

Anne gave a splutter of laughter. "Hard to be sure yet, but I think Lord Wellington's suspicions might well be correct. Good girl, Pearl. Lie down now and let him suckle. You've still got some work to do."

There were five puppies, born over the next few hours. The sixth was tiny and Anne knew with a sinking heart that this one was too small. She persisted though, repeatedly massaging its chest and blowing gently into its mouth. Brett watched her sympathetically.

"Leave it, ma'am. He's too small. Even if you get him back, he won't make it."

"He might. I want to give it another minute or two."

"Give him to me."

Anne turned. Brat must have entered the stable without her noticing. She came forward, holding out her hands for the lifeless puppy.

"It is growing late and you must be cold and stiff from kneeling in the hay all this time. I will try."

Anne passed over the puppy and got painfully to her feet. She had not realised how late it had grown. Sunset would not be for another hour or more but the evening was much cooler. She watched Brat for a moment, decided that as a

77

farmer's daughter she knew what she was doing and walked to the stable door. Outside, she could hear the regular bustle of the little town, packed full of headquarters staff and their servants. There was another sound in the distance. Anne listened, puzzled. It was unmistakably gunfire.

"Is it finished, ma'am?"

Kuhn must have been watching from the house and seen her emerge. Anne gave a weary smile as he approached.

"I think so. Brat is trying to revive our smallest one. I'm not sure he's going to make it but the other five are feeding very well. Morrison has gone to make sure the room in the tower is ready for them and warm enough and his Lordship's grooms and orderlies will take turns to watch them and make sure she doesn't lie on them. I think Morrison has set up a box with a rail. Theo, what's that firing? Surely they're not still fighting at San Sebastian?"

"No, ma'am. It comes from the direction of the pass at Maya, we think. General Murray has sent one of his officers out to meet Lord Wellington. We have been hearing heavy gunfire for several hours."

"I didn't notice, I've been too busy." Anne turned as Brat called her. She returned to the stall and looked down. To her surprise, the Spanish girl was carefully settling the tiny puppy beside his litter mates, guiding his mouth to one of Pearl's teats.

"I don't believe it. You did it, Ariana!"

Brat looked up, her face alight. "I was about to give up. We will have to watch this one carefully though, he is very small. Still, he is sucking well."

"Thank goodness. Four dogs and two bitches. And Pearl seems very well, which is what his Lordship will be concerned about. Brett, I need to wash and change. Will you let me know when they're settled in the tower room and I'll come up to check on her."

"I will, ma'am. Well done. Can see now why they like to have you helping in the surgeon's tents."

Anne smiled. "This is a lot easier. Though I am tired."

"Are we going back to Vera tonight, Señora?"

Anne hesitated then shook her head. "No. I was hoping to, but I think we should wait until his Lordship is back. San Sebastian is not a problem for us, but I'd like to know a little more about that gunfire before I decide to ride back to Vera. Do you agree, Captain Kuhn?"

"I was going to insist upon it, ma'am. If there is any possibility that the Light Division is marching out immediately, we should not go. We may miss them and we have no information."

"Very well. Come and help me change, Ariana, and we'll await Lord Wellington's return."

Chapter Six

Paul awoke to the sound of a horse ridden fast, slowing in the clearing before his tent. He was out of bed and pulling on his boots by the time a sentry appeared at the tent flap.

"Orders from General Alten, sir. It's urgent."

Paul felt his stomach lurch with anxiety, more than he would usually expect at the prospect of action. He pulled on his jacket, glancing around at the rumpled mattress, all too aware of the absence of his wife. Silently he cursed Lord Wellington, his hunting bitch and Marshal Soult who was presumably responsible for this sudden alert. Logically he knew that Anne was at headquarters and that Lord Wellington would ensure her safety but he hated being apart from her on the march. He was grateful that Kuhn was with her. He had enormous faith in his young German ADC.

Jenson limped in with a covered lantern and with his usual unruffled calm, began to light lamps. It soothed Paul a little and he took a deep breath and smiled at his orderly.

"Better send him in, Jenson. Let's find out what's going on. Where the bloody hell is my brigade-major? Is he still asleep?"

"Not much chance of it with that racket, sir," Fenwick said, ducking into the tent. Paul could hear it now, the call of bugles from the other brigades of the Light Division. Fenwick saluted and Paul returned it, wondering how his acting brigade-major managed to look so immaculate three minutes out of his bed. Manson would have greeted him looking like an irate hedgehog with his dark hair standing on end. Paul felt a little rush of sentimentality and wished Manson would recover more quickly and get back to the brigade. He liked Fenwick but missed his predecessor badly. Another man followed Fenwick into the tent.

"Cornet Bradley, sir with orders from General Alten. I'll make sure the rest of them are up and moving."

Paul smiled at the young cavalry officer and took the letter he was holding out. Alten wrote in a clear hand and his orders were always blissfully brief and to the point. As he read, Fenwick left the tent and Johnny Wheeler appeared, fully dressed, with Lieutenant-Colonel Gervase Clevedon behind him. A moment later Colonel Norton appeared. Paul finished the letter and looked up.

"We're to march as soon as possible. Back towards Yanzi initially then possibly on to San Estevan. We'll probably receive more orders on the march."

"Soult?" Johnny asked.

"Soult. I knew that arsehole was about to do something annoying. Cornet Bradley, the General says you can fill us in on the rest. Speak freely, lad."

Bradley saluted again and seemed unable to say a word. His uniform was unfamiliar to Paul, with dull yellow facings and white lace. He was clearly not one of Scovell's men so Paul assumed that the 9th Dragoon Guards must have just arrived to take up their attachment to the Light Division. It was not surprising that this boy looked so overwhelmed. The newcomers must have barely had time to take a breath.

"At ease, Cornet Bradley. 9th Dragoon Guards?"

"Yes, sir. Just arrived."

"Did you even get time to put up your tents?"

"Barely, sir."

"Blame bloody Soult. Tell me what you know while Jenson gets us some tea."

The boy seemed to relax a little. "Sir, General Alten received orders from Lord Wellington. The assault on San Sebastian has failed and the French have attacked the passes at Maya and Roncesvalles."

Paul felt a little chill. "I'm guessing we didn't hold them."

"I think Roncesvalles held, sir, but there was heavy fighting at Maya. Casualties on both sides."

Paul looked at his officers. "That must be the gunfire we heard yesterday," he said. "I assumed it was San Sebastian, though the direction felt wrong. But it's hard to tell in these mountains. Anything else, Mr Bradley?"

"Only this, sir. General Alten said to give it to you personally."

Paul took the letter and was relieved at the familiar elegant script. He opened it and read quickly. Anne had clearly written in haste to ensure that her letter could go off with Wellington's orders.

"It's from Nan. She's remaining at headquarters for the time being. There are plenty of medical and administrative staff there and Wellington has got some Spanish infantry doing guard duty. She tells me not to worry."

There was a long silence in the tent, then Johnny stirred. "I'd better get back to my battalion, sir."

"I'll get out there and see…" Clevedon began.

"Oh fuck off, both of you. Wait until your wives or fiancées are out here with the bloody French approaching and see how you feel. Stay and get a drink at least. George Kelly already has the fire going and it'll be another half an hour before Kempt gets Barnard out of bed."

There was laughter, although it was a little forced. Paul waved them to camp chairs and pulled out a box of tack biscuits. He had given orders for basic rations to be given to each man, knowing that the commissary wagons could be unpredictable even on a good day and wholly unreliable in difficult country.

Jenson and Charlie Bannan brought tin cups of tea through and Paul wrapped his hands around his, trying to remember where he had put his gloves the previous day. He finished drinking, listening to the sound of his brigade scrambling into order outside. His officers left one by one and the young cavalry cornet set off back to Alten's headquarters. It was becoming lighter outside. Paul got up reluctantly, looking around the tent. His servants were experts at packing up a camp quickly and Ross Mackenzie and the other quartermasters would have his baggage train on the road long before either of the other brigades. Paul noticed Anne's possessions scattered around with a pang and wished her maid was here to pack properly for her.

Jenson removed the cups and reappeared a few minutes later, just as Paul was buckling on his sword. He turned to find his orderly holding out his riding gloves. Paul's greatcoat was over his arm.

"You'll need this until the sun comes up, sir."

Paul took the gloves and allowed Jenson to help him into his coat. "What in God's name would I do without you, Freddie?"

"Ride without gloves some days, sir. The grooms are bringing the horses up."

Paul stepped outside and almost bumped into Alison Macdonald who was approaching the tent flap. She stepped back quickly and stumbled and he caught her arm to steady her.

"Sorry, lass. Are you all right?"

"Yes, sir. I thought…I wondered…that is, as Mrs van Daan isn't back yet and Brat is with her, I thought you might like me to pack her things for you. Only if you want me to, sir."

Paul's face softened into a smile. "Yes," he said gratefully. "Thank you Alison, it's been bothering me."

She flashed him a smile and disappeared into the tent and Paul surveyed the apparent chaos of his brigade. It was rapidly beginning to form up into some kind of order. Paul looked around.

"Private Bannan, where are you?"

"Here, sir."

Charlie saluted smartly and Paul laughed and ruffled his hair. "One of these days you'll be doing that in uniform, Charlie. Unless you change your mind when we get back to England."

"I won't do that, sir. Want to serve in the 110th under you. Hope to make Sergeant-Major one day, like RSM Carter."

"If you carry on as you're going, Charlie, you might end up as an officer, like Captain Manson. Right now, though, I want you to take charge of Craufurd on the march. Jenson will help you but if Craufurd decides to take off after rabbits it's your job to get him back. Agreed?"

Bannan was staring at him with astonished eyes. "A…an officer, sir? Me? But my Da's just a rifleman."

"My great-grandfather started out as an apprentice printer in Antwerp, lad. It's not where you start out that matters, it's where you end up. If Craufurd gets tired or if we're travelling on mountain paths, I want you both in the carriage, by the way. I don't trust that idiot dog not to go over the edge and take you with him and my wife would never forgive me."

Charlie saluted again and raced away in search of Craufurd. Paul watched him for a moment, unexpectedly charmed by the thought of a future where he had no need to spend his life killing Frenchmen and might have some time to help a bright, enthusiastic nine-year-old fulfil his dreams. Jenson's voice broke in on his reverie.

"You might want these, sir."

Paul turned to see his orderly holding out his hat in one hand and his riding whip in the other. He grinned and took both.

"I hope I improve before noon, Jenson, just in case the French attack."

"You'll be all right if they do, sir. A fight always seems to wake you up a bit."

The Light Division marched out of Vera, heading towards the Bidassoa River in the direction of Lesaca. Paul rode at the head of his brigade with Johnny Wheeler beside him and tried to keep his mind firmly on his job and away from his wife. It was impossible to do so. He had no idea where Wellington had gone, though he presumed his chief had headed out to meet General Sir Rowland Hill and whatever remained of the troops who had retreated from the high passes. The information he had received was frustratingly vague and Alten did not seem to know much more. Paul wished he had accompanied Anne to headquarters. He might well have done so if it had not been for his meeting with Captain White. Not only would he have been privy to Wellington's thoughts and movements but he would also have been able to escort his wife back to the brigade in time for them to march out. He did not know exactly where she was or when he would see her again. They had been apart for too long during this campaign, with Anne tied to Vitoria dealing with their wounded men, while he made pointless marches across the countryside chasing the French. Paul hated it.

Once across the river, they marched south along the left bank during a misty morning, with sunlight attempting to push its way through the clouds. As the miles increased between the division and Lesaca, Paul felt his mood drop even further. He replied to Johnny's cheerful conversation as well as he could and tried to pretend everything was normal but he suspected he was doing a poor job. Eventually his friend confirmed it.

"Would you like me to shut up, sir?"

Paul could not help smiling. "I'm sorry. I'm a miserable bastard sometimes."

"You're not. I understand. There's no point in me telling you that she'll be all right, because…"

There was a shout from along the lines. Paul heard his name and reined in, peering back through the mist. A cavalry trooper wearing the distinctive red band of Scovell's staff corps was cantering up from the back of the lines.

"General van Daan, there's an officer approaching. Says he's one of your staff, he's asking permission to pass our rear guard." The young trooper sounded apologetic. "We've got half a dozen of the 9th dragoon guards with an officer who looks about twelve-years-old at the back, sir. They're a bit enthusiastic. I think it's one of your ADCs. A Captain Kuhn from the KGL?"

Paul stared at him for a long moment, his heart leaping with happiness. He tried to contain it. "Is he alone?"

"I've not seen him, sir, but I understand it's a small party."

"Send them up, Trooper. And thank you."

The sound of galloping horses reached him within five minutes. A gap was opening up between Paul's brigade and the rear of the second but he knew he would easily make it up. The riders came into sight: Kuhn at the head in his distinctive dark green jacket with lighter trousers. Behind him were two women and another man. Paul watched them come, his eyes on the woman dressed in a wine red riding habit riding an elegant black mare. The party drew closer and then as if by prior agreement, three of them fell back slightly to allow Anne to approach her husband. Rufus whickered a greeting to Bella, Anne's mare. They were old friends.

Anne reined in beside him, smiling broadly. Paul studied the lovely face. He was assailed by memories of so many meetings and partings over the years. This time they had been apart for only a day but it felt longer. She reached out her gloved hand and he took it and raised it to his lips, then looked up into her eyes.

"Bonny lass, what the devil are you doing here?"

"Joining my husband and his brigade, love. I hope you don't mind?"

"How did you find us?"

"I interrogated his Lordship's ADCs. They were reluctant to tell me anything since it was clear that Lord Wellington had decided I would be safer in Lesaca. Luckily I managed to corner Captain Graham who told me his orders. I knew the division would be passing close by, so we got ourselves ready and Theo went to keep a lookout. We knew it wouldn't take long to catch up. I must say the cavalrymen who are forming the rear guard were a little difficult, but Theo became very precise and very German and they were quickly intimidated. Are they Davy's 9th dragoon guards?"

"Yes. They'll clearly need some training. Move closer. I'd just been convincing myself I wouldn't see you for weeks. I need some reassurance."

Anne laughed and edged Bella closer. Paul leaned over and kissed her on the lips. It lasted until the two horses became bored, which was long before Paul was ready for it to end. They parted smiling, both horses restive.

"I'm hoping the baggage wagons are following?"

"Yes, Mackenzie is in charge. Alison Macdonald came up to offer to pack up your things. I've left Craufurd with Charlie. How is Pearl?"

"Very well. Six puppies, four males and two bitches. One of the males is very small, I didn't think we were going to be able to revive him, but Ariana managed it. Her list of talents never ceases to amaze me. I've left detailed instructions with the local grooms as to how they are to manage things and have promised a hefty bonus for every puppy that remains alive."

Paul began to laugh. He could not believe how quickly his mood had soared. "How much is it costing us to keep these blasted puppies alive for Lord Wellington to complain about, girl of my heart?"

Anne was laughing back at him. "We can afford it, General. Ariana has ridden back to remind Captain O'Reilly of her existence. May I ride with you or do I need to…"

"Yes. Stay with me, bonny lass. You can move to the back if we look likely to see action, but I need you to cheer me up. Poor Colonel Wheeler has been trying to make conversation with a depressed mute."

"It's true ma'am," Johnny said cheerfully, moving his horse forward. "Very happy to see you. I don't mind what we talk about as long as it includes actual conversation. Michael O'Reilly was right. The difference you make to him is shocking. Welcome back."

***

It was the beginning of three miserable days. The Light Division camped at the village of Sumbilla and rested through the following day to prepare for a night march which proved one of the worst Simon Carlyon had ever experienced. Horses, men and baggage wagons had to make their way along narrow tracks in complete darkness. Some of the paths ran alongside terrifying precipices where a stumble could send a man to his death. The route was crossed by several streams, fast-flowing from the recent rains, and Simon listened to his men cursing as they slithered over slippery stones and then marched on to the sound of gentle sloshing from wet shoes and boots. There was none of the usual good-natured banter among the officers and men. Everyone concentrated on keeping their feet or their horses firmly on the track. Progress felt agonisingly slow.

Simon was worried about his men. At least a third of them were relatively new recruits, sent out to replace those lost to death or injury at Vitoria and were not yet hardened to long marches in appalling conditions. There was little time to rest and with the baggage wagons struggling to keep up, men had only the rations they carried. It was a relief, as the sky began to lighten into a faint misty dawn, to see the outline of a church bell tower rising above the red tiled roofs of the village of Zubieta.

Simon was cold and damp and his horse was plodding with weariness but he forced himself to turn back along the straggling column to check once again that all his company had made it intact through the long miserable night. He thought of the women at the back of the long column, struggling in heavy skirts and carrying baggage and children and sent up a brief prayer that they had all arrived safely. As the perilous nature of the march had become obvious, Anne van Daan had dropped back with her maidservant to supervise the camp followers and baggage-train and Simon knew that any woman who was

84

struggling too much would have been unceremoniously dumped onto a wagon or into Anne's own carriage. He wondered if Anne was regretting her decision to leave the comfort of Wellington's headquarters in Lesaca, then dismissed the thought. His former sister-in-law had endured worse conditions than this to be with her husband.

Reaching the back of the line, Simon found that Sergeant May had been about the same business, counting heads and barking questions about any missing men. He waited until May had finished before asking:

"Anyone missing, May?"

"No, sir. Two men fell out on that last climb, Porter and Agnew, but we just had a message to say that Mrs van Daan picked them up in one of the wagons and they're fine."

"It's no surprise that Porter didn't make it," Simon said grimly. "He looked as though he'd not had a square meal for years when he arrived and we've not had time to fatten him up yet."

"If you don't mind me saying so, sir, nobody's getting fat on army rations. I also think Porter's undersized for a reason. He can barely lift that musket."

Simon eyed his Sergeant thoughtfully. "Underage, you think?"

"Definitely, sir. I don't know which cross-eyed drunken bastard of a recruiting sergeant let him sign up, but he bloody shouldn't be here. I've spent the past few weeks trying to make sure his messmates don't steal his rations and half his bloody kit but I don't have eyes in the back of my head."

"Have you caught anybody yet?"

"If I had, you'd have heard about it, sir. Me and Paisley are pretty sure who's giving him a hard time but he's not talking about it and you know what the rest of them are like about tale bearers."

"Fair enough, but he's going to get himself killed if he's too weak to fight. I'll speak to Mrs van Daan and get her to keep him with the sick and wounded for the time being. She'll come up with an excuse. He can make himself useful there for a bit until we stop for a few days and then I'll talk to him. Thank you, Sergeant."

"Any news of the French yet, sir?"

"No. I'm hoping we'll find out more soon. I'll let you know." Simon ran his eyes along the column, suddenly aware of another absence. "Have you seen Mr Fox anywhere, May?"

May gave an expressive snort of disgust. "Ho. I think you'll find him with the baggage wagons as well, sir. He disappeared early on, told Mr Middleton he was suffering from a disordered stomach."

Simon swore and made no attempt to hide it. "A disordered stomach? I thought that was last week when he was supposed to be supervising picket duty."

"Maybe the young gentleman has a delicate constitution, sir."

"The young gentleman is an idle bastard who's frightened of a day's work, Sergeant. Who's due to set the pickets today?"

"Lieutenant Trevithick, sir."

"Well he's getting the day off. I am going to find Mr Fox and return him to his rightful duties, Sergeant. Probably with a boot print on his arse. Stand them down and let them rest. We should get orders any minute and I'm hoping they involve a camp and some hot food."

Simon found Ensign Laurence Fox seated on a wooden crate beside the baggage wagons, watching as Anne directed the unloading of tents and cooking equipment. He was holding a silver hip flask to his lips, his pale eyes on Anne's trim form. She was clearly unaware of his scrutiny but something in Fox's expression infuriated Simon. He walked up to his junior and removed the flask, stoppering it firmly. Fox choked on the brandy in surprise and uttered an oath. Simon stood glaring down at him and Fox suddenly realised it was his company officer and scrambled awkwardly to his feet, saluting.

"Sorry, sir, you made me jump."

"You're going to be a lot more sorry before the end of today, Mr Fox." Simon kept his voice low so that the men unloading the wagons could not hear. "This is the second time in a week that you've been absent from your post without good reason."

"I had reason, sir. Sickness. Must have been something I've eaten; I was as sick as a dog earlier. Couldn't possibly have…"

Simon lost his temper. "I once walked beside a man who was so badly wounded and burning with fever that he could barely put one foot in front of the other. He dragged himself mile after mile in fucking agony without so much as complaining. This isn't winter quarters or some fancy posting in Brighton for the summer, it's a bloody campaign. We're at war, the French are marching and your place is with your men. If you need to throw up or empty your bowels, find a bush and deal with it and then get moving again."

"Are you putting me on a charge, sir?"

"Not a chance of it," Simon said flatly. "Major-General van Daan doesn't like officers being under arrest during a campaign, he says they have better things to do. Get yourself over to your men. You can relieve Mr Trevithick on picket duty as you've had a nice rest in the baggage wagon. I've asked Sergeant Paisley to keep an eye on you and if you disappear again, I'm going to punch you. Now get moving."

Fox turned on his heel and walked away. It was lighter now, with a pale sunlight pushing its way through the clouds. Simon turned to survey the village. Paul had chosen the slopes above it for his camp site, high rolling hills covered in springy meadow grass. In the distance Simon could hear the gentle tinkling of cow bells from a herd grazing higher up. He could also see a sprinkling of red coats between the Light Division camps and the cattle and he grinned. The men posted on guard duty would be from the 110th, under reliable NCOs, and any infantryman or rifleman showing interest in roast beef or mutton would be given short shrift. He knew his commander's habits by now.

"I see Mr Fox has left us already."

Simon turned. "He's on picket duty, ma'am."

Anne was laughing. "I presume he's feeling better."

"I didn't ask him. Should I have? I'm sorry, I should have checked with you first."

"I have no issues with Mr Fox going back to his duties. No medical issues anyway."

Simon regarded her with interest. He had known Anne since childhood and had a good deal of respect for her shrewdness. "What about non-medical issues?"

Anne shrugged. "There's nothing physically wrong with him, Simon. Paul believes he's trying to get himself arrested and possibly cashiered to avoid combat. He may well be right, but it's more than that. He seems to me to be trying to avoid everything, even his fellow officers."

"He doesn't seem to have many friends."

"He doesn't have any. The men despise him and I think the officers are beginning to do so as well, especially since word got around that he appeared to have been absent without leave during the battle. The few friends he had made are keeping their distance now."

"Nobody wants to be associated with a coward, ma'am."

"That's utterly ridiculous," Anne said angrily. "Fear isn't contagious."

"Actually in battle, it rather is."

She looked at him for a moment then gave a reluctant smile. "Touché. I agree with Paul that Fox doesn't want to be here and he shouldn't be. I think he and Johnny are hoping that eventually he will crack under the pressure and simply resign his commission."

"Don't you agree, ma'am?"

"I think if he was going to do so, he'd have done it by now. There's something more to this story, Simon. He keeps turning up here with a new ailment or injury and I've been trying to get him to talk to me, but all he can manage are a few platitudes and some very poor attempts at flirtation."

"Just take care with that, ma'am."

"Simon, I am better qualified than most women to judge when a man might pose some kind of threat to me and I can tell you categorically that Laurence Fox does not. If we were not trying to fend off a French invasion I would keep him around a little in the hope that he would eventually tell me what's going on, but as it is all I can do is keep an eye on him. Just do the same, would you? Paul and Johnny are too exasperated with him to see what I see, but I'm honestly worried about him."

Simon felt a little chill. "You don't think he'd harm himself, do you?"

"I can't be sure that he wouldn't. Paul's methods generally work you know, even with the most difficult young officers."

Simon could not help smiling. "I've reason to know that, ma'am."

"You were not that difficult, Simon. Just angry and grieving. All the same…I know Paul chose to put Fox in your company because you're a conscientious officer who won't let him neglect his duties. But I think he might have chosen better than he realises. I think you're in a very good position to understand what it's like not to fit in. At least at the start. Just watch him, that's all I ask."

Simon said nothing for a moment. "I will," he said finally. "Thank you for telling me this. I've been cursing the little blighter for being a damned nuisance in a dangerous situation. Perhaps there is more to it. I don't think there's a chance he'll open up to me, but I can certainly keep an eye on him."

A hand descended onto his shoulder and Simon jumped and swore. His commanding officer laughed and went to kiss Anne.

"You've got bad nerves, Captain Carlyon. Stop flirting with my wife and come and join us. I've just been speaking to Alten and I need to break the bad news that we've another long march ahead of us tomorrow."

"Damn. Excuse my language, ma'am, but we could do without it. This country isn't easy and some of the men are exhausted."

"Some of the baggage animals are struggling and I've no idea how we're going to get those guns up the mountain," Anne said.

"We'll have to carry them if necessary. Alten is sending the baggage wagons by another road. I want the men fed and rested today. We've no idea where Soult is, which means we could encounter him at any moment." Paul studied his wife and Anne gave a crooked smile.

"Are you wishing I'd stayed in Lesaca, General?"

"Yes. No. This is turning into a nightmare, but if it all goes wrong and we have to make a fast retreat I'd rather you were with me. You made the right decision, girl of my heart."

"Do we have any more information about what has happened?"

"The usual fuck-up," Paul said grimly. "Soult managed to pull the army back together somewhere around Bayonne and has launched attacks on several fronts over the high passes. Wellington has told Graham at San Sebastian to get the Royal Navy to re-embark his guns. He won't risk them falling into enemy hands."

"Is that likely?" Simon asked, startled. "I hadn't realised…"

"We're not marching through the night for the good of our health, Captain. He's trying to cover all routes to Pamplona while making sure the various parts of the army don't get cut off from each other. As we knew from the start, this is a bastard of an area to defend. I don't know the details yet but it seems that the Fourth Division were attacked at Roncesvalles and Cole didn't like the odds, especially in heavy fog, so withdrew his men towards Pamplona. Stewart's men put up a fight at Maya but Hill pulled them back when he realised Roncesvalles was lost."

"So the French hold both passes?" Anne asked. Simon admired the steadiness of her voice. He had yet to see his remarkable sister-in-law panic.

"At the moment. They don't seem to be following up that quickly though. Alten tells me that Wellington thinks they're unsure of our numbers or deployment so they're being cautious. He wants us to block the Dona Maria pass to the south of here." Paul reached for her hand. "The route is horrendous, bonny lass. We can't manage the baggage wagons and your carriage but there's a good road down towards Pamplona. You could go with them but I'd rather you didn't."

"I'm staying with you, Paul. We'll manage with pack mules, I'll speak to the muleteers. Go on, go and brief your officers. I have plenty to do here."

As Simon fell into step beside his commander, Paul said:

"I passed Mr Fox on my way to find my wife. Has he been in trouble again?"

"Not really, sir. He went to the surgeons – some kind of stomach disorder, I believe, but he's all right now."

"Don't treat me like an idiot, Captain. I suspect my wife thinks I'm mishandling Fox."

"She didn't say that, sir. But she is worried about him." Simon shot him a glance and decided to take a risk. "Having spoken with her, I'm beginning to think she might have a point. He's become completely isolated from the rest of us."

"I wonder why?"

Simon grinned. "He's bloody irritating, sir, but I don't wish him harm. Your wife asked me to keep an eye on him, that's all."

Paul's mouth twisted into a wry smile. "I think he's an arsehole, Simon but I'm not infallible, I've been wrong before. I want him out of my brigade and if it takes a court martial to do it then I will. But if either you or my wife can drag out what the hell is wrong with him and it helps, I wish you well. Just don't leave him in charge of your men unsupervised. I wouldn't trust the little toad to sit the right way on his horse."

"Yes, sir." Simon shot him a look. "Are you worried? About our position here, sir?"

"I'm more worried about where we're going next," Paul said grimly. "We don't know what the hell is happening elsewhere. I wish we were with Wellington. This feels like fucking chaos to me."

***

Four days of marching and countermarching, with limited information and repeated changes of orders, tried Paul's temper sorely. The weather was wet and miserable and the roads did not improve. There were no opportunities to set up a full camp and the commissary wagons could not always reach the column, which meant that the men were hungry as well as tired. Wellington had given orders for the Light Division to march eastwards in the hope of turning Soult's flank if necessary.

Paul attended daily briefing meetings with General Alten. The Hanoverian freely shared what news he had with his brigade commanders but even his generally placid temper seemed frayed by the uncertainty and poor conditions. As far as they were aware, Soult was continuing to march on Pamplona, frantically trying to pull his separated army together for an attack. Paul supposed that the French, like the Allies, were struggling with communication difficulties and lack of provisions and unlike Wellington, they did not have supply depots within reach. Their only hope was to strike quickly and force the Allies to abandon supplies and baggage.

Paul did not think they would succeed. Wellington had been taken by surprise and was scrambling to catch up but the French did not have the men or the logistical framework in place. Paul thought they would have to withdraw. His only concern was how many men the Allies would lose in forcing them to do so.

News arrived at Lecumberri where the exhausted men were finally greeted with their supply wagons and sufficient food. Fires were lit and Paul gave orders that his officers and NCOs were to concentrate on getting the men fed and some of their kit dried out. He had no idea when they would receive further orders but he wanted his men as well rested as possible. Lecumberri was a typical small Basque village with little to see and no reason for the troops to go wandering off. Sentries were posted and Anne organised a small party to visit the village to see what fresh provisions might be available to buy. She returned in triumph two hours later with bread, cabbages and turnips along with several covered pails of fresh milk.

"As the women and children haven't managed to meet up with us yet, I'm going to give the milk to the sick men. It will help to build up their strength."

Paul studied her. It had been a long four days. Anne's riding habit was splashed with mud and her hair was bundled up into a simple knot. There were dark circles under her eyes. Paul suspected he did not look much better. Conditions had made it difficult to sleep much and they were all bone-weary.

"Do me a favour bonny lass. Take your own advice and drink some yourself, will you? I know it's easier on horseback but you still look exhausted."

"I look a fright, don't I?"

"You look like my beautiful wife. As she looks after a week without a proper wash, decent food and a good night's sleep, obviously."

Anne laughed aloud and stood on tiptoe to kiss him. "Which is the same as saying I look a fright. It's lucky you love me anyway. I'm going to try to catch some sleep once we've eaten. We've marched and stopped at such weird times this week that I think my body is confused about whether it's day or night. Do you…"

"General van Daan."

Paul turned. "What is it, Captain Fenwick?"

"Message from General Alten, sir. He wants to see you at headquarters immediately. Sorry, sir."

Paul's heart sank. "Christ almighty, not again. What now? Has he even had time to set up a headquarters?"

"Apparently he's quartered in a farm about a mile to the west, sir. Cornet Robinson here will show you the way."

Paul groaned, put his arms about Anne and leaned his brow on the top of her head. "Sometimes desertion sounds like a sensible option," he said. "Save me some food will you, girl of my heart?"

"Of course." Anne studied him and he could read the concern in her dark eyes. "Come straight back, Paul. If there's to be another night march, you need to rest."

"I will. Jenson, will you bring Rufus round please? No need to come with me, you should get some rest yourself."

"I've already got Felix saddled up sir, so I'll come."

Paul watched as his orderly limped forward, holding both bridles. "You are my nursemaid," he said glumly. "I am haunted by a fucking nursemaid with a wooden leg."

"You can probably outrun me, sir, if you get a head start."

Paul took hold of the bridle with a grin. "I'd end up circling back to look for you. I'm too used to you by now. Come on, let's get this over with. I wonder what hoops his Lordship wants us to jump through now?"

They found Alten eating bacon, eggs and fresh bread in a big farmhouse kitchen. Paul's mouth watered at the smell of the food. He saluted and the German waved him to a bench.

"Sit down, General. When the others arrive, Señora Mendia and her daughter will serve breakfast for you all. There is coffee too, with milk. Tell Sergeant Jenson he also will be given food if he goes to the stables, there is a room where the farmhands eat and my orderlies and grooms are being served there.

Paul yelled the message to Jenson then sat down and accepted a pottery cup from a sharp-eyed girl of around sixteen. He smiled his thanks and she blushed and sped back to the fireplace where her mother wielded several skillets in iron brackets and the mouth-watering smell of frying bacon filled the air. Paul sipped the coffee and let its heat flood through him, warming his tired body. He closed his eyes, concentrating on the bitter flavour and the sheer relief of being temporarily comfortable.

"Are you all right, General?"

Paul opened his eyes. "Yes, sir. Sorry. Just a bit tired, but we all are. Don't think I don't know you're trying to soften me up here. We've got another night march ahead of us haven't we?"

Alten gave a wry smile. "Yes. There is good news, because Lord Wellington has defeated Soult at a place called Sorauren and they have begun a retreat."

Paul felt his spirits lift a little. "Thank God for that. Though I'm guessing the bad news is that he's going to send us chasing headlong in pursuit."

"I have orders to march across country to try to cut them off. It will be a difficult route, I believe."

"There's no such thing as an easy march here, sir. I'm worried about the men; some of them are already exhausted. They'll need food and rest today."

"I am going to order them to be under arms at midnight. They must rest until then of course. How is your wife? Had we known how difficult this would be, she could have remained in Lesaca."

"She was never going to remain in Lesaca, sir. She's very tired, like the rest of us, but she'll be all right. I just hope we catch them this time. I've spent enough time on this campaign making pointless forced marches after the French."

"We shall do our best, General. I think I see the others coming. I have also invited Colonel Scovell of the Staff Cavalry Corps and Colonel Fraser of the 9th Dragoon Guards since they are to accompany the division. Have you met Colonel Fraser before?"

"I don't think so, sir. They're new out here and I don't think I've run into them anywhere else."

Paul rose to greet Kempt, Skerrett and Scovell. He did not recognise Colonel Fraser, a stocky Scotsman with a receding hairline and an enormous moustache. To his surprise, however, he did recognise his companion, a tall dark haired officer in his thirties who looked around the kitchen with an air of faint distaste as though it was beneath him to eat in such humble surroundings. Paul almost swore at the sight of him.

Alten was also on his feet, making the introductions. He looked rather surprised at the sight of the second officer and Fraser was quick with an explanation.

"This is Major Welby, General. He's on limited duties at present due to an accident in Santander so he has been acting as an informal ADC. Making himself generally useful."

"That has to be a first for you, Welby," Paul said, before he could stop himself.

Welby's good-looking face flushed a dark red. Paul could almost hear him gritting his teeth. He hoped it hurt.

"Well well," Colonel Fraser said jovially. "You know one another then, sir? Old friends, eh?"

"No. We were acquainted at school many years ago. As a matter of fact, we were both sent down at the same time. Which is the only thing we have in common."

Alten made a small sound which might have been a cough but Paul suspected was a hastily suppressed laugh. Kempt was openly grinning and Skerrett looked somewhat embarrassed. Fraser did not seem to know what to say. Paul kept his eyes on Major Welby, waiting for him to speak. He could see the effort it was costing the man to keep silent. Fortunately, Alten intervened.

"An interesting story, General van Daan. I would like to hear it some time. You are both welcome to join me for breakfast, Colonel Fraser while I tell you Lord Wellington's news – and his orders. Come, be seated."

Alten's voice was polite but firm and Paul grinned at him and took his seat obediently. He considered Alten a friend and the Hanoverian was very lenient with him but he recognised an instruction to stop baiting Welby.

They ate well, listening to Alten explaining their orders and the proposed march. Paul felt his heart sink at the prospect. Wellington had made a stand against Soult's advancing troops on a hillside above the little village of

Sorauren, stopping them dead. Initially, Wellington's men were heavily outnumbered but Soult had seemed to lose his nerve and postponed the assault on the ridge. By the time he attacked the following day, British and Portuguese reinforcements were close by and Wellington had sent the Sixth Division against Soult's flank. As more Allied troops reached the field, the French commander bowed to the inevitable and ordered a retreat.

Paul forgot about Welby as he listened to Alten's unemotional voice reading the report. Behind it he could hear a fierce and bloody battle, hotly contested by both sides and he knew casualties would be high. He could not help wondering about his friends in other divisions. The loss of Lieutenant-Colonel Henry Cadogan on the heights above Vitoria was still raw.

Alten finished his report and put down the letter. "It seems that the news is good, though we must wait to discover the cost in lives," he said seriously. "But for now the French retreat. They will possibly try to cut us off from San Sebastian but our scouts report that they seem to be aiming for San Esteban and the route back into France."

"Is it over then, sir?" Kempt asked. "He's not expecting them to stand?"

"His Lordship writes that their army is spent, with many losses. Also their defeat means they have no access to our supply depots and they are running out of food for both men and horses. He believes they will retreat as fast as possible. We are to march at speed to cut them off. The route will be difficult, across country with few real roads."

"The route will be appalling, sir," Paul said grimly. He was trying to visualise Fenwick's map. "I know we don't have our baggage wagons with us, but what about Ross's guns?"

"We will have to get them there somehow, General. I have my orders. For now you should finish eating and return to your brigades. The men must rest as much as possible during the day."

At the end of the meal, Alten signalled to Paul to wait behind. When the others had gone he poured the last of the coffee into their cups.

"I perceive that you have a problem with Major Welby of the 9th Dragoon Guards, General."

"I'm sorry about that, sir, I was being childish. Welby has that effect on me but I'll keep it under control."

"You were at school together?"

"Yes, at Eton. He was a bully there and I doubt he's improved much. We've run into one another a few times over the years and I keep up with regimental gossip. He's an unpleasant man and a poor officer, but we've never actually served in the same place before now."

"Try to ignore him if you can, General. It should not be difficult. You outrank him considerably, even though he seems a little older than you. No reason to rub salt into that wound."

"Point taken, sir. I'll do my best to avoid him as long as he does the same. I'd love to know what this accident was in Santander, mind. He's got a reputation as a hot-head and has fought a few duels over the years."

"With you, General?"

Paul gave a reminiscent grin. "Not since Eton, where I handed him his arse in a fencing bout. He did challenge me once years ago at a party in Lisbon, just after Vimeiro. Something to do with a female friend of mine though for the life of me I can't remember the details."

"Did you fight him?"

"Good God, no. I told him to fuck off."

Alten laughed aloud. "Continue to practice that restraint, Paul. This is not the time."

"Don't worry about it, sir, I can't imagine what would persuade me to fight Cecil Welby these days, he's not worth the time. I should get back to my men. If you need help with the route, may I suggest…?"

"I have already had the same advice from Colonel Scovell and with your permission I will borrow your brigade-major and his excellent map. Have you news of Captain Manson?"

"We had a letter with the last post to reach us and he's much better. I think we'll be seeing him soon, if his lady love ever lets him escape."

"I am glad, since I know you miss him. Go back to your brigade, General and make sure your wife rests instead of spending the day taking care of everybody else. I know her."

"So do I, sir. I promise I'll make sure. Thank you for breakfast."

Jenson waited outside with the horses. As they walked their mounts back along the track towards their bivouac, Jenson said:

"Interesting story about Major Welby, sir. I was talking to his groom over breakfast. Nice lad, name of Harrison, comes from Dorset."

Paul shot him an amused look. "What would I do without your nose for gossip, Jenson? Spill it."

"Seems Major Welby got himself into an unfortunate entanglement with a young female and looked set to become leg-shackled. She even came out to Spain to marry him in Santander."

"Welby?" Paul said in astonishment. "Good God, the poor woman. Did anything come of it?"

"Seems not, sir. Harrison's not sure what happened, but the lady went back home betrothed to someone else."

Paul gave a shout of laughter. "Oh good girl, whoever she is! She must have seen a way out at the last minute and run like a rabbit. Was Welby broken-hearted?"

"Not at all, sir. Harrison said he was as happy as a grig. I was coming to the best bit. Welby went out on a spree to celebrate his lucky escape with some of his fellow officers."

"I bet she celebrated a lot more, but go on."

"Got himself drunk as a Mersey ferryman and went the wrong way down a dark alley on his way back to his billet. Robbed and badly beaten; they broke his nose and his arm. That's why he's on light duties."

"I thought there was something odd about his face." Paul was still laughing. "I take my hat off to the footpads of Santander. They couldn't have found a more deserving victim. Thank you, Jenson, I needed a good laugh today."

Chapter Seven

Over the next few days, Gabriel Bonnet watched the disintegration of Marshal Soult's grand invasion with a sense of grim inevitability. He was by no means the longest serving officer in the brigade, but by now he was the most cynical. Bonnet objected to the term and preferred to think of himself as a realist. Any fool with a few years of campaigning behind him should have been able to see the stupidity of trying to conduct a long range campaign across such difficult terrain with less than four days supplies on hand. The British army on the other hand was well-supplied, well-equipped and well-entrenched on the other side of the mountains. Wellington might have made mistakes with the disposition of his troops, but Soult had never had any hope of taking more than temporary advantage of it.

Bonnet had always struggled with authority figures and rarely found a senior officer he could truly respect. He thought wistfully on occasion of Marshal Suchet who was not perfect, but who genuinely seemed to have a grasp of both tactics and logistics. Possibly Soult did too. Bonnet had decided a long time ago that most of the stupid decisions made by generals in Bonaparte's army stemmed from the fact that none of them were capable of saying no to their Emperor. On the rare occasions somebody was forced to do so, Bonaparte refused to hear it. Bonnet thought the man must be completely delusional by now and resented every unnecessary death under his command caused by the Emperor's intransigence. He tried to keep his opinions to himself as much as possible, though it was a relief to share them with Bianca and with Captain Cavel. Soult's army began their retreat with battered morale and Bonnet did not think it would help any of them to hear a battalion commander giving his frank assessment of the Emperor. Cavel maintained a steady loyalty to Bonaparte but did not seem to mind listening to Bonnet's grumbling.

D'Erlon led his division down from the bloody combat at Maya with orders to get in touch with the rest of Soult's columns as quickly as possible, but in the mountains and valleys of the Spanish Pyrenees it proved an impossible task. They saw several bodies of horsemen in the distance but could not tell if they were French or Allied cavalry. Heavy mist made marching miserable, soaking their clothing and slowing their progress to a crawl to avoid disaster on the narrow mountain tracks.

D'Erlon halted his division at Elizondo. It was a pretty town, bisected by the Baztan River with a number of impressive houses and a collection of cottages and small businesses lining the winding cobbled streets. Most windows were shuttered and doors bolted as the French marched through. Bonnet had been told that an Allied division had only just marched out of the town and he did not blame the occupants for either evacuating or remaining within doors. They were probably praying that neither army decided to start sacking the town. Bonnet could have reassured them that they were safe from D'Erlon's battered, exhausted men. The division had left more than a thousand dead and wounded up in the passes and although the Allies had withdrawn, Bonnet would not have called it a French victory.

British troops were apparently very close in the village of Irurita which made it very likely that the 30th would be in action again soon. Bonnet took a roll call, wrote up the returns of dead, wounded and missing men and waited impatiently for orders. None came. D'Erlon seemed reluctant to attack, either because he was waiting for news of the other columns or because he hoped that the weather would improve. Instead, it grew worse, with a spectacular thunderstorm during the night which kept the French huddled in what shelter they could find. Bonnet had broken into a feed store and wedged as many of his officers and their horses inside as he could manage.

He stood in the doorway with his arm about Bianca, watching the storm break over the mountains. It was a breathtaking sight, the inky-black sky torn apart with brilliant flashes of lightning. The rain fell in a deluge. It was so heavy that some of the stragglers who had fallen behind for various reasons could be seen staggering down the road, battered by the sheer force of the rainfall. Bonnet could feel his wife shivering in her wet cloak and he put both his arms about her and held her close, hoping that it would warm them both.

"Are you all right, sweetheart? I'm sorry, this is bloody miserable."

"For all of us, Gabriel. You are as cold as I am. Come, let us go inside. At least this door may keep the wind out a little."

Morning came, bringing with it a watery sunlight showing a drenched landscape and Bonnet emerged, shivering. He gave orders to his men to search for firewood, though he was not optimistic that they would find anything dry enough to burn. Bianca and Manuel, Bonnet's Spanish groom, managed a small blaze using wood from a broken-up feed trough and Bonnet was gulping down weak coffee and eating the last of his tack biscuits when he was summoned to Chassé's headquarters in the town to receive orders.

"The British have marched out," Chassé told them. "The General has sent a message up to D'Erlon and we're expecting orders to pursue as soon as possible. I'm told they were in a worse state than us, they tried to come over the pass in the dark. Make sure the men are ready to march as soon as the orders arrive."

"Any news of the supply wagons, sir?" Bonnet asked. "The men are out of rations and there's nothing to find here."

"They're supposed to be on their way to Elizondo now," Chassé said. Bonnet could tell by his expression what he thought of that information. "He'll probably leave half a battalion to escort them on to us once they arrive."

"Maybe he should leave the 30th, sir. We've only got about half a battalion left."

Chassé gave a grim smile. "You're not the only ones, Colonel. But you're definitely one of the worst. Don't think I don't know what your men did up there and what they lost because of it. I'll make sure it's acknowledged."

"Thank you, sir, though I'd prefer to know that my dead were buried and my wounded on their way to hospital. It's all right, I know you've no more clue than I have."

"When I have news, I'll tell you. My word on it. Now get them moving."

The retirement of the British seemed to have spurred D'Erlon into action and by midday the three divisions were on the road. As they crossed the Velate River, then turned towards the town of Lanz, Bonnet saw evidence that the tale of the enemy's miserable night march must have been true. The pass was cluttered with the wreckage of baggage wagons and gun carriages. One or two seemed to have gone over the edge and lay shattered at the foot of steep cliffs. On one occasion Bonnet saw a body in a red coat lying beside that of a mule, testament to the appalling conditions they had endured. He shivered a little and moved his own horse further away from the edge.

The column reached Lanz and bivouacked for the night. Bonnet was awoken at dawn with a summons from Chassé He returned to find a pot suspended over the fire and his wife slicing what looked like turnip into it. Bonnet paused to admire the view, reflecting that Bianca's ability to create a meal from almost nothing made him the luckiest man in the army. She seemed to sense his regard and turned to look at him. Her hair was coming loose from its pins at the side and the steam formed it into little wispy curls around her face. She smiled and Bonnet felt his heart melt.

"Where on earth did you find turnips? Don't tell me the English carry root vegetables in their knapsacks now. No wonder they're so slow."

Bianca gave a laugh. "No, Captain Cavel managed to buy these from the cottage he took shelter in. There was a farmer, his son and a pretty wife and I think she was charmed by his good looks."

"Or grateful for his protection," Bonnet said grimly.

"Manuel did manage to loot half a spiced sausage though. And I have picked some dandelions and nettles. It will make a good stew."

Bonnet glanced around him, seeing the smoke from dozens of camp fires. Damp wood gave off a particular odour but the usual accompanying smell of food cooking was missing. The men of D'Armagnac's division were hungry and it was going to get worse. He looked back at his wife.

"What in God's name did I ever do without you, Bianca?"

98

She dropped the last of the turnip into the pot, set down her sharp little knife and went into his arms. Her hair smelled of smoke and her cloak was still damp under his hands. As she hugged him close to her, Bonnet felt a sudden desperate longing to be free of this place, of his responsibilities and obligations to his men. He wanted to go back to Paris, to his mother's apartment above her bakery, redolent with the small of freshly baked bread and pastries. He wanted to build a home for Bianca and find a profession that did not oblige them to sleep in the open in freezing rain. He wanted to stop risking his life and taking the lives of other men. He wanted peace.

"What is it, Gabriel?"

Bonnet realised to his surprise that there were tears on his cheeks and Bianca was studying him in concern. He wiped them away and kissed her very gently.

"I love you, little bird. I don't say that often enough."

Her smile was luminous. "You show me every day. That is what matters. Go and find Captain Cavel or he will miss his breakfast."

Bonnet kissed her soundly and departed in search of his friend.

***

Supply wagons finally arrived on the following morning. The rations were limited and Bonnet's officers and NCOs supervised their distribution carefully. Nothing was being held back and the troops were given further orders to raid the mountain villages in the immediate vicinity for food. Bonnet called in his officers, painfully aware of those missing due to death or injury, and gave his own orders. He had no idea how much food would be available in these remote villages and hamlets but he was grimly aware that they were just as likely to come back with half a dozen bottles of wine as a basket of bread and with battle looking increasingly likely, he had no wish to be commanding drunken troops.

"Do you think the Marshal will fight tomorrow, Gabriel?" Bianca asked as they watched the foraging parties setting off. "Is that why he is trying to collect supplies now?"

"Yes," Bonnet said. He turned, peering into the distance. It was misty again but he could both hear and smell the enemy. Their cooking fires flickered dimly through the fog and the smells wafting across suggested that they were having better luck with their supply train than Soult's men. The French campaign had been reliant on some quick victories and the capture of Wellington's supplies. Apart from what they had picked up from the deserted camp up at Maya and the wrecked carts and wagons of the British night march, they had captured precisely nothing and Bonnet was not optimistic.

"Can you win?"

"I think the biggest win will be if we can retreat out of here with our army mostly intact," Bonnet said bluntly, since there was no one around to hear him. "And I think Soult knows it. I'm told he's already had a bit of a kicking at some place called Sorauren. He seems to be hanging around in the hope of reversing that, now that our column is close enough to join in, but I don't think he has a hope in hell of relieving either Pamplona or San Sebastian. I think he's going to fight because he's got no option. And possibly because he doesn't want to have to report back to fucking Bonaparte that he ran like a rabbit at the sight of Wellington."

"Do they have more men?"

"It seems likely. They were scattered all over the place but they've had time to regroup while we've been sitting on our arses waiting for orders."

"Should General D'Erlon have attacked sooner?"

"Bonaparte will think so, that's for damned sure, if this goes badly wrong."

Bianca took his arm and hugged it against her. "Gabriel, if this does go wrong it will not be the first time. I shall say what I always say. Please take care. I find I do not care very much who wins or loses any more, as long as you come back to me at the end."

Bonnet kissed her. "I find I agree with you," he said wryly. "Over there, hiding in that mist, is an English general by the name of Rowland Hill. Which is a bloody silly name. I don't know much about the man except that he's one of Wellington's finest, but the way we're sitting here looking at each other, I've a feeling we're about to find out. If this battle starts unexpectedly, Bianca, I want you to go up to the farmhouse Cavel showed us. Use his name as well as mine; tell them you're an officer's wife. Take Manuel and my spare horses. Stay there. If we're routed, I want you out of the way when the Allied troops come through."

"I promise, Gabriel."

"Try to keep Manuel safe. The Spanish and Portuguese can be bastards to men who serve the enemy and I've grown attached to him."

"I will, husband."

Bonnet grinned, knowing that she was well aware how much he liked it when she called him that. He did not think Bianca herself would be too much at risk as long as she could get hold of a British officer and explain her status. She had been captured once before and Bonnet had not yet got over his frantic terror that she might be dead or in some way harmed. He had risked everything to retrieve her and would do so again if he was able, but he wanted her safe above all else.

"Ask for Van Daan and his wife," he said abruptly. "If you should get picked up, use his name. I've no idea if the Light Division is here but even if they're not, he's well-known and well-regarded and it will keep you safe."

"Gabriel, why are you so worried? You are not usually this bad."

Bonnet was not sure himself. "God knows. Maybe I'm getting old. Or just tired of this fucking war. I hope they do find a few bottles of wine up in those villages. I'm not sure about the men, but I could do with a drink myself to calm me down."

There was little food to be found in the villages. The foraging parties straggled back into camp throughout the day and Bonnet observed that some of them had indeed found wine to be an excellent substitute. His own men, under the strict supervision of their officers, were completely sober although Cavel delivered a dozen bottles of local wine to his delighted Colonel. Perhaps because they were less inebriated, the men of the 30th had managed to acquire a goat and half a dozen chickens and Bianca hurried into action, supervising the butchering and distribution.

It was very little to share between so many, but after days of nothing but hard biscuit and weak stew, roast meat felt like a feast. Bonnet shared the wine with his officers, since there was no point in carrying it into battle or leaving it for the British to loot if they won. After some thought, he sent Cavel with a bottle to General Chassé and was rewarded with a cheerful note of thanks and a bag of apples. Bonnet was pleased with the exchange and sat beside his wife watching the sun go down and eating the fruit. It occurred to him that his most successful relationships with senior officers often revolved around food. Marshal Suchet's penchant for his company had a lot to do with Bianca's cooking.

The attack was ordered early and Marshal Soult rode up personally to supervise. The Allied troops had moved out of the village and taken up a far more defensible position along the edge of a thickly wooded ridge. Hill's right was posted on rocky ground and Bonnet, inspecting the distant troops through his folding telescope, thought it looked very solid but his left, out towards the village of Buenza was more strung out and Bonnet decided that if he were D'Erlon he would concentrate his main attack there.

By the time the Marshal arrived, D'Erlon had already thrown out a screen of skirmishers and musket fire crackled up and down the line. It was echoed in the distance by more serious firing which suggested that the other section of the army was also engaged over towards the village of Sorauren once more. Presumably Soult was confident that Wellington's troops could be held there or he would have remained with the main force.

D'Armagnac's division was under orders to make a feinted attack on the stronger right, while Abbé and Maransin were to attack the left in an attempt to take the summit of the hill. Most of the troops facing Bonnet's section of the line seemed to be Portuguese, with a section of redcoats in support. Many French officers were contemptuous of both Portuguese and Spanish troops, assuming that they would break easily. Bonnet had recently faced Portuguese troops on the bloody field of Vitoria and it was his experience that they were as tough as their British allies.

Once within range there was a fierce exchange of musket fire, made more difficult for the French who were firing uphill. Bonnet's men managed to get off several satisfying volleys which did considerable damage to the front of the Portuguese line. He was listening intently to the drummers for a sudden change in orders. Chassé had told him it was their job to keep the Portuguese busy while the other two columns routed the weaker left of the enemy line. It was a feint rather than a serious assault and could be called off at any moment if something went wrong.

Given their orders, Bonnet had expected that most of the action would involve firepower but he quickly realised that D'Armagnac had decided to press forward. The Portuguese had been badly hit in those first punishing volleys and Bonnet could see them scrambling to fill gaps in their line, their officers bellowing orders. Bugles sounded their haunting call above the rolling clouds of smoke and the Portuguese troops struggled to re-form.

Bonnet halted his men in line to get off another volley. They were much closer to the enemy now and he could see the Portuguese clearly: a mixture of the blue infantry jackets and dull brown of some of the light infantry. The red-coated British troops made a splash of solid colour in their midst. There were not many of them but Bonnet was not sure that mattered. The Portuguese seemed to have fallen back into line very quickly and as Bonnet's men fired, the volley was answered at almost the same moment.

Bonnet yelled a warning but it was pointless. The musket fire ripped into his front line, cutting down half a dozen men without mercy. Several others were hit by spent balls or flying debris. One man, a young recruit from Cavel's company, was on the ground screaming: half his arm shot away. The shattered remains lay beside him in a pool of blood, obscenely bright against the green of the grass.

Bonnet was thrown onto his back where he lay winded for a moment, not sure if he had been hit, then realised something was lying across his legs. He sat up, pushing the heavy weight away from him. The man was dead and Bonnet was soaked in his blood, but he was uninjured. Around him, his battalion was in chaos, some of them already falling back. Bonnet swept the ground with a long look and saw that the rest of Chassé's brigade was picking itself up and moving forward. The other brigades were even further ahead. That devastating volley had missed them entirely and they were part way up the ridge, firing into the Portuguese ranks.

For a moment, Bonnet considered letting his men break and run. It would get him into trouble, but it would save their lives and he wondered if that might be worthwhile. They had lost so many during these past weeks and Bonnet was sick of watching them suffer and die and not even being able to bury them properly.

Ahead of him, General Chassé turned and yelled, waving an arm. Bonnet could not hear his words, having been deafened by musket fire, but his gesture was clear enough. Faced with a direct order, his years of training and experience took over and he was moving forward before he had time to think; shouting orders to his remaining officers and NCOs to move the battalion further to the left to cut off any attempt by the enemy to turn D'Armagnac's flank.

It took them out of the direct line of fire for a time. Bonnet knew how close they had come to breaking and fell back to supervise the men at the rear, allowing Major Faure to lead them on. Some of the men had already begun to run and Bonnet chased after them, roaring at them to get back into line. They obeyed without question, even more terrified of the menacing figure of their Colonel, sword in hand, covered in blood and with his face blackened by the

102

smoke. Bonnet was glad he looked convincing. He had never been closer to running away himself in his life.

The need to rally his men steadied him though and by the time he joined Faure and Cavel at the front again, he had recovered his courage and found an extra spur of sheer fury. D'Armagnac seemed to have utterly ignored his orders to make a feint attack and was fully engaged against the enemy. The Portuguese showed no sign of breaking. They were as steady as any troops Bonnet had fought against. He was furious with the General for his arrogant assumption that these men would not stand.

Since he could not take it out on D'Armagnac, he vented his anger the Portuguese. Coming up the slope on the right of the enemy line, he hurled himself into a bitter hand-to-hand fight, with bayonets and swords. Further along the line there was still sporadic firing but that was impossible here without either side hitting their own men. It was the kind of brutal combat which Bonnet both hated and excelled at. His height, strength and sheer bloody-mindedness drove him forward into the Portuguese line, his men alongside him, pushing the enemy back into the trees.

Once there, Bonnet's trained skirmishers were in their element, but they were faced with an enemy who were just as skilled. There was plenty of cover in the dim forest, and dappled sunlit glades became death traps as the two sides stalked each other. An occasional burst of firing and a shout of pain was followed by eerie silence within the woods as the battle continued to rage outside. Bonnet knew he must be coming up close to the flank of the main Portuguese lines but he was suddenly worried. He knew nothing about the progress of the main battle and if he sent his men in only to discover that the rest of D'Armagnac's column was in retreat, he would have nowhere to run and his men would be slaughtered.

He began calling them in, concentrating on the advanced skirmishers and noticing that the Portuguese caçadores seemed to have melted away through the trees ahead of them. It seemed to confirm his suspicion that there had been some shift in the enemy line but he had no idea if it was forward or back. His battalion had completed its task and driven in the Portuguese right, but Bonnet decided he was going no further without information. He summoned Cavel and gave him a low voiced instruction, then concentrated on getting his men formed up into some kind of order in the woody glades while he waited. He had no idea how long they had been fighting and his pocket watch gave him no useful information as he had forgotten to wind it. It felt like several hours.

Bonnet was about to ask Faure if he knew the time when there was a crashing sound and Cavel appeared from between the trees. One look at his expression told Bonnet all he needed to know.

"We're retreating?"

"Falling back down the slope. Bloody D'Armagnac pushed it too far. If we carry on through here we'll end up at the back of their lines. Might as well surrender straight away at that point."

"Fuck it." Bonnet thought rapidly. He was furious with the General but he also knew he had been guilty of exactly the same thing with this foray into the woods. His men had performed brilliantly but that was not what they were supposed to be doing at all. Their feinted attack had turned into a full scale battle and it did not sound as though the French were winning it. Bonnet wondered briefly how the attack on Hill's left was going, up towards the summit.

He looked around him at his battered men and made a quick decision. "We retreat," he said shortly. "I'm not leading a gallant charge to the death here, it's not my style. Running retreat through the woods, fast as you can and don't stop to fight until we're back with Chassé. Get them moving, Major Faure. It's going to take ten minutes for those skirmishers to realise they're on the winning side and we're like sitting ducks in these fucking woods. Back to the brigade, it's our only chance."

The men of the 30th ran. One or two paused to look behind them and their officers and NCOs bellowed at them to keep moving. There was no point in silence or concealment; the enemy knew perfectly well where they were and Bonnet thought their only hope was that the caçadores would be delayed waiting for the order to pursue. Men stumbled over tree roots and leaped over fallen bodies, both French and Portuguese. At one point they came across two of their men, both wounded, hobbling back towards the tree line. A man pulled up uncertainly beside them and Faure shouted at him to carry on. They would either make it or would be killed or taken prisoner but there was no point in losing more men in an attempt to help them.

Bonnet could already see the light beyond the trees when he heard shots behind him and shouted orders in English: many of the Portuguese battalions had British officers. Here in the forest they were fairly safe. He knew the danger point would be when they emerged onto the grassy slope and had to race down to the protection of the French lines. They could not afford to pause to get their bearings or to decide the best line to take. Once in the open, the Portuguese could line up their muskets and shoot them in the back without mercy until they were out of range. Bonnet tried to visualise the lay of the land in his head.

"Faure, Cavel. Get to the front and lead them down. Don't stop and don't look back. Straight to Chassé's brigade. I'll bring up the rear."

"I will do that, Colonel…"

"Don't be a fucking idiot, Faure. I'm coming last because I'm not as fast as you." Bonnet could barely speak, he was so out of breath. His lungs were burning with pain and his legs already felt leaden. This would be the second time in a year he had fled for his life and almost been cut down or taken prisoner and he knew he had been lucky at Vitoria. He took a deep, agonising breath.

"Cavel, they're yours," he bellowed. "Get them out of here."

His men burst through the trees into full light and Bonnet paused, leaning against a tree trunk, gasping as they raced past him. He had no idea how many were still alive or if any more had fallen dead or wounded in the forest, but he made himself remain still until the last man he could see bounded past him and down the slope. The sounds of pursuit were close by and for one insane moment, Bonnet was tempted to raise his hands in surrender. It would hurt less than another frantic run down the slope and Bonnet was beginning to wonder if he was about to have a heart attack. Then he remembered he had promised Bianca he would come back so he heaved himself off the tree, turned and began to run.

Downhill it was easier and he followed the swarm of blue jackets ahead of him as his men charged ahead. Behind him he could still hear shouted orders and then the muskets exploded. Grass flew up to his right, so close that Bonnet flinched and stumbled, almost falling. His downwards momentum kept him going however and the next volley came nowhere near him. As he had suspected, they had orders not to follow for fear of being cut off. He had made it.

For the first time, Bonnet slowed a little, surveying the battlefield. D'Armagnac's troops had been driven more than halfway back down the slope. Bonnet had a good view across the ridge and he could see dead and wounded men from both sides scattered across the hillside. All the bitter fighting of that morning had gained D'Armagnac's men no ground at all.

His men were reaching the lines now, falling in behind the rest of Chassé's brigade. Bonnet pushed himself onwards and into relative safety. By the time he arrived he was struggling to catch his breath at all. He stood for a long moment at the back of the ranks, the sounds of battle all around him, coughing violently until he was sick on the ground. A hand rested on his back and a water bottle was pushed into his hand.

"Sip it slowly or you'll choke yourself."

Bonnet obeyed and gradually the mist cleared from his vision. He looked up and was surprised to find Chassé himself. He passed the bottle back and Chassé took it with his left hand. His right arm was soaked in blood and a junior surgeon was winding a bandage about it in a somewhat haphazard fashion.

"You're wounded, sir."

"Not serious. You sound worse than I do."

"I'm getting too old for this," Bonnet said, trying to make it sound like a joke.

"Aren't we all? Orders to pull back and regroup then make another assault."

"Oh they're fucking joking."

"They're not. If bloody D'Armagnac had followed orders we could have held this lot steady all day, but he had to try and be a fucking hero."

Bonnet, aware of his own unheroic retreat merely grunted. Chassé grinned.

"That was a bloody good charge, Colonel. Shame you had to pull back, but you made the right decision and you got every one of them back alive."

"We left two wounded men up there, sir."

"No you didn't. They limped down the hill while you were heaving your guts up. The caçadores chose not to fire at them. Your Major just sent them back to the surgeons."

Bonnet felt his spirits lift a little. He straightened. "You should go back to the surgeons yourself, sir."

"Ha! I might have a bloody arm but I'm still in better condition than you. We just had word that after getting lost in the woods for a bit, Abbé has turned their flank, out on their left. If we can hold on here, these Portuguese bastards will have to pull back."

"You mean we're winning this fight?" Bonnet said in astonishment. His brigade commander gave a crack of laughter.

"Unlikely, isn't it? Keep your men at the rear for a while though, they've done enough. They've lost enough, I saw the damage those volleys did."

Bonnet tried to hide his relief. "Yes, sir. Be all right after a breather."

"Good. Go and take it. I'll need you on your feet."

**

Bianca found him late that night, waking him from a restless sleep wrapped in his cloak on the hard ground. Bonnet jumped at the feeling of her hand on his arm and sat up, rubbing sleep from his eyes. When he realised who it was, he relaxed and reached out for her as she settled beside him in the darkness.

"What the devil are you doing here, wife? I thought you safely tucked away in a farm cottage."

"The farm cottage is full of wounded men and I was worried about you. They said your brigade took many losses. I'm sorry, Gabriel but I had to know."

Bonnet drew her down to lie in his arms. "Don't be, I'm glad you're here," he whispered. "We had a bastard of a day but won the field, or so I hear. All to no fucking purpose though, because bloody Wellington blew the rest of the army away at Sorauren for the second time in a week and we're now waiting to find out which way we're going to retreat."

"Back to France?"

"Soult isn't admitting it, but the rest of the army knows we're running with our tails between our legs again. I'm fucking sick of it." Bonnet forced himself to stop speaking. It was after midnight, he was exhausted and he knew they must be on the move at first light. Hill's battered forces had retreated in good enough order to form up again nearby. Bonnet had no idea of the number of dead and wounded on both sides but he was dreading a resumption of the fighting tomorrow, before his men had had a chance to recover. He could have spent an hour ranting about the stupidity and waste of lives of this campaign but he needed rest.

Bianca snuggled close to him, kissed him very gently on the lips and then on each cheek. "Sleep, *querido*," she whispered softly. "Wherever we must go, we will go together. I love you."

Bonnet felt his mouth curve into a smile, something he would not have thought possible an hour earlier.

"Did you bring Manuel?"

"Yes."

"And the baggage mules?"

"Yes."

"I don't suppose there's any breakfast?"

"Some apples and half a loaf of bread that I bought from the farmer. If you do not go to sleep, I am not sharing it with you."

"I'm sleeping," Bonnet said drowsily. He was not sure he was going to do so easily but he lay listening to her breathing beside him in the darkness The sounds of snoring men, braying mules and restless horses faded quickly into nothing and he drifted into sleep.

Chapter Eight

By the time the Light Division approached the River Bidassoa again, they had endured four days of exhausting forced marches, several of them through the night. To obey Wellington's orders, Alten had pushed his men hard across country in appalling conditions. A night march across the Santa Cruz mountains had seen men collapsing from exhaustion along the way. They moved at a snail's pace, trying to light their way with blazing torches.

Paul thanked God that most of the women, children and camp followers had taken a different route with the baggage wagons. He wished Anne had done the same thing. Most of the officers chose to walk, leading their horses carefully alongside sheer precipices. Many of Paul's officers had hoisted exhausted men up onto their mounts to avoid leaving them behind. Anne's black mare, Bella, carried a Portuguese caçadore and behind her, young Private Porter clung precariously to the chestnut gelding being led by Brat.

Putting his wife ahead of army protocol, Paul walked beside Anne as much as he could. His wife prided herself on her ability to cope with appalling conditions and had endured several dreadful retreats over the past few years, but there was something terrifying about this endless shuffling through the darkness in constant fear of a missed step which might take them over the edge of a cliff to their death. Both Anne and Brat were very quiet and Paul tried hard not to worry about his wife all the time since he could do nothing to ease her misery

During the daytime he insisted she snatch what sleep she could. Paul slept little, spending his time checking on the sick men, meeting with Alten and the other brigadiers to receive the latest news and orders and riding back up the paths they had crossed the night before to guide in stragglers. Food was scarce and what was available was given to the sick men.

As news of Wellington's victories and the retreat of the French continued to come in, Alten pushed his men harder in an attempt to cut off a fleeing French column. Officers and men tried to grumble quietly but Paul had good hearing. The Light Division had grown very attached to their Hanoverian commander and Paul had never before heard them complain this much but the men were being pushed to breaking point and their officers were growing angry.

Paul understood, but he did not blame Alten, who had been placed in an impossible position by Wellington's constantly changing orders.

Between midnight and midday on the 1st of August the division had marched more than twenty miles and were greeted with the unwelcome news that the French were still just ahead of them. Paul gave orders for his men to rest. There was no food left and both men and horses were exhausted. He settled his wife in the shelter of some bushes out of the way of a brisk wind, then went in search of Alten and further orders.

His commander was seated on a crumbling stone wall reading a letter. A cavalryman in the uniform of the Staff Cavalry Corps hovered nearby, clearly awaiting a response. Paul studied Alten's face and swore under his breath. He had never seen Alten look so exhausted and so miserable. It was as if the German had taken on the suffering of every man of his division who had collapsed by the wayside. Paul wondered if he was aware of what was being said in the lines. He hoped not. Alten was a good man; a kind man as well as a good officer and he would find it hard to know that some of his officers were holding him responsible for the misery of the past few days.

Alten looked up and managed the ghost of a smile. "General van Daan. Have you yet managed to rest? Always when I look around me, you are there. Do you not require sleep?"

"I'm dreaming of it, sir. Though if you see me every time you look up, that suggests that you're not getting enough sleep either. Further orders?"

Alten nodded. "We have missed them, but his Lordship hopes we might still be able to catch them. I am to send the Rifles out after them as quickly as possible, with other troops in support. The rest of the brigade should remain here. I intend to send the first brigade; the 43rd can…"

"Send us, sir."

Alten paused. "The first…"

"I agree you want the rifles out there, but the 43rd have been dropping like flies. They're exhausted."

"We are all exhausted, General."

"I'm volunteering, sir. With your permission, I'll leave my wife and her maid here, you can take care of them for me. She needs rest. We'll take a few cavalry troopers with us. If we need further support I can send a runner back. The first brigade has been at the front of every action. Give them a break."

After a moment, Alten nodded. "Very well, General, I will issue the orders. Please ask your wife and her companion to join me. My orderlies have gone in search of some food. If they find any I will make sure she eats something. You may take ten troopers to act as messengers. Are you in need of fresh horses? My own spare mounts are…"

"It's all right, sir, we've walked them for most of the way, they're fine. A bit hungry, but I've let them graze where they could. Get some rest or Nan will start fussing over you, and believe me you don't want that."

Alten gave a tired smile. "Good luck, General. And be careful. I would not wish to answer to either your wife or Lord Wellington for further disasters."

Paul realised that his commander knew very well what was being said in the lines and he was suddenly angry. "You're not answerable for the long list of fuck ups during this war, sir. And believe me, if I hear any man of mine saying otherwise, he'll be taking an unexpected dip in the Bidassoa, whether he can swim or not. I'll keep you informed."

Alten smiled, and this time it was a far better effort. "Thank you, Paul. Sometimes I remember that there were those at Horse Guards who believed you and I could not work together. It has been a pleasure, this past year, proving them wrong."

***

They marched at speed, eight miles from the village of Yanzi down a winding track towards the River Bidassoa. The 95th Rifles under Colonel Andrew Barnard took the lead and Paul led the men of the 110th in support. He was aware that there was no need for him to accompany his regiment. Lieutenant-Colonel Gervase Clevedon was an old friend and an experienced officer and more than capable of supporting the Rifles, but after days of pointless marching Paul was itching for a sight of the French and he knew that neither Barnard or Clevedon would mind.

The road climbed steeply on the left bank of the river. The rocky surface was like huge steps, with slabs of overlapping stone. Paul was riding Nero, his second horse, having decided that Rufus had done enough and earned a rest. The big black gelding stepped delicately over the slippery surface and Paul peered down at the river rushing far below and was glad that he was making this ride in broad daylight.

At around four o'clock, a messenger ran back from the front of the column and Paul rode up along with Clevedon to join Barnard at the head. He knew as soon as he approached the Irishman that the enemy was close by. There was dust floating in the air and over on the right bank the sunlight picked out occasional flashes of brilliance off bayonets.

"They're here," Barnard said softly. "After days of chasing shadows, the bastards are just over there."

"Within range?"

"They fucking will be."

Paul grinned. "The bridge?"

"We'll catch up with them if it bloody kills us, sir."

"I believe you. I'm going back to my men, you're in the lead here. Send word if you need me."

Barnard flashed him a brilliant smile. He had struggled initially when his temporary but long-term command of the brigade had been handed over to Sir James Kempt. It had been made slightly worse when Paul had received his promotion to major-general and had retained command of his own brigade. Paul was younger than Barnard and had not served for as long. Wellington could recommend but not not insist on promotions and had learned over the years

110

which battles to pick and choose. On that occasion he had chosen to push for Paul's promotion and Barnard had gone back to being a battalion commander. Paul thought his friend had handled it very well and hoped he would get his reward in the end. He also hoped that Barnard would stop feeling the need to prove himself time and again by taking ridiculous risks in battle, but he knew better than to say so.

They had almost reached the summit of the mountain and the men were struggling, still exhausted after their previous long marches, but the prospect of action seemed to give them new energy. Paul held a steady pace, not wanting them to tire themselves out. It was growing later and the air was still with a hint of evening's early glow when abruptly Barnard called a halt. Paul rode up to join him and reined in alongside looking down over the river. The French were there, a straggling column of blue coats.

"Are the Spanish still holding the bridge?" Paul asked, not taking his eyes from the column.

"No, I sent out scouts. They were driven off by voltigeurs earlier. The French know we're here, the officers have been keeping an eye on us. I think they'll be waiting for us at the bridge."

"Alten sent word that they've got the Fourth Division hot on their heels. Poor bastards are about to get stuck between the two of us. All right, get them moving down the hill, Colonel. We'll come in if you need us."

Released from their even-paced march, Barnard's leading companies raced down the hill to meet the French who were already across the bridge and moving into position to meet them. Paul watched the action from further up the slope, keeping the 110th at arms and ready, with their officers dismounted. He was not sure if they would be required. The 95th were experts at this kind of skirmishing and the French were probably demoralised and much depleted in numbers after their recent disasters. On the other hand, the riflemen were exhausted as well.

The initial skirmishing went well, with the green jacketed riflemen moving smoothly into cover as they approached the bridge. Paul watched appreciatively as the men worked in pairs, one firing while the other reloaded, moving from one shelter to another. They were fast and lethal despite their weariness and the French voltigeurs were beginning to fall back towards the bridge. Paul did not blame them. If he had been in command he would have set them to hold the bridge while their comrades streamed past rather than deliberately engaging the enemy but he suspected that the French command structure was, temporarily at least, in utter chaos. The passing troops seemed to have their wounded with them which was slowing them down. Paul thought that at some point they would have to run and he was mentally making plans to pick up the injured men and get them to a hospital when there was a sudden sharp crackle of firing and a bellow from Colonel Barnard which made him spin around.

There was a small wood up to the left of the bridge which ran steeply up the mountain slope and Paul saw immediately that he had been wrong about

111

the French leadership. An officer with imagination had sent his men through the forest on the far side, out of sight of Barnard's men, and they had appeared at the tree line in perfect order and were firing muskets directly down onto the riflemen who were diving for any cover they could find.

Paul swore. "Clevedon, get them up in support. Companies two to five take the direct route, proceed slowly and let them see you but stay out of range. You're in command, Colonel. The rest, follow me, we're going the long way round."

It was a steep scramble up the rocky slope to the left of the forest and Paul felt it in his calves and back, already aching from the past week. He forced himself to remain at the head of his troops. Ashford, who led his first company and Giles Fenwick climbed on either side of him and Paul kept his eyes on the trees as he heard the first crackle of musket fire from Clevedon's men. There was no sign of the French on this side of the forest and Paul suspected they were being kept busy by the other four companies of the 110th.

As Clevedon's men made the advance, the rifles must have emerged from cover and Paul could hear sporadic firing from Barnard's men again. The firing sounded muffled as he made his way cautiously between the trees. It was growing darker, with twilight almost upon them and Paul strained his eyes in search of the French ahead of him.

The wood was not large and he saw them quickly, their backs to his approaching men as they fired down on the Rifles and the 110th. Paul held up his hand to halt his companies then made a gesture to Ashford and Fenwick to take their two sections forward. He had no need to give further orders. His men were very experienced in this kind of fighting and the French had no idea that they were about to be attacked from the rear until the first shots rang out.

It was over very quickly and Paul approved the speed with which the French officer called the retreat. The voltigeurs ran, bounding back down the slope leaving half a dozen dead or wounded scattered along the tree line. Several more fell as they ran the gauntlet of Clevedon's muskets and Barnard's rifles and they did not stop running until they were across the bridge and safely behind a solid wall of infantrymen, who had been set to guard it. Paul led his men back down to the path, reflecting that they would have lost none at all if they had not attempted to cross in the first place. Neither he nor Barnard had any intention of attempting to force the crossing and watching their men being shot down on the narrow bridge. He had seen the French under Ney attempt it at the Coa several years earlier and the memory of the piled bodies, cut down by musket volleys, had never left him.

Once the voltigeurs had retreated, Paul turned his attention to the remainder of the French. He realised they were looking at the rear guard, with baggage mules and wagons as well as the wounded. The main army had eluded Wellington once again but these battered and bedraggled troops were at the mercy of the riflemen and the 110th. They were trapped on a narrow road, with the river on one side and a steep rocky cliff on the other and were well within range of both rifles and muskets on the opposite bank above them. Paul watched as Barnard and Clevedon placed their men along the river line in an almost leisurely manner. There was no need to hurry now. The distance was no more than thirty or forty yards and the British had the advantage of height, with the slopes looking down onto the retreating French. Barnard gave the order and Clevedon followed it up. The men took aim and began to fire at will.

The French troops knew what was about to happen to them and Paul could see them beginning to panic. Men who had been marching in an orderly manner were starting to run, overtaking those carrying the wounded and in some cases pushing them to one side. Wounded men who were being helped along by comrades, or carried on makeshift stretchers and blankets, were dropped and abandoned. They lay where they fell, bloody and unable to rise and Paul could hear their voices raised in frantic appeals for quarter. He felt sick. As he opened his mouth to speak, he heard Clevedon's cut-glass accent raised in sudden fury.

"Not the wounded! Any man firing at one of them will wish he hadn't."

"You heard the officer of the 110th, riflemen," Barnard's voice floated back above the crackle of firing. "They've only got muskets, they won't be able to hit them anyway, but you might. So don't."

Paul grinned, deciding he would deal with the Irishman later. Half his companies already had rifles and the rest of them used the new Light Infantry land-pattern muskets which were also issued to the 43rd and 52nd. They were not as accurate as the Baker rifle but at this distance, with the French packed so closely together, it would be hard for anyone to miss.

Across the river, some of the French infantry were trying to return fire but it was impossible to hit the British at such an upward angle and with such good cover. A contingent of cavalry had drawn their swords and were trying to force their way through their hapless infantry to take a steep pass, which seemed to be the only way out of the trap. Some of the infantry were retaliating furiously, trying to beat the cavalry back.

Paul felt a wave of sheer rage. "Hammond, Cooper, Scofield. Take out that fucking cavalry officer before he lets his troopers trample over their own men to get out of this."

Half a dozen men led by Sergeant Hammond scrambled to a better vantage point and took aim. Paul felt a sense of satisfaction as the cavalry officer and several of his troopers fell. Their horses ran free, weaving between the infantry. The other dragoons, finding no immediate escape, had begun beating the terrified foot soldiers with the flats of their swords to speed them along.

It sickened Paul. He realised that further along the bank, Barnard had stopped calling out orders and encouragement to his men to fire. The French were in full flight, abandoning baggage and knapsacks in favour of speed.

"Sir?"

Paul turned to see Clevedon beside him and read his own distaste in the other man's grey eyes. "Permission to order them to cease fire, sir?"

"Yes. God yes. Fenwick, get down to Colonel Barnard with the same order, will you? This isn't war, it's fucking murder."

"Yes, sir, although there's not much need. The men are stopping firing of their own accord. Nobody has the stomach for this."

"Once they're past and the bridge is clear, I want a message over to the Fourth Division. They can loot the baggage to their hearts content but I want the wounded taken care of first or I am going to stick Sir Lowry Cole's head on a pike."

"I might phrase that a bit differently, sir, I think he's senior to you, but I'll make sure he gets the point," Fenwick said gravely. He took off at a run towards Barnard's command post, sure-footed on the steep uneven ground. Paul watched him go and found himself smiling. He was looking forward to the return of Captain Manson from sick leave but he had no regrets in his choice of temporary brigade-major. Spending more time with Giles Fenwick had given him a new value for the man and turned mutual respect into friendship.

It was full dark by the time Paul led his weary men back to join the rest of the Light Division who had bivouacked further along the river. Fires had been lit though there was little food available. Paul went in search of his wife and found her seated beside an impressive blaze with her friends. There was a surprising smell of fish which made Paul's empty stomach growl. Anne rose and came forward to kiss him.

"Is everything all right?"

"Yes, though we had some skirmishing. We missed the main army, slaughtered a few of the rear guard and picked up about twenty prisoners, all of them wounded."

"Do I need to have a look?"

"Barnard's surgeon is over there with Daniels, bonny lass. I don't think you'll be needed but I'm sure they'll call you if you are. What on earth is that smell?"

"Trout, sir," Michael O'Reilly said placidly. "Also a couple of eels. It wasn't much, but we've saved some for you and Colonel Clevedon."

"You've been fishing?" Paul asked in astonishment. "How?"

"Ask Brat," Michael said. Anne's maid was approaching with two mess tins containing cooked fish and a tack biscuit. Paul took his, paused and looked at Anne.

"Have you eaten?"

"I've had plenty. Only a short march tomorrow and we'll be back at our old camp site near Vera. Anne watched him eat for a moment then rose and returned with a bottle of wine. Paul stared as she poured several cups then passed one to him and another to Clevedon. She looked around.

"Where's Giles? We've saved him some food as well."

"He rode over with a message to Cole from me but he'll be back soon. Put me out of my misery, girl of my heart. Where did the wine come from?"

Anne laughed. "Lord Wellington stopped off, he's on his way back to Lesaca. He had a great deal to say about you taking your men in support of Colonel Barnard instead of allowing the 43rd to do its job. He was quite short with General Alten, I thought, but I explained that it was wholly your idea and then distracted him by talking about Pearl and the puppies. He left me two bottles of this and informed me he would send Colonel Murray in search of better accommodation for me when we are back at Vera."

Paul sipped the wine and felt its warmth seeping through his entire body. He closed his eyes and thought about puppies. It was very soothing.

Giles Fenwick rode in just as the group was breaking up for the night. Paul dismissed the others to sleep and sat by the dying fire, finishing the wine while his brigade-major ate.

"You must be exhausted. Was Cole all right?"

"Yes, sir. I like General Cole. He'd already got men out to bring in the French wounded. Poor bastards. I think they're just relieved it's over. Even a prison camp must look better than what they've just been through. I was talking to one of them. A young lieutenant from Rheims. He tells me morale wasn't good at the beginning of this campaign but it's in the dust now. Most of them just wish Bonaparte would sign a peace treaty and stay within his own borders."

"I suspect that's a pipe dream. It sounds wonderful but I'd find it hard to sleep at night waiting for that bastard to build up his army and launch another invasion. I'm not sure he'll ever stop until we kick him out for good."

"I agree with you, sir. And there should be some justice for the thousands who have died for his uncontrollable ambition. I don't think I could support any kind of peace that left him free and in power."

"For Antonio?"

"For Antonio and all the people I saw slaughtered in Castro Urdiales earlier this year. And throughout the rest of this war. Even the men who died of that bloody fever in Walcheren wouldn't have been there if it hadn't been for that bastard Bonaparte."

Paul drained his cup and stood up. "We'll finish him, Giles. I don't know what the politicians and diplomats are thinking but I don't see Wellington signing another peace treaty he doesn't agree with and he's no longer the junior general. His opinion counts. Get some sleep. I'm hoping we'll be reunited with the rest of our baggage wagons tomorrow and we can finally get some rest for a few days. Goodnight, Captain. And thank you."

"Goodnight, sir."

Paul watched as the younger man settled himself, wrapped in his shabby cloak on the ground, and then went to join Anne.

***

D'Armagnac's brigade staggered across the border into France in darkness and by the time they received the order to stop and rest, Bonnet was almost asleep on his feet. He had kept his men together throughout the long agonising days of the retreat through a mixture of cajoling and bullying. His wife applied the same strategies to him when he sat late into the night by the camp fire, considering desertion.

115

There was rest at last on the outskirts of the little town of St Jean de Luz and in the pale light of dawn the supply wagons, which had never managed to reach them on the long hungry march, rolled into camp. Bonnet dragged himself from an exhausted sleep and harried his remaining officers and NCOs to prevent the men storming the wagons and possibly slaughtering the pack animals as well. Order was restored, the division was fed and the chefs de battalion were given orders to rest their men, count their losses and make up the returns for headquarters. Soult settled to recover from the retreat and presumably to write his excuses and explanations to his Imperial master.

Losses were alarming. More than a third of Bonnet's battalion was missing; either dead, captured or seriously wounded. He had lost a dozen wounded men during the frantic retreat along the Bidassoa. He had no idea if they had survived or not. He had been forced to shout orders at his men to leave them to the mercy of the Allied troops. Passionately he hoped they had been picked up and taken care of.

For a time he had lost track of his wife in the chaos and had endured three agonising hours before she appeared, along with Manuel. She had abandoned some of their baggage in favour of mounting herself and their servant on the mule and made it into camp unscathed, though she was covered in mud and badly bruised from a fall in the dark. Bonnet took her into his arms and held her for a long time.

"I've had enough of this," he growled. "Fucking Soult. Fucking Bonaparte. Are you all right, Bianca?"

"Yes. So very tired though, and sore. This stupid animal got loose in the confusion and when I managed to catch him he kicked me. I thought he had broken my hip."

"If he's done you any serious injury I'll break his bloody neck."

"No, it is just badly bruised. I will be fine, Gabriel and we must forgive him because once we got hold of him and calmed him down he carried us nobly for several miles. If he had not done so, I think we would have been taken because the British were not far behind us. We lost many men, did we not?"

"Yes. I still don't have the final numbers because I've not heard back from the field hospitals yet. They're talking about sending some of the units back to Bayonne on garrison duty until they can recruit more men, but I don't think it'll be us. Apparently D'Erlon's column is in better shape than most."

"Can they recruit more men?"

"While women still give birth and boys grow to manhood, he'll have a regular stream of conscripts. But they'll be too young with no time to train them properly and no experience." Bonnet took a long breath. "I'm going to shut up now before I start yelling it aloud and get myself arrested. Come and get some food, Bianca and then I want the surgeon to take a look at you, just to be sure."

Bianca hugged him. "What will happen now, Gabriel? Will he try again?"

"I suppose he'll have to. Not immediately. He'll have to consider his resources and come up with a new plan. In the meantime we all go back to sitting

116

on our arses staring at Wellington's men who are doing exactly the same with us. At the moment I just need some proper food and a good night's sleep. Just in case the arseholes decide we're in better shape than we are and order a surprise night march through impossible terrain to fight an enemy who holds all the advantages and probably has more troops by now. Oh wait, though. Didn't we just do all that?"

Bianca smiled somewhat tearfully and kissed him. "You definitely need food, Gabriel. Come, we shall collect our rations and then see what else I can find to cook."

"Let Manuel do it. You're hurt."

"I am also hungry and Manuel cannot cook. Do not fuss over me, Gabriel, I am very well. Just thankful to be back with you."

Bonnet surveyed her sternly. "Next time, you're staying with me, I don't care what the regulations say. Go and rest, I'll bring the food to you. Have we lost the bedding?"

"No, but I am afraid we lost the tent."

"Never mind, it had holes in it anyway. I hope the redcoat who loots it gets soaked in the night and develops pneumonia. I'll be back soon."

***

Paul's new camp was situated three miles from the previous site, in a small valley bisected by a fast stream which flowed into the Bidassoa. He was overseeing the setting up of tents and a baggage park when he was joined by Johnny Wheeler and Colonel Andrew Barnard who had ridden over from the second brigade which was once again camped close to the little town of Vera.

"Do you think we'll get a week off now, sir?" Johnny asked, surveying the neat lines of the emerging camp.

"If you'll excuse me mentioning it, Wheeler, some of us were working hard while you lot lounged around eating your way through your rations."

Barnard's voice was loaded with sarcasm and Paul grinned. Their arrival back at Vera had been greeted with the unwelcome news that the French had occupied the heights of Santa Barbara and surrounding hills again and needed to be driven off. Most of the Light Division had not eaten properly for days and some of the men were faint with hunger and exhaustion when the order came for Kempt's brigade to attack. Fortunately it coincided with the late arrival of the commissariat wagons and Kempt's men had stood wolfing down dry tack biscuits while loading their weapons. After their exertions of the previous day, Paul was happy to stand back and watch the other brigade make the advance and Barnard's men, the 43rd and two Portuguese battalions had taken the hill without firing a shot as the French withdrew.

From there, Alten gave orders to recapture the nearby Ibanteli Mountain, a sharply defined summit which guarded the route to another of the passes into France and which currently stood in the way of direct communication with the Fourth Division. Barnard had led the attack with his riflemen in two

117

wings, supported by the 43rd. Fog made the assault particularly difficult and Paul had stood with his officers listening to the muffled sounds of fighting, wishing he could persuade Alten to let him go in to support the first brigade. He had unhappy memories of several actions which were hampered by fog during Massena's retreat and he wondered if Alten was expecting too much of Barnard's men.

By the time the fog began to lift however, the 95th were making themselves masters of the summit and the French were in full retreat; racing down the slopes into the valley towards France so quickly that many of them left caps, pouches and equipment behind. The action was not costly for Barnard's men and Alten congratulated them, gave his orders about encampments and retired to his chosen headquarters in a solid farmhouse on the edge of the valley.

Paul knew perfectly well why his camp had been relocated from its previous position. He surveyed the little valley with satisfaction and waited for Barnard to speak. It did not take long.

"How in God's name do you do it, Van Daan? I've been in this bloody army for eight years longer than you and I'm around the same number older than you. It's not the fucking promotions that I mind so much, it's the fact that every time we stop for longer than a few days you end up living in the lap of luxury with the locals treating you like visiting royalty."

Paul laughed aloud. "Don't exaggerate, Andrew. I've seen the farm you're billeted on and they're going to fatten you up like a chosen calf. Just behave yourself with the farmer's wife, she's very attractive and she likes the look of you."

Barnard grinned "I like the look of her as well, but I'm not that stupid, General. Faced with the choice of a comfortable billet for a week or two and a roll in the hay I know which I'm choosing. She's even given Antoine the run of her kitchen."

"That's good. I await a dinner invitation," Paul said placidly. Barnard's French cook was excellent, if slightly temperamental. He had been taken prisoner at Salamanca the previous year and had accepted Barnard's offer of employment in preference to transportation to a prison camp. As far as Paul could tell the arrangement worked very well.

"You'll get one. All the same, look at this, for God's sake."

Paul admired his new headquarters. The big three storied house was from the seventeenth century, painted a bright terracotta with double wooden eaves and a high stone wall surrounding it. A small cupola was set at the front of the house above the dark grey tiled roof. There were wrought iron balconies at the upper windows and shady gardens with a fountain playing on the front carriage drive.

"It's very nice isn't it?"

"I hate you."

Paul laughed and capitulated. "Don't be an idiot, Colonel, you know perfectly well that Murray found this on orders from Wellington. That's why he moved our camp site. Nor has it anything to do with his affection for me. He

118

spends ninety per cent of his time working out how to thrash Bonaparte and manage the Spanish and Portuguese governments and the final ten per cent worrying about the comfort and safety of my wife. The house belongs to the Lordship of Oñate, but as the current incumbent is a long way away he isn't going to mind us moving in. There's a couple who live in one of the estate cottages and act as caretakers. They're helping my wife allocate the rooms now. It's a bit musty and a bit damp but so much better than a tent."

Barnard snorted. "In a previous era they'd have burned your wife as a witch."

"I've thought that myself, to be honest, but I'm fully prepared to make the most of her magic. I'd invite you to dinner tomorrow but we've been summoned to dine with Lord Wellington. I think he wants Nan to inspect the puppies and have a look at Pearl."

"Good God, I'd forgotten about that. What on earth is he going to do with them?"

"Unless he's changed his mind, it's my job to find homes for them." Paul eyed his friend thoughtfully. "Andrew, you're a single man with no responsibilities. A dog might be just the thing…"

"I have an entire battalion under my command and I'm not taking on a damned puppy," Barnard said forcefully. After a moment he added:

"Have you thought about Skerrett? He could do with cheering up a bit."

"Interesting idea. I'll ask him. Or maybe Nan should. She's hard to resist."

"Witchcraft, as I said. Is that the only reason for your visit to headquarters, do you know?"

"I've no idea but if there's any news, I'll let you know."

Barnard gave an ironic salute. "You're a friend and a gentleman, General van Daan as well as an invaluable source of headquarters gossip. Talking of which, Colonel Wheeler, there's a rumour going around that you're a fortunate man. Is it true?"

Johnny smiled. "More than I can describe, sir. She's said yes so all I need to do now is get through the rest of this war and get home to marry her."

"What's her name?"

"Miss Mary Ludlow. You'll probably have heard that my uncle died and I inherited his estate in Derbyshire. Miss Ludlow is the daughter of my estate manager."

"She sounds perfect for you. Congratulations. As your brigadier is off hobnobbing with the aristocracy tomorrow, why don't you join me for dinner and we'll celebrate?"

"I'd like that, thank you."

"Don't let him get you drunk, Colonel. The French are very close."

"Miserable bastard," Barnard said dispassionately. "Don't worry about it, Wheeler, he won't be there. We can do what we like."

It was four miles from Paul's camp to Wellington's headquarters in Lesaca. Paul was accompanied by Anne and followed by Jenson and Anne's

119

Portuguese groom. He was also accompanied by Ensign Laurence Fox and thoroughly enjoyed his wife's surprised expression. It was customary for Paul to take one of his junior officers when he went to dine with his Lordship. He generally took his Brigade Major or one of his ADCs, but as he went to find Captain Theo Kuhn of the King's German Legion to issue the invitation, he caught sight of Fox.

It was the first time Paul had seen him since the march and he paused. Most of the senior officers had found accommodation in the house and a lot of the juniors had begged space in the farm cottages. Some of them were sharing one of the small barns and Paul had paused outside to listen the previous evening. It was clear that his juniors had managed to find enough local girls to hold an impromptu dance and Paul admired both their relentless high spirits and their energy. Ensign Laurence Fox had pitched his tent instead. It was isolated on the edge of the lines of the 112th and Fox was sitting in a camp chair outside with a portable desk balanced on his lap, writing a letter.

Paul hesitated. Given Fox's record since he had joined the 112th earlier in the year he would not usually have chosen him to attend at headquarters, but Simon Carlyon's remarks had stayed with him. He stood watching Fox for a moment, then changed course and went to join him. Fox seemed deep in thought and did not hear his approach. At the last minute he looked up, saw Paul and got up so hastily that he overset his chair and tipped the writing desk onto the floor. The inkpot spilled a dark pool onto the grass. Fox snatched up his letter just in time and stood staring down at the chaos. Belatedly he remembered where he was, transferred his papers to his left hand and managed an awkward salute. Paul returned it gravely. If this had been one of his favourite juniors he would have roasted him unmercifully but he was aware that he did not have that kind of relationship with Fox and it would have been unkind.

"Sorry Mr Fox, I didn't mean to make you jump that badly. People generally hear me coming for miles. Writing home?"

"Yes, sir. I'm writing to my brother."

"I hope that wasn't the last of your ink. If it was, let me know. My wife always keeps a good supply."

"No, sir. Thank you sir. I've got more."

Fox wore a shuttered expression which bothered Paul. When he had first met the younger man he had been exasperated by his arrogance as well as his complete lack of respect for his senior officers. That belligerence seemed to have vanished and Paul wondered why. He had a feeling that both he and Johnny had somehow missed something during the chaotic few weeks since the battle.

"I was looking for you," he said. "My wife and I are invited to dine at headquarters today and I generally take one of my junior officers. I'd like you to accompany us. We'll be riding over because I can't get my wife to use her carriage unless there's a thunderstorm in progress."

Fox's mouth was hanging open. "With Lord Wellington, sir?"

"Yes. It's an informal dinner so don't worry. One or two of his staff will probably be there."

120

"But…why me, sir? Surely Lieutenant Powell or Captain Kuhn would be better. Or Captain Fenwick."

Paul regarded him in surprise. "They've all dined at headquarters many times, Ensign. I thought you might like the opportunity."

"I'd feel awkward, sir."

"Good God, why? Your service record hasn't been that impressive so far, but your table manners are perfectly good. It's just dinner."

Paul could have bitten his tongue the moment he said it. Fox's fair skin flushed a dark red and he wore the mutinous expression which was familiar to Paul.

"Thank you, sir, but I'd really rather not. Like I said, I'd feel awkward and I think you'd be happier with another officer."

Paul opened his mouth to snap out a response but managed to stop himself just in time. "Request refused, Mr Fox," he said as gently as he could manage. "Get yourself changed and join us, please."

Fox was mostly silent on the ride to Lesaca but Anne was in good spirits which made his sullenness less obvious. Paul forced himself not to react to it, talked to his wife and questioned his orderly about the progress of young Private Porter who had been temporarily assigned to assist Jenson about his many duties. When they were ushered into Lord Wellington's presence, Paul watched Fox carefully but was relieved to see that whatever his objections, Fox could produce good manners when he chose.

He was seeing Wellington at his best. On his return to Lesaca the Commander-in-Chief had been suffering badly from lumbago but he seemed to have recovered and was in good spirits. As Paul had guessed, it was an informal dinner. Most of the other guests were members of Wellington's staff. Colonel Lord Fitzroy Somerset was his young military secretary, General Miguel Alava was one of his Spanish liaison officers and Major-General Sir George Murray was his newly returned and much valued quartermaster-general. There was a fourth man present and Paul smiled broadly then went forward to shake his outstretched hand.

"Richard, it's good to see you. I thought you were a permanent fixture at San Sebastian."

Major-General Sir Richard Fletcher returned his smile. "I have been. His Lordship wanted to consult with me about one or two matters, so very kindly invited me over for a few days."

"Is Sir Thomas Graham not here?"

"I shall be returning with Sir Richard to receive the latest news on the resumption of the siege," Wellington said smoothly. "Today is purely social, General. The only business I am willing to discuss today is the welfare of my hunting bitch and the progress of her offspring."

"How are they, my Lord?" Anne asked. "I'm longing to see them and so sorry that I was obliged to leave so suddenly. Did they all survive?"

"They did, thanks to the excellent instructions you left for my grooms. I wish you had remained, ma'am, not because of the puppies but because it would have spared you a very unpleasant time upon the road. I have been hearing of your trials from General Alten, who was full of praise for your courage and fortitude. But it was unnecessary. You would have been much safer here."

"I was not worried for my safety, sir. I just wanted to be with my husband."

"That, I surmised," Wellington said dryly. "When we have dined you shall accompany me to see Pearl. I think she is recovering well from the birth."

"And the puppies? They were so small when I saw them, it was difficult to imagine what they would look like as they grew."

Wellington attempted a frown. "Well they do not look like my pure-bred hunting greyhound, ma'am."

"I don't suppose they do, sir."

His Lordship's lips twitched into a reluctant smile. "They are surprisingly attractive," he admitted unexpectedly. "I had a visit from a Spanish gentleman who resides locally. He is interested in hunting and I took him to meet Pearl and the puppies. To my surprise, he has requested permission to visit your billet to meet their sire. I attempted to describe the creature but I fear I ran out of words. Still, he is interested, if you would permit it, General?"

"Of course," Anne said instantly. "I'm always willing to show off my dog, sir, you know how I feel about him."

"If I did not, ma'am, I would have been a lot more angry," Wellington said pointedly. Anne laughed.

"I'd love to know more about Craufurd's pedigree," she said. "He has the oddest habits sometimes. We have sheep in the pastures behind the house and he's fascinated by them."

"I'm sure he is."

"Not as dinner, sir. He behaves rather as if he's herding them. Given his long coat I'm beginning to wonder if he's crossed with a sheepdog."

Wellington raised surprised brows. "I had never considered that. It might also explain his protectiveness of you, ma'am. Despite my irritation, I have always admired that."

They were still talking about dogs as Wellington led her into the dining room. Paul watched them, smiling, then glanced at Fox. He thought that the boy was looking a little happier. He came to attention as he saw Paul's eyes upon him and Paul shook his head.

"At ease, Mr Fox. As his Lordship said, this is a social occasion. Lord Fitzroy, tell me the truth while he's out of earshot. How much time has he spent with those dogs since he got back?"

Somerset gave a splutter of laughter. "Yesterday he could barely walk with his back pain, sir. I had to attend him in his bedroom to take dictation. And yet when General Alava went looking for him about an invitation, he was not there."

Alava smiled at Fox. "I found him sitting on a folding camp chair in that draughty barn watching them feed. He had his valet carry it down there for him. His Lordship does not like others to see that he has a softer side, Mr Fox,

122

but it appears without fail in the presence of dogs, horses, children and Mrs van Daan. Come, we must go in or he will begin to shout."

"Not once he's got my wife to himself. He wouldn't notice we were missing for half an hour."

"True. But also I am hungry. After dinner, General van Daan, I need to speak with you a little. I will not raise it before his Lordship because he is determined not to speak of business today, but when he goes to fuss over his dogs I will steal you away for a few minutes. Now Mr Fox, you shall sit between me and Lord Fitzroy and we shall speak of our own dogs. Which part of the country are you from and is it good hunting country?"

Paul was seated between Murray and Fletcher. With Fox being happily drawn out of his shell by Somerset and the Spaniard, and Anne occupying all Wellington's attention, he caught up on family news with both Fletcher and Murray then asked about the progress of the siege. He had known both men for many years. Fletcher was Wellington's chief engineer and he and Paul had become friends during the building of the defensive lines of Torres Vedras back in 1809. Fletcher had been badly wounded during a French sortie at Badajoz the previous year and had gone back to England to recover but had returned in time for Vitoria and was currently trying to manage both the blockading of Pamplona and the siege at San Sebastian. There was a chronic shortage of good engineering officers and virtually no trained sappers, so that Fletcher had to manage as best he could using local labour or untrained infantrymen to dig his trenches and build redoubts.

"If I had even half the resources of the French we wouldn't struggle as much as we do every time we have to attack a citadel," Fletcher commented bitterly, nodding to the servant to refill his wine glass. "I lost several good officers at Burgos who haven't been replaced yet. Sometimes I feel as though I'm trying to do this without any support at all."

"You sound like Dr McGrigor with the medical services," Paul said sympathetically. "Ever since Vitoria when he got a proper look at our surgeons' equipment, which we paid for out of our own pocket by the way, he's been trying to work out a way to get Wellington to increase provision."

"McGrigor is a good man," Murray said. "Seems to know how to manage his Lordship, which is more than most people do. How's your young brigade-major doing, Van Daan? Recovering, I hope?"

"Captain Manson? Yes, he's apparently doing very well. He's making noises about returning but I've told him if he comes back before he's fully fit, he'll regret it."

"You must miss him."

"I do, although I've been very happy with his temporary replacement. It was a snap decision and if I'd thought about it for longer I'm not sure I'd have gone with Fenwick, but I'm glad I did."

"What about Colonel Swanson?" Murray asked. "Have you heard from him?"

"I've had a couple of letters, though my wife hears more regularly from Keren. He's joined his father in our parish church as curate. I think he's recovering, though I doubt he'd tell me if he wasn't. He wouldn't want to worry me."

"He's a good man; I know Lord Wellington values him highly. A loss to the army. And a more personal loss to you, I imagine."

"He's been my best friend since we were boys together," Paul said. He wished Murray would change the subject though he knew the man was only trying to be sympathetic. He was not sure he would ever come to terms with Carl Swanson's absence from his battalion, though he fully respected his friend's decision not to return and try to carry on after the loss of his left hand at Vitoria. He tried not to think about it too much and during the long days of fighting and marching he could push it to the back of his mind for a time, but as he sat beside the camp fire at night or around his mess table for dinner he caught himself looking for Carl, waiting for him to arrive. It was a nagging ache which only time could heal but Paul wished that time would hurry up. He was sick of feeling this way.

When the meal was over he was pleased that Somerset towed Fox away to introduce him to some of the other young ADCs. Paul had not heard much of their conversation but suspected the two men had found some kind of common acquaintance or family connection in Fox's home county of Cumberland. It was a relief to see Fox in animated conversation with somebody. Thinking about it, Paul realised that he had not actually seen the boy with any of his former friends in the brigade since the week they had spent in San Estevan. He wondered if rumours had spread about Fox's supposed disappearance during the battle at Vitoria. Simon Carlyon had thought that an accusation of cowardice might leave the younger man isolated but there was no evidence against Fox and no charges had been brought. It had been Fox's first major battle and Paul thought that most of his officers would give the boy a second chance at the very least.

He was still puzzling over the matter as he walked with Anne, Wellington and Alava down to the stable to visit Pearl and her puppies. Anne knelt in the straw stroking Pearl's silky grey head, oblivious to the risk of stains on her yellow silk skirts. Wellington crouched beside her pointing out the different patchy colouring on some of the puppies and laughing with her as they tumbled over each other.

"If he remains like that for too long he will not be able to stand up," Alava said dispassionately. "His back is not yet better."

"Nan will get him up." Paul glanced at the Spaniard. "What did you want to speak to me about, General?"

"Let us go outside. We will walk back to the house and drink a glass of wine and I shall explain. I should warn you that I am asking for a small favour."

Paul gave him a sideways look. "Small?"

Alava gave a flourish of his hand. "Perhaps a little bigger than small."

Paul laughed as the Spaniard stood back to allow him to go through into a small parlour. He got on well with Alava.

"Out with it then, before he comes back in search of brandy to help with the pain."

"You know that of my many duties, one is to act as liaison with the various Spanish commanders. Sometimes this duty is more difficult that at others."

"I should think it would be hellish, but carry on."

"This week, I was approached by a gentleman – an old acquaintance of mine. Colonel Anaya has a problem within his regiment."

Alava poured brandy and Paul accepted the glass with thanks. He sipped it.

"Go on," he said suspiciously.

"Anaya commands the 1st Mallorcan regiment. They serve in the Second Spanish Division under Espana. The troops are mostly from the island although some of the officers are from other parts of Spain. One of them is a gentleman of little fortune but good birth by the name of Captain Don Ángel Cortez. He and one of his fellow captains distinguished themselves during the siege of Tarragona – the first siege, you will understand. They were both wounded and went to Mallorca to recover."

"This is taking far too long if you want to avoid sharing the tale with his Lordship, General. What is Don Ángel's particular problem?"

"He is Spanish and noble," Alava said in disgusted tones which Paul appreciated, given Alava's own impressively noble lineage. "He has both a temper and a sense of honour."

"Oh dear Lord. Has he been duelling?"

"He has. Twice within the past month. The first was with a fellow officer, new to the regiment. The second was with the man's younger brother who challenged him over the first duel."

"Did he kill either of them?"

"Fortunately not. However, it has been decided that they must find another posting for Cortez. He is a brave soldier with a distinguished service record, you understand. But…"

"But he ran up against a man with better connections," Paul said shrewdly. "I'm not sure I can help you, General."

"But you may. They have suggested to Lord Wellington that Cortez be given some kind of headquarters post, possibly in intelligence. He is very good, but difficult and may do better working alone."

"Then it's George Scovell you should be talking to, though I'm not sure he's recruiting. Since King Joseph's cipher fell into our hands and was thoroughly cracked, he's been getting all the news he needs. But also, we're almost in France. There's not the same need for the exploring officers to map the countryside and watch the enemy. He's still got Fenwick on call when he needs him and one or two others, but I'm not sure…"

"Lord Wellington understands that it is not that we need him, General. It is that Espana wants to be rid of him. Perhaps he could be useful to assist

125

Captain Fenwick at need. A temporary posting, but with honour. Away from his regiment so that things can cool down."

Paul suddenly realised that he was being dense. "You're not talking about him coming to headquarters, are you, Miguel?"

"No," Alava said apologetically. "Lord Wellington will not have him. He says he has enough young hotheads ready to quarrel at a word and does not require another. But if he is to work with Captain Fenwick…"

"Is Wellington trying to land me with this blasted man?"

"It was just a suggestion. Lord Wellington said that he thought a Spanish intelligence officer might be useful, especially as he speaks fluent French as well. But if he comes, it must be seen that it is not a punishment. To join the very famous third brigade of the Light Division can only be seen as an honour."

"Oh for God's sake," Paul said in exasperation. He finished the brandy and set down the glass. Alava refilled it immediately. "Has this already been decided? And why the hell are you sneaking around behind Wellington's back if it has?"

"It has not. Lord Wellington, most surprisingly, has said that you have had enough to deal with and he will not see you saddled with this man, especially given your views on duelling."

Paul picked up the glass, staring at Alava in astonishment. "Are you sure that's what he said?"

"I was there myself, General."

"Good God, how extraordinary. Do you think he's all right? He was a bit odd last month now I come to think about it."

Alava laughed and touched his own refilled glass to Paul's. "I think he understands that these past weeks have been hard for you, Paul. He is not without sympathy to those he calls friends. At least, not always."

"That's true. Oh blast it, General, you want me to tell him I'll take this Cortez don't you?"

"I would consider myself in your debt."

"Well I don't want him. But I'll speak to Wellington and tell him I'll at least see the man. I can't do more than that. And not today because I'll need to speak to Fenwick first."

"Of course. I am grateful that you will at least consider it."

Paul sipped the brandy, his eyes on the other man. "Why do you care, Miguel?"

Alava shrugged. "I feel sorry for him," he said simply. "I have a feeling that the provocation may have been very great."

"Do you know what it was about?"

"Only rumours. If you are to see him, I think you should ask him yourself."

"All right." Paul put his glass down. "Stop bribing me with brandy, you've got your way. I'm going to collect my wife and my junior officer and go

126

home to sleep it off. Is he all right, Miguel? He seems it, but I've hardly seen him. It's been a tough few weeks. Is he getting treatment for his back?"

Alava gave a faint smile. "He is well. Angry with himself because he believes he made an error, but relieved, I think. He worries about you also."

"He doesn't need to, I'm fine. Let's hope San Sebastian doesn't turn into another Burgos though. We don't need it through the winter months. At least we've got Fletcher back and I've a lot of faith in him. As for his Lordship, perhaps these puppies will distract him for a while."

Chapter Nine

Captain Leo Manson woke early from habit. With no reason to get up, he lay quietly for a while. A chink of light through the curtains at the long windows grew steadily brighter and he could just see a sliver of blue sky. The tavern was still and silent. Accustomed to late hours, its inhabitants tended to sleep through the early morning. Manson was used to the noise of an army camp which was never really quiet at all and could not remain asleep once it was light, no matter how much he wanted to. He did not mind at present. His time here, with this woman, was very limited and Manson was reluctant to waste too much of it sleeping.

Turning his head carefully so as not to disturb her, Manson surveyed his companion. She was still soundly asleep, her attractive face peaceful, framed by a riot of dark hair on the pillow. He could remember his first nights with Diana Periera when she had not seemed to sleep much at all. They had been apart for most of the intervening year, apart from a few precious weeks during winter quarters, but they had corresponded regularly. The frequency of her letters had made Manson the butt of good-natured banter from his fellow officers, especially those who knew that Diana's tavern was also the local brothel. Manson tried to ignore the jokes as best he could and was deeply appreciative of his close friends who defended his choice without hesitation, no matter how incomprehensible they found it.

Manson had not expected to see Diana again so soon but he had received a bad leg wound during the recent bloody encounter at Vitoria and needed to convalesce. He could easily have done so at the army hospital in Vitoria, which now had a small unit for officers attached to it, but his commanding officer had suggested that Manson return to the little border town of Elvas and to Diana for his recovery. Manson was passionately grateful to him and Diana had welcomed him, fussed over him and for a few short weeks made him feel loved in a way that he had never felt before. Manson was recovering faster than the army surgeons had thought possible and dreaded leaving her.

Diana murmured in her sleep then turned over and opened her eyes. She smiled at the sight of Manson lying watching her.

"How long have you been staring at me, Captain Manson?"

"I've no idea. Time stands still when I'm looking at you."

Diana gave an unromantic peal of laughter and Manson laughed with her, pulled the pillow from under her head and hit her gently with it. She rolled away, snatching at his pillow and retaliated. The fight lasted for several minutes until Diana called a halt by scrambling out of bed.

"No. Stop it. Those are expensive feather pillows and if you break one, I am giving you the job of collecting every one of the feathers to re-stuff it. It will take you hours."

Manson grinned but lowered the pillow. "Spoilsport. I was enjoying the opportunity of a little training there."

"If you've been fighting the French with feather pillows, no wonder you ended up wounded, love. You should try a sword next time."

Manson made a gesture, acknowledging the hit and moved to sit on the edge of the bed. Diana was pulling on her shift but she came quickly to his side. "You haven't hurt yourself, have you?"

"No, it feels fine." Manson stretched out his long leg. On his last visit to the local Portuguese surgeon, the protective bandages had been removed and Manson had been instructed to exercise the limb: gently at first, not putting too much strain on it. There were two ragged scars on his thigh where pieces of stone had been removed but they were already much less red and angry. The leg ached badly if Manson did too much but he could already walk without using a stick and two days earlier had made his first attempts at riding a horse. Manson respected the surgeon but preferred to manage his own convalescence and he knew that if he could not ride, he was of no use to his battalion. Riding had been painful, stretching the damaged muscles in a different way to walking, but he was determined to persist.

"I wondered if you'd done too much yesterday," Diana said, watching as Manson limped to the clothes chest by the window. Manson heard the anxiety in her tone and took out a clean shirt then looked round at her with a grin.

"I wondered if I'd done too much last night, but I've woken in a remarkably good mood. It must be good exercise. I should tell Dr Daniels to prescribe it."

Diana gave a little splutter of laughter. "I don't think he needs to prescribe that particular form of exercise to a battalion of redcoats, Leo. Though he probably has to prescribe other remedies when they acquire a dose of the pox. Are you hungry? I'm going to the market early, I was going to eat when I got back but if you…"

"I'll walk down with you."

Warm brown eyes surveyed him lovingly. "You don't have to, Leo. I'm grateful to Major-General van Daan for letting me take care of you like this but I'm not sure how he'd feel about his brigade-major helping the local brothel keeper to do her shopping."

"Knowing Major-General van Daan he'd probably offer to carry your basket himself. Anyway I think the citizens of Elvas are getting used to me. They probably think I'm your new business partner."

129

Diana was twisting her long dark hair up into a knot in front of the wooden framed mirror on her dressing table. "At least there are no British troops stationed here at present. I've seen some curious looks from the Portuguese garrison, but their officers can hardly make a fuss, given that..."

She broke off and Manson felt a familiar frisson of discomfort. They did not talk in detail about her profession. While he was staying with her, Diana had devoted herself entirely to him. She had told Manson that the proceeds from the tavern and the rent from the other girls who plied their trade from her bright, clean rooms was more than enough to support her and Emilio, her bartender and general manager. Manson thought she was probably telling the truth; he had seen how popular the tavern was with the townspeople, the Portuguese garrison and passing travellers. Still, he worried that he was a charge on her while preventing her from earning her living and he flinched every time she avoided a difficult subject.

They walked hand in hand through the busy market and Manson watched with enjoyment as Diana haggled over mutton, rice and fruit and placed an order for a delivery of preserved fish. He was always slightly surprised at how little regard the locals paid to Diana's shocking reputation. She seemed well-liked in the town and was treated like any other prosperous businesswoman. Manson wondered if that was a cultural difference or an effect of these long years of war. In most English market towns she would have been shunned.

They stopped at the wine merchant's to place an order and lingered to taste a new Spanish wine from the Douro region which Senhor Luis informed them was selling well. As they left the shop and started to walk along the unpaved road towards the tavern, Manson said:

"I wish you'd let me pay my way, Diana. This isn't fair. If I was billeted at your tavern in the usual way, I'd be expected to pay for my bed and board."

Diana shot him a sideways glance. "The last soldiers billeted on me in the usual way raped my girls and beat me when I objected, Leo. You risked your life to arrest them."

"That was my job. This is different. I've been living like a prince; I have to have cost you money, aside from..."

He stopped, realising what he had been about to say and felt himself flush. "I'm sorry, I shouldn't have said that."

To his surprise, Diana made a little growling noise in her throat. It sounded like an angry puppy and drove all rational thought out of Manson's head. He stared at her in astonishment and she set down the rush bag of olives she was carrying, put her hands on her hips and said:

"Put that basket down."

"Why?"

"Because I am going to shout at you and I cannot do it while you are carrying my shopping."

Manson looked at the heavy basket then back at her. "That isn't a very good incentive to put it down, Diana."

"Put it down."

Manson obeyed and eyed her warily. "What have I done wrong?"

"Nothing. Of course you have done nothing wrong, Leo, you never do. You are kind and considerate and affectionate…every day I am happy that you are part of my life."

"I'm happy too."

"But I am not happy that we need to tread so carefully with our words. I think when you first…when we first decided that this was to be more than one or two nights in bed together…did we not agree that we would not be so careful?"

Manson thought about it and smiled. "Yes. But it was easier to do that in a letter."

"Does it hurt you that I allow other men to share my bed for money?"

Manson almost winced but he could not refuse to answer her. She was right, they had agreed last year to be frank with each other.

"Yes," he admitted. "I hate it. But I also worry that you're giving up your income to take care of me and you won't even let me pay rent. I…"

"If you pay me rent, Leo, I will feel like a prostitute and you have never made me feel that way."

Manson was completely silenced. Diana allowed the silence to go on for a long time. Eventually she spoke in a quieter tone. "You cannot pay me rent because you are not some passing army officer billeted at my tavern. You are my lover and you are currently my guest. If you were billeted somewhere else and I travelled to stay with you, would you allow me to pay you rent?"

"No. God no. But Diana…"

"Why not, since you live on your officer's pay? Which is considerably less than I earn, by the way."

Manson could not speak for a moment. Eventually he said:

"You make a very valid point, Diana. But it is the way of the world that a man is expected to support a woman. It bothers me that I can't do that."

"It bothers me that we talk of money at a time like this. How many more weeks do we have, Leo? Two? Possibly three? I am watching you and I can see you pushing yourself so that you can recover sooner and go back."

"Oh love, that's not because I don't want to stay. It's just…"

"I know. It is your duty. The regiment is also your first love and I think it always will be. Once you can ride properly and walk for more than half an hour without that leg giving way, you will be on your way and I accept that. But for the time that we have left, I have set everything else to one side to spend it with you. I expect you to do the same for me."

Manson felt his heart breaking. He reached out and took her into his arms, completely ignoring the surprised stare from a farmer driving a loaded cart down towards the market.

"Love, I'm sorry. I can't lie to you so I end up trying not to say anything at all."

"I know you do. Please stop. I bought this little piece of prosperity as a prostitute. I am not at all ashamed of that."

131

"I'm not ashamed either. But Diana…"

He saw her expression change and she raised her hand to his lips quickly, touching them with two fingers to silence him.

"Don't, Leo. I can see by your face that you are going to say something very special, but you mustn't. It will only hurt both of us more when it has to end."

"What utter nonsense," Manson said calmly. "Where do you come by these ideas, Diana? It will hurt exactly the same, whatever I say. Of course, it may never come to that, because I may be killed in the next engagement."

"Don't say that."

"What am I allowed to say then? I can't say that I love you, although I do. I can't say that I hate what you have to do, because that would put unfair pressure on you to stop. I can't talk about all the things that could happen between now and the end of the war, including my death, because it will only upset you. All I want is to be with you, but I'm not allowed to say that either, because everybody would think I was mad. Including you."

Diana stood looking at him and Manson braced himself for a scolding. Unexpectedly her expression softened. She stood on tiptoe and kissed him very gently.

"I love you too."

She laughed at his expression of astonishment. Manson rallied quickly, determined not to allow this moment to escape him. "Is that permitted now? We've made some progress."

"I am never going to allow you to ruin yourself for me, Leo. It would make both of us miserable."

"And I'm telling you that I don't make plans for what happens after this war because I don't know if I'm going to survive it. One day, if I do, I will probably stand outside your tavern and ask you to come home to England with me and you're probably going to say no."

"I am."

"That's going to break my heart, but it'll be your decision. But that could be a year away, or two or more. What I will tell you, since we are talking of it, is that if I'm killed, you'll be notified as if you were my wife, and anything I have goes to you. It's not a great deal, but there's some prize money and the sale of my horses and goods."

"Leo!"

"You've just told me that you're going to break my heart one day, love. I'm admitting that I might break yours, although if I do it will be unintentionally. But I don't intend to spend the time we do have worrying about that. I want to enjoy every minute together."

Diana stretched up to kiss him again. "I had forgotten how very straightforward you are, Leo Manson. I agree. Let's not talk of it again."

"No, let's talk of it. It's part of who you are and how you came to be here, just as the men I've killed are part of me. I'm not going to carry on avoiding it. I have decided we will have three more weeks, even if I could possibly go back before then."

"I don't want you to get into trouble, Leo."

Manson picked up the heavy basket. "He'd give me six months if I asked for it," he admitted. "I'm not going to though. In the meantime, I intend to enjoy every moment. Starting with breakfast with the loveliest woman in Portugal."

"Who is also a prostitute."

"The loveliest prostitute in Portugal," Manson said determinedly. Diana cocked her head to one side and looked thoughtful.

"Although now that I come to think of it, I cannot remember the last time a man paid me to go to bed with him. Apart from you incessantly trying to do so."

Manson gaped at her as she walked ahead of him then limped faster to catch up. "I do not. And what do you mean?"

"Just that since you left in the winter, I realise I have got out of the habit of it. I seem to have become dreadfully choosy."

"Diana, are you trying to tell me that you are in fact no longer earning your living as a prostitute?"

"Well I have not formally resigned my occupation, Captain. Just that recently I have been feeling more secure." She glanced at him with a little deprecating smile. "I was always so afraid that I would never have enough. That I must snatch at every opportunity in case something went wrong and I was left on my own and penniless again."

"Given what happened to you at fifteen, Diana, that makes perfect sense."

"I think for years all I thought about was survival. The war did not help, of course. But recently...I do not believe I told you that I have been making enquiries about the purchase of another property. A hotel."

Manson was astonished. "In Elvas?"

"No, in Oporto, where I was born. I like it here, but it is a quiet little town and once the war is over and the armies have moved on...Oporto is a thriving port and trade will pick up again once Bonaparte is gone." She gave him a quick look. "I have not wholly decided. Once you have gone back to your regiment, I had intended to travel to Oporto again to meet with the current owner and to look..."

"Not without a proper escort you won't," Manson said before he could stop himself. Diana gave him a look and he held up his hands in a gesture of surrender. "Sorry. I meant to say, please don't travel without a proper escort. The French may be a long way away but there are too many soldiers travelling back to the lines from sick leave and they have a bad reputation. There are also local bandits and army deserters. I'm not trying to interfere with your life, Diana, I'm just..."

"Yes you are," Diana said in matter-of-fact tones. She pushed open the door to the tavern and Emilio leaned his broom up against the wall and hurried forward to take the baskets.

"I'm trying not to." Manson took a deep breath. Diana gave a sudden giggle.

"It is very funny watching you squirm, Leo, but it is unkind of me. I have arranged a passage on a merchant ship. Emilio must remain to run the tavern, but I will take my groom with me and I have hired a personal maid to make me look respectable. Although if a very handsome English officer could find the time to make part of the journey with me, I should not object."

Manson's heart lifted a little. "Truly? I would love to, Diana. I've promised the General that I'll return by way of Vitoria to see how Sergeant-Major Carter is doing, but I should easily be able to catch a passage from Oporto to Santander or one of the other northern ports. In fact it will be an easier journey as well as rather more enjoyable for the first part of it."

"Then it is settled."

Manson followed her through into the parlour and waited while she spoke to her cook about breakfast. When they were alone again he said:

"Diana, why haven't you told me any of this before? This can't have happened overnight, you've been planning it."

She flushed a little. "I have. I thought...I was going to write to you about it."

"That makes no sense."

"I suppose it does not. Leo, it's difficult to explain. I wanted to share this with you. I wanted to tell you how excited I am about this. A new start."

"I sense a but."

"But I was afraid that you would take it to mean something that it does not."

Manson had suspected as much. He thought about it for a moment then decided to say it. "I see. You thought I would see this as a way that we could be together after the war. A respectable business for you."

"Yes."

"Is that what you intend? Respectability?"

"I don't like that word, it is so...so English."

"And it is such nonsense."

"Yes. But it means something, Leo. If I buy this hotel, I don't intend to run it as a brothel. I would like to make it the best hotel in Oporto and have Lord Wellington as my guest. I would like you to visit me there. But I will still be a former prostitute and that will never change. If I tried to make a life with you, every party would be a nightmare, wondering if I would be seated next to one of your senior officers whom I'd previously slept with."

"Not if I leave the army."

"If you left the army for me, you would wake up in five years time missing your career and your friends, wondering how high you could have gone if you hadn't married me."

134

"I might wonder. That doesn't mean I'd be unhappy."

"I would be. You are a remarkable man, Leo Manson. If I watched you limit yourself because of me, I would be miserable and it would tear me apart. Which would tear you apart. I'm sorry. I know you would risk anything for me but I am not as brave as you are. Can you understand that and love me anyway?"

Manson could see tears sparkling in her brown eyes. He walked towards her and put his arms about her. She snuggled into his chest and hugged him tightly and he bent to kiss the top of her head.

"I do love you anyway and I'm not going to argue with you. What is the point of spending our next few weeks fighting over something that might never happen? Let's carry on as we are, as friends and lovers. When this war finally ends, we'll have to have the conversation anyway. I know what you intend to say and I'm not going to spend the intervening time nagging you to change your mind. On that day, you can send me away. Don't waste our time now reminding me of it."

She looked up at him, her cheeks wet with tears but she was smiling as well. "Leo, you really are the most charmingly straightforward man I have ever met. Thank you. And I love you."

"I love you too, Diana. Come and have breakfast with me and tell me all about this hotel."

***

More than twenty years active service had given Johnny Wheeler a good appreciation of the value of rest time. He welcomed a few days of respite after the exertions of the past week and once the forward pickets were in place and orders were given regarding the maintenance of discipline in camp, Johnny gave instructions to his servant and invited his favourite junior officer to dinner.

With the temporary combining of the 115th and 112th into a provisional battalion, Simon Carlyon was formally under Johnny's command for the first time and it pleased both of them enormously. Johnny had not always got on so well with Anne's former brother-in-law but their shared experience of the appalling retreat from Madrid at the end of the previous year had brought them very close. Johnny owed his life to Simon. They had also become friends.

There was a small parlour at the back of the Casa Martinez which Anne had set aside for the use of any officer wishing to entertain privately. The brigade officers dined together in two big reception rooms, crammed onto every table Anne had been able to find. Mealtimes were noisy and sometimes chaotic, since with the need for picket duty and the knowledge that the French were very close and could launch at attack at any moment, it was difficult to know how many would be seated at any one meal.

Anne rose to the challenge with her usual confidence, spending hours with Sergeant Kelly planning meals and riding out daily to source supplies from local farms. Paul had given orders that while drinking was allowed, drunkenness would not be tolerated, given the proximity of the enemy. His officers complied with good-natured grumbling and some pointed remarks about the amount of wine consumed by the first brigade which was encamped far closer to the French than the third. Paul's response was short, explicit and extremely profane and his officers remained cheerfully sober, at least within sight of their commander.

Johnny's servant, with help from Kelly, had provided two courses with mutton, fish and an excellent chicken salad with a sharp tangy dressing which was new to Johnny. For the first part of the meal they talked mostly about the food. Kelly had a passion for trying new recipes and local dishes. He seldom had the chance to experiment on campaign when he was cooking over open fires with the most basic of ingredients, but even then some new spice might arouse his interest. Johnny and Simon laughed over one or two of his more eccentric dishes, including the meal during their pursuit of the French after Vitoria when Kelly's over-enthusiastic use of the local pimento spice had practically burned their mouths.

"I much prefer this," Simon said with a sigh of content when his plate was clean. "It's remarkable what he manages to come up with though, in the most appalling circumstances. We must be the best-fed troops in the army. I've never really understood Kelly's status though. Is he actually a sergeant?"

"I believe so. We met him in Dublin years ago, he was cooking for the officers' mess. At the time he'd been put on barrack duty because of an injury he sustained in Haiti which almost killed him. While he was recovering, somebody discovered that his mother had cooked for a very wealthy Anglo-Irish family and he'd grown up helping her. He was put onto kitchen duty and, after the first meal he cooked for us, I saw a familiar gleam in the General's eyes which told me when we marched out of there, George Kelly would be coming with us."

"So he wasn't originally from the 110th? How on earth did the General manage that?"

"It was remarkably simple. At least it was if your mind works like the General's. He organised a medical discharge for him and then got him re-enlisted into the 110th and promoted him to sergeant."

"Is that actually allowed?"

Johnny grinned and shrugged. "I don't think anybody cared enough to argue about it. As for George, his army pay is supplemented by a hefty bonus from General van Daan, which he is saving to buy his own chop house in London or Dublin when he's ready to retire." Johnny speared the last piece of chicken. "I for one think the whole arrangement is excellent."

"And what about Sergeant Jenson? How does that work?"

"Don't you know about Jenson? He was in the light company when the General first got his captaincy. Over my head, by the way, because he could afford it and I couldn't. Jenson was wounded at Assaye and had to have the lower half of his leg amputated. I was injured on the same day, quite badly. So was the General although he was still on his feet. I lay in the medical tent watching while Dr Norris performed the amputation. They were short of orderlies so Captain

136

van Daan, who was about twenty-two at the time, held the leg still during the surgery. I think Jenson was nineteen."

"Dear God."

"I'm not sure I could have done it. We were sent home. We'd lost more than a third of our men in that campaign and a lot of us were on the sick list for a while. Jenson was left with the choice of a medical discharge or at best, doing barrack duty if he could manage with a wooden leg. If they couldn't find him something he'd probably have ended up in the workhouse or begging on the streets. He struggled with the wooden leg to start with, but the General was absolutely determined he was going to do it. He could hardly walk himself. I can remember them limping up and down the deck of that troop ship all the way from India to England. He got Jenson acting as his valet and orderly and it was obvious they got on really well, but a man with a wooden leg can't march so he couldn't come on campaign with us."

"Unless he could ride," Simon said softly.

Johnny smiled. "Unless he could ride. Paul spent that summer in Melton Mowbray teaching him, though I don't think he had any idea that Jenson was going to develop such an affinity for horses. Once again, I believe he takes army pay with a bonus from the General. Not that he needs a retirement fund. Nobody is ever going to separate those two."

Simon refilled both wine glasses. "I'm glad you told me, sir, I've always wondered."

"A little slice of regimental history. Is that the last of the wine?"

"I brought another bottle but we probably shouldn't."

"We probably should. I agree with the principle but neither of us is going to get drunk on two bottles and we've earned a celebration after the past few weeks. I gather the General has got you playing nursemaid to Ensign Fox, the little bastard. How is it going? I must say I think you've been good for him, nobody has had to pour him into bed in a drunken stupor for weeks."

To Johnny's surprise, Simon did not laugh. He sipped the wine then set down his glass. "I don't think he's got anybody to drink with, sir."

"What do you mean?"

"I've been watching him for the past few days. Mrs van Daan put me onto it. I think she's spoken to the General as well. I mean, when he first arrived he was a complete pain, but he got on all right with his fellow subalterns, didn't he?"

"As far as I can tell. In fact, I had to speak to one or two of them. I didn't want them picking up his drinking and idling habits. He was friendly with Hughes for a while and then he seemed to be spending a lot of time with some of the juniors from the 115th. Onslow and Smith, I think."

"Well he's not now. But what is really odd is that while all our juniors have found some kind of billet, even if it's just shared space in the barn, Fox has pitched his tent alongside the men."

Johnny was silent. He did not like Fox and was very sure that the younger man had no place in the army, but he disliked the idea that any man was

137

being ostracised. He had seen it happen from time to time during his early years. The officers' mess had a series of unwritten rules, one of which was that it was a place for gentlemen and that within its confines, all had equal rights. In practice that was nonsense and considerations of rank counted for just as much in the mess as on the battlefield. However, in most regiments a senior officer would not interfere if his juniors voted to exclude or isolate a member for unacceptable behaviour.

Johnny knew that the second battalion of the 110th had taken such a vote against Ross Mackenzie after he reported a popular officer for drunkenness during the Walcheren campaign. He had heard his General on the subject and he had absolutely no doubt that such brutal ostracising of a fellow officer would not be permitted in Paul van Daan's mess.

"Have they voted to send him to Coventry?" Johnny asked quietly.

"Apparently not. I spoke to several of them and they assured me there's space in that barn for him and his kit if he wants to join them. He's chosen not to. I asked him and he said he prefers to be on his own."

"What about his behaviour?"

"He fell out several times during those ghastly night marches and ended up with the hospital wagons. I hauled him out and sent him back on duty. Since then he's done his picket duty, turned up for meals and went to dinner at headquarters with the General, though apparently he didn't want to. I actually don't have anything to complain about, sir, except that he's cut himself off from his fellow officers completely and won't say why."

"Well there's a reason," Johnny said. "And whatever they're saying, some of them know what it is. If that was Hughes or Smith or any of the others, his friends would be over there persecuting them until they either joined the mess or explained what was wrong."

"Any ideas?" Simon said, rather plaintively. "Honestly sir, I'm stumped."

"Not an earthly clue," Johnny said. "Whatever the problem, we need to get him out of here. He doesn't want to be here, he's not suited to the army and he can't work with his fellow officers if he won't speak to them. What a bloody mess. I'll talk to General van Daan again. Perhaps his wife can have a word. I don't think I'm very good at this."

Simon smiled. "You were bloody good at it with me, sir."

"Oh come on, Simon, there's no comparison. You arrived here trailing your brother's bloody legacy like a dead weight behind you. You just had to learn to put it down; it was obvious what was needed there. With Fox, I honestly don't know. But we can't keep taking the poor little bastard into battle in the state he's in. He'll get himself and everyone around him killed."

"Perhaps the General can find him a job that doesn't require him to fight, though I've no idea what." Simon had said it idly but Johnny stared at him as a thought struck him.

"Say that again."

"A job. Some sort of administrative posting. I wasn't serious, sir. I can't imagine what you'd find for Fox to do."

"Nor can I. But he managed it for Longford and I'd have sworn he was unemployable. You're a genius, Simon."

"Who's Longford?"

"Never mind. Go and get that second bottle, Captain and let's talk about something more cheerful. How do you think the provisional battalion is working out?"

***

Marshal Soult's army, having been driven back over the Pyrenees, seemed to have settled into its former position. With the Spanish still blockading Pamplona and Graham's army continuing to besiege San Sebastian, the Light Division had nothing to do but wait for orders.

Movement around the various encampments was limited by the proximity of the enemy. Paul walked or rode down to the banks of the Bidassoa most mornings to watch the progress of the French defences. They were so close that it was not necessary to use a telescope to watch as they built field works and rough redoubts. The advanced French pickets could just as easily watch the Light Division troops as they went about their business and some of the Allied men seemed to regard it as a form of entertainment to observe what was going on in the French camp.

"They're bloody mad," Giles Fenwick informed Paul as he gave his morning report. "Yesterday evening some of the French gave a dance for some local women. I'd ridden down with Tom Oakley to see Harry Smith and found him and the rest of his brigade cavorting about on the opposite side of the river to the music with a dozen voltigeurs cheering and yelling encouragement from the other side."

Paul burst out laughing. "Tell me Colonel Barnard was in the middle of it."

"Of course he was," Fenwick said. "Mr Oakley joined in with enthusiasm. There must be something wrong with me. All I could think about was how many of the bastards the riflemen could have taken down if they'd been waving rifles instead of bottles."

Paul felt a tug of sympathy. He studied his brigade-major, trying to decide what to say. Fenwick seemed to realise it and gave a twisted smile.

"It's all right, sir; I know it's me. They're just men. Most of them probably don't even want to be there and why shouldn't they have a laugh across the river with our lads?"

"That's not what you're thinking, Captain. You're saying what you think I want to hear."

"I don't want you to think I'm a lunatic."

"You're not a lunatic, Giles. Stop it."

139

Fenwick shrugged. "All right. I hate them. I look at those uniforms and I don't see the men behind them. I see the men who threw a man out of a window and caught him on bayonets for entertainment. The men who raped women until it killed them. The men who drove a good man to kill the woman he cared about and her daughter rather than leave them to be tortured then butchered. The men who bayonetted Antonio over and over."

Fenwick stopped abruptly. Paul could see that his hands were clenched on the desk, the knuckles white. He rose and took a step towards the sideboard which held the brandy.

"No," Fenwick said quickly. Paul turned in surprise and the other man forced a smile. "No thank you, sir. It's too early."

Paul sat down. "It's up to you, Giles, but it's medicinal."

"I know. The problem is that for a couple of weeks after Castro Urdiales I was taking a lot of medicine. I don't think it really helped."

"I see."

"I served with Captain Liam O'Hara for a while so I know the damage an officer can do with a drop or two to steady the nerves. I don't need it. Look, sir, I'm sorry. I try not to talk about it. Please don't worry, I won't…"

"I'm not worried, Giles. You're doing an excellent job as brigade-major and if Manson wasn't coming back I'd give you the job permanently. There's nothing wrong with you. You just need time to get over something fucking awful happening. And the French did it. When I see them waving and smiling in an informal truce I don't forget that the same men will be trying to blow my head off in a few days time and I certainly don't forget what they did to my wife last year. There's nothing wrong with you."

Fenwick was silent for a while then looked up and gave a rather better effort at a smile. "Thank you. I need somebody to tell me that every now and then. Sometimes I wonder if I'll ever be fit for polite society again. I think something might be broken in me."

"It can be mended. If you'd seen the state of me after Assaye you'd realise how well I understand. It took a couple of years before I was really over it. As for wanting to kill every Frenchman in sight, I'm glad nobody could see inside my head the week after they blew up that church. Is there anything else I need to know about?"

"You might already have heard it, sir, but Colonel Barnard tells me that the Rifles are planning a dinner on the banks of the Bidassoa to celebrate the anniversary of the formation of the Rifle Corps."

"Oh dear God."

"It did occur to me that maybe we should take extra precautions."

"Personally, I'll be heading for deep cover. But you're right. I doubt the French will have orders to attack the drunken bastards but it won't hurt to make it obvious that we've posted extra – and very sober – pickets along the line. Leave it with me, I'll talk to Kempt and Skerrett." Paul reached for a letter on the table he was using as a desk. "This arrived yesterday. The contingent of

140

Light Division reinforcements we spoke about is expected to arrive within a week."

"So we're expecting them in two weeks then, sir?"

"If we're lucky. There are two new junior officers with them: one for the 110th and one for the 112th. The rest are new recruits spread across all three regiments. They should have done some basic training at Melton but this is not the best time for them to join."

"Poor bastards," Fenwick said dispassionately.

"Definitely. The officers are both very young: sixteen and seventeen I believe. Don't pull that face, Giles or I shall cry."

"Sorry sir, couldn't help it."

"Mr Black is for Harker's company and Mr Everton is for Michael's. They'll both look after them as best they can but keep an eye on them as well, Giles."

"I'll try, sir. There's one other thing. Carlyon tells me you've got young Fox on some kind of attachment as ADC. Is that right?"

"Starting tomorrow. You're pulling that face again, Captain."

"Why?"

"Because he's a fucking liability and I need him out of combat," Paul said flatly. "I don't know what's wrong with him, Giles, but Simon Carlyon would rather work with one junior short than have to rely on him. And he's never fucking there anyway. He can ride a horse and carry a letter. I'm handing him over to Evan Powell for a while until we get into winter quarters and I've got time to deal with him properly. In his place, I'm informally seconding one of my Portuguese officers to work with Simon. He wants the experience, he's desperate for promotion. You might remember him – Lieutenant Ronaldo from Freineda?""

"Isn't he married to old Rivero's daughter? The woman who gave evidence at Stewart's trial?"

"That's right. He's a good man, very willing to learn and I think he's grateful that we stepped in when that bastard Vane was persecuting his wife. And his English is excellent. Simon is happy, so I'm happy. I'm told there are rumblings through the brigade that Fox doesn't deserve this and I know…"

"Those aren't the only rumblings about Ensign Fox, sir."

Paul stopped and stared at Fenwick. "Do you know something about this?"

"Not much. I don't know how much you've heard, sir, but was there some kind of scandal attached to Fox before he joined up?"

"So I've been told," Paul said slowly. "I've no inkling what it was about but it was the reason his older brother insisted on the army. I should have asked you before, Giles, you know the right people. Any idea?"

"I'm sorry but no. But what I did hear, very unofficially from Tom…Tom Oakley, I mean…is that some of Fox's recent unpopularity has something to do with a rumour from home."

"Good God. Do you know what kind of rumour?"

"I'm afraid not. Sorry, sir."

"Where did it come from? I mean it has to be recent. He's been fucking irritating from the day he arrived, but this isolation is new."

"The 9th Dragoon Guards," Fenwick said succinctly. "Someone knew the family and knew the story. Nobody is talking and I haven't pushed it. They're all adamant that there's been no mess vote to exclude him but there are a lot of awkward mutterings about him not fitting in. Do you want me to find out?"

"I wish I could have two brigade-majors," Paul said wistfully. It had been a passing remark but it drew a real smile from Fenwick, which pleased him. "Let's leave it for now, Giles. The last thing I want is to stir up any bad feeling in the brigade when we could be facing a major action. I'll deal with them later. Fox is out of the way and if he's treated as a member of my staff for a while it will make his isolation less obvious. Interestingly, he actually did very well when I took him to headquarters; it's clear they know nothing about this. Keep an ear open though and you can tell Oakley to do the same. He seems reliable."

"He is, sir."

Paul studied him. "You get on well with him, don't you?"

Fenwick laughed. "Yes," he admitted. "It's hard not to. He is the most uncomplicated fellow I've met in a long time. And he's a bloody good officer. I tried hard to be cynical about him but he's just…really nice."

Paul laughed as well. "Never underestimate the value of really nice, Giles. It's what I miss in Carl and what I value in Johnny. Will you do something for me?"

"Of course, sir."

"Take the day off. You can't ride far in these circumstances, but it's a fine day. Take Oakley and go fishing, or go for a walk or just sit in the sun and drink wine. Ride to Lesaca and enquire after his Lordship's puppies. If he's there, he'll be delighted to show them to you; other than the siege at San Sebastian they're his favourite topic of conversation. Take the day off."

Fenwick rose and saluted. He was smiling naturally now. "I will, sir. Thank you."

Chapter Ten

At Lord Wellington's invitation, Anne accompanied Paul on an inspection of the siege works at San Sebastian. While not especially fond of listening to detailed accounts of plans to blow up a town and its garrison, she was glad of the distraction. The Light Division was suffering from some of the usual disciplinary problems associated with a period in camp and Anne suspected it was being made worse by being confined to the lines. The Allied and French armies had been watching each other warily for more than two weeks now, still with no sign of movement from either, but it was impossible to relax. As the siege progressed, Soult must surely be making plans for another attempt to relieve the town.

Paul was in a particularly bad mood owing to the fact that he had been co-opted onto a disciplinary board at a General Court Martial for the past two days. Courts martial were rare in his brigade, reserved only for the most serious crimes and Paul's officers were encouraged to find less formal ways of punishing minor infractions. Generally he went out of his way to dodge the unpleasant duty of sitting on a board, but the request had come directly from Alten and was couched in terms that Paul could not ignore.

It had felt like a long two days. When he was not in court, Anne offered wine and sympathy and listened to his detailed complaints about army regulations, the charges brought and the punishments inflicted. Anne knew how much he hated it and was relieved when it was over. He returned in the late afternoon on the second day, kissed her lovingly and told her he was going for a ride. Anne watched him go, then went in search of information.

She found Jenson at the horse lines, rubbing down his horse. He paused to salute her then continued his work. When Felix was fed, watered and settled he limped over to join Anne.

"What happened, Freddie?"

"Death penalty. Two of them."

"Oh no." Anne sighed. "Did he vote for it?"

"He voted for the guilty verdict but tried to argue a reduced sentence. It was never going to work. It wasn't just desertion, they'd robbed a local farm as well and they'd a record a mile long."

143

"Did they attack anyone?"

"No and that was the point the General tried to make. They stole a chicken and some cabbages but didn't touch the farmer or his family. But the combination of that and the desertion did it. Also they'd been missing for a week after Vitoria. They had it coming, ma'am. But you know how he is."

"I do. Thank goodness it's over. He's ridden off for a bit but he won't go far. Lord Wellington has sent an invitation to go to San Sebastian tomorrow, to the siege lines. Hopefully they will have done something wrong and he'll be able to vent his spleen by explaining that to Lord Wellington and Sir Thomas Graham."

"They've got my sympathy, ma'am, but I'm not stepping in to save them. Let someone else get it for a change."

"Has he been dreadful, Freddie? I should have come with you."

"On the way back I found myself counting the number of times he used the word 'fuck' in a sentence. I think he might have broken his previous record. Sorry, ma'am. Shouldn't have said that. It's been a long day."

Anne laughed aloud. "Go and rest, Sergeant and enjoy your dinner. You've earned it."

"Yes, ma'am. Good luck with him. You're about to earn yours as well."

Paul was unusually quiet when he returned. After dinner Anne suggested a walk. They wandered through the lines hand in hand with Craufurd padding peacefully beside them. It was a fine evening and they walked up a steep track towards the Santa Barbara heights. Somewhere high above them, Skerrett's brigade were encamped in far less comfortable conditions. It was damp and often windy on the hilltops and mountain slopes and the men shivered in tents and cursed Wellington's decision to leave the army's greatcoats in storage at the beginning of this campaign. It meant that they had less to carry on the march but the weather in these mountains was unpredictable even in summer. Anne was already worried about how long it would take for the commissariat to transport the greatcoats up to the army in time for the colder weather.

The sun was beginning to sink below the horizon when Paul and Anne paused and turned to look westwards over his camp. Further to the north were the crowded lines of Kempt's encampment and, between trees and shrubs, the winding waters of the Bidassoa sparkled gold in the warm evening light. Beyond the river Anne could see the French. The smoke from their cooking fires drifted into the air and she could catch glimpses of men in blue coats moving about, cooking their meal, drinking their wine ration and standing on picket duty watching the Allies doing the same.

It was a little hazy and small clouds of insects hovered above puddles and marshy areas on the hillside. Craufurd became fascinated by a butterfly and followed it between little clumps of blue wildflowers. Paul grinned.

"He's going to eat that thing in a minute."

"I do hope not, it's very pretty. He might not though. He spent almost two hours playing with a dragonfly in the stream a few days ago but made no attempt to actually catch it. I think he was put off eating insects when that bee stung him on the nose at San Millan."

"Well it was a valuable lesson then. I wish he'd learn to eat mosquitoes. Though I have to say things have improved a lot since Brat constructed that muslin tent around the mattress. She's the most remarkably useful female. Do you think Michael is serious about her?"

Anne shot him a glance. "Yes, I think he may be."

"He's said nothing to me."

"You hoot with laughter every time he mentions her name, Paul. It's not much of an incentive to confide."

Paul tried to look repentant. "Do I? Sorry, I'll try to remember not to. When I was younger and in such a mess with my love life he used to tease me mercilessly. But we're all older now and I'd like to see him settled. He's one of my best friends and I'm learning to value those all the more for losing some of them. I keep thinking about those two men. One of them was an old hand. The other was only twenty-one."

"I'm sorry, Paul. Will you need to attend the hanging?"

"No, thank God. They're both from the 43rd. I did what I could; I don't want to watch it." Paul put his arm about her and drew her closer. "They didn't even seem that frightened. It's as if they knew it was coming and just accepted it. After all, it's not that much worse than civilian life. Back in England they could easily have been hanged for such terrible crimes as picking pockets, cutting down trees and stealing a loaf of bread from a market stall. The army has actually given them several chances."

Anne's heart ached for him. "But that doesn't help at all."

"Not one whit. If they'd transfer them over to the 110th I could turn them into soldiers. Not model citizens perhaps, but men who could fight and be proud of it. Especially the younger one. He's a boy and he's going to die." Paul took a deep, steadying breath. "I need to stop talking about it. Why am I talking about it? Look at how beautiful this is. And I'm standing here with you. Do we have any wine left?"

"Plenty. I bought more at an extortionate price from the sutler who supplies headquarters in Lesaca."

"Let's go back to the Casa Martinez, collect the wine and lock our bedroom door. I'm tired of the army tonight. I just want you."

"I'm right here, General. Always."

Paul bent to kiss her, very gently. "For some reason, I'm remembering the night Major-General Craufurd died. I lay in your arms that night with my heart completely broken. Somehow you healed it. You always do."

"It's what we do, Paul. For each other."

He smiled more naturally. "Let's go and do it all over again then. Only I'm sending Craufurd to sleep with Charlie tonight. It's very distracting knowing that your dog might suddenly remember how much he loves you and jump on me when things are just getting interesting."

Anne gave a peal of laughter. "Oh don't. It was funny though."

145

"We clearly have different definitions of that word, girl of my heart. Craufurd, here. Leave the butterfly alone."

***

On the ride over to San Sebastian the following morning, Paul's mood had improved though he was still quieter than usual. Anne rode beside Lord Wellington with her husband on her other side. His Lordship filled any conversational gaps with a lengthy account of the siege works, the plans for an assault within the next week and his concerns about the morale and condition of the Fifth Division, which had suffered badly during the first assault. Paul listened, asking an occasional question. Anne wondered if Wellington had noticed that Paul was not his usual ebullient self. She suspected not. While on campaign, the Commander-in-Chief tended to be completely absorbed in his work with no time and little patience. Paul's quiet attention suited him very well at present and it would not have occurred to him that there was anything wrong.

Despite herself, Anne became interested in the conversation. She had not visited the siege lines so far, partly because she had joined the Light Division on its lengthy and occasionally pointless marches in pursuit of the French and partly because her time had been equally divided between helping to manage the new camp and supervising the headquarters puppies. His Lordship had moved from being furious at Pearl's pregnancy and scathing about the results to being overly-anxious about the puppies' well-being. Anne was not surprised. Wellington often seemed to have a better rapport with animals than with people.

It had proved impossible to make another attack on San Sebastian immediately after the failure of the first assault on the 25th of July partly because supplies of ammunition were dangerously low. There was also the problem of Soult's unexpected attack across the border, which had absorbed all of Wellington's attention for a time. He had issued orders to Graham to embark his guns aboard the Royal Navy ships to prevent their capture should the campaign go badly wrong. Still furious at the abandonment of the Allied guns by Sir John Murray at Tarragona the previous month, Wellington had no intention of losing any more artillery.

There had been several meetings since then between Wellington, his engineering officers and Sir Thomas Graham to discuss what had gone wrong during the first assault. Sir Richard Fletcher and several of his engineering officers had been slightly wounded during the fighting. At least one had not survived his injuries. Anne remembered the heavy losses among the Royal Engineers during the assault on Badajoz the previous year. Men volunteered for the Forlorn Hope but the forward position of the engineering officers during an assault was taken for granted.

"Is Fletcher back on his feet yet, sir?" Paul asked, when Wellington's lengthy description of trenches and artillery batteries finally ran dry.

"Yes, yes, it was a minor wound, thank God. I need him at his best. He wasn't there when we planned that assault you know. I'd left him and Burgoyne behind at Pamplona. Major Smith from the engineers and Colonel Dickson planned the attack. Fletcher seemed to agree with it when he arrived, but he did express some doubts." Wellington was silent for a moment. "I have a great regard for Fletcher, as you know General, but sometimes I wish he would be more decided in his opinions. He is too easy, too willing to allow himself to be overridden. I need my officers to tell me the truth."

Anne caught Paul's eye and saw the gleam of amusement. "Do you, sir?" he said cordially. "That's good to know, because there has been the odd occasion over the years where you've given the impression you need your officers to keep their opinions to themselves and do as they're told."

Wellington snorted and managed an impressive glare, given that he had to do it sideways. "As though that has ever made the slightest difference to you, Van Daan. I have heard a lifetime's worth of your opinions during the past few years."

"And you'll continue to hear them, sir, if I think they need to be heard," Paul said placidly.

"I am in no doubt of that. I wish you to accompany me on a tour of the siege lines along with Fletcher and Burgoyne."

"And Sir Thomas Graham, I hope, sir."

"Of course he'll be there; he is in command," Wellington snapped. Paul looked as though he was about to say more but caught Anne's eye again and managed to stop himself.

"Is he fully fit again, sir?" he asked instead. Wellington looked as though he was about to return another dismissive answer but after a long pause he said:

"His eyes are beginning to trouble him again, I believe. I have immense faith in his ability, but I begin to wonder if his health issues may occasionally affect his energy. I wish to speak to you about the Fifth Division, General. Opinion is divided about their performance during the assault. Oswald assures me they fought valiantly but I've heard differently from one or two of the engineering officers. They sustained considerable losses and I am concerned that their morale may be affected."

"Oswald is a good man, sir. I'd be inclined to trust his word."

"Whatever the truth of it, he is unlikely to command them during the next attack. I have heard from Leith and expect him to arrive any day now. General Oswald will of course return to command his brigade."

Paul did not immediately reply. Anne could guess what he was thinking and hoped he would try to phrase it tactfully.

"Sir, I'm about to give you one of those unwelcome opinions."

"Oh for God's sake, what now?"

"Even if Leith gets here in time, I'd let Oswald lead the fifth for the assault."

"It is Leith's division, General."

"I know it is. But to be replaced after that first failure is going to make Oswald feel as though he's being punished for it. More to the point, it will look

147

that way to the rest of the army. The man has a career ahead of him, he doesn't need to carry that."

"I am not punishing him. If Leith does not arrive, he will remain in command. Nobody will think less of him." Wellington gave a grim smile. "After all, my attachment to matters of rank and seniority are well known."

Paul smiled back. "That's true," he admitted. "All the same, after I made a colossal mess at Alba de Tormes, you made a point of putting me in command at the Retiro in Madrid. There were definitely men of higher rank than me who could have taken that place. You did it to demonstrate that you hadn't lost confidence in me."

"What makes you think that, General?" Wellington sounded surprised.

"Because I know you. I wasn't the best choice that day. I hadn't fully recovered from my wounds."

"I remember that," Anne said crisply. Her husband shot her a grin. His determination to return to the field before he was ready had been the cause of one of their more impressive marital quarrels.

Wellington did not reply immediately. Anne thought that he was in an unusually mellow mood and seemed to be enjoying both the ride and the conversation. She wondered if he really wanted Paul's opinion on the progress of the siege or if this was just an excuse to spend time with one of the few real friends he possessed in the army. Eventually he gave a little snort.

"Ha! Well perhaps you are right on this occasion. It must have been one of my rare moments of sentimentality. I reserve them for very few people."

"I'm well aware of that, sir."

Wellington shot him a look, then unexpectedly gave a proper smile. It made him look ten years younger.

"I stand by my decision, General van Daan. Both about you and about Oswald. But you should have observed that if I am obliged to send a very competent officer back to his brigade – or indeed to his battalion – I usually try to give him plenty of opportunities to shine thereafter. I would not be concerned for General Oswald."

Paul began to laugh. "Yes, you do. In fact you've almost overdone it with Barnard. Don't let him get himself killed in the process, will you? I'm very attached to the drunken Irish bastard."

"So am I," Wellington admitted. "Tell me, what is this I hear about a proposed celebration for the 95th? Was this Barnard's idea? Is it being properly managed?"

The rest of the ride was occupied very pleasantly with Paul's description of the anniversary dinner planned by the officers of the Rifles and of his own precautions to ensure that the French were not tempted to take advantage of the celebrations. Anne listened admiringly. At such a crucial point in his campaign, Wellington might well have taken exception to the dinner and sent a blistering letter to the battalion commanders cancelling the plans, but her husband was managing him superbly. His account of the riflemen's efforts to construct a table big enough to seat the seventy or so officers who would not be required for duty made Wellington laugh aloud. Paul's description of the canopy, supported by tree branches, which was supposed to keep them dry in inclement weather caused the Commander-in-Chief such mirth that several of his staff members turned to stare and Lord Fitzroy Somerset trotted his horse forward to find out what was causing it.

"They must be mad," Wellington said when he could speak again. "Am I to understand that you have taken responsibility for ensuring the camp is properly guarded during this event, General?"

"Yes, my lads will cover it, with support from the 43rd and 52nd and both Kempt and Skerrett are fully aware."

"I should probably put a stop to it, but it has given me such entertainment that they may proceed. I rely upon you to observe it, General. I want a full account if they are drenched by a rainstorm or if high winds blow them all into the Bidassoa." Wellington started to laugh again. He managed to bring himself under control with a visible effort and looked at Anne. "Are you invited to this dinner, ma'am?"

Anne smiled. "No, my Lord. I'm taking care of Juana Smith for the occasion, since we all agree that the language and the amount of wine consumed is likely to make it unsuitable for ladies."

Wellington snorted again. "As if that has ever troubled either you or Juanita before now. I agree that your presence might constrain some of them to better behaviour though and that would never do. Look – San Sebastian. I believe this is the first time you have visited? Lord Fitzroy, send a message ahead to Sir Thomas. We shall have breakfast in Oyarzun I believe, before riding on to the edge of the siege works.

"I'll go myself, my Lord."

As Somerset cantered ahead, Wellington looked over at Paul. A gleam of amusement still lurked in the blue eyes.

"Is it wrong of me to hope for rain on that day, General?"

"Not at all, sir. I've always known you had a funny sense of humour."

***

Sir Thomas Graham occupied a square, yellow-stone house in the centre of the little town of Oyarzun, some seven miles from San Sebastian. He came out to greet his visitors and Paul could see from his expression that he had been expecting a military briefing rather than a social occasion which included a lady. Graham bowed to Anne very politely and made enquiries about her well-being, while Wellington, having landed his second-in-command with an awkward social problem, immediately began an in-depth conversation with Colonel Alexander Dickson, who commanded the artillery, and Sir Richard Fletcher, his chief engineer. He waved at Paul to join them. Anne flashed him a reassuring smile and turned back to the rather flustered Graham.

"Sir Thomas, you do not need to tell me that you had no idea that I would be here. You probably did not know that you were going to be expected to provide breakfast for so large a party either. Please don't worry, his Lordship does this all the time. He once did it to a group of bewildered Spaniards on the way to Talavera. They had no idea what on earth to do with me."

"I'm sure they were delighted nevertheless, ma'am. As am I; it has been too long. I'm just embarrassed at my poor hospitality when you were so generous with yours during winter quarters."

"Think nothing of it. If you will lend me one of your ADCs, I shall find out where we can buy enough food and organise everything."

Graham almost sagged in relief and Paul managed not to laugh out loud. "Ma'am, I shouldn't impose on you like this. One or two of my staff are billeted at a tavern in the next street, they might be able to help. And there's a bakery…"

"Excellent. Go and talk to his Lordship, sir. I'll arrange it."

"Thank you, ma'am. Are you…that is to say, will you all be staying the night?"

"I honestly don't know, Sir Thomas. It was not mentioned but if this takes all day, his Lordship may decide to do so rather than ride back in the dark. Probably best to be prepared."

"Of course, ma'am. I'll speak to my servant. This is a big place, they'll be able to find a room for you and the rest of us will manage."

"Thank you, sir."

Anne moved away and Graham joined Wellington's party. Paul saluted gravely. "Everything all right, Sir Thomas?"

"Thanks to your wife. Wonderful woman. Excellent address and such presence of mind." Graham noticed Wellington looking at him and bowed. "If you will come into the parlour, my Lord, I can show you on the map where we have reached before we ride out to inspect the work."

Breakfast was a small feast of bread, cheese, cold meat and some very good local cider. Anne sat between Captain, the Earl of March and Lieutenant, the Marquess of Worcester, dividing her attention cheerfully between them. The conversation around the rest of the table was all of military matters but Worcester and March, who were both in their early twenties, paid no attention to anything other than their companion. Paul tried not to show his amusement too obviously and wondered how long it would take for Wellington to become irritated.

Fortunately the meal was drawing to a close by the time his commander noticed. Paul saw Wellington's mouth tighten. He was preparing to draw his fire when Anne rose gracefully, shaking out the skirts of her wine-coloured riding habit. Chairs scraped on the wooden floorboards as every man got to his feet. Anne gave a little bow to Wellington, smiling.

"With your permission, my Lord, I'll withdraw and leave you gentlemen to your maps and charts. I would like to ride over to the siege lines with you afterwards however, if I won't be in the way?"

"You could never be in the way, ma'am," Wellington said immediately. "We will be just a few minutes, I promise you. Graham, perhaps one of your people could bring Mrs van Daan some tea?"

Paul watched her leave, escorted by one of Graham's servants. He glanced over at March who caught his eye and blew out his cheeks in a gesture of relief. Paul smiled benignly at the younger man's naivety and counted silently in his head.

"Lord March. Lord Worcester. Now that I have regained your attention, perhaps you would favour me with your opinion of the practicality of the plan of attack that Sir Thomas just outlined?" Wellington asked crisply. "Or did the cider cause you to drift off to sleep during his briefing?"

Paul settled back in his chair and waited for the storm.

***

With March and Worcester riding at the back of the party looking noticeably subdued, Wellington led them at a brisk canter towards the siege lines. The town of San Sebastian was built on a low peninsula which ran from south to north and ended in the rugged hill of Monte Orgullo. The castle of La Mota was perched on the hilltop in a formidably defensible position. To the west of the peninsula was a bay with the tiny island of Santa Clara guarding the entrance. To the east ran the estuary of the Urumea River. The city was flanked by a wall which Paul estimated to be about eight feet high It ran along the river bank and the edge of the western bay.

The party rode up to a vantage point on one of the neighbouring hills where Graham had installed a picket from the Fifth Division and from one of the Spanish brigades. The view of the town was excellent from here and Graham took over as tour guide, pointing out the various defences and features. The tide seemed to be in and the sea lapped against the foot of the containing wall. Paul eyed it thoughtfully.

"How far does the tide go out?" he asked. "Could you cross it?"

"Yes, at low tide you can see a strip of land there. Perfectly fordable." Graham pointed again. "On the landward side there's a wall, as you can see, with a fairly deep ditch. Then there's that bastion and a hornwork beyond it. They've guns up in the castle and a couple of other batteries on Monte Orgullo on either side. The rest of their guns are positioned around the defences."

"That's going to be a nightmare for any storming party," Paul said, running his eyes over the town. "But you have excellent positions for your guns on these hills, sir, and apart from the castle there doesn't seem to be anywhere for them to hide."

"No," Wellington said. "It does not seem that the French paid a great deal of attention to the defences of San Sebastian until very recently. Unfortunately, there is no hope of starving them out even if we had time, which we most certainly do not. It is proving impossible to maintain a complete blockade from the sea. It seems the Royal Navy is unable to provide me with enough ships and the French are constantly running the blockade to bring in food and ammunition."

151

"What about water supplies, sir?" Anne asked. Sir Thomas shot her a surprised glance but Wellington did not hesitate to reply. When discussing military matters he often seemed to forget that Anne was both a female and a civilian and spoke to her as if she was a junior officer asking intelligent questions.

"Our men cut off the aqueduct before the first attempt on the town but we have been told that they have several wells. They will not die of thirst."

"There was a collection of houses and several convents outside the hornwork, ma'am which they destroyed early on," Graham said, adjusting quickly to his company. "They left one, the Convent of San Bartolomeo, which they fortified and put a garrison in. We stormed that last month, then built batteries out on the Chofre Sandhills to breach the walls."

Paul had already heard several accounts of the failed storming. Depending on the storyteller, blame had been apportioned to Graham, the Royal Engineers and Artillery, the men of the Fifth Division, General Oswald and Lord Wellington himself. He listened now to Wellington and Graham's account to Anne and thought, not for the first time, that it was an army custom to pick apart every defeat and disaster like vultures on a corpse. He had often wondered why they did not spend as much time dissecting the anatomy of success when it occurred since that might well be a far more valuable lesson for the future.

After a while Wellington led them down to the sandhills to the east of the town and summoned Paul to inspect the siege works, leaving Anne in the care of Lord March, who did not seem to see it as the punishment it was intended to be. Paul listened to his chief discussing ways and means with Fletcher and Dickson and realised that he intended to begin the bombardment very soon. He wondered why he was here. Wellington often included him in briefings where he had no right to be simply because he liked to be able to discuss ideas with him afterwards but Paul had a strong sense that the plan of attack here had already been decided.

He listened mostly in silence, not attempting to make suggestions but weighing up the various ideas for his own benefit. Since the failed attempt in July, more siege equipment, guns and ammunition had been brought in by the Royal Navy, although Wellington railed at how long it seemed to be taking. Once again the main attack was to come from the eastern flank by the river and the batteries prepared to enlarge the original breaches, blowing away the French's attempts to repair them. Other guns would fire from the San Bartolomeo redoubt down onto the hornwork and the San Juan bastion.

It was late afternoon before Wellington seemed satisfied and Paul was hot and tired and becoming hungry. Lord March had found Anne a comfortable spot under some trees by the river and as the party began to break up, Paul walked his horse back over the dunes and went to join them. He found his wife seated elegantly on March's coat on the sand. The young Earl was sprawled out beside her. He was in the process of describing Lord Wellington's furious explosion of wrath at a Spanish groom who had clumsily allowed the puppies to escape their pen during the night, resulting in half the household being summoned outside in various states of undress to recapture them. Anne was laughing until she cried. Paul stood watching until the Earl finished his tale, then dismounted, leading his horse to where March had tethered his own and Anne's mounts.

March got to his feet hastily, saluting. Paul waved a hand to indicate that no formality was necessary and went to kiss Anne.

"Have they finished?"

"I think so. It was interesting, though I'm not sure what it has to do with me. Have you spent the entire day flirting with my wife, March?"

"Yes, sir. Lord Wellington's orders."

"I'm not sure that's quite how he phrased it, but I admire your interpretation of his instructions." Paul surveyed his wife and smiled. "I must say you look very comfortable and surprisingly cool sitting there."

"Lord March has been looking after me very well, General. Do you have any idea if we are riding back to camp tonight?"

"I believe we're dining here then going back to Lesaca. His Lordship has offered us a bed for the night and I'm going to accept because I'm not doing that ride in the dark with you and no proper escort. We'll leave early tomorrow."

With time to prepare, Graham's cook had managed a very creditable dinner with roast pork, stewed mutton and a very good rice dish. Wellington did not linger over the wine, being eager to get underway. Paul observed his wife disappearing into the kitchen quarters in the chaos of their departure and grinned, knowing that a generous vail to the cook was likely to yield the recipe she wanted. She returned in time for her groom to help her into the saddle looking remarkably smug.

"Well done," Paul said softly as they trotted out of the stable yard. "George will be delighted."

"He was a very nice man and also gave me a recipe for a kind of tortilla that's easy to cook over a camp fire," Anne said. "I'm looking forward to trying it. I think Lord Wellington is calling you to ride up with him, love."

"I do hope we're not going to talk about parallels and breaching batteries all the way back. I might have had enough of that today. Lord March, keep my wife company again, will you? I'm being summoned."

"Gladly, General van Daan."

"Behave yourself, girl of my heart and don't elope with the Earl."

"Go away, Paul."

Paul grinned and cantered up to join Wellington. To his surprise, his Lordship touched his heel to Copenhagen's flank and pulled ahead of the rest of his party. Paul kept pace with him until they were some way ahead. Wellington slowed to a walk.

"I wanted to speak privately with you, General." Wellington gave him a sideways glance. "About the assault."

Paul felt a little jolt of concern. Wellington knew perfectly well how much he disliked siege warfare. Thus far there had been no indication that the Light Division would be involved in the second attack on San Sebastian but Paul had a feeling that was about to change. He said nothing. There was a long pause. Abruptly, Wellington said:

"Sometimes I feel as though you are able to read my mind."

"You can clearly read mine just now, sir."

"I read it perfectly, General."

"Sorry about the bad language then."

Wellington gave a splutter of laughter. "I am sorry to be the bearer of bad news."

"You've improved your delivery though, sir. You used to make announcements like this in the middle of briefing meetings just for the fun of watching me blow up."

"I must have mellowed. It isn't as bad as you are thinking, Paul, I'm not sending in the entire Light Division. I want volunteers from those divisions close enough. Fifty from each brigade plus fifty from the Portuguese. I will write the orders when I get back."

"Why, sir? I mean what difference will that many men make?"

"I think when the Fifth Division discovers that I am sending in men with experience in storming a breach to show them how it is done, it will improve their morale remarkably."

"I think when the Fifth Division realises you're implying that they're either cowardly or incompetent, they're going to pissed off with both you and the poor volunteers. Are you intending to send my men in as a Forlorn Hope?"

"Only if they volunteer for that, General. Otherwise it will be up to Oswald or Leith, whichever is in command."

Paul managed to say nothing immediately. It felt like a heroic effort. Eventually he said:

"Who is commanding the Light Division contingent?"

"I believe General Alten has a man in mind. Not a major-general, that would not be appropriate. Are you asking…?"

"No. I'd like my men to be as far back as possible."

"That will be up to Sir Thomas Graham, General. I intend to give permission for senior officers to view the action from the hills however, should you wish…"

"I don't," Paul said shortly. "It's not a fucking cricket match and I'd rather stay with the rest of my brigade and pray that they all come back. And keep an eye on the bloody French, because if they've got wind of an assault, I wouldn't put it past Soult to have another try."

Wellington gave a grim smile. "I was hoping you would say that, General. I will feel much more comfortable knowing your brigade is alert along the river banks. I'm sorry. I know this is not the news you wished to hear. Sometimes I must make difficult decisions."

"We all have to, sir." Paul looked at his chief and managed a smile. "I fucking hate sieges, you know."

"I have heard you mention that before," Wellington said. "I hope you intend to stay the night in Lesaca. I have a remarkable port that I would like you to try and if we get back early enough I would like to challenge you to a game of chess, if you are not too angry with me."

Paul sighed. "It's not you," he said. "I'm just getting tired of watching my friends getting maimed or killed. We did so well for a few years, but it seems to be catching up with me now."

"I understand." Wellington glanced round at the members of his household. Anne was riding between Somerset and March. Paul could hear them laughing at something she had said. "At times they exasperate me beyond measure, but I would hate to lose any one of them. Come, we shall canter while the light is still good enough. Otherwise Copenhagen will become bored and you know how restive he gets."

Paul took his cue, because he knew Wellington expected it. He gave the chestnut stallion a disgusted look. "If that animal kicks out at Rufus because he's in a bad mood, sir, I'm going to castrate him."

"You had better keep a safe distance then," his chief retorted. He flicked the reins, setting Copenhagen into swift movement.

***

The dinner for the officers of the 95th went off without a hitch much to Paul's surprise. Anne had been watching the preparations with considerable amusement and admiration for the officers' ingenuity. They had dug two long parallel trenches to act as seats, with wooden boards laid along each side and down the centre to act as benches and tables. Each battalion provided its own tin plate, cutlery and wine cups and some of the men acted as servitors for the evening. The canopy of branches which had been erected overhead was more decorative than practical, though Anne supposed that tent canvases could have been thrown over it in case of bad weather.

It was not needed. The afternoon was sunny and the evening skies clear. The band of the first battalion provided the music and the sounds of merriment floated to the rest of the Light Division as well as across the river to the French. There were endless toasts and as the wine flowed freely, the songs became more vulgar. Anne had walked down with Paul to share a cup of wine with some of their friends attending the dinner but removed herself prudently as the officers became more drunk. She was not in the least bothered by raucous drinking songs but she knew that her presence would inhibit at least some of the officers. Instead, she sat with Paul and some of their friends on the slopes of the hillside watching the celebrations from a distance and laughing at some of the more outlandish toasts which could be heard clearly on the still evening air.

"I wonder how many of them understand English," Johnny said, indicating a group of blue-coated French officers who had walked down to the river to watch the spectacle. Captain Cadoux of the second battalion, an elegant gentleman in his early thirties, was standing on the bench with the air of a man giving a speech in Parliament, reciting an appallingly explicit salute to the sexual failures of the Emperor Napoleon.

"I'm hoping they can't understand that, or some loyal subject of the Emperor is going to have a go at blowing Cadoux's pretty head off," Giles Fenwick said. "I'm trying to decide whether to ruin his day tomorrow by telling him you were within earshot of this, ma'am. He'd die of embarrassment. I'm quite impressed though, I didn't know Daniel was so eloquent."

"Or so creative," Michael O'Reilly said. "I wonder if he made all that up or if these rumours about Bonaparte are actually going around."

"I think they're from some kind of gutter press publication," Lieutenant Powell said. "I'm sure I've read them somewhere before. Maybe a poem or some such thing."

Paul surveyed his young ADC with interest. "I didn't know you were interested in poetry, Mr Powell. The things I learn about my officers. Do you by any chance write it as well?"

There was a ripple of laughter through the group. Powell laughed as well, though Anne suspected the fading light hid a blush.

"I don't, sir. Couldn't put together a rhyme if you paid me. If my memory is correct though, neither could the author of that broadsheet. There was a lot of that kind of thing going around a few years ago. Mostly about Bonaparte, though the Prince Regent came in for his fair share as well."

"In Prinny's case it might well be true," Fenwick said lazily. "Do you think we need to remain on full alert, sir, or can we share a cup or two of wine up here? I have a very good madeira I'd like to share."

Paul stared at him in surprise. "Have you been playing cards again, Captain? Or come into an inheritance?"

Fenwick laughed, getting to his feet. "Neither, sir. I have a cousin who is considerably wealthier than I am, who recently ran a promising newcomer at Newmarket and won handsomely. One of the more eccentric bets was the entire wine cellar of a prominent member of the peerage, whom I shall not name but who must have been as sick as a dog to have to hand it over."

Paul began to laugh. "That story is so unlikely it has to be true. Did your share of it arrive with the last delivery of supplies?"

"Yes, sir. He must have bribed the army transport service I'm afraid."

"We've all done that," Paul said equably. "It's a generous offer, Captain, thank you. I don't intend to get as drunk as the Rifles down there, but I think we can enjoy a glass or two on such a beautiful evening. I think our peaceful interlude is about to come to an abrupt end once those guns start up tomorrow morning. It'll take a few days to make a practicable breach, but I'm not convinced Marshal Soult is going to sit around twiddling his thumbs watching it happen. Get a couple of the men to help you carry it up here."

They sat until late sipping the wine and watching as the officers of the 95th began to stagger towards their beds. Some of them were still singing, their arms about each other's shoulders, swearing eternal friendship in slurred tones. Michael O'Reilly built a small fire on a broad slab of rock and he, Brat and Juana Smith collected a pile of branches from the small copses of trees which were scattered across the slopes. Paul sat with Anne leaning against him, her body

156

warm and relaxed in the shelter of his arm. He felt peaceful and happy, listening to his friends swap stories from previous campaigns.

On evenings like this he had learned to quell thoughts of the next month, the next week or even the next day. Army life was unpredictable and he had more than once been awakened from sleeping in his wife's arms to sudden frantic activity and the approach of danger. At the same time he thought that most people, particularly eager boys dreaming of military glory, had no idea that days like this were far more common than days spent engaging the enemy.

In his younger days Paul had found the tedium of army life difficult to bear and had acquired a reputation for restlessness. Some of that would never change and he suspected that his low tolerance for boredom probably explained why his men were so well-trained. Still, he thought six years of constant war had taught him to value the peaceful days, particularly now that he had Anne beside him. He bent his head and kissed her lightly and she smiled up at him through the flickering firelight.

Eventually they ran out of both wine and firewood and it was growing colder so they rose, doused the glowing embers and made their way cautiously across the slope towards their billets. It was darker than Paul had realised and their progress was slow. Michael had drunk rather more than the others and was inclined to be amorous, trying to kiss Brat as they stumbled down the slope towards the valley. Brat scolded him lightly but did not seem to be making any serious objection, although Paul was not sure if that was because she was having to hold him up.

"We should have brought a lantern," Anne said somewhat breathlessly as they arrived on more level ground on the valley floor. "Is your leg all right, Colonel Wheeler."

"Perfectly, ma'am. I am as sure-footed as a mountain goat," Johnny said gravely, making Anne giggle. Her mirth was infectious and they began their cautious way along the track towards the hamlet laughing at their clumsiness in the darkness.

Paul decided that Michael was not the only one who was slightly tipsy. The madeira had been too good and the rule about not drinking too much had definitely gone up in smoke after the second bottle. He took in several deep breaths of cool night air, trying to clear his head properly and took Anne's arm firmly.

"Let's try not to break any ankles here. God knows what time it is, I must have gone mad getting drunk on a hillside with you lot, with the French less than a mile away. Slow down a bit, Captain Fenwick. You might have excellent night vision but the rest of us can't see a bloody thing."

"I don't know why, we've had enough sodding practice this past month," Michael said. "If Alten turns up asking questions, we can just tell him it's a training exercise."

"That'd work until he got close enough to see that you can't walk in a straight line," Johnny observed.

There was a faint mist on the valley floor, but ahead Paul realised he could see a light. He peered at it, trying to work out if they were closer to the Casa Martinez than he had realised, but the light was moving and it was followed by a second and then a third. Paul began to laugh.

"Never mind, troops, there's a rescue party on its way. Jenson never lets me down, though I hope he's not wandering around himself in the dark on a wooden leg."

They made their way carefully forward and the bobbing lights resolved themselves into four covered lanterns, held on short poles by Captain Ross Mackenzie, his Quartermaster-Sergeant and Sergeants Cooper and Dawson. Paul greeted them cheerfully.

"Very good to see you, Captain. Thank you for the relieving force, we lost track of the time thanks to Captain Fenwick's generosity. I hope you're not here to tell me the house is under attack by Marshal Soult?"

Mackenzie laughed. "No, sir, everything's quiet. Sergeant Jenson came to find me to tell me you weren't back yet. We were a bit concerned you might miss your way without lights."

"I think we'd have found our way but it was going to be slow going." Paul fell into step beside his quartermaster, running his eyes over the Scot's slightly rumpled appearance. "Did he have to get you out of bed, Captain?"

"I wasn't asleep, sir."

"I was," Cooper said.

"So was I, sir," Rory Stewart said morosely. "Tucked up nice and warm when the Captain came to tell me I needed to go out in the middle of the night to retrieve a bunch of drunken officers who couldn't find their way home in the dark. Never heard such a tale, in all my days in the..."

"Oh fuck off, Stewart." Paul was laughing so much he missed his footing despite the improved lighting and stumbled. "If it wasn't too dark to see where the bloody river was, you'd be head first in it by now."

"You know what, sir?" Stewart said cordially. "This is one time I might fancy my chances in a bout with you. How much have you had, for God's sake?"

"Too much. It's going to take me a month to live this down after everything I said about drinking."

"More than a month, sir," Cooper assured him, reaching out to steady Fenwick who had also tripped. "Wonder how much it's worth to keep quiet about this?"

"I wonder how much picket duty it would take before Gisele forgets what you look like and runs off with a Rifleman?" Paul responded and the party dissolved into laughter again.

Lights were burning at the Casa and it was warm in the big square hallway. Paul watched his friends making their way carefully up the stairs and turned to Mackenzie.

"Ross, thank you. I'm sorry you had to get out of your bed, I was an idiot," he said softly. "Must be the influence of the Rifles. Don't tell Barnard about this or he'll roast me for a year."

158

"I have it on good authority that Barnard's orderly had to pour him into his bed, sir. He wouldn't have noticed if you'd danced along that table of theirs."

"I'm not quite that bad. I might check on Michael though, before I go to bed. He was distinctly jug-bitten."

"Do you want me to go, sir?"

"No, I'll do it. Get yourself back to bed. Goodnight."

He had forgotten that Michael was sharing a room with Fenwick. He found Giles in shirt sleeves and without his boots on, helping Brat to manoeuvre the Irishman into the big bed. Paul stood in the doorway laughing for a moment as Michael tried hard to draw Brat onto the bed with him and instead managed to unbalance Giles. Brat scrambled back out of reach as both men collapsed onto the bed and lay there, helpless with laughter. Brat put her hands on her hips with an exclamation of exasperation in Spanish. Paul went forward, grinning.

"Go to bed, Brat, it's all right. I'll deal with him."

She gave him a grateful smile. "Thank you, General. He will be very sorry tomorrow. As will Captain Fenwick." She gave Giles a severe look. "This reminds me of that night in Oporto."

"At least I didn't knock you out this time. Good night, Brat."

With Fenwick's help, Paul managed to get Michael's boots off and settled him on his side. Michael was already snoring. Paul looked over at his brigade-major with a smile.

"What the fuck was in that wine, Captain?"

"I think it was stronger than we realised. I must tell my bloody cousin that he could have endangered the safety of the brigade by sending me that. I wonder if he'd tried it himself and thought this would be funny? Sorry, sir."

"Don't be, it's been a very good evening. Goodnight, Giles."

He had reached the door before he became aware of the sounds. He froze, listening. Giles heard it at the same time and ran to the long windows, pushing open the casement. Paul went to stand beside him. They could see nothing out in the cool night except faint tendrils of mist and the swaying of trees and bushes in the light breeze, but there was no mistaking what they were hearing.

"It's started."

"Yes." Paul stood listening for a moment to the distant boom of gunfire. The sound was curiously flattened by distance but he had no doubt that he was listening to the beginning of the bombardment of San Sebastian.

"Poor bastards," Giles said very quietly. Paul wondered if he meant the French garrison or the townspeople then realised that with Giles, it would definitely be the latter. He suddenly felt completely sober.

"Get some sleep, Captain. It may be a long day tomorrow. Goodnight."

Chapter Eleven

Paul was in the big dining room reading a letter from Leo Manson when the official request arrived from Alten for volunteers to assist at the storming of San Sebastian. The bombardment had been clearly audible for several days. Alten had ridden over in the company of Lord Wellington to watch the progress of the attack and both Kempt and Skerrett had joined him. Paul declined the invitation and Alten did not ask why.

Paul was not sure himself. It was illogical, but he had no part to play in this particular combat and was uncomfortable with the role of spectator. In addition, now that he knew that some of his men would be required to join the storming parties, he would be unable to stop himself assessing the ground, selecting and discarding the best and worst points of entry and worrying that Graham, or Wellington, or Leith, who had arrived back to take command of his division just in time for the assault, might make the wrong decision and get all of them killed.

Paul read the letter twice through, sighed and went to the door, calling for Jenson, who appeared from the direction of the kitchen. Paul waved the letter at him.

"Find Captain Fenwick for me, will you, Jenson? We need to select our volunteers. I'm going to call a general parade this evening and the company officers can speak to their men. It'll give them tonight to think about it and we'll start taking names tomorrow."

"Any idea when it's happening, sir?"

"According to Alten, either the 30th or 31st, but that might change. They've not decided yet. Apparently the navy have taken the island of Santa Clara and the Fifth Division have beaten back at least one French sortie. Wellington has the bit between his teeth this time; if Graham looks as though he's faltering he'll step in and take over."

"I'm surprised he's not already done that, sir."

"Even he can't be in two places at once and I think he's reluctant to get bogged down at San Sebastian in case Soult has another try with a relief column. He's been caught like that once already, he won't want it happening again."

There was a sombre air over the brigade as the parade broke up that evening. The Light Division had been asked to provide fifty men from each brigade, including the Portuguese, which meant a contingent of two hundred men. Another two hundred volunteers would join them from the Guards and the King's German Legion brigades of the First Division plus two hundred from the Fourth Division. With the word out, Paul did not join his officers in the big dining room which doubled as a mess room. Instead he walked through the overgrown garden at the back of the house to a wooden fence which overlooked a wide meadow. Paul had commandeered it as his baggage park and horse lines. As always, there was constant activity through the evening as grooms and servants fed and watered the officers' horses and pack animals. Paul leaned on the fence, watching a Portuguese muleteer trying to examine the fetlock of a stubborn mule which looked as if it was trying to land a kick on him.

"Are you all right, sir?"

He turned to see Johnny Wheeler beside him. "Jesus, Colonel, don't creep up on me like that."

"You were a long way away."

"Woolgathering. I hate this business of volunteers. We're a regiment for God's sake and then a brigade. We should fight together or not at all."

"What you mean is, you hate the thought of any other commander in charge of your men when you're not there in case they bugger it up and you can't do anything about it."

"Well, yes. Leith is back, did you know? According to Kempt, who was over there this morning, he's absolutely furious about the slur on the honour of the Fifth Division and has flatly refused to allow any of the volunteers to lead the storming parties. They'll be kept back in reserve."

"Surely that's a good thing, sir?"

"Yes, as long as he doesn't see another way which is too risky for his beloved fucking division and decide to send our lads through it first to see if it works or not."

"You absolutely can't stand not being in control, can you?"

"No. I'm not even in control of who goes."

"The company officers are saying there are an awful lot of volunteers this time."

"I'll just bet there are. Well for a start, we are pulling out any man I don't trust to behave himself with the locals when he gets in there. That ought to weed out a few. I'd rather not send anyone with a family, but I might not be able to enforce that one because so many of them have got local girlfriends now. As for the officers…"

"How many are we sending?"

"Not that many. The Light Division contingent is commanded by Lieutenant-Colonel John Hunt from the 52nd. I'm glad of that; I like Hunt, he's

161

a good man. From our brigade we're sending two subalterns, four sergeants and forty rank and file from the British regiments and one Portuguese officer, a sergeant and ten men. They've also asked for volunteers for a captain to assist Hunt. Those will be chosen by drawing lots. Fucking gambling with my officers' lives. I'm tempted to announce that I'll kick the arse of any officer who volunteers but I can't do that."

Johnny put his hand on Paul's shoulder. "At twenty-one, sir, you would volunteer for literally anything. Except picket duty of course, which involved a lot of standing around and keeping your mouth shut. Those were never your strong points. And if you had the opportunity you'd volunteer now, just to stop somebody else from going."

Paul could not help laughing. "You know me too bloody well, Wheeler. Barnard did volunteer, by the way and put up a huge argument about being allowed to lead the Light Division men in, but he has been firmly refused. He's fairly pissed off about it but I'm glad. Andrew doesn't have a good record with sieges and I'd hate to lose him."

It was growing darker and the sky had clouded over. Paul shivered, though he was not really cold. His friend's hand felt warm on his shoulder even through his jacket. Paul put his own hand briefly over Johnny's.

"If I've not already mentioned it, Colonel Wheeler, I'm bloody glad you came back from sick leave. I don't know what I'd do if I'd lost both you and Carl. Keep safe, will you?"

"I do try to. Stop standing out here giving yourself the horrors. Come and have a drink, we don't have to sit in the mess if you don't want to. I've got some good brandy in my room and it won't give us the headache that Fenwick's bloody madeira did."

Paul laughed and rolled his eyes. "If I was Fenwick I'd kick his cousin the next time he sees him. In fact I might do it myself the next time I'm in London. Even Nan woke up with a sore head. I would love a glass of brandy, Johnny. It might steady my nerves for when I see the names on that bloody list."

They began to walk back towards the house. "Are you wanting a say in the selection from each battalion?" Johnny asked.

"No. There's no point. You know what I'm like, I'm going to yell whoever it is. Gervase will agree the final list from the 110th and you and Norton can split the difference between the 112th and 115th. I've agreed that any captain who wants to volunteer should submit his name directly to Lieutenant-Colonel Hunt. I'm staying out of it."

"That's a very good decision, sir."

"It was my wife's idea, which is why it's a very good decision. I was entirely prepared to stamp around yelling at any man who raised his hand, but she pointed out that we have to do this. And everybody else thinks it's their chance at glory. There's something wrong with me. Lead me to the brandy, Colonel."

***

162

The negotiations and discussions over the volunteers for San Sebastian took place against the background noise of the distant crashing of Graham's guns, battering down the town's defences. Johnny sat with Lieutenant-Colonel Philip Norton studying the lists of volunteers from the provisional battalion provided by his Adjutant. Given Paul's stated objection to including men likely to run wild once inside the town walls it was possible to remove a dozen applicants without further consideration. Johnny knew all of the men from his battalion personally to some degree. After some thought, he removed another man who had a pregnant wife and two older children. This still left too many.

It was more difficult for Norton, who had only commanded the 115th for six months but, like Johnny, he knew the troublemakers by the frequency with which their names came up before him. He removed two other men, one because he was still troubled by a shoulder wound received at Vitoria and the other because he was a recent recruit and Norton's NCOs had expressed doubts that he was actually of age. After some discussion, Norton suggested they should make the final selection by either length of service or sticking a pin in the lists while blindfolded. Johnny decided on the latter. It was done and Johnny went for brandy, poured for them both then leaned back in his chair and sighed.

"I wonder if Clevedon has finished?" Norton said. Johnny smiled tiredly.

"Like us, he was making his final decision today. The men will be informed and they'll be called for over the next couple of days. If anything happens to prevent one of them from going, like illness, we'll just take the next man on the list."

"Do we know who the two officers are going to be?"

"Yes. That's going by seniority out of those who applied, so it will be Jackman from the 110th and Hardy from the 115th. We'd initially agreed to make that selection by drawing lots but the General discovered that young Evan Powell was keen to go and he changed his mind rapidly."

Norton gave a little laugh. "He'd never have allowed that."

"I wouldn't have been keen myself. Seniority is better because there can be no argument about preferential treatment." Johnny sighed again. "I'm going to call Thompson to take this over to Fenwick and Russell. Then it's off my desk and I can enjoy this brandy and try not to think about it."

Norton eyed him sympathetically. "Is it going to be bad, sir? I've not been over there."

"According to the General, it is likely to be a bloody nightmare and I wish our lads weren't involved. I just hope Leith maintains his dignified temper tantrum and refuses to allow them any meaningful role in it, but I'm not optimistic. He's going to need all the men he can get."

The men chosen to form the Light Division contingent were informed by their company officers and Paul assembled them on an uneven field at the front of the Casa the following morning with the two officers. They were joined by ten men from his Portuguese battalion under Lieutenant Ronaldo who had

163

asked to be released from his temporary secondment to Simon Carlyon's company to join the assault. Johnny knew Paul had given permission reluctantly. He knew Ronaldo's wife and in-laws very well from his time billeted close to the family home near Freineda and would have preferred a man without family, but the Portuguese battalion had made their choice by drawing lots and Ronaldo was the clear winner with no objections from his brother officers.

Johnny, Norton and Lieutenant-Colonel Gervase Clevedon had chosen to join Paul as he spoke to the men. The speech was brief, thanking them for their courage and determination to uphold the honour of their regiments, their brigade and their division. He also reminded them of the behaviour he expected of them towards any remaining civilians of San Sebastian once the town was taken. Paul was good at this, his voice carrying clearly on the crisp morning air. Johnny listened, remembering other such moments and other such speeches. Generally Paul would have saved his words for the moments before the attack began when the danger was immediate and the men needed the encouragement, but Paul would not be there when these men went over the breach into San Sebastian. Johnny hated it and he knew his friend did too.

In the distance another man was approaching from the house. Michael O'Reilly had clearly come to lend support to the occasion, making his way across the wet grass with his long stride. Paul finished his speech and the men cheered loudly. Paul gave permission for Sergeant Coates, the most senior NCO among the volunteers, to dismiss them. He turned to meet Michael.

"You're too late, Captain O'Reilly. If you want to hear the best of my speeches you need to get moving a lot earlier than this. Never mind, I'm hoping Colonel Wheeler made notes. He's saving them for my biography."

"I am not writing your biography, sir. I wouldn't know what it was safe to put in and what I should leave out for legal reasons." Johnny studied Michael. He thought the Irishman looked unusually grave and a little pale. "Are you all right, Captain? You look a bit peaky."

Paul immediately turned his full attention to his friend. "Actually, you look half-dead. Didn't you sleep, or are you coming down with something?"

Michael saluted very formally. "I'm well enough, sir. I've just come from a meeting with Colonel Hunt from the 52nd. He sent for me to tell me I'll be his second-in-command at San Sebastian. I won the ballot."

Johnny made a little squawk of surprise. It sounded ridiculous but he could not help himself. He heard Norton catch his breath beside him. Paul made no sound at all. He had frozen, but the expression on his face made Johnny wish that he had remained in bed and then gone for a leisurely breakfast this morning, rather than joining the small parade. Michael said nothing. His dark eyes were on his commanding officer's face. Johnny knew with absolute certainty that the white face and worried frown had nothing to do with either illness or apprehension about the coming battle. Michael O'Reilly had far worse problems than that. Eventually Paul took a long deep breath. His voice came out at full volume and most of the men, who had already crossed the field on their way back to camp, turned back to stare in surprise.

"Are you out of your fucking mind, Captain O'Reilly? What in God's name made you think I would agree to this piece of fucking insanity, don't you know me better than that? I've no idea what's wrong with you, but you are not volunteering to get yourself killed under any commander outside this brigade. Get back over there and tell Hunt that I've refused permission and you are not fucking going."

Michael did not speak for a moment. When he did, his voice was deliberately steady.

"I am going, sir. I put my name into the ballot, the same as the other officers. I've the right to volunteer for this. I'm sorry if you're angry but you're not going to change my mind."

"You're clearly out of your bloody mind," Paul said furiously. "What's got into you, Michael? You're not usually this fucking stupid. Generally we all stand back and politely applaud the boys of the Forlorn Hope as they jostle to get themselves killed going over the breaches. When I'm ordered to storm a citadel, I'll do my job as well as I can, but I'm not idiotic enough to stand in the firing line if I don't have to. Think about it, use your brain. You don't need to do this. I'll speak to Hunt and tell him I've refused permission; he'll hand it on to the next poor bastard in line who will be delighted and we can all move on."

"I don't want you to do that, sir. I don't need your permission, you don't command my regiment. If I needed permission at all, I'd have to ask Colonel Wheeler. But I don't. I've thought about this, I didn't do it lightly."

Johnny held his breath. He was horrified at Michael's decision but did not think yelling at him was likely to change his mind. Paul's temper was unpredictable but it seldom lasted for long, especially with his closest friends, and Johnny thought a calm discussion was needed here.

Paul looked as though he was silently counting to ten. Michael continued to stand to attention. Nobody else spoke or moved, though out of the corner of his eye, Johnny could see that they had an interested audience from some of the volunteers who had moved back to within earshot. Johnny turned towards them, raised his arm and pointed in the direction of the camp. Several of them moved immediately but Sergeant Coates and Sergeant Barforth lingered. Johnny began to walk towards them and they both saluted immediately and went on their way. Johnny reflected that it hardly mattered. They had heard enough and by noon, the tale of Captain O'Reilly's quarrel with his brigade commander would have reached every man in the third brigade and be making its way through the rest of the Light Division.

Paul let out his breath in a whoosh. "Michael, I've no fucking idea what's going on in your head right now, but let's stop making a gift of it to the entire Light Division," he said quietly. "Come on, we'll talk inside, I'll get George to bring some tea into the small parlour. Do you want Johnny to join us? I'd ask my wife, but she's not feeling that well this morning so I've told them to take breakfast up to her."

"Is she all right, sir?" Michael said quickly. Paul gave a faint smile.

"She's fine, it's just female problems. Colonel Wheeler, join us, would you? We're going to need the voice of reason in there."

Nothing more was said until they were seated around the wooden table with the tea tray before them. Paul wrapped his hands around the cup as he drank, as if he was cold, though Johnny suspected it was more for comfort. He felt in need of comfort himself. Michael had not touched his cup yet.

Eventually Paul set down his cup and broke the silence. "Why have you done this, Michael? Death or glory is not generally your style."

"I'm not intending to die, sir. I've survived a fair few sieges in my time. I'm not stupid and I know how to duck."

"Anybody can get themselves killed going over those breaches. Ask Major-General Robert Craufurd. I don't think he exactly planned to die at Ciudad Rodrigo." Paul studied his friend. "Talk to me, Michael. Is everything all right? I've a feeling I've not been much use to you as a friend recently. In fact I know I've not. The humour of your situation was too much for me. I am sorry. But if something's gone wrong, there are better ways to fix it."

Michael stared at him in surprise and then laughed. "Is that what you're thinking? Jesus, sir, have you been reading gothic romances in your spare time? This isn't a suicide attempt. If I wanted to kill myself – and I don't – I'd borrow Hammond's rifle and blow my head off. Far more reliable."

"I didn't really think it was," Paul said. "But then what?"

Michael did not respond immediately. He sat with his eyes on his untouched tea cup. Johnny was beginning to wonder if he had forgotten the question when the Irishman looked up, directly at Paul.

"It's difficult for you to understand, sir, because you've never been where I am. Colonel Wheeler will probably get it. I'm stuck. I'm thirty-four and a captain without purchase. We both know that's where I'm staying. I've got years of experience in the army, but most of them don't count because I served them in the ranks. I was only commissioned four years ago and you've shoved my promotions through into dead men's shoes but you can't do that any more. The right to purchase up to major goes by seniority and date of commission which means I'm going to get passed over for every snotty-nosed brat who had his first commission bought for him at the age of fifteen by his wealthy uncle. Evan Powell will make major before I do and much as I like him, that pisses me off."

There was a long painful silence in the room. Paul reached for the teapot and refilled his cup. "You're right," he said in matter-of-fact tones. "It pisses me off as well. Michael, you know that I…"

"You've done everything you can for me, sir, but it's out of your hands now and you know it. Even if a majority became vacant in the brigade, and I bloody hope it doesn't because those men are my friends and I don't want them dead, there are too many good men ahead of me. It will go to them, and it should. But that leaves me nowhere."

"Christ Michael, I'm sorry. I didn't realise how much it mattered to you. But this is not the way."

166

"It hasn't always mattered this much, but it's different now." Michael took a long deep breath. "It's not just me. I want to be married. I want a family and I want a future. I've little enough to offer her but I think she'll take me as I am. I want to offer her more. I want promotion and the opportunities that come with it."

"You should have bloody well come to me, Michael," Paul said angrily. "We're friends. Yes, I've been something of an arsehole about your relationship with Brat, but if I'd realised it was this serious you know perfectly well I'd have sat up and taken notice. I agree, promotion within the brigade is not likely, but there'll be other opportunities. I can ask around, make sure people know you're looking. We can..."

"It's unlikely to work, sir," Johnny said quietly. He was watching Michael with painful understanding. "He came up from the ranks. You and I know he's one of the best officers in the army, but outside this brigade they'll just see a former Irish sergeant who shouldn't be allowed to sit in the mess with the gentlemen. At least, some of them will. Look at how Dodd struggled, even when he had the money to purchase up."

He could see the frustration on Paul's expressive face. "It's bloody ridiculous," he growled. "This is why we lose excellent officers who volunteer for the Forlorn Hope because it's the only way they can think of to get noticed. But Michael..."

"I know you'll do your best for me, sir, but Colonel Wheeler is right. I need more. I need to get noticed, not just within this brigade but elsewhere. I need to be mentioned in dispatches."

"You managed that earlier this year."

"I don't think that letter reached the right people, sir. I'm not naïve. San Sebastian isn't going to bring me my promotion. But there will be other opportunities and I intend to take every one of them."

Paul sat back in his chair and rolled his eyes, making a little growl of sheer frustration. "Michael, for God's sake don't turn into Andrew Barnard in front of my eyes, I can't stand it. I thought I'd bloody lost you on that pointless mission to Castro Urdiales. I can't go into every battle wondering if you're about to go haring off in search of glory and promotion."

"Don't be bloody ridiculous, Paul, I'm not going to abandon my men halfway through a fight." Michael gave a little smile. "Calm down about it, would you? This is why I didn't tell you what I meant to do. No point in stirring you up when I didn't even know that I'd get it."

"What does Brat think about it?" Johnny asked. "Does she understand why you're doing this?"

Michael said nothing. Johnny stared at him in slowly dawning realisation but Paul, with more personal experience, was much quicker.

"You haven't told her, have you?"

"Not yet," Michael said. For the first time he sounded defensive. "As I just said, there was no point until I was certain. I'll speak to her..."

Paul got up. "You'll speak to her now," he said flatly. "We'll vacate the room, you can bring her in here. I've got no idea how far your relationship has progressed, Michael, but watching the two of you it seems to me that she had a right to be consulted on this before you went storming in."

"Are you telling me that's what you've always done?"

"Not always. Those are the occasions you'll see me walking about white faced and sleep-deprived after a night on Johnny's floorboards. You were a bloody idiot to do this, in my opinion, but I understand your reasoning even if I don't agree with it. But I'm not sure you understand how little your promotion is going to matter to a woman like Brat. Get her and tell her. If you need medical attention afterwards, I'll call Nan."

Michael stood up. Johnny thought that he had seemed remarkably calm under the onslaught of his commanding officer's fury earlier but he looked far less confident now. "I thought I might ask her to come for a walk."

"Good idea," Paul said. "Wait until you're in the middle of a nice wide meadow with no weapons close by. But not too far. We need to be able to hear you if you're screaming for help. Maybe you should borrow a bugle."

"She could use the bugle to hit him with," Johnny pointed out.

"Good point. No bugle. Go and find her, Michael."

When the Irishman had gone, Paul sat down again and emptied the teapot into their two cups. It was tepid but Johnny drank it anyway.

"Poor bastard."

Paul sighed. "I feel guilty. I've been wondering what's holding him back from speaking to Brat since it's obvious how he feels about her. He'd have told me if I'd not been teased him so much about her."

"He might not have, sir."

Paul eyed him. "Because I have a blind spot?" he asked shrewdly.

"You understand far better than most of the others. I've seen you tie yourself in knots trying to ensure promotions go to the best man and you've stuck your neck out a few times. But you can't really know how it feels. I've seen you lend the purchase price to a bright youngster that you want to bring on. But it's more difficult for Michael."

"It bloody shouldn't be." Paul finished his cold tea. "Do you think it will work for him?"

"I think if he comes to the attention of Wellington or Graham or Hill, they can apply pressure far better than you can."

"And then he takes a majority out of my brigade and I lose him."

"You can't ask him to remain a captain for the rest of his life just to stay with us."

"I know. I don't." Paul rose again. "I'm going to see how my wife is feeling. Those guns are intensifying, aren't they? I don't think it will be long. Christ, I wish this was over. I wonder how Michael is getting on?"

***

Michael found Brat in the kitchen in conversation with George Kelly. He waited in the doorway watching her in silence until she noticed him and gave her quick, sunny smile.

"I did not see you there, Michael. Are you looking for me or are you searching for food?"

"I've barely eaten my breakfast, Brat. Even I can't eat again yet. Will you come for a walk? I want to talk to you."

She went willingly, taking his arm to stroll through the long grass of the meadow beyond the house. Michael led her carefully away from the lines of tents and the baggage park. He felt a sick heaviness in his stomach which had nothing to do with fear of the battle to come. He had managed to avoid thinking about her reaction when he told her what he had done simply by telling himself that many officers had put their names forward and it was unlikely that his would be chosen. His commanding officer had responded exactly as he had expected and he had been ready to deal with that. He had no idea how to deal with Brat.

"What is wrong, Michael?"

They were in the centre of the meadow, with cows grazing at the far end and a small stream bubbling alongside a straggling hedge. Michael stopped, ironically aware that this was exactly the location suggested by his commanding officer.

"Listen Brat, I've something to tell you. I've not mentioned it before, because I wasn't sure anything would come of it, but…the truth is, I volunteered for the assault on San Sebastian. I heard this morning that I've been chosen as second-in-command to Colonel Hunt who is to command the Light Division contingent when they…"

Brat threw off his arm so violently that he almost stumbled. She whirled to face him. "You volunteered?"

"There was a ballot," Michael said steadily. "My name came up."

"Your name would not have been there had you not submitted it."

"That's true. Look, Brat, I can see that you're angry but let me explain."

"In the way that you explained to me when you left me crying in Castro Urdiales and went to be a hero in a fight that was not yours?"

"It's not the same."

"No, it is not. Then we were trapped in a town of desperate people and the garrison had not enough officers. Then I could understand that it felt like a duty. Here you were one of many, squabbling over a place that nobody should have wanted. Why?"

Her face was flushed and the brilliant blue-green eyes were stormy and dark. She looked furious. Michael summoned his arguments.

"I'm thinking ahead," he said. "Brat…you know my situation. I'm stuck at captain and likely to stay that way. I need to do something if I'm ever going to achieve promotion. The fact that I began in the ranks means I'm years behind my fellow officers in terms of seniority and…"

"Do not speak to me of this nonsense!" Brat said furiously. "I do not wish to hear it. Who cares if you are a captain, a major or a donkey handler? You

169

spend your life trying to get yourself killed. I do not see why you must make this extra effort."

"I care," Michael said in desperate tones. "And you should care. I need to advance if I am ever to…if we are ever to…"

"Ever to what?"

"You know what I am talking about."

"I have absolutely no idea."

"If I'm ever to be in a position to afford a wife. A family."

It was said and Michael could not believe he had said it so badly. He stood glaring at her in the middle of the field, wondering if he looked as foolish as he felt. Brat stood looking at him for a long time. Then she said:

"And where do you intend to find this wife and family that you seek, Captain O'Reilly?"

"I don't know," Michael said. His voice had dropped. He felt suddenly tired and hopeless and very stupid. "I don't know. I thought…perhaps I was wrong. Brat, we've never had this conversation, but I hoped…I believed…"

"What did you believe, Michael? That I would wish you to volunteer for this…this thing? Why?"

"Because it's time I started to look to the future, Brat. If we are ever to…"

Brat's bubbling anger exploded into fury. "What is this thing that we are to do?" she spat. "You speak in vague words and riddles and mutter things as though I cannot possibly understand them, but you tell me nothing of what you want and I am becoming tired of it! Do you think if you become a major, it will make everything simple between us? This is nonsense. You do not need to fight in the breach of San Sebastian, Michael. You simply need to talk to me."

"I did it for us, Brat. For you."

Brat hit him. The slap caught him on the jaw rather than the cheek and did not particularly hurt but it shocked Michael. He put his hand to his face and stared at her in disbelief. For a moment he thought she was going to hit him again, then she seemed to realise that she had hurt herself and took her right hand in her left rather gingerly. He felt a rush of concern.

"Let me see that."

She took a step back, cradling her hand against her breast. "No. I do not wish you to touch me."

"Brat, you just hit me very hard on my jaw and I'm telling you now that it didn't hurt me but I think it's hurt you. Let me look."

"No! You have just tried to blame me for what you have done and I will not…"

"I've not blamed you for anything, urchin, I'm just trying to explain. If you would just stop shouting at me and listen."

Abruptly the anger seemed to drain from her face and she began to cry. She turned away from him as if she could not bear to let him see her tears. Michael stood frozen for a moment then stepped forward and put his hands on her shoulders, turning her round firmly. She had lowered her head. Panic gave

170

him wisdom and he made no attempt to make her look up but simply gathered her into his arms so that her slight, taut body was against his and held her close, kissing the red curls and murmuring soothingly. She turned her face into his chest and sobbed. Michael felt as though his heart was breaking.

"I'm sorry," he said finally. "I've made such a mull of this. I've been telling myself that you would understand. That I couldn't speak to you formally until I had some kind of a future to offer you. I love you, querida. You must know that by now. I want you to be my wife, but how can I propose marriage when I've nothing but my army pay and a wandering life to give you? I thought that at least this would show you that I'm serious about our future. Have I got this whole thing wrong? Do you not want me, urchin? Because if that's the case, I should probably..."

She pulled back and looked up at him from tear-drenched eyes. "Of course I want you, you big idiot," she said fiercely. "I want you now, not in some imagined future when everything is different. How do I even know if I will like Major O'Reilly? I know that I love Captain O'Reilly, but he may change and no longer care for me."

"I'm never going to stop caring for you, Brat."

"Then care for me now."

There was a lump in his throat which made it difficult to speak. He swallowed twice, hoping it had cleared but his voice still came out croaky and unsteady.

"If I survive this, will you marry me?"

She did not speak for a moment. Then she said:

"I would rather marry you if you do not do this."

"I can't withdraw. I would look like a coward. It might not matter to a fine young buck with the money for his next promotion tucked into his pocket, but they're waiting for me to prove that I can't sustain the character of a gentleman. I'm sorry, Brat. Probably I shouldn't have done this, but it's done now."

He watched her consider the matter, his heart beating fast with sheer terror in case she said no. Finally she moved, and it was towards him rather than away. Michael took her into his arms and kissed her with desperate passion. It lasted for a long time. He suspected that neither wanted to end the kiss and move back into conversation, but it had to be done.

Finally he raised his head and looked down at her. "Thank you," he said very gently. "I'm sorry. Will it help if I promise I'll never do anything else like this without talking to you first?"

"It will only help if you survive."

"Then I'll survive. You've not answered me, by the way."

For the first time, she smiled. "Always, you are so impatient. Should I not take time to consider the matter?"

"You can have as long as you want, urchin."

She made a little sound of sheer exasperation and moved into his arms again. "Suddenly you are so serious and that is not what I am used to. I do not need to consider, Michael. I just need you to come back to me."

"When I do, can we be married?"

She eyed him for a moment. "Are you allowed to be married in a Spanish church?"

"You mean a Catholic church? Yes. They don't need to know the details, I'm not inviting Lord Wellington anyway."

"I would like to invite Mrs van Daan."

"I doubt if you could keep her away, querida." Michael realised that he was smiling. He was not sure he would ever be able to stop. "Let's do it as soon as we can. I can't believe I was stupid enough to wait this long."

"This week, you are stupid enough for anything."

He began to laugh. "Are you going to continue to insult me for the rest of our married life, Ariana?"

"It will depend on whether you deserve it." Brat studied him quizzically. "Am I now to be Ariana to you?"

He stopped laughing and looked at her. Her expression was serious but her eyes were smiling. Michael realised he was trying to memorise her face, as though he might need to visualise every detail during the coming days. He was suddenly furious with himself for thinking that he needed to prove himself in some way, when previously, she had followed him willingly into danger simply because she loved him. He gave a crooked smile.

"At some point, urchin, we're going to have to get accustomed to that. At least in polite circles."

"I do not think I belong in polite circles, Michael, but for you I will try. Although if we suddenly become so formal, I think Major-General van Daan will laugh himself into a fit. Does he know that you have done this thing?"

"Yes. He yelled. My ears are still ringing."

"Good. Does he know that you...that we..."

"He doesn't know I was about to propose to you. I didn't know that myself until just now. I knew I wanted to but I wanted to give you time. You're so much younger than I am..."

"Do not start that again or I will shout louder than Major-General van Daan." Brat drew back from him a little. "You have a very hard jaw."

Michael raised his hand to feel it then dropped it again feeling foolish. "I'd never thought about it. I've had a punch or two over the years which have hurt a lot, but I'm not sure you've had boxing training. Does your hand still hurt?"

"Yes. It serves me right, I should not have hit you. I lost my temper, I'm sorry."

"Brat, I definitely asked for it. Let me look at that."

She gave a sharp gasp of pain as he prodded her hand. Michael studied it and realised to his dismay that it was distinctly swollen.

"Move your fingers."

172

Brat attempted to do so and stopped immediately. "It is very painful," she said.

"Christ, I hope you've not broken it. I think you should let Mrs van Daan or Dr Daniels look at it."

"I cannot tell Dr Daniels that I injured my hand hitting you, Michael. It is ridiculous."

"Mrs van Daan then. She'll think it was perfectly sensible and probably arrange for somebody to teach you how to do it again without hurting yourself. Come along."

She dissolved into slightly tearful giggles. "I am such a fool."

"You've just agreed to be my wife, Brat. I can't argue with you."

Brat took his arm and they made their way back across the meadow. She was silent for a while and Michael worried about how much pain she was in, but when she spoke it was clear that her injury was not on her mind.

"Do you know when it will be?"

"In a couple of days. They'll let us know." Michael turned to look at her and her expression tore at his heart. "I'm going to speak to the General and ask for some unofficial furlough, urchin. I'd rather like to spend all of my waking hours with you."

Brat gave him a little smile. She did not reply but allowed him to lead her into the house in search of Anne.

***

Michael was settling to sleep when Fenwick appeared at the door of their shared room. His friend made no attempt to come in and close the door. Michael sat up. He thought Giles looked tired and unhappy and he suspected that he knew why.

"News, Giles?"

"Orders just came. You're to march out tomorrow to join Leith's men in the trenches. I've no idea if they'll storm tomorrow night or the following day. There's been some talk of an assault in daylight this time."

Michael groaned. "I'd hoped for another day. I should go and tell Brat."

"I thought she was still here."

"No, I sent her to bed. No point in her sitting up all night fretting."

"Do you think she'll fret any less if she knows you're moving out tomorrow? It's not a dawn march." Giles yawned. "I have some work to finish in the parlour. If she's still about, I'll tell her. Go to sleep, Captain O'Reilly. You're going to need it."

Michael lay back reluctantly. He was suddenly wide awake, his whole being aware of the coming battle and of his new position as an engaged man. He had told nobody but Anne and Paul of his proposal. This was not the time for a celebration. He was keenly aware of what he had done to Brat, making his feelings known at the same time as telling her that he had volunteered to fight. He was furious with himself for not speaking to her first.

173

Anne had inspected her hand and decided that it was not badly hurt though it was possible she had cracked a bone.

"Either that or it's just very bruised. I'm going to bind it up for a few days, Ariana, just to stop you using it until the swelling goes down. I'm also going to give you a sling. After that, we'll see. Don't look at me like that. You are formally off duty until the assault is over. Alison can help me if I need it, but I won't be attending any parties. Go. Be with your fiancé. And congratulations, both of you. I wish we could celebrate properly, but we'll attend to that later."

Brat had spent the day at his side. She had not reproved him again about his impetuous decision to volunteer and they had not spoken of the coming battle. Instead they walked through the meadows until rain drove them within doors and then they sat talking. Anne arranged for dinner to be sent up to Michael's room and Fenwick had tactfully remained absent.

The house was still and quiet. After the heavy rain during the afternoon, the night was warm and the sky very clear and spangled with stars. Michael got up and went to the window to look out. He could not see the French lines from here: they were obscured by a bank of trees, but he knew they were there. In the distance, the guns still boomed relentlessly at San Sebastian but close at hand he could hear an owl hooting as it swooped over the hills in search of prey.

"Michael."

He turned quickly. She was standing by the closed door watching him. She still wore the white muslin gown, with a dark shawl thrown about her shoulders. She had already abandoned the sling. Her auburn curls were loose on her shoulders. Brat had worn her hair short for several years when she had dressed as a boy. It had begun to grow in earnest now and Anne had showed her how to put it up in a simple knot, with carefully arranged curls framing her face. The new hairstyle turned her from girl to young woman in an hour and Michael could not decide whether he was captivated or terrified. Looking at her now, he decided that he would always like her better like this. He went forward and took her good hand in his.

"Damn Fenwick. Did he wake you up?"

"No, I was not asleep. He told me it will be tomorrow. Are you all right, Michael?"

He gave a little smile. "I always have a knot in my stomach before a fight, *querida*. Nothing to worry about. Come and look at these stars. You can stay with me until Giles comes to bed, he said something about some work to do."

"He is not working. He is sleeping on the sofa in the parlour. I found him some blankets and a pillow."

Michael froze. "What? Why?"

"I asked him to. He said he would be very comfortable. I think it is true, you know what he is like, he can sleep anywhere. He told me I should make the most of it, so I am here."

Michael released her hand. "Brat, no."

"Do you not wish to?"

174

"Of course I wish to." Michael was suddenly painfully aware of exactly how much he wished to. It was almost comedic that just the thought of making love to her had such an immediate effect on him. He was thankful for his long, loose shirt which concealed a great deal. "But love, I'm not sure this is such a good idea. I've been dreaming of this for months, you know I have. But we're going to be married, as soon as I can arrange it. If I…if we…if it happens now, what I'm killed? What if I leave you with a child and I'm not there to support you? We should wait."

"We are not going to wait," Brat snapped. "I have been waiting and I am tired of it. No, do not speak again, you have nothing sensible to say. If you had not done this foolish thing, we could have been married in the usual way and I would have waited. But tomorrow you are going to fight the French when you do not have to. Again. Last time, there was no opportunity to do this. If I let you send me away we will have lost another opportunity. This is not the first time I have done this, Michael. But it is the first time I have ever actually wanted to do it, with any man. I am not wasting that because of your scruples. I believe you will come back to me. But in case you do not, then you owe me this night."

Unexpectedly, Michael felt tears sitting heavily in his eyes. He tried to blink them back then changed his mind and let them fall. He moved towards her again and drew her into his arms.

"Ariana, there is nothing in the world I want more than to make love to you," he breathed. "But if there's a child and I don't come back…"

She reached up and wound an arm about his neck, pressing her body close against his. "Then I will raise your son or your daughter to be proud of the father they had. As I am proud of you. As I will always be proud of you."

There was no more resistance in him and he did not even try. He kissed her long and hard, feeling the urgency of her response and decided that he was being an idiot and that she was wiser than he.

"Then come to bed with me, *a mhuirnín*."

"I do not know that word. What does it mean?"

Michael scooped her up into his arms for no other reason than that he wanted to enjoy how light and slender she was. He felt a ridiculous sense of possessive joy that he had never experienced before.

"I'll teach you," he said, carrying her to the bed. "In a while."

Chapter Twelve

Michael awoke early to the sound of a light tapping on his door. For a moment he was confused in the grey half-light. Then he remembered and moved quickly so that she would not be disturbed. He wrapped a blanket around his waist and padded to the door, opening it a crack. Giles Fenwick stood in the hallway in shirt sleeves. His fair hair was rumpled and he looked barely awake.

"I'm sorry," he said in low tones. "This just came; it's your orders. No immediate rush, they want the volunteers to form up at Alten's headquarters at noon."

"Are we going in tonight?"

"No, it'll be in daylight tomorrow. It's dependent on the tides."

"Well that will be fucking fun. Thanks, Giles. For everything."

"Get back in there and lock the door. I'll make sure you're not disturbed until you're ready to come out."

"Mrs van Daan is going to murder me for this."

"No, she won't. If you come back in one piece you'll marry the girl, which will make us all very happy. If you don't, she'll be furious with you but she can hardly stab you if you're already dead. Come and see me before you leave."

"I will."

Michael bolted the door and turned. He was not surprised to find her awake, sitting up with the covers drawn up around her breasts. Her hair was a tumbled mass of curls and her eyes were fixed on his face, wide with anxiety.

"Do you have to leave now?"

He went forward quickly, sliding under the blankets and drawing her to sit with her head on his shoulder. "No, *querida*, not right now. We're assembling at noon, we have a little time."

Brat's lips curved into a little smile. "I am not sure that I have the energy."

"I could probably convince myself, but I'm not going to. I need to conserve my strength for the fight."

He broke off, wishing he had not said it, but she did not flinch. Instead, she snuggled into him. "That was very lovely."

176

"That was perfect, Ariana. You're perfect."

She gave a little giggle. "You know that I am not. I am barely used to wearing skirts again and I have no idea how to make polite conversation. And I have a terrible temper. I hit you."

"You're perfect to me."

She reached up to caress his face very gently. "I love you, Michael. Please be as careful as you can. Now that I know, finally, what I want, I cannot bear to lose it."

"I'll come back to you, Ariana."

"Do not promise."

"I cannot promise. But I will do everything in my power."

"That, I will trust." She flashed him her impish smile. "It seems that suddenly you are more comfortable calling me Ariana."

"Somehow it feels very natural. Are you all right? Afterwards I lay there wondering if I should have been more gentle. Less...oh I don't know." Michael saw her expression and could not help laughing. "Don't look at me like that, it's terrifying."

"Good. You are about to start talking nonsense about how young and delicate I am, which is ridiculous when you know that I am very strong."

"I wasn't thinking of that. I was thinking of what was done to you when you were younger. I was worried it might bring back unhappy memories. I didn't want to frighten you, but I forgot all about it when we were...well, you know."

"You have become remarkably tongue-tied," Brat said dispassionately.

"It seems to be the effect you have on me. Perhaps if you were wearing more clothes, I'd regain my fluent tongue."

"I rather like to see you stammering and blushing like a schoolboy." Brat leaned forward and kissed him very gently on the lips. "Stop worrying, Michael. I also wondered how I would be. I have discovered that sharing a bed with the man I love has nothing to do with those creatures. It is a very great relief to me."

"Me too." Michael slid down under the covers again and drew her into his arms. They lay quietly for a while, her head pillowed on his shoulder. He could not remember the last time he had felt this peaceful and this settled. He did not want it to end but he knew it must.

The knowledge reminded him that there was something he wanted her to know. He hated the constant reminders that he was marching out to battle and might not come back, but this one thing felt too important to leave unsaid.

"Ariana, I've something to say to you."

"Is it bad? You sound very serious suddenly."

She sounded genuinely anxious and he planted a kiss on her forehead. "No *cáilín*, it's nothing bad. It's simply that there's something I want you to know. In case..."

"Do not say it."

"I have to, Ariana, because if there's any chance that last night results in a child, I want you to tell my son or my daughter. I've spoken a little of the foolishness of my youth and the reason I joined the army."

"You have. I remember you talked of it on our way to Castro Urdiales."

"I told you then I joined under a new name, when the rebellion failed."

"You did."

"I've never told my original name to a living soul since that day, not even my best friends. I want you to know it, Ariana. I'll not be going back to it. I couldn't now. But it's the name my mother and father gave me."

Brat sat up, her eyes on his face again. They were wide with surprise. "You wish me to know?"

"I want you to know all of me. When I come back and we're married, I'll tell you the whole sorry story and you can laugh at the fool of a boy I once was. I don't have time to do that now."

"What is your real name, Michael?"

"My real name is Michael O'Reilly. I've lived my life under it. But back then I was Ciaran Donnelly, the son of a respectable schoolmaster from Sligo."

"Ciaran." She seemed to be testing it on her tongue, learning the sound of it. "Ciaran Donnelly."

She looked so serious that Michael could not help laughing. "It sounds a lot better when you say it. It must be the Spanish accent."

"It is a very pretty name, Ciaran Donnelly. I am so happy you told me, even if I must never say it outside of our room."

"I wanted you to know."

"What was your father's name? And your mother's?"

"He was the same, I was named for him. My mother was born Naoise Murphy. I'd a younger sister as well. They lost four children between me and her, she was ten years my junior, still a child when I left. Maura. She used to follow me about…"

He broke off, surprised to realise that he was crying. She moved back into his arms immediately and drew his head down onto her breast, stroking his hair, murmuring soothing words in Spanish. Michael cried for a long time. When the storm of his tears was over he did not move. He felt peaceful and loved and much better.

He had no idea how long he had lain there in her arms when she stirred a little.

"I want to stay like this forever, *querido*, but we cannot. You must be up and eat something so that you are ready for battle. And you must spend some time with the General and Giles and your other friends."

"I'm very happy here."

"They also need to wish you luck."

Michael thought about it and suddenly saw the funny side. "I've been into battle so many times in my life, Ariana and it has never before been this dramatic. Why does everybody think I'm about to die? I've never died before and I don't intend to this time. This is extremely silly, urchin."

She sat up, looking down at him. "Make sure you don't."

"I'm not in the least worried about the French. It bothers me more that those nosy bastards know that you spent the night in here. If any one of them says a single word to bring a blush to your cheeks, I'm going to punch them."

"Michael, I sold myself to soldiers to survive and most of them know it. I am not going to blush. I think it is you who are a little embarrassed."

Michael thought about it and decided it was true. "I'm still going to punch them," he said. "Come on, let's get some breakfast."

***

Paul rode over to Alten's headquarters to see his men march out towards San Sebastian. He stood beside Michael looking over the neat lines. Two hundred men of the 95th, 52nd, 43rd and the Portuguese caçadores were lined up before Lieutenant-Colonel Hunt.

"A reliable source has informed me that you won't be going over first," Paul said quietly. "Leith is sticking to his intention to let the fifth lead the way in. He's got Oswald acting as his informal ADC. It's good of Oswald, partly because he has every right to be pissed off at being superseded at the last minute and partly because he's still not fully recovered from the wound he received during the last assault. Both of them are adamant that they want the fifth to have the chance to prove themselves and redeem their reputation."

"Poor bastards."

"Yes. But I'm not sorry. My source – which is impeccable by the way – also informs me that the men of the fifth share their officers' annoyance at the slur upon their honour and are likely to give the gallant volunteers from the first, the fourth and the Light Division a good deal of lip when they get there. I'm only telling you so that you know to keep an eye on those gentlemen who are likely to respond to such lip with a punch in the face. We don't need fisticuffs in the trenches before you even get the order to attack."

Michael grinned. "Thanks for the warning, sir. I'll speak to them before they get there and make sure they know my views. And yours. Thank your impeccable source – also known as Captain Fenwick - for me, will you? What time did you get the poor bastard up this morning to do this reconnaissance?"

"I had nothing to do with it; he rode over there during the night of his own accord."

"Christ, no wonder he looked exhausted this morning."

Paul gave him a thoughtful look. "I was a little concerned you'd be tired yourself, but you look remarkably rested."

"Happiness will do that to you, sir. You should know."

"I do. Fight well, Captain. When you get back, my wife is arranging a dinner for your particular friends to celebrate your betrothal."

"Tell her to save it for the wedding breakfast."

179

Paul raised enquiring eyebrows and Michael smiled. "I rode over to Vera with Brat earlier, to see Father Xavier at San Esteban Church. I wanted to make my confession, it's been a while."

Paul could not help laughing, though he knew Michael was perfectly serious. "I see. Did your lady love also make confession?"

"Yes."

"I imagine after that, he's agreed to marry you the minute you're available."

"He more or less told me to just show up," Michael admitted with a grin.

"Nan and I want to be there, Michael."

"I'd like you to, sir, but we need to keep this very quiet. Nobody will care within the brigade, but I don't want you to get into trouble over my religious beliefs."

"If anybody asks me I will inform them that you agreed to a Catholic service for Brat's sake and the rest of it is none of their business. We'll be there and I believe Captain Fenwick has informed your lady that he's giving the bride away."

"He did. Thank you, Paul. You know how much it means to me."

"I do. You'd better go, Hunt is looking at his watch. Good luck, Michael."

Paul watched as the small contingent marched out in regimental order, with the Portuguese bringing up the rear. There was a knot of anxiety in his gut which he had tried hard to conceal from his friend. Michael had enough to do and did not need to go into battle carrying the weight of other men's fears. Brat had said her farewells back at the Casa and Paul approved her decision.

Paul watched the departing troops until they rounded a bend in the road and were out of sight behind a copse of trees. He was aware of something nagging at him, a faint instinct that something was wrong. It bothered him because he had experienced such feelings before and generally they were not without foundation. The troops were in perfect order and clearly ready for the fray. He had spoken to his men as a group and individually to those of them he knew well. They had his orders about their conduct and he had complete faith in Michael and the three other officers, including Lieutenant Ronaldo who commanded the small group of Portuguese from his brigade. There was nothing wrong, but still something chafed at the back of his mind.

He turned at the sound of footsteps and found General Alten approaching. He saluted and Alten returned the salute.

"I suspected I would find you here, General van Daan."

"I wasn't going to let him go without waving him off, sir."

"If you wish, you may accompany him further. Lord Wellington has given permission for some of the senior officers to ride over to watch the storming. I am going and have deputised General Kempt to command in my absence."

"What about Skerrett?"

"He will also remain in command of his brigade. Colonel Wheeler is a very able deputy."

Paul was tempted but something held him back. He thought about it then shook his head. "I don't think I will, sir. I think if you're away, I'd rather be at hand, just in case. And also, I think standing watching my men go over the breach without me would probably give me a heart attack. I'll be better off here."

Alten smiled. "I understand. I will send news when I have it. I was in search of Colonel Barnard to ask if he wished to accompany me but it appears he has ridden off on his own business. He was very disappointed at my refusal to allow him to lead the party, though I explained that the decision came from Lord Wellington. Perhaps he needed some time alone."

"Perhaps he's gone off to find a quiet roadside posada for a drink or two. It wouldn't be the first time. I'll ask his orderly if he knows and see if I can find him. I'm glad he couldn't go. He seems determined to earn a brigade command by behaving like a lunatic in every battle just now, I don't think..."

Paul stopped. He stared at his commander who looked back at him with a puzzled frown. Paul thought back to his conversation with Michael. One or two of the other Light Division senior officers had been out to watch their men depart but he had not seen Barnard and it suddenly occurred to him how strange that was. Andrew Barnard was an excellent and very popular officer, in part because of his good relationship with his men. Paul could think of no reason why he would not have been there to see them off, regardless of his own disappointment.

"He wasn't here," he breathed. "He wasn't here to wave off his men."

"As I said, he was chagrined not to be allowed..."

"That wouldn't matter a damn to Andrew Barnard. He'd have stood to attention and saluted them regardless of how he felt, though he might have gone off to get drunk afterwards."

Alten opened his mouth to speak again then closed it, studying Paul's face. Paul was trying to conjure up a picture of the men marching out, trying to work out the exact moment he had felt that niggling sense of disquiet and why he was suddenly sure it had something to do with Barnard.

Paul had an excellent visual memory and suspected that along with a good eye for terrain, it was what made him a successful battle commander. It was something he shared with Wellington who seemed to be able to remember the peculiar features of a landscape without effort when deciding how to place his troops. Paul closed his eyes, remembering the men of the 110th, 112th and 115th marching past him, saluting. Behind them had been the Portuguese and Lieutenant Ronaldo had given him a broad smile along with his salute. Ahead of them, the green jackets of the 95th made a striking contrast to the red coats of Paul's men. Many of the riflemen had saluted as well, although one tall figure wearing a battered shako had been looking in the opposite direction, away from Paul. He had been slightly out of step too, as though he was a new recruit or at least a man who did not regularly take part in drill practice. The reinforcements

181

had not yet arrived although they had landed and were marching down from Santander. The man must have been…

"Fucking hell!" Paul bellowed. Alten jumped violently.

"General?"

"Bloody Andrew Barnard is with them. He's gone without permission. Jenson, where's my horse? I'm going after him and I'm going to wring his fucking neck. This is getting absolutely ridiculous, he needs a full-time nursemaid and I don't have the time."

Alten was staring at him in complete bewilderment. "General, I do not understand. He could not have been there, I would have seen him."

"He was bloody there, sir. He was in the ranks with a borrowed rifle and the nastiest looking hat I've seen in a long time."

"Are you telling me he disguised himself?" Alten sounded astonished.

"Yes. I can't believe I didn't realise what I was seeing. Jenson, where the hell are you with my horse?"

"I'm coming, sir. You told me to water them and rub them down. I'm not a bleeding miracle worker; I'm going as fast as I can."

Alten gave the limping orderly a wide-eyed stare at the tone of his voice but Paul went forward immediately to take Rufus' bridle.

"I'm sorry, Jenson. I'm in a bit of a temper."

"I would never have known that, sir. Where are we going?"

"You can take Felix back to the house. I'm riding after the volunteers to kick Colonel Barnard's arse for him. It won't take long, he's on foot. I'll see you back…"

"There is no need, General van Daan, unless you have changed your mind about accompanying me to watch the storming," Alten said gently but firmly. "I am about to set off and will easily overtake them. I will remove Colonel Barnard and ensure that he remains well away from the action and I will speak to him privately about his rash conduct. I will also ensure that Major-General Kempt is made aware of it."

Paul was silent for a moment. He was longing for a legitimate target for his anger but he knew that Alten was right. "You'd rather I didn't rip his head off in front of two hundred men about to go into battle, sir?"

"I think it is probably best."

"I think you're right," Paul said regretfully. "It's not my job, he's not even in my brigade. Thank God, because I'd kill him. I'm angry enough about Captain O'Reilly, but at least he has a reason. Would you mention to Barnard, though, in the middle of your quiet and reasoned reprimand that he's lucky you were here? If I'd caught up with him I'd have shoved that borrowed rifle right up his Irish arse."

"I will be sure to explain his good fortune, General. My best wishes to your very lovely wife."

***

182

After fifteen minutes in the trenches outside San Sebastian, Michael was grateful for his commander's warning about the unhappiness of the Fifth Division. He marched his men into position and settled them down in their bivouac, which was effectively a muddy hole. It was clear from the expressions and grumbling discontent of those men of Robinson's brigade who were closest to him, that the Fifth Division were deeply resentful of the inclusion of the volunteers. Being unable to complain to Lord Wellington they were going to take it out on the newcomers.

Hunt's men had marched initially to Lesaca where they spent a relatively comfortable night in tents. The officers were invited to dine with some of the headquarters staff and Michael was surprised and ridiculously pleased when Lord Wellington appeared and hauled him off, along with Lieutenant-Colonel Hunt, to inspect the rapidly growing puppies. Michael did not know Hunt particularly well, though he knew Paul was friendly with him. He was a cheerful red-head in his early thirties who did not seem overawed by his unexpected invitation from the Commander-in-Chief and talked readily about dogs, hunting and his wife and young children back in England.

From Lesaca, the volunteers marched on to Oyarzun where they once again set up camp. Sir Thomas Graham invited the commanding officers of the various volunteer contingents to dine with him and Michael enjoyed his meal and reflected that there were some distinct advantages to seniority which he had not really experienced before now. He knew that this elevation was very temporary but he decided that he could get used to it, though he felt a pang of sympathy for the subalterns and men huddled in their tents listening to the rain fall.

At midnight they were marched on to an assembly point in a convent at the edge of the lines to await final orders. Michael managed to get some sleep but was awoken after only a few hours with orders to take the men into the trenches in a reserve position.

It was still raining. Michael gave orders to the men to eat their rations before they became too waterlogged and hoped the deluge would dampen the enthusiasm of the Fifth. It did not. If anything, their increased discomfort made Robinson's men more imaginative in their taunts and some of Michael's men were clearly feeling the strain. Sergeant Coates of the 110th was visibly gritting his teeth and one or two of the men were muttering insults under their breath. They were getting louder and Michael sighed, pulled himself out of the mud and squelched along the trench.

"Smithy, are you under the impression you're whispering? Because if you are, you've gone bloody deaf. I can hear you from down there and if the fellow with the bald head hears what you just called him he's going to be climbing over here for a boxing match."

"That's all right, Captain. I need something to do."

"You've got something to do and it's not baiting the men of the fifth into a brawl. Settle down and try to get some sleep, we've a bit of a town to

183

storm in a few hours. If you get into a fight with those arseholes I'm going to drown you in the outer works, they must be filling up nicely."

"If this rain keeps up you won't need to, sir, we're all going to drown right here," Sergeant Barforth said morosely. "I keep telling them to pipe down and ignore it, but it's not bloody easy, the things they're saying."

"They think the honour of their division has been impugned by our presence, Sergeant. They'll forget about it once they're in a fight."

"If that bastard with the red hair says one more thing about my wife, he's going to be in a fight sooner than he thinks, sir," Sergeant Bowlby said grimly. Michael turned to look at him in surprise. The Sergeant's expression suggested that further intervention was going to be needed.

Wearily he hauled himself to the top of the ditch. There was an unpleasant squelching sound as the muddy trench reluctantly released him. He trudged forward, scrambling over the top of one trench and dropping down quickly into the one in front. In this weather there was no danger from French musketry even if any were within range but he kept low instinctively.

Up close he could see that the group of men from Robinson's brigade sported the white facings of the 47th Foot. Michael made his way past them, taking care to either tread on them or splash mud over them as much as possible. They grumbled quietly but could not complain openly to an officer.

He reached a small group of officers huddled in blankets, passing a bottle between them. They looked chilled and miserable and Michael greeted them amiably enough and exchanged pleasantries about the dreadful weather and the miseries of siege warfare. They replied civilly but it was quickly clear that they shared their men's resentment. Nobody offered him a drink.

With his social obligations out of the way, Michael looked over the bedraggled lines. "It's going to feel like a long night in this."

"It's more like morning already," the Captain agreed. "I've been wishing they'd ordered a night attack but they can't do it with the tides being so essential. Did you volunteer, Captain?"

"Yes, we all did. Two hundred of us from the Light Division."

"Going to show our men how it's done?" one of the lieutenants said with a hint of sarcasm. Michael regarded him tolerantly and decided not to take the bait.

"Not if we're being used in support, which we apparently are," he said mildly. "To be honest I'm glad of it. That breach looks like the camp rubbish heap the day we march out and I'm not sure I liked what I saw of the defences behind it. We're all going to lose a lot of men, Lieutenant."

"We lost a lot of men last time," the Captain said.

"That being so, I'd hate the losses to start early because your men can't keep their mouths shut. I'm doing my best to keep it calm, but they're all on a short fuse today. I'd appreciate a bit of help. Can you tell your men to stop shouting insults over the trenches at the volunteers and start yelling them at the French if they're bored."

"Sensitive fellows are they?" the Captain said. He did not seem particularly concerned.

"As I said, they're on a short fuse. And so am I. If I have to step in to stop a brawl because you can't control your troops, Captain, two things are going to happen. The first is that I'll countermand my orders to show restraint and tell them they can kick the shit out of any man of the Fifth that looks at them the wrong way. It shouldn't take long, our lot are well-rested, well-fed and better trained than any of yours. The second is that I'll be taking the names of the ringleaders which Major-General van Daan has assured me will be passed directly on to Major-General Leith with a recommendation they be court-martialled for being drunk on duty. The charges will stick. Nobody in their right minds are going to believe that a sober man would think it a good idea to start a fight with the 110th hours before a major assault because their feelings are hurt. Of course they're fucking drunk." Michael looked pointedly at the bottle in the young Ensign's hand. "While I'm about it, I'll add your names to the list. Leith would like that, I'm sure."

"I'm not bloody drunk," the Captain spluttered indignantly.

"Good. Then you'll be sensible enough to recognise that I'm deadly serious. If you won't discipline your men, I fucking will and you along with them. Good morning, gentlemen."

Michael turned away and did not look back as he slithered through the mud back to his own place in the trench. He did not need to. He could hear the Captain giving orders to his juniors to speak to the men, uttering dire threats of retribution if the taunting did not cease.

Back in his muddy refuge he settled down again, wondering if there was any chance of getting more sleep. A voice reached him through the darkness.

"Everything all right, sir? They've gone awful quiet."

"Yes thank you, Sergeant Coates. I think they've decided to go to sleep."

"Good idea, sir. Give the drunken twats the chance to sleep it off before they have to fight. Fancy a drink?"

Michael took the brandy bottle, trying not to laugh too loudly. He took a swig and passed it back along the line.

"Very funny, Coates. Now go to fucking sleep."

***

It was foggy the following morning with an eerie mist obscuring the river, the sea and parts of the town from view. The rain had finally stopped in the early hours and Michael had slept a little, though he was cold and damp and seemed to ache right into his bones.

He awoke to discover that Paul had sent his bandsmen with a supply wagon to the back of the lines and as soon as there was enough light for them to see where they were going, Michael saw them making their way forward with covered camp kettles of hot black tea. The men crowded around, filling tin cups and accepting hard tack biscuits with as much delight as if they had been offered a feast. Michael took his own cup and stood watching. He realised that the 110th bandsmen had brewed enough tea for the rest of the Light Division volunteers as well. It was a typical Van Daan gesture which cost nothing but some time and effort but made a huge difference to the men's morale.

Lieutenant-Colonel Hunt joined him as he surveyed the breach, his hands wrapped around a tin cup. "Three rousing cheers for your General, O'Reilly. He's saved my life this morning. If Lord Wellington hears about this, he'll go straight up the wall, coddling the troops like this. How does he get away with it?"

"Mostly his Lordship pretends not to notice," Michael said with a grin. "If it's brought to his attention he'll shout a bit and then Mrs van Daan will step in with an apology, claiming that it was all her idea. Women are allowed to be soft, so he'll pat her hand indulgently and forgive her, pretending to forget that he's speaking to a woman who can amputate a limb faster than a junior surgeon. It's a convenient fiction which prevents Wellington from feeling too lenient and often saves General van Daan from getting cashiered."

Hunt almost choked on his tea. "Is any of that true?"

"It's all true, sir, I've seen it working for years. I'm told that we're to be used as a screen of skirmishers. Is that right?"

Hunt grunted, handing his cup back to Drummer Edwards who had come to collect it. "Bloody stupid idea. Leith don't want his precious division to feel slighted so they'll go over first. He's leaving the First and the Fourth Division volunteers in reserve and he wants me to take our men along with two hundred German light infantry to the front trenches to try and provide a screen of fire to protect the stormers."

Michael surveyed the looming bulk of San Sebastian where the width of the breach was becoming more visible through the mist. "With four hundred men? That's ridiculous, we'll be spread too thin. And they have far too much cover, we'll barely be able to touch them. What on earth's the point?"

"Not sure there is a point, old boy. I kicked up a rare dust to get myself this duty. They wanted to give it to that glory hunter Napier, but I asserted my seniority and won the day. I'm beginning to wish I'd stayed where I was and let him do it." Hunt shot him a glance. "Why did you do it, O'Reilly?"

Michael kept his eyes on the town. "You can probably work it out, sir. I'm sure the whole Light Division knows my history."

"Very few of the Light Division give a damn about your history, Captain. My Colonel would kill for an officer of your experience. The trouble is that with the length of service rules, he wouldn't be allowed to take you over some pink-cheeked boy who's never been out of England but who joined up as a bloody child. I'm sorry you're in this position, it's ridiculous."

"It's all right, sir. I've come further than I'd any right to expect thanks to the sheer bloody-mindedness of General van Daan. But my personal circumstances are set to change and I want advancement. I'm not naïve enough to think they'll pin a major's insignia on my arm for one battle, but I know that the more I'm seen the better chance I'll have of a one-off promotion. They do happen."

"Getting married, are you?"

"Yes, sir."

"Is she back in Ireland?"

"No, she's a few miles away chewing on her finger nails in case I get myself killed. She's a young Spanish woman attached to the Van Daans' household. We met in Madrid last year."

"Did you, by God? Good to know something positive came out of that. I wish you happiness, Captain. Don't get yourself killed. Though it sounds as though that's very unlikely given that we're doing nothing more interesting than shooting at walls."

Michael ran his eyes over the wide breach. The mist was lifting further with every passing minute. He heard a bugle call, followed by another.

"I wouldn't be so sure of that, sir. I think Leith might find he needs all the men he's got to storm this bloody place."

"Well let's hope if he wants our men, we can still find them if he's got them strung out along this front line," Hunt said grimly. "Come on, Captain. Morning tea is over."

The French garrison under General Rey had apparently lacked artillery from the beginning of the siege and much of his stock had been damaged or destroyed by the relentless bombardment. Intelligence suggested he intended to rely on mines and muskets to defend the town but it was clear from even a brief observation of French activity in the breach that he was actually depending on the sheer drop at the back of the breach to keep Leith's men at bay.

Even during these final hours before the attack, Rey did not allow his garrison to rest from their unending struggle to keep the breach clear. The pounding of artillery toppled rubble and other debris inwards from the breach. As quickly as it fell, the French removed it, risking their lives to maintain that lethal descent. Michael watched them through his telescope as he waited for the final orders. Like ants, they scrambled over the fallen masonry, forming chains to keep the back of the breach clear. Graham's mortar batteries continued to fire bombs into the space between the old ramparts and the new stone wall which Rey had built as a second line of defence and Michael shuddered to imagine what it must be like for those work parties, labouring to remove the debris as quickly as it fell. He had seen men carried out, covered in blood. It was impossible to tell if they were dead or alive but he knew Rey would have them removed anyway. A dead man could be used as a ladder as well as a chunk of stone and Michael had seen them piled high in the breach at Ciudad Rodrigo for their comrades to clamber over.

Once Leith's men climbed the breach there were only two ways into the town which avoided the sheer drop. One was against the Amezqueta Tower at the north end and the other was a narrow opening in the curtain wall to the south. It was possible to see that the French had blocked the gap so that it was only wide enough for one man. The breach was wholly exposed to fire from both directions as well as from the eastern side of the hornwork defences which had not been demolished.

There were loopholes along the new stone wall behind the breach. Michael could not see if they were occupied by muskets or small artillery but he could imagine the carnage they were going to cause among men trying to find a way through. He had no idea about the positioning of mines and was thankful that, at the start of the assault at least, that would not be his problem.

The storming was to be led by Robinson's brigade. Spry's Portuguese and Hay's depleted brigade would initially be left in reserve along with the remainder of the volunteers. Hunt took command of his small band of light troops, including a contingent of both German and Portuguese borrowed from other brigades, and made his way along the front trenches with Michael as the storming parties formed up, trying to decide the best positions to make them count. It was a disheartening task, given that the French were well concealed behind their defences, but there were a few areas where the enemy would probably find themselves exposed as they attempted to fire.

Michael's men were spread out along the front, facing the hornwork, a fortification with two pointed demi-bastions which gave extra protection to the southern end of the town. Of the British light infantry regiments present, the green-jacketed 95th were all equipped with rifles, which were slower to load but more accurate than the standard-issue muskets. Over the years of the war rifles had been issued to many of the Portuguese and King's German Legion and more recently to some of the light companies of other regiments.

Paul had acquired rifles for the 110th light company as far back as 1809 and had gradually managed to introduce them to the rest of the regiment in the teeth of official opposition. Michael suspected he had simply purchased them and waited for the noise to die down. It was often his way of instituting reforms. It meant that most of the men under Michael's command today carried a weapon that they could at least aim properly.

Hunt had placed his riflemen at intervals along the front trench with his muskets further to the south to link up with the rest of the volunteer skirmishers under Michael. They made a thin line, with both contingents of muskets grouped together in the centre so that they could direct volleys onto any Frenchman within reach. Michael could hear the men grumbling as they settled to wait for the order to fire. He was not surprised. None of them had volunteered for this to be told to remain at a safe distance and shoot at shadows.

The mist cleared fully at around eight o'clock to reveal a dark sky filled with heavy clouds. It was very hot with the uncomfortable threat of a looming storm. As soon as the town was fully visible the Allied batteries opened up. They kept up a thundering bombardment of the defences throughout the early part of the morning. Michael watched the various storming parties forming up and tried not to think about what might happen to these men over the next few hours. He had not taken part in the storming of Badajoz, having been wounded in the trenches before the attack, but he remembered the horror of Ciudad Rodrigo very well. The young lieutenant in command of the Forlorn Hope was standing with his men, talking and laughing and Michael did not think he was much older than twenty. He wanted to walk over there and tell the boy to stand down, that he did not need to die today. Suddenly he was furious with the unknown officer, furious with himself and furious with the dreams of honour and glory that made men sacrifice their lives in a hopeless cause. Still he knew that somebody must be first over the breach. He was just grateful it was not going to be him.

Michael dropped back down into the trench, splashing into a muddy puddle which had not yet dried after the night's rain. He reached into his jacket for his pocket watch, wishing time would move faster. He hated this waiting.

"You've got another three-quarters of an hour, Captain. They're advancing at eleven to catch the low tide. Some of the Portuguese are going in that way."

Michael jumped and whirled around. The fair-haired man in a shabby red coat had slid noiselessly into the ditch behind him.

"Fenwick, what the bloody hell are you doing down here? Did I see your name on the list of volunteers?"

"Don't be an idiot, Michael, do I look like a man who would volunteer for a fuck-up like this?"

"You were at Castro Urdiales."

"That was an accident."

"How do you know this is going to be a fuck-up?" Michael enquired.

"Because sieges always are."

"Be specific, Giles."

"I am here to be specific. I've just come from a conversation with Sir Thomas Graham, Sir Richard Fletcher and Sir James Leith where I was so specific that they're going to complain about me as soon as they manage to work out whether I'm working for Lord Wellington or General van Daan this week."

"Who are you working for this week?"

"I'm operating as a private individual at present but none of them need to know that. The General will cover for me anyway. Listen to me, Michael, because we don't have much time. Do not take your men over that breach."

Michael stared at him owlishly. "Giles, that's exactly what I came here to do. As it happens, it's looking unlikely. They want the glory to go to Leith's men so we're stuck down here acting as sharpshooters."

"Bloody good thing too, but that's not going to last. That breach is fucking useless. There's a sheer drop on the other side of it and they've got their last pieces of working artillery trained on it as well as every musket they can find. Anybody going up there is going to get either shot down, blown to pieces or fall over the edge and break his bloody neck."

Michael thought of the young officer and forced his mind away from it and back to his friend's words. "I'm pretty sure they know all this, Giles."

"So they tell me. I don't think they have a fucking clue how good those inner defences are. They're not getting over that breach in these conditions and I don't think they should try but they've made it clear that the decision has been made. I've just been over to the Portuguese and spoken to Major Snodgrass and it turns out their officers also did a little illicit reconnaissance last night and have come to a similar conclusion. Where's Hunt?"

"Over there."

Giles slithered along the back of the trench to find the Colonel and returned with him in tow. Hunt looked slightly bewildered but did not argue, merely bent over the rough sketch Giles had pulled out of his pocket.

"They're going to send you in at some point. They don't have enough troops here, it's a bloody disgrace. Though rumour has it that Wellington might be fighting on two fronts again, a message just came in that Soult is on the move."

"Oh fuck," Michael breathed.

"Don't worry about it, Michael. The General is up there and he is not sitting on his arse doing nothing. Concentrate on this. The only way through is to get around their inner curtain wall; you'll be dead if you try to go over it. They've got both ends covered but they're going to lose men and I'm hoping once they start firing those bastard guns, our artillery will be able to take them out. If they send you in, you need to make for here."

He pointed to an area under the northern tower. Michael studied it and saw a heavily marked square. "What is it?"

"A house. At least, the remains of a house. They pulled down all the houses along that row when they were building that bloody wall to make sure there was no cover for our men and nothing to help them scale the wall. But for some reason they didn't finish the job down here. It's half ruined and frankly a hazard in its own right, it looks as though it could come down in a strong breeze. But it's there and if you can get to it, you can get down the other side and hit those bastards on the wall from behind."

Hunt leaned over the map. "Is it defended?"

"There are only a few sentries and I suspect they'll quickly be called onto the main breach because that's where the attack is coming from. Even if they've worked out the weakness, they'll assume we don't know it's there."

"How do we know it's there?" Hunt asked.

"Because I was up there."

Hunt swivelled an appalled gaze onto Giles. "You climbed up there? How? Why? Did you have authorisation? Who ordered…?"

"Don't ask him, sir," Michael broke in hastily. "He's an intelligence officer, it's what he does. You won't get a straight answer out of him anyway."

Hunt glowered at him. "And I'm supposed to take his word…"

"Yes," Michael said with finality. "The only problem might be that we're ordered to the opposite end of the breach."

"Get lost in the chaos," Giles said flatly. "It happens all the time in sieges. Remember Badajoz?"

"I wasn't there. And nor were you, now that I think of it, you were scaring the shit out of Antonio around Salamanca at the time."

"I've heard enough accounts." Giles cocked his head at the sound of a bugle. "They're forming up for the first assault. Keep your men around the northern tower as far as possible. When you're ordered in it will be natural to send you that way."

"And how are we going to find our way, Captain?" Hunt said snappily.

Giles regarded him with a kindly eye. "I thought I might stick around and come with you," he said.

Michael swore furiously. "You bloody well won't, Fenwick. You've done your job. Thank you. But you're not one of the volunteers. Over on the slopes of Monte Olia there's a lovely spot for watching the action. Get yourself over there. That's an order."

"You can't order me anywhere, Michael, we've already established that. Colonel Hunt could, but I'm hoping he won't. I was over at Monte Olia earlier on, it's quite a sight. Some of the officers have ridden over from the Bastan with a day's holiday to see the spectacle. There are some navy men and some new recruits just landed at Pasajes. And then we have a few hundred locals all in their Sunday best. They've come in from Pasajes, Renteria, Oyarzun, and Hernani. There are these big stone slabs down the hillside which are like seats at an open air theatre. Some of the ladies were passing around sugar drops. Colonel Hunt can give me any order he likes, I am not going over there to sit and watch the French slaughtering more of my friends if there's anything I can do to prevent it."

There was a long difficult silence. Michael could not decide whether he wanted to hit his friend or embrace him but he did neither. Hunt looked momentarily bewildered and Michael did not blame him. It was difficult for an officer not accustomed to Fenwick's equivocal position in the army to know where he fitted into the chain of command.

"You can order him to leave, sir, if you want to," Michael said finally. "I can't, he outranks me by date of commission."

"Would you, if you could?"

"No," Michael said. "He won't go anyway, there'd be no point. He'll just drift out of sight and reappear when he's needed and there's no longer any way of getting rid of him. Besides which, he's bloody useful in a fight and he might just get us in there if this is going wrong."

"Even if he does, what are we going to do with so few men?"

"I never know that until it's happening, sir."

Unexpectedly, Hunt grinned. "Good point, O'Reilly. You can stay, Captain Fenwick. But for the purposes of this action, you are under Captain O'Reilly's command, is that clear?"

"Yes, sir. Thank you."

Michael watched as Hunt walked back towards the rest of his men. "You're not going to be thanking him in an hour, Giles."

Giles had his watch in his hand. "Ten minutes, actually," he said in neutral tones. "Where do you want me?"

Chapter Thirteen

It was a few minutes before eleven when the Forlorn Hope scrambled up out of the trenches and charged forward towards the breach. Giles watched them go with a heavy heart. The young lieutenant led about twenty men from the 4th Infantry straight towards the centre. It seemed oddly quiet without the deafening artillery of the past few hours, though there was still a lively crackling of muskets from both sides, along with the occasional distinctive sound of a rifle.

The young lieutenant was wearing an old-fashioned hat with a feather instead of the regulation shako. Giles wondered where on earth he had found it and why he thought it was a good idea. As he ran he snatched it from his head and waved it to urge on his men. He was faster than they and reached the foot of the breach several yards ahead of them. As he began to climb there was a crash of muskets. Giles saw his body jerk violently, hit several times. He tumbled backwards and lay sprawled across the foot of the rubble. His men surged past and over him as if he was not there. Giles closed his eyes for a moment, not wanting to look. Beside him he heard Michael murmuring what sounded like the words of a prayer, presumably for the dead man's soul.

An explosion ripped through the air as one of the French mines went up, but it was further back and did no damage to the stormers and supporting troops who were climbing the breach. Above them, the apparently deserted curtain wall was suddenly swarming with defenders as the French scrambled to their allotted posts. Michael whirled around, bellowing orders to his sharp shooters and Giles watched him, making no attempt to intervene. Hunt had not needed to tell him to follow the Irishman's orders in a battle. Giles had served with him at Castro Urdiales and knew how good he was.

The French troops manning the wall waited in their loopholes as the first men of Robinson's brigade reached the crest of the breach. It was difficult to climb, consisting mainly of huge blocks of stone with very little filling of small rubble in between. The lead columns made it to the top and then stopped abruptly. Giles thought they almost seemed to rock back on their heels and he knew why. The stormers were faced with a sheer drop on the other side and had no way of crossing it and climbing up the facing wall.

192

They were given no time to consider what to do next. The muskets fired and the front ranks of Robinson's men were cut down. Some fell forward into the gap between the breach and the wall while others went backwards, tumbling down the breach to lie like broken dolls over the great chunks of stone.

Around Giles, the Light Division volunteers fired intermittently at any Frenchman they could see. Several of the near gunners were shot down and others appeared to take their place. The far guns were well out of range. Michael was moving between his men, encouraging them. Giles thought it was probably more to give himself something to do than because he thought they needed his orders. What they needed was action. Helpless anger was written across every countenance as they watched the Fifth Division being shot down.

Officer after officer led more men up the breach and ran into the same merciless wall of fire with no way to pass over the drop. It was like watching some kind of mass suicide though Giles, with silent fury, would have called it murder. He thanked God his commanding officer had not elected to join the spectators on the mountain slopes. He had a sudden vivid picture of Paul sliding down the mountainside in search of Graham, Leith or Robinson and a further vision of what he was likely to do when he found them. Whatever was happening back in Vera with Marshal Soult's attack, Giles was glad Paul was there and not here.

The air was thick with smoke now and Giles could feel the acrid taste of it at the back of his throat. He coughed, which made it even worse and he had to stand still for a moment, choking. A hand grasped his and shoved a water bottle into it. Giles drank gratefully and stood for a moment, catching his breath.

"Thanks, Michael," he croaked finally.

"You're welcome. Don't you dare expire, I have enough to do."

"I don't have anything useful to do here. Do you mind if I run over to the headquarters staff? I'd like to find out what's going on and they might need a messenger."

"Be my guest. You're not really under my command, Fenwick."

Giles gave a crooked smile. "I am if you need me, Michael."

He threaded his way back through the trenches, among men waiting for the order to advance. They were pale-faced and sweating in the morning heat. Giles saw white knuckles clutching hard on weapons. All eyes were raised to the breach where men continued to scramble upwards. Another French volley blew the next row apart. Guns from either side blasted canister shot down onto those still climbing. Giles looked away, unable to bear it.

He found General Sir James Leith on the beach outside the sea-wall opposite the advanced trench. He was accompanied by General Oswald whom he had recently replaced in command and by Wellington's chief engineer, Sir Richard Fletcher. Leith was giving orders to a staff member to bring forward new troops from the approaches while Fletcher and Oswald had their heads bent over a plan of the town. Fletcher looked up and saw Giles. He nodded to him and gave a faint acknowledging smile then looked back at the map.

"The Portuguese are on their way with orders to attack the smaller breach here."

"Did they lose many in the crossing?" Leith said, moving to join the two men. They were all shouting to make themselves heard over the deafening cacophony of gunfire.

"A fair few were cut down by grape shot, but they're over. It was deeper than we anticipated, they were up to their knees in water, trying to manage quick time while wading."

"They did bloody well but they still have to get over that breach and the French have got their guns trained on it."

"It's narrow as well, there's no way to take it in a rush" Fletcher said. "I've sent Lieutenant Gathin, one of my acting engineers, to lead in the Portuguese but we're going to need to find a way to silence those guns. They don't have many but they're well aimed. Captain Fenwick, do you have a message?"

"No, sir. To be honest, I was wondering if Sir James might find a use for me as messenger. I'm not needed anywhere else and I can't stand to join the spectators."

Leith gave a grim smile. "As long as you refrain from trying to tell me my job, Fenwick, you can remain. The rest of my staff are already running around the field, you could be useful. I..."

There was a crackle of musket fire which sounded alarmingly close. It was drowned out immediately by the deafening crash of a volley from the top of the breach but Giles was startled to see stone chips fly off a large rock less than three feet away from him. He realised that some French muskets had found the range to the beach and he spun around instinctively looking for cover. There was a pile of rubble, presumably from the original town walls. He swung back to the commanders.

"Sir, get behind here..."

Leith and Oswald were both on their knees in the sand and for a moment Giles thought that Oswald was hit. Then he realised the blood on his hands came from Fletcher who lay very still. Oswald looked up and his expression was distraught.

"He's dead. I think he's dead."

Giles ran forward, forgetting about the danger of being shot down. He dropped to his knees beside Fletcher but he knew already that there was nothing he could do. The engineer had been shot directly through the neck and the damage was appalling. Giles suspected the ball had smashed his spine and he would have died in an instant.

Nobody spoke for a long time. The shocked silence was broken as more bullets struck the ground beside them, throwing up sand and water into their faces. Giles scrambled to his feet and reached out a hand to help Oswald, who had been wounded during the previous assault and moved awkwardly. They scrambled quickly to a more sheltered position behind the ruined stonework.

194

"Fenwick, get yourself up to the back and bring a stretcher party down to take Sir Richard's body to the rear," Leith said. His voice was strained and Giles could see that he was trying to bring himself under control. He felt a fierce admiration for Leith's contained manner. Fletcher had been a well-respected and talented officer, much valued by Lord Wellington. He was also a close personal friend of Paul van Daan and Giles dreaded having to tell his commanding officer about his death.

He took off at a run to the back of the trenches and accompanied the stretcher back to the beach then helped the men lift Fletcher's body carefully onto it. There was nothing to cover him with. Giles walked beside the stretcher back up to the rear of the lines where the surgeons had set up a series of tents and were treating the wounded as they were brought out. There were already too many of them, lying scattered over the ground waiting their turn. Giles made enquiries and was directed to take Sir Richard's body to a sheltered area at the end of the furthest earth works where several other bodies were neatly laid out.

To his relief, a servant came forward with a sheet and showed them where to lay Sir Richard. The body was carefully wrapped in the makeshift shroud. The other bodies were also covered with bloodstained sheets. Giles stood looking down at them, wondering if these were all officers or simply men valued enough by their comrades to warrant careful treatment. At the end of the line the shroud was topped by a battered old-fashioned hat with a broken feather. There was blood on the hat.

"Lieutenant Maguire, sir," the servant said, following his gaze. "Led the Forlorn Hope but never made it to the top. Twenty-one today, he was. Brave lad."

"Brave?" Giles echoed. His voice sounded hollow and curiously detached. "Yes, I suppose he was. I wonder if that will be a comfort to his family."

The man stared at him blankly. Giles wondered if he had just accidentally spoken in Spanish. He had done so occasionally in the past when making the switch between his work as an intelligence officer and a return to normal life but since going back to the 110th to command a company earlier in the year he thought he had stopped doing it. The man made no further enquiries and Giles was not sure so he nodded and returned to the beach to find Sir James Leith reading a note from Sir Thomas Graham who was currently over with the batteries on the Chofre sand dunes. There was no sign of Oswald.

Leith looked up at his approach. "There you are. General Oswald has just been taken up to the surgeon's tents: he's been hit in the face. Not sure if it's shot or flying debris."

"You're injured yourself, sir," Giles said quietly. Leith touched a bloody gash across his forehead.

"This? It's nothing, just a piece of stone. I'm told Robinson is down, I don't know how bad he is. And my ADC was wounded bringing this message. I need you to take a reply to Sir Thomas at the Chofre batteries."

"Yes, sir."

"Don't get yourself killed for God's sake, I'm running out of officers."

Giles took the scribbled note, saluted and turned to survey the route he must take. Behind him he heard Leith calling out orders to bring the next contingent of reserves forward for the attack. Giles wondered if Hunt's men would be among them. He thought of Michael beginning the dangerous scramble up the breach and tried to force his mind away from the picture. It would not improve the odds if he took himself back down to join the attack.

Instead he set off at a run towards the river, following the line recently taken by the Portuguese troops in reverse. It was horribly easy to follow the route because a scattering of dead and wounded men showed him the way. By now the Portuguese had entered the bloody fray at the lesser breach. They would have been under fire from the town the entire way but they had not faltered. Giles splashed into the river, gasping at the cold, trying not to look too closely at the men who had not made it. The water lapping onto the sandy bank was faintly pink.

Giles felt very exposed with his back to the town as he waded across towards the breaching batteries. The air was thick with smoke and he moved carefully, trying not to flinch at the crackle of muskets from the defenders and the crash of the Allied guns. He knew that his sense of vulnerability was wholly illusory; the French had plenty of targets climbing the breaches or racing out of the trenches across the beach. They were unlikely to start shooting at a solitary man crossing the river in the wrong direction, even if they could see him through the gun smoke. Nevertheless the itch between his shoulder blades did not disappear until he was out of the water and running up to the first gun crew shouting enquiries about the whereabouts of Sir Thomas Graham.

Sir Thomas was in conference with several artillery officers who seemed to be arguing passionately about something. Giles moved to where he could be seen and then waited, listening. He realised with some astonishment that the discussion appeared to be about turning the guns directly onto the breach and the hornwork.

Graham caught sight of him and held up a hand, stilling the artillery officer. "Fenwick, is that for me?"

"Yes, sir. From Sir James Leith."

Giles handed over the note and stood waiting. Graham unfolded it and read quickly. He did not move or speak for a long moment and Giles had to remind himself to breathe. He could sense the other man's struggle to make a decision. Graham looked terrible. His face was black with smoke like all of them and streaked with sweat. Both his eyes were bloodshot and the left one seemed to be permanently weeping. Giles knew that the General had been forced to go home the previous year because of a serious eye infection which had threatened his sight. He had apparently made a good recovery but Giles suspected that battlefield conditions had caused the symptoms to return. It looked so sore that he found himself blinking in sympathy.

Graham turned back to the artillery officers abruptly. "Colonel Dickson, Sir James Leith reports that while he will continue to feed reinforcements from the trenches into the breaches there has been little success. Those men who reach the summit are slaughtered where they stand. We are losing too many. He has ordered the volunteers from other divisions to take their turn in the assault but we need to do something more, before the tide makes further assaults impossible."

"You have my recommendation, sir."

Graham hesitated for a moment longer then gave an abrupt nod. "Very well. Give the orders. All batteries to be redeployed from their current fire on the enemy guns on Castle Hill. As soon as the guns are in place, they are to open fire on on the high curtain, over the heads of our men."

Giles swore. He had not realised he had said the words aloud until both Graham and Dickson turned to stare at him in utter astonishment. Giles thought irrelevantly that neither of them would have looked that surprised if it had been Major-General van Daan standing here.

"I beg your pardon, Captain?"

"My apologies, Sir Thomas, I was just shocked. I mean surely that's impossible."

"I think you forget yourself, Captain," Graham said, but Giles thought he detected sympathy in the rebuke. "I have given the order."

He turned away to speak to some of the other officers. Dickson bellowed an order and the gun crews scrambled into a flurry of movement as though they had been awaiting his word. Giles stood staring at them, frozen with horror.

"Are you all right, Fenwick?" Dickson sounded genuinely concerned.

"No, I'm bloody not," Giles said furiously. He knew that his manner was not appropriate to Dickson's rank but he could not help himself. "Has he gone mad?"

"It's not as much of a risk as it sounds, Captain. We've got the exact range, we've been blowing the place apart for days. And currently our men aren't getting to the top at all. Look at them, they've been pinned down on the slope and they're lying there waiting to be picked off by those bloody muskets. They can't move without getting their heads blown off, they've lost at least half of their officers and the remaining half can't get the men to follow them to the top. Once we clear those ramparts they'll be able to find a way in at either end of the curtain wall. Unless something changes they're in no danger."

Giles stared up at the breach. Dickson was right; the assault had completely stalled and men were lying flat over the slope. The only movement came from a group of men who had formed up at the foot of the breach.

"Something did just change," he said. "Leith has just ordered in the fucking Light Division. I'm going over there."

He began to run. Behind him he heard Dickson's voice yelling at him to come back but he ignored it. Later today or tomorrow, if he survived the next few hours, he might find himself in trouble for failing to obey a senior officer. As he splashed into the river and back up the beach on the other side, Giles decided that was a problem for another day.

***

As Colonel Hunt had predicted, the men of the Light Division were scattered through the advanced trench when the order came to lead them onto the breach. Hunt found Michael with a dozen men who were successfully pinning down a group of infuriated French musket men close to the northern tower.

Michael had appropriated a rifle from one of the 95th who had gone down with a ball through his shoulder. The rifleman had protested loudly at the theft of his weapon but Michael ignored him. He felt considerably better now that he could shoot somebody and in this chaos there was nobody to point out that officers did not carry rifles although Hunt's expression suggested that he might have something to say in different circumstances.

"We've orders to lead the next advance, Captain. To show them the way, I'm told."

Michael looked around him. "Are they being bloody funny, sir? They know the fucking way, they just can't get there without getting their fucking heads blown off."

"Very eloquently put, Captain," Hunt said dryly. His face was pale under its coating of black powder. Michael suspected he did not look much better himself. "I've distributed what ammunition I have and asked for more. How are you supplied?"

"Well enough sir. Will we go with the men we have?"

"I'll lead them on. See if you can round up a few more and follow us up as quickly as you can."

"Yes, sir."

Michael watched, feeling slightly sick as Hunt led his party forward to the foot of the breach. As they began to climb, they had to detour around men already lying flat over the stones. On seeing the Light Division men climbing upwards one or two of the men scrambled up to follow them but most remained where they were. Michael did not blame them. He wondered briefly what would happen if his search for the rest of his men proved fruitless, or at least if he pretended it had. Could he save their lives by simply failing to lead them in or would they be scooped up by some other troops ordered into the breach afterwards? It did not really matter. He owed it to Hunt to take in what support he could find and he did not have it in him to fail in his duty.

He raced along the trenches, now very bare of men, calling his NCOs by name. Lieutenant Ronaldo came to meet him with his small contingent of caçadores and behind him was Sergeant Coates with twenty men from the third brigade along with four from the 43rd who seemed to have become separated from their fellows. By the time he joined up with Lieutenant Jackman and Ensign Hardy at the foot of the breach, Michael thought he had most of the volunteers he had started with. He wondered what had happened to the others and hoped

198

they had not been shot while trying to take down the French muskets, but he would not know until after the battle.

Michael looked upwards. He could still see Hunt and his men climbing steadily towards the summit. They were getting very close. Surveying the slope, Michael groaned inwardly. It was worse than he had realised. He wished he had spoken to Hunt to suggest that they make their way directly towards the northern edge of the breach as Giles had suggested but it was too late now and he could not fail to go in support of the Colonel. Uttering a silent prayer, he grasped the edge of one of the lower blocks of stone and began to pull himself up.

It was a gruelling climb. Michael had no breath for speech but he heard one or two of his men shouting to the others who were lying below the summit, urging them to get up and join the renewed assault. Several of the men he passed were wounded, crying out for help that he could not give. Some lay inert and silent and would cry no more. Michael wondered bitterly what the toll would be after this day's work. The first assault had been costly enough. If Graham failed a second time all these men would have died in vain.

Halfway up, Michael's hands and knees were scraped and bloody from crawling over the stones. He paused, waving to his men to halt for a moment. Partly it was to catch their breath but he also wanted to see how Hunt was doing. While his men rested, Michael tucked himself in behind an enormous piece of masonry for cover and peered upwards.

Hunt was at the top of the breach with a party of around twenty men. The stuttering sound of musket fire indicated that the French were already on to him and Michael saw a man go down. For a moment it looked as though Hunt himself was hit as he staggered backwards. One of his men caught him and the Colonel doubled up but did not fall. He was waving his arms frantically at his men to get down and they obeyed, dropping flat to the rocks while Hunt seemed to catch his breath.

The incessant noise of artillery and muskets drowned out any possibility of hearing what the Colonel was yelling at his men but his arm gestures were very expressive and Michael realised he was about to attempt the edge of the curtain wall where Giles had described the way down into the town. Michael wondered if the ruined house had survived the past hours of battle, but it was almost certainly their best chance. As Hunt urged his small party on, Michael got up, waving his small band to their feet. He had seldom been so reluctant to advance in the face of enemy fire but Hunt's stubborn courage made it impossible to retreat.

The fire was heavier here and Hunt was losing both officers and men. Scrambling past three red-coated bodies, Michael flinched at the sight of Lieutenant Harvest of the 52nd. The younger man lay on his back, head pointing down the rocky slope, his eyes staring blindly up into the smoke-filled sky. Lieutenant Ronaldo who was climbing beside Michael made a little sound of distress, quickly silenced so as not to alarm his men. Michael shot him a quick approving look, though he was not sure the Portuguese could see it properly in the rolling fog of battle.

Michael changed direction and took a diagonal route across the front of the breach, trying to keep as low as possible to avoid the periodic volleys from French muskets. He was only a few feet away from Hunt now. The Colonel had only a dozen of his own men left standing but he seemed to have acquired a collection of Portuguese caçadores who had lost their officer. Hunt was at the edge of the breach peering down. One of the Portuguese was carrying the regimental colours and as Hunt was about to step over the crest of the slope he reached out and pushed it into the Colonel's hand.

Michael was finally close enough to make himself heard and he called out. Hunt glanced back. He managed a smile that looked more like a grimace, his teeth showing white in his blackened face. Seeing Ronaldo and his Portuguese with Michael he hoisted the flag a little in salute and then turned and took a step forward over the top.

There was an enormous crash of artillery followed immediately by a ferocious volley of muskets and Michael was completely blinded. Just ahead there was a confused jumble of cries and shouts of warning. Michael dropped flat to the stones again, bellowing at his men to do the same. There was no point in blundering forward until the smoke cleared a little. He remained still, his heart hammering, his eyes watering with the effort of trying to see through the black cloud.

Eventually it cleared a little. Hunt was down though still moving and several of his men had also been hit. One of them was crawling towards him, frantically checking for injuries. It looked as though he had been hit in the leg. His trousers were soaked with blood and he lay back, his eyes closed and his face rigid with the effort of not crying out with the pain.

The Portuguese flag lay where it had fallen beside Hunt. Michael was trying to work out how to move the injured men away from the breach so that they would not impede another attempted rush on the narrow traverse which protected the open end of the curtain wall. He was surprised at a sudden movement to his left and turned his head to see Ronaldo on his feet, yelling in Portuguese.

Michael screamed an order but he knew he would be ignored. Ronaldo's men were getting up and clambering forward. They were joined by the remains of Hunt's caçadores who had temporarily stalled at the crest of the breach. They flung themselves towards the gap and Ronaldo bent to scoop up the fallen colours.

The musket ball took him fully in the chest as he straightened, so close at hand that it took him off his feet and hurled him backwards down the slope. More fire raked across the Portuguese front and half a dozen men were hit and went down. The rest threw themselves flat to the ground, arms covering their heads as both bullets and sharp pieces of stonework flew around them. Michael closed his eyes, unable to bear it.

His men were trapped, too close to the lethal fire into the breach even to raise their heads. He lay there for what must have been several minutes, trying to decide what to do. The firing had paused, probably because the French saw

200

no point in wasting valuable ammunition on what might have been dead and dying men. Michael did not even know how many of his men still lived.

Ahead of him, unexpectedly, he heard a familiar voice. "Captain O'Reilly, the Colonel's alive. Should we try and get him out of here?"

Sergeant Coates' voice was hoarse but he was clearly alive and uninjured and it brought Michael firmly back to reality and a sense of his duty. Cautiously he raised his head and looked around. The men closest to him all seemed to have survived so far. Michael knew that the moment they moved, the French would be on to them again but they might not fire on one or two men helping the wounded.

"All right, Coates," he yelled. "If he can be moved, let's get him down. Take it nice and slowly and keep your hands off your rifle. Nobody else move."

Coates and a private from the 52nd who had a bloody arm moved towards Hunt and helped him to shuffle down the slope towards Michael. Hunt had been shot in the lower leg below the knee but to Michael's surprise he seemed to be able to walk a little. He was shaking with pain, an unmistakable tremor in his voice.

"Sorry, O'Reilly. Damned mess. Not much use to you now. None of them will be, all my officers are dead or wounded. Apart from Andrews over there. He'll…"

"That's enough, sir. Your fight is done. Let them get you out of here. Coates…"

"I'll get Griffith and Dobbins to help him down, sir, they're both wounded anyway, though they can walk. Fletcher's dead. Not sure about Smithy, it doesn't look good."

"Oh fuck this place," Michael breathed, closing his eyes again. "What about Sergeant Bowlby? And Barforth?"

"Barforth's over there with a bloody big hole in his left arm. Young Blount is with him. I don't know where Bowlby is, I lost him on the way up here. Hope he's all right."

"So do I. Tell them to get themselves over to Mr Ronaldo. I think he's dead, but if he's not, they're to get him out of here however they can. Any of the others wounded, send them down to the surgeons."

"What about you, sir?"

"I'm fine."

Shrewd dark eyes met Michael's gaze steadily. "If we make another try at that breach, sir, we're not going to be fine at all."

Michael could not speak for a moment. Finally he managed to get his voice under control. "I can't retreat, Coates. Look around you. Get yourself down with some of the wounded."

"Not a chance of it, sir."

"Stubborn bastard. How many have we got left able to fight?"

Coates raised himself cautiously, peering around. The wounded men were beginning to make a clumsy retreat, some of them crawling back down the rocky slope. Michael called out, his voice carrying more easily in the temporary lull. Men began to move, scrambling over the rocks to join him. There were more than he had realised. Apart from the Portuguese who had joined Ronaldo in his heroic dash for the crest, Michael's men had managed to keep low. He had lost some. Both Sergeant Bowlby and Ensign Hardy were missing.

Lieutenant Jackman was there. Michael surveyed him for a long moment. Jackman looked back defiantly.

"Lift your right arm."

Jackman did not move. Michael surveyed the bloodstained coat then looked up at Jackman's face. "Lift your right arm, Mr Jackman. It's an order."

Jackman reached over with his left and raised the bloody right sleeve. His face contorted with pain and he made a little sound but continued to lift his arm. Michael did not know if he wanted to laugh or cry.

"At ease, Mr Jackman. I can't take you in like that, you'll get yourself killed. More to the point, you might get these men killed and we've lost too many already. Down to the surgeons. It's an order."

"Permission to remain here, sir."

"Why the fuck do you want to stay here if you can't fight, Jackman? It's a bloody death trap."

"So that I can tell the General what happened. If...if..."

Michael tried not to think about that. "All right, you bloody hero. Stay there, keep your head down and if this goes wrong surrender. Don't try to follow us in."

There was a flurry of musket fire from the centre of the breach but it quickly died away. The French knew they had Graham's men pinned down for the time being and they were not wasting ammunition trying to hit men lying flat on the slopes. They had reached an impasse which could not last. Michael considered how to break it.

"All right," he said finally. "We're not doing another death or glory charge without a plan. There's some kind of small artillery piece up in that tower and there are muskets ahead in the earthworks and up on the end of the curtain wall. Our aim is not to let them realise we're moving forward. We're going to move very gradually and very quietly, on our bellies if necessary until we can see our targets. Coates, you're taking the curtain wall. Any man with a rifle goes first, the muskets provide a volley to cover their reload. I'll do the same on the other side. Sort out your ammunition and share it equally so nobody runs out early. Pass the orders round and divide the men, Coates."

There was something almost comedic about the movement of Michael's troops as they shuffled rather than ran into position, but there was nothing amusing about the expressions of concentration on their faces. Michael felt a combination of pride and panic. He had known some of these men since he had been a sergeant in the light company years ago. Some were strangers from other battalions of the Light Division. There were a few Portuguese. All shared a sense of grim determination and Michael was terrified that he was about to lead them all to their death.

202

When they were in position Michael waited for a long agonising moment to make sure that the French were not about to open fire. He raised his hand, looking over at Coates and his men, took a deep breath and then dropped his hand in a silent signal to open fire.

In one smooth movement he got to his feet, swinging his borrowed rifle up to his shoulder. He had already identified his target, a blue-coated artilleryman whose flank was exposed by a broken tower wall. The man was facing out towards the main breach and had no reason to expect a renewed attack from this corner. Michael took careful aim and fired. He heard the scream of pain but saw nothing more because he had already ducked back into cover. To his left, concealed between two enormous blocks of fallen stone, a rifleman he did not know was on his feet, his rifle trained on the gun emplacement. He waited for so long that Michael thought they would see him and cut him down but then he fired and a body tumbled forward into the long traverse below the tower. It was immediately joined by another Frenchman, shot down by Coates' men on the opposite side.

It was working. A group of men racing into an open breach were easy to cut down. Twenty or so well-trained individuals picking off chosen targets was a different matter. This was the kind of skirmish fighting that Michael understood best and he had carefully chosen his position. He was not going to defeat a French garrison like this, but he had every intention of disabling that gun and of driving the men at the end of the curtain wall into cover. After that he would take his chance at the breach and see if Giles was right about getting men into the town that way.

Concentrating on his task, Michael lost track of time, but there was no more activity from the tower gun and only a few desultory shots coming from the wall. Michael called out to Coates and the Cornish Sergeant slithered over the rocks, keeping low.

"We're holding them, sir, we've got them pinned down. And I think the gun crew is dead. They'll try to get more men up here but we've got some time. Permission to scout ahead and see…"

"Go."

Coates vanished over the edge of the breach. To Michael's relief no shots followed him. He realised, with momentary surprise, that Graham's batteries out on the sand dunes also seemed to have fallen silent and he wondered why. Perhaps they were repositioning the guns to more effectively target the small amount of French artillery. Michael hoped they did not manage to find the range on this tower within the next ten minutes.

Coates was back, his head appearing over the top of the breach so unexpectedly that Michael swore and knocked down the musket of a man of the 52nd who had raised it reflexively.

"Coates, you bloody idiot you're going to get your head blown off. What's going on?"

"Sorry sir," Coates said softly, moving closer. There's a way down and it's currently clear though it's a bit of a scramble. Takes you into the street behind that bastard wall. There's a couple of partly ruined houses, we could hole up in there and take stock. Should be able to come up behind them."

"With twenty men," Michael said. It sounded completely ridiculous.

"Twenty Light Bobs, sir."

"I should never have brought you with me Coates, you're a lunatic. All right, you're in the lead, take them straight into cover. You, rifleman, what's your name?"

"Hope, sir. First battalion."

"You're one of Barnard's lot. No wonder you're bloody mad. You can also shoot so you're bringing up the rear with me. Rifle trained on that corner and if you see anything move, shoot it. I'll take this side."

"Yes, sir." Hope looked faintly pleased. "You're not a bad shot yourself for an officer. Did you by any chance…?"

"Yes, I came up from the ranks. No, this is not my rifle and I'd forgotten how bloody heavy they are. I'll tell you the rest later. Ready?"

"Ready, sir."

They rose cautiously, moving out of cover with rifles and muskets at the ready, scanning the breach for signs of French activity. There was still firing from further along the breach but in this corner nothing stirred. The French artillery from the opposite end of the breach still thundered out defiance, though Michael was not sure what it was shooting at since it could not possibly reach the men who had halted below the parapet of the main breach. There was still no sound from the Allied guns on the sandhills and once again Michael wondered why. It was oddly quiet, as though for a brief moment everything around him had paused. Even the smoke had cleared a little. Michael waited as his small party filed to the crest of the breach, his hands sweating on his rifle, his eyes scanning for signs that the French had spotted their movement.

There was a sound from below, at the foot of the breach. It was a bugle, sounding clear and pure against the crackle of musket fire and the rumble of the remaining French guns. Michael had been hearing bugles all morning, calling men to their muster points from the trenches, but this one froze him in his tracks. Ahead of him, Sergeant Coates also turned, outlined in an appallingly exposed position just over the top of the breach. The men were trained to understand the various regulation bugle calls. It was often the only way to communicate orders in the mind-numbing noise of the battlefield. In addition, most regiments had developed their own distinctive bugle calls to summon in their own men. This could be particularly important for light infantry, where skirmishers might be strung out over a wide area to cover advancing troops.

There were no advancing troops now, just a lone officer in a red coat waving his hat above his head, with a bugler standing beside him, repeating the call. Michael could not see the officer's face and did not need to. There was only one man it could possibly be. He wondered for a moment if Giles Fenwick had gone mad. Every man on the breach from the 110th had turned, knowing the sound of their regimental call.

Giles made no attempt to yell orders which could not possibly have been heard. When he realised Michael had seen him he threw out his arms and dropped them, palms flat to the ground. The gesture was unmistakeable.

"Down!" Michael screamed. He was already moving himself, falling awkwardly between two huge blocks. Around him his men dropped like stones. Coates was the last to do so, having to scramble back up over the breach, but he skidded to a painful halt beside Michael, one cheek cut open and bleeding where he had scraped it on a rock.

"What the bloody hell...?"

The Allied artillery fired and the air seemed to shake. Michael was a long way off but instinctively found himself burying his head in his arms. He had not heard that kind of concerted firing since the last hours of the bombardment before the storming and his ears, already ringing from the shooting around him, were filled with an echoing buzzing sound. He lay still, as stones and masonry rained down around him, wondering what in God's name had just happened.

Michael raised his head very cautiously and surveyed the slope across the breach where the trapped Allied infantry still lay below the crest. For a moment he could not work out what had happened but as he looked, there was another enormous crash as the batteries fired again. Shot whistled low over the heads of the trapped men on the slope and smashed down onto the French troops manning the wall.

The destruction was appalling. Bodies were flung into the air, ripped apart so that they fell in bloody pieces onto the wall and into the deep ravine which had protected them for the past few hours. Several defenders towards the centre of the breach still stood in position but Michael realised that their heads had been completely shot away leaving only their bodies in a grotesque parody of soldiers guarding the breach. Michael pushed himself to his knees, bent over the gap in the rock and was sick.

One of the younger riflemen lying nearby made as if to rise and Michael reached out an arm, shoving him flat again. "Don't move, they're not done yet."

As he spoke the guns fired again. There was a screaming whistle which seemed to rush close above him and he clamped his arms over his head, yelling pointlessly to his men to do the same. The small tower which held the gun rocked above them, showering them with debris. On the other side of the breach the end of the curtain wall was blown away and more stone tumbled down into the ditch below. There were cries from some of the defenders closest to Michael.

The guns continued their barrage for about twenty minutes. After the first few hits, Michael gained enough confidence to push himself into a sitting position behind his covering rock, though he was careful to keep his head very low. He had never before been in the position of seeing his own army firing over his head and it was both terrifying and strangely exhilarating. The Allied gunners knew their range from long practice during the days of the bombardment and were able to concentrate their fire on the sections of the wall most closely packed

205

with enemy troops. The Frenchmen had no hope of returning fire and those who were not wiped out in the initial cannonades were fleeing down into the town.

Unexpectedly, beyond the curtain wall there was another explosion. It was bigger than anything the Allied guns had managed, ripping apart that section of the wall and throwing huge chunks of debris and more bodies into the air. It looked as though a building had been blown apart and it cleared the ramparts of the remaining Frenchmen. They were either dead or on the run.

"What in God's name was that?" Coates breathed close to Michael's ear.

"That was some kind of munitions store, I've seen it before. Whatever we just blew up was destined to rain down on the heads of our men. I hope it took a few of the fuckers with it. Come on, Sergeant. I think that will finish it."

Across the width of the breach men were stirring and some of the officers were beginning to shout orders, getting their men ready for another rush on the breach. Michael peered down through the swirling mist of cannon fire trying to see if anybody was signalling that the barrage of fire was ending. He suspected they were although he could not immediately see anything.

The murky clouds began to drift clear and Michael could see more men running into place at the foot of the breach. The guns had fallen silent as their crews worked quickly to reposition them towards the more distant defences of the town. The barrage was followed by a long, almost eerie silence, broken only by the whimpering of some of the French who had survived the cannonade. Then an English voice shouted. It was taken up by another and then more as those officers who had been pinned down with their men across the breach realised that they were free to advance.

Michael looked around at his men who were stirring as though coming out of a trance. "Up!" he bellowed. "They're not all fucking dead yet. Coates, lead them in. What the hell are you staring at? We lost men up here, we've earned the right to…"

"Sir, it's Captain Fenwick. He's down. And the bugler."

Michael froze then scrambled to stand beside the Sergeant. He could see clearly now where the two men lay. Giles was face down and the bugler was lying on his back. It was impossible to see from up here if they were dead or wounded but nobody was going to help them. Every man was focused on the renewed assault. Agonisingly Michael knew he needed to do the same. At any moment some of the survivors from Robinson's brigade would be racing towards this part of the breach and he wanted his men to be first. His duty lay ahead of him. Below lay a friend whose timely warning had probably saved Michael's life and might well have cost his.

"Sir, permission to withdraw. Can't fight like this."

Michael turned to look at Coates in complete astonishment. Coates was holding a hand to his face. It was an ugly gash and there was blood dripping down onto his jacket but Michael was not fooled for a moment. He had seen Nick Coates in action with a wound which had almost killed him and he had not stopped until he had fallen unconscious. Coates met his gaze steadily.

"I think you're right, Coates. Can't fight with your eye full of blood. Get yourself down to the surgeons, lad and if you find any of our wounded on the way…"

"I'll do that right now, sir."

Coates took off, bounding down the slope at terrifying speed. Michael watched for a moment then turned back to his small group of men.

"Come on then," he roared, lifting his rifle. "San Sebastian is ours, boys. Let's go and take it."

Chapter Fourteen

Several supply wagons rumbled up the narrow track towards the San Marcial heights late in the afternoon, with the welcome news that two more were on their way. General Manuel Freire, who had only recently succeeded to command the Army of Galicia and its associated battalions currently posted at San Marcial, must have had news of their approach because the wagons were immediately surrounded by guards to prevent the starving Spanish troops looting them and to ensure an orderly distribution of the meagre rations.

Captain Ángel Cortez sent his junior officers to supervise the collection of food. It was not nearly enough and the wagons had not even come from the Spanish commissariat but from British stores. Lord Wellington, from his current command post on the heights of the Peñas de Aya, had reluctantly ordered his own commissariat to provide some succour to his hungry allies. The Spanish supply system seemed to have broken down again and Wellington was aware that starving men would not be fit enough to fight.

Ángel collected his own tack biscuits and morsel of tough mutton and went in search of his friend. He found Captain Óscar García perched on a broken wall trying hard not to bolt down the food. He grinned at Ángel and waved his arm expansively.

"Join me, Captain Cortez. Only the finest food served here."

Ángel could not help smiling. García had that effect on him, however bad his mood. He sat down and bit into the tasteless food, trying to remember when he had last eaten properly. It felt like a long time.

"Any news?" he asked.

"You know everything I know, Ángel. General Freire has orders to hold this section of the line against a possible French attack. Lord Wellington's agents report that Soult will make a final push to reach San Sebastian once the assault begins tomorrow so he is moving troops into position to protect Sir Thomas Graham's men. We have this delightful area to defend. Nothing new."

"I wondered. I don't get invited to social gatherings these days."

García frowned. "There are no social gatherings, Captain. You're not being left out."

Ángel finished his food and looked up with a wry smile. "Yes I am, Óscar. I'm not an imbecile. If it were not for this new French advance, I'd have been packed off to join the British with this entirely fabricated job as an intelligence officer which is very clearly an excuse to get me out of the way."

García sighed. "I'm sorry, Ángel . I wish there was something I could do. I tried to speak to the Colonel on your behalf..."

"I told you not to do that," Ángel snapped.

"I know you did. I ignored you. He listened but then said that two duels and two officers badly injured and out of action was not acceptable in time of war. Though honestly, I think it might have helped if you had confided in him what the original duel was about."

"It was my own affair."

"You haven't even told me."

"It was a personal matter, García and you know that I do not like to share such things."

"I know that you are a very stubborn man." García sighed again. "When I spoke to the Colonel, he told me that if you had not been such a good officer, Ángel, he would have dismissed you from the regiment. As it is, Captain Torres and his younger brother seem unlikely to return. The Colonel understands that their father is looking for a staff posting in Madrid for the Captain. His brother will return to his studies."

"The Captain will do very well there. If nobody runs him through before then."

García gave an unwilling laugh. "You are incorrigible, Ángel . I wish I knew what he said to you. Either nobody knows or nobody will speak of it. I am dying of curiosity."

"It will do you good," Ángel said unsympathetically. "You are far too inquisitive."

"And you have no interest in your fellow man beyond his fighting experience. Unless he insults you of course, in which case your only interest is in killing him."

Ángel slid off the wall, his hand on his sword hilt. His friend vaulted athletically over the broken stones, using them as a barrier. He held up his hands, laughing.

"Do not. Do not do it, Ángel, they will dismiss you."

"I do not care."

"They will arrest you and try you for murder."

"No they won't. They will shake my hand for ridding the army of a nuisance and reinstate me to my battalion. I don't know why I didn't think of this before."

They dodged around the broken wall, moving to left and right. A few of the men had turned to watch them in surprise. García was laughing too much to concentrate and Ángel waited until he was fully distracted then jumped over the wall and took the younger man in a painful head lock. He could feel García's body shaking with mirth.

209

"Do you yield?"

"Not at all."

Ángel drew his sword halfway out of its sheath. "I will cut your throat without hesitation, García. Do you yield?"

"No."

Ángel stepped hard onto his foot and García gave an anguished yelp. Ángel released him and he hopped to the wall and sat down, feeling through the soft leather of his boot for injury.

"Do you think they'll arrest you if I complain you've broken my foot?"

"No." Ángel studied him with some concern. "Have I?"

García wriggled his foot and stood up, testing it. "No. But it bloody hurt."

"I'm sorry. I trod harder than I intended."

"You do everything more than you intended, Captain. That's why you should never fight duels." García was smiling, which took the sting out of his words. Ángel smiled back. He could not help it. For almost two years he had eaten, slept, fought and occasionally almost died with this man at his side and no matter how black his mood, García could always drag a smile from him. It was infuriating. It had also, at times, kept Ángel sane.

"I would never fight a duel with you, García; it would be like fighting a child."

"You would never fight a duel with me, Ángel, because I am not stupid enough to accept your challenge. Anyway, you are afraid of what my wife would do to you if you killed me."

"That is very true," Ángel admitted. "Have you heard from her?"

García shook his head, sitting down on the wall again. He moved up to make space for Ángel and reached into his coat pocket for his silver flask.

"No, but it means nothing. The post is probably sitting in some dusty office while two Spanish officers argue about whose duty it is to arrange for it to be sent on to the next staging point, or whether we should be responsible for our own mail at all instead of leaving it to the British. As we leave everything else to the British."

"Including feeding our men," Ángel agreed. "I am sorry, Óscar. But you are right, the letter will come."

"It is just not knowing," García said, almost apologetically. "She must have given birth by now. I know that she is young and healthy and safe with her family and friends. She was so confident that it would go well. But…"

"But we all know occasions when it has not." Ángel took a swig of brandy and passed the flask back to his friend. "I cannot give you empty reassurances, García. But somehow I think when the news arrives it will be of a happy event and a new son or daughter."

"I am sure you are right. I just wish it would come."

"In the meantime, it is your duty to keep yourself alive to meet your child. Which means getting enough sleep the night before a battle."

García laughed and got to his feet. "You are like my childhood nursemaid, Captain."

"I promised your wife I would be so, García. I must get back to my men and so should you. Goodnight."

The heat of the day had given way to a chilly night, with mist swirling above the Spanish bivouac. Ángel did a final inspection of his company, spoke to his junior officers and settled on the hard ground wrapped in his cloak.

He lay awake for a long time, listening to the rumbling snores of the men around him. It was not the cold nor the discomfort that made it impossible to settle. Ángel had served in both French and Spanish armies for fifteen years now and could sleep anywhere if he was tired enough. Tonight though, when he needed the rest, he was thinking about García, who at the tender age of twenty-three was about to become a father for the first time. He was trying hard not to think about Dona Raquel García, giving birth to her first child on the distant island of Mallorca without her husband to support her. Ángel had been reassuring his friend daily that she would be all right. Partly this was to help García. Mostly it was because Ángel could not bring himself to contemplate the possibility that anything might happen to Raquel.

If he closed his eyes he could see her clearly; a tall curvaceous girl with honey-gold curls and sparkling blue eyes. She was the daughter of a wealthy glassmaker and Ángel and García were billeted in her family home when they arrived in Mallorca dressed in rags and badly wounded after the fall of Tarragona. As a tradesman's daughter she was not a suitable wife for a Spanish aristocrat, however impoverished he might be. She was also too respectable for a casual seduction so Ángel had set temptation firmly aside and tried to ignore his growing attraction to her.

He realised too late that García, who was equally well-born, did not give a damn about the disapproval of his wealthy family and was more than willing to marry a tradesman's daughter if he loved her enough. Ángel was appalled at his friend's choice and only realised afterwards that his anger was driven by jealousy rather than social disapproval.

Since their wedding, García and his wife had spent more time apart than together but the long winter quarters had enabled him to take some leave to visit her. He had tried hard to persuade his friend to go with him. Ángel had refused steadfastly. Distance had enabled him to manage his feelings for Raquel but he was terrified that weeks staying in her parents' house, seeing her with García, would be too much to bear. He had received the news that she was carrying her first child with a mixture of happiness for her and García and sheer misery for himself.

Ángel had been alone all his adult life and had thought loneliness an inevitable consequence of being a soldier. His hatred of the French invaders had consumed him until he had convinced himself that the commonplace joys of a wife, a home and a family were both impossible and unwanted. García and Raquel had taught him differently. He was glad for his friend but found it bitterly hard to watch.

211

He slept finally but restlessly, dreaming of Raquel. Eventually he opened his eyes to find a heavy grey fog shrouding the camp and closed them again imagining the lingering softness of her hair under his hands and the warm tone of her voice, saying his name. She had a lovely voice, always hovering on the edge of laughter. To a man raised in a home where no laughter was ever heard it had been intoxicating and it was not surprising he had fallen so hard and so unsuitably. It was his job now to manage his feelings so that García never knew of them.

Around him, the camp was stirring into life. Ángel got up and went to rouse his company. There was no more food and Freire had issued orders that no fires should be lit until the position of the French became clear. Nobody doubted that Soult would advance today; the only question was which part of the Allied line would bear the brunt of the attack.

Wellington had been preparing for another French advance at the same time as planning for a new attack on San Sebastian. New redoubts and earthworks had been built all along the line and over the past few days he had moved his forces into position and given orders to his various commanders in case Soult made a move. On the heights of San Marcial Freire's orders were simply to stand and, if possible, to push the enemy back. Depending on numbers and the determination of the attacking force, Ángel thought it could be done.

The slopes of San Marcial were scattered with shrubs and brushwood, thicker in some areas than others. Ángel stood at the crest as the battalion formed up behind him, straining his eyes to peer through the fog. They were out there, he was sure of it, though until the mist cleared there was no way to tell how close they were. Full ebb tide on the Bidassoa would not be until around noon but some of the fords would have been low enough to enable troops to cross unseen. There was no doubt at all that Soult was on the move; British observers from the high points of the Pena de la Aya and the Ibanteli had seen considerable French activity.

"Captain Cortez, are your men ready?"

Ángel turned to see his battalion commander approaching. Colonel Anaya was in his forties, sparely built, with a pronounced nose and fierce dark eyes. He was a fearless soldier and a good leader and, until his recent troubles, Ángel had enjoyed serving under him.

A lot of Spanish troops had adopted the British habit of saluting a senior officer but Ángel did not like it, so he bowed.

"As you see, Colonel, they are fully at arms and eager to fight."

Anaya ran his eyes over the waiting troops and nodded. "I hope this clears soon. Waiting is not good for morale."

"Their morale is good, sir. Especially considering they are so hungry."

Anaya acknowledged his point with an expressive grunt which told Ángel everything he needed to know about his commander's views of the Spanish commissariat.

"If they kill enough Frenchmen, they can steal their rations," Anaya said.

212

"If they have any. I'm not sure Soult is any better supplied than we are."

"That should make it a fair contest then, Captain."

"I think we have the advantage, sir. That is a very steep hill."

Anaya grinned which pleased Ángel. He had not seen the Colonel smile at him for weeks. "Make sure they don't pursue too far and get cut off," he said. "I know what you're like, Cortez."

"Are you suggesting that I would risk my men in an attempt to retrieve my honour, Colonel?" Ángel tried to keep his voice even, but he could hear the rising irritation. Anaya heard it too and sighed, shaking his head.

"Do not be so quick to anger, Cortez. It is why you are in this mess in the first place. I'm not for one moment suggesting you'll lead a suicidal charge to evade your new posting. I simply wanted to remind you that we have a lot of raw recruits and you'll need to watch them."

Ángel felt rather foolish. He gave another stiff bow. "Of course, Colonel."

Anaya studied him for a long moment. "I wish you were not so difficult, Cortez. You are such a good soldier."

Ángel was surprised. "Thank you, Colonel. I have tried…I believe I have learned much since coming under your command. After Tarragona, I thought I had little left to learn, but…"

To his surprise the Colonel laughed aloud. "That's honest of you, Cortez. It was very obviously true. But your management of your men is much better than it was. If only I could say the same for your relationship with your fellow officers."

"I get on well enough with most of them, sir."

"You get on very well with García you mean, and he manages them for you. I'm still surprised he didn't manage to prevent those duels, you know."

"He did not know about them, sir."

"That is what puzzles me. Generally, he knows everything about you. Why in God's name did you fight Torres, Cortez?"

"It was a private matter, Colonel. I prefer not to say."

"Along with every other officer in the battalion. I asked García and he informed me that you refused to tell him any more than you told me. I am surprised none of the others have not broken the silence, somebody must have known and they are usually like a gaggle of gossiping women. All I can assume is that he insulted you in the worst way possible."

"I cannot say, sir."

"My only consolation is that given what you did to him, it is unlikely that the affront will be repeated."

"That was my intention, Colonel."

Anaya looked exasperated. "It would have been easier to keep you, Cortez, if there were mitigating circumstances. I have told you this."

"I know you have, sir. I am sorry, but it is a matter of honour."

"Then I shall not press you now, although I urge you to reconsider."

213

The Colonel took a handkerchief from his pocket and wiped perspiration from his brow. Ángel was faintly envious. He no longer possessed a handkerchief and if he wiped his face on his grubby coat sleeve he would end up with a muddy streak. The air was warm and heavy, as though a thunderstorm threatened. Ángel hoped it would hold off. Heavy rain would mean damp powder and could leave Freire's men defending the San Marcial heights with nothing but bayonets.

"What time is it, sir?"

Anaya took out his watch. "A quarter to eight. Is it my imagination, or is the mist beginning to clear?"

Ángel peered into the thick haze again. He was not sure at first but as he stared, he realised that the fog was becoming more patchy with low trees and bushes becoming visible halfway up the slope. The Colonel stood beside him looking as if he was willing it to clear.

A light breeze fluttered the leaves of a stunted olive tree and the mist swirled again. This time Ángel could see much further and he caught his breath at an unexpected stir of colour and movement in the distance. Anaya swore softly under his breath.

"They're here," he whispered. "They must have crossed early this morning in that damned fog before any of us was out of our bed rolls. They're already here and they'll be massing for an attack. I need to let Freire know…"

He was interrupted by a roar of cannon. They could not possibly be Spanish guns. General Giron, in command of the Spanish forces in the vicinity of Irun had only twelve guns and most gunners from the various divisional batteries had been called into action at San Sebastian. Ángel whirled around, looking across at the massed Spanish troops. He could hear shouts of warning and a scramble into cover further down the line but it did not look as though much damage had been done.

All along the Spanish front bugles were sounding and those battalions late to form up were hurrying into line. The mist was clearing quickly and the French troops at the foot of the wide slope were clearly visible. Freire sent out his orders rapidly and his men moved forward to take up a position to the front of an old defensive trench about two-thirds of the way up the slope. The troops moved smoothly into place and waited for orders. More shells fell and there was a limited response from Giron's few guns but neither side seemed to be doing much damage. Ángel had the feeling that the artillery was more for show than as part of a serious attack. If the French wanted to take San Marcial they were going to have to do it the hard way.

As the enemy surged forward, Freire ordered his light companies forward in a skirmish line. Ángel had a clear view down the slope now and could see the French tirailleurs climbing ahead of the main force to engage. The air was already filled with the crackle of musket fire and the smell of smoke as the two sides moved closer together. The Spanish had the advantage of the higher ground and were making excellent use of the bushes and small groups of trees

214

for cover. The French pushed forward, and beyond them, the main columns were beginning to advance behind their skirmishers.

Ángel could feel the usual pre-battle nerves twisting his stomach into a knot as he watched them come. It was difficult to assess numbers given the uneven terrain but the bottom of the slope was a mass of blue coats. As they began the steep climb though, the columns seemed to be breaking up. There were too many shrubs and trees and areas of tangled undergrowth to make a smooth advance possible. Ahead of the main force, the French skirmishers had reached their limit and were now pinned down by the Spanish light troops. They could go no further without risking being cut down by the Spaniards who had found good cover higher up the slope and were firing at any Frenchman who raised his head. A few bodies were strewn across the hillside and the tirailleurs remained firmly in place.

The French columns continued to climb and were coming up level with their skirmishers. There was no longer any order to their forces; they were making their way up the slope however they could. Ángel realised, with some awe, that the front line, ragged and undisciplined, was beginning to merge with the rear of their skirmish line. The whole French column had somehow turned into a disorganised mass. They appeared almost leaderless, though there were clearly officers present, intent only on reaching the top of that steep slope.

Ángel realised he was straining his ears, listening for a bellowed order to halt, to call them into line. It did not come. It was as if the officers were as blinkered as the men, concentrating only on progress without a thought of what waited them at the top of the hill. He wondered if their unconcern was due to an inherent contempt for Spanish troops, who had fled before them so many times. Ángel had been part of a number of unnecessary, undisciplined routs in the face of a determined French advance but he knew it was not about to happen here. Freire's men were in good order and excellent spirits, despite their empty stomachs, and they were not about to give way.

Freire held his nerve until the last possible moment then gave the order to charge. His bellow was so loud that Ángel heard it from further down the line over musket fire and the crash of distant guns, ahead of any individual battalion orders. He drew his sword, raised it above his head and roared to his men to advance, then without bothering to check if they followed him, he launched himself down the hill onto the French.

The men followed. Ángel could hear them on either side of him, could hear the thunder of a thousand feet across the slope, the explosion of muskets as those at the front took aim and fired at the enemy. Some of the first straggling line fell to the ground. Those behind them stopped, looking up at the Spanish troops advancing towards them. They were covering the ground quickly, not faltering as an occasional French shot blew a gap in the line.

Ángel's men crashed into the front rank of the French column. His sword was raised but he had to search for a target because the line was so disordered. He found one: a broad infantryman who seemed inclined to stand, his bayonet steady in enormous hands. He parried Ángel's slashing sword, eyes fixed on his face, looking for a sign that his guard was about to drop. Ángel pressed forward. He had learned the hard way that there was no place for finesse during a battle, though his strength and his skill at swordplay undoubtedly gave him an advantage over most opponents. He slashed high, making the Frenchman sway backwards, temporarily off-balance. Ángel followed through with brutal thoroughness and the man fell forward as he withdrew his sword, the bayonet falling from lifeless hands. Ángel swung around to make sure he was not about to be bayonetted from behind and realised that in those few minutes the tide had turned and there was no Frenchman within reach.

They were retreating back down the hill at speed. Freire's men charged after them, rolling the French columns ahead of them. Some of them stumbled and fell in their panic and the Spanish bayonetted them on the ground, giving no mercy. Later, prisoners might be taken but in this first rush no quarter was asked or given. Freire's men swept on down the hill, swerving around clumps of bushes and leaping over fallen men. Ángel felt a rush of sheer exhilaration as he ran with them. He had fought in many battles, some of them victories, but he had never before been part of such a successful charge as part of a purely Spanish force.

The order to halt came before his men reached the foot of the slope and was quickly called across the line. Bugles sounded and officers and NCOs yelled to their men to stop. Ángel pulled up, raising his voice in concert with the others. He knew this was the danger point, particularly in such a successful rout of the enemy. Inexperienced men could easily get carried away and, as Anaya had pointed out earlier, there were a lot of raw troops in this army.

Looking around him Ángel felt a lift of pride at the sight of his company and his battalion. They had come to rest in a rough line, looking down over the French who were still running. It was unbelievably satisfying to watch them go, heading towards a knoll on the river bank. There was another body of troops waiting there in reserve and behind them Ángel could see activity on the water as men toiled in the hot morning air, building a temporary bridge over the Bidassoa. The sight cooled Ángel's enthusiasm slightly. If the French could successfully bridge the river, here and further up, it would enable them to continue to bring troops over even when the water was at its highest. Ángel wondered how many men Soult had at his disposal and how many he was prepared to send against Freire's small force on the heights of San Marcial. The victory had been sweet but the day was not over.

Freire sounded the retreat and the Spanish trudged back up the hill to their former position. Men were sent out to bring fresh water along the line. There were several springs and a well in the old hermitage on the summit of the hill which meant the troops had plenty to drink even though food was in short supply. Ángel watched as his men drank, splashed cold water over sweating faces and swapped stories of the short but satisfying charge. He had lost none of his company although one of the new recruits had been carried away to the surgeons with a dangerous looking bayonet wound. A few men had minor

216

injuries which were being patched up by their comrades using makeshift bandages. Ángel stopped to speak to one of them and was assured that Private Asensio was fit enough to fight again that day. Asensio was one of the new men, the twenty-year-old son of a Mallorcan farmer and the determination in his voice made Ángel smile. He was never particularly easy with the men, although the past two years in command of this company had taught him the value of taking an interest in their welfare. He complimented Asensio on his fortitude and warned him against foolish heroics should the pain become worse, then walked over to Captain García's company in search of his friend.

He found García deep in conversation with one of his sergeants. His smoke-blackened face looked worried, with a deep frown furrowing his brow. Ángel ran his eyes over him in quick concern but García was unharmed. He went forward to join his friend.

"Is everything all right, Captain?"

"No," García said. He turned to perform the same brief safety check. It warmed Ángel who had never quite got used having a friend who cared enough worry about him during a fight. "Did you lose anybody?"

"One man took a bayonet to the stomach. He has been taken to the surgeon, I've no idea how serious it will be. Several minor injuries. What of you?"

"Like you, only one serious, but it is young Valls. He tripped over during the first charge and according to Sergeant Morata here, landed at the feet of a French infantryman who stabbed him several times before Morata got to him."

"I hope the French bastard did not survive the experience, Sergeant?"

"He did not, Captain. But I fear for Private Valls, he was badly wounded."

"I'm sorry, García," Ángel said sympathetically. "I hope it isn't as bad as it looked."

García dismissed his Sergeant and took a long drink from his water bottle. He looked pale and very upset. "I feel responsible," he said.

"You are not responsible, Óscar. Valls wanted to join. He was desperate to join. He knew it would not be possible to do so on Mallorca, so he took a fishing boat to Sagunto then made his way to our camp. I think that shows more dedication than any other man in this regiment."

"He'd never have done that if I hadn't told him how to manage it, Ángel. And promised him that I'd accept him into my company."

"He should have been able to sign his name in the book at the barracks in Palma along with the other new recruits. He should have marched out with the rest of us with his family waving him off and cheering him and showing their pride. He should never have had to leave his home in order to join the Spanish army. It is a disgrace. I just hope the men of his company have welcomed him as they should."

García managed a grin despite his tired misery. "Half of them are from the mainland anyway and have no idea that the Xuerta people are not allowed to

217

join the army on their home island. The other half are from Mallorca but they're good men and respected Valls for his courage and dedication. There were one or two who were inclined to shun him because of his heritage..."

"I know."

"But since you threatened to hang Private Carvajal from the nearest tree on the way to Pamplona they have behaved very well."

"I am glad to hear it."

"I'm not looking forward to writing to Raquel about this. The Valls family have worked in the glass factory for generations. She'll be upset."

"Don't you dare write to her until you know anything for sure," Ángel said firmly. "You are assuming the worst of this, García, which is not like you. Valls traces his ancestry back to a Mallorcan Jew who stood shouting defiance at the Inquisition when they burned him to death. He is tougher than you imagine. He might come through this."

García put a hand on his friend's shoulder. "I hope so. I hope your man makes it as well."

Ángel turned to survey the river banks where the French army was milling about while its officers struggled to bring order again. Some men were cautiously making their way up the lower slopes to bring in the wounded. There was an isolated flurry of shots from along the Spanish line, quickly ordered into silence and the French were left unmolested to retrieve their men.

"It won't be long," García said.

"No." Ángel pointed to a long train of men on the far bank of the river. "It will be low tide in less than an hour and he'll bring his reserves over by the fords; they won't need to wait for that bridge to be finished. He should have waited for them in the first place, the arrogant bastard."

"Why would he do that? This place is only defended by the Spanish and it's well-known that we run at the first sign of battle."

Ángel glanced at his friend who was surveying the distant French with watchful dark eyes.

"Not these Spaniards. Not this time."

"Definitely not," García said. "I look forward to showing them what we can do. I still owe them for half a dozen bayonet wounds at Tarragona."

Ángel raised his left hand and flexed his fingers instinctively. These days there was no pain, just a little stiffness in the muscles and a loss of feeling in part of his smallest finger. The hand was crossed with white scars.

"I have a grudge of my own from Tarragona," he said. "I wonder if he is still alive? I wonder if he is out there somewhere?"

"The big French officer? I wonder myself sometimes. I hope I never see him on the field, Ángel. I know he half crippled you, but he also saved both our lives and gave us our freedom that day. I'd hate to have to kill him."

"I would not hesitate," Ángel said grimly.

"Let us hope it does not come to that." García turned at a shout from behind him. "Colonel Anaya wants to speak to us, I think. He probably has orders."

Ángel paused, his eyes still on the distant French. It was very clear that they were preparing to bring their reserves across for a second attack. He watched for a moment, remembering.

"I hope you are out there," he said softly. "I really hope you are."

Chapter Fifteen

Michael was exhausted; a numbing tiredness which flooded both his body and his mind, so that it was becoming difficult to think clearly. The sights and sounds of the death throes of San Sebastian were an assault on all his senses and he realised he was having to concentrate to put one foot in front of the other.

Once over the wall, the remains of the Light Division stormers, pitifully few, fought their way through the narrow streets of the town. Michael could hear sounds of battle on all sides. The streets were laid out in a fairly regular grid pattern and the survivors of the French garrison initially made a series of defensive stands in the houses and shops. Rey had clearly made efforts to barricade the town in case the Allied troops broke in and Michael thought his efforts surprisingly effective, but there were not enough French troops to man the defences. Those who made the attempt were exhausted by the long hours of fighting in the breaches and there were very few reserves. Rey had thrown all his forces along the walls, trusting that the defences of San Sebastian were unassailable. Once Graham's men were inside the town, the French could do nothing but fall back.

Their orderly retreat quickly turned into a headlong flight to the castle, where Rey intended to make his last stand. Michael's small band joined men of the Fifth Division racing through the streets in pursuit. Musket and rifle fire echoed off stone walls as the Allies advanced through broad squares and narrow alleys. Initially they were systematic about it, clearing each building of French troops as they went through, but Michael knew that would not last. He had seen men during a storming before and there were already small bands of men disappearing inside houses from which they failed to emerge.

The French were driven back through the town. Occasionally Michael's men met fierce resistance across one street but there were too many side-streets and alleys which could be used to outflank them. Some of the barricades were unmanned; there were simply not enough men to defend them. At one corner a young French officer put up a spirited resistance with around twenty men, protected by barrels filled with broken stonework. A dozen men of the Fifth Division were desperately trying to dislodge them.

Michael yelled at his men to halt and looked around him. Visibility was terrible as the narrow streets filled with smoke. He could see the red glow of flames rising above the eastern side of the town and he supposed that the combination of Allied artillery and the disastrous explosion of French munitions had started the conflagration. Michael wondered how quickly it would spread. Too many of these houses were built wholly or partly from wood and many of the roofs were thatched. Once the fire took hold these streets would become a death trap and he wanted his men out of here before then.

In front of him rose an elegant stone house with elaborate wooden balconies overlooking the street. It was perfect for his purpose and he could see that the thick door had already been broken down. Possibly the Fifth Division had already begun to loot this street, but Michael suspected that actually the damage had been done by the French, using whatever materials they could find to build makeshift defences.

He led his men into the house and up the narrow staircase, throwing open doors as they went to ensure that no French snipers lurked within. The rooms were empty; their furnishings showing signs of a hasty departure with drawers and cupboards left open and beds unmade. There was wealth and prosperity here and Michael sent up a quick silent prayer that these people had made it out of the town before the storming.

The balconies were exactly what he had wanted. Michael placed his rifles and muskets to his liking, peering down through the thickening smoke at the little party of Frenchmen.

"Ready to fire, sir."

"Not yet. Terry, get yourself down there and haul those fucking idiots from Hay's brigade out of the way before they get caught in the cross fire."

"Yes, sir."

Michael watched as his Sergeant approached the men. There was no officer with them and their NCO, a burly sergeant with blood dripping from his left arm, seemed inclined to argue the point with Terry, though some of the men had the wit to look up as Terry pointed and began to back away rapidly at the sight of the waiting Light Division men. The Sergeant remained stubbornly in place with a few die-hards and Michael groaned.

"I'm tempted just to shoot him. Nobody will ever know it was us."

"No need for that, sir," one of the riflemen said cheerfully. "Permission to move him?"

Michael understood and stepped back. "Granted, Rifleman Hope."

Hope stepped forward, settling his rifle into his shoulder and took careful aim. The crack echoed around the small balcony, making Michael's ears ring. The shot hit the ground terrifyingly close to the Sergeant's feet. It was further away from Terry who dived back towards the broken doorway and into cover. He had no way of knowing where the shot had come from and was clearly taking no chances. Michael could hear his feet clattering on the stairs and repressed a grin as he burst into the room, swearing furiously.

The Sergeant and his men had scattered as the shot hit. It clearly unnerved the remaining infantrymen who remained at a cautious distance as their Sergeant finally looked up at the balcony, his expression shocked. Michael stepped forward and raised his voice to a bellow.

"Get out of the way you bloody imbecile before we blow your fucking head off. Move!"

The Sergeant moved, melting away into the chaos after his men, presumably before the officer above him had time to ask his name and regiment. The commotion had also alerted the French to their danger and Michael could hear the young officer shouting orders to run but there was no time. The crash of musket and rifle fire was unbearably loud and it was followed by the screams of wounded and dying Frenchmen. The survivors fled without need for a second volley, abandoning their defensive position in a frantic rush for the temporary safety of the castle.

Michael looked around him as his men began methodically cleaning and reloading their weapons. He was struck by their monumental calm. It sounded as though hell itself was opening up in the streets outside but these men, from battalions across the Light Division, behaved as though they were on a training exercise. Michael's body ached with tiredness and his brain was full of anxiety for Giles and the other men who had fallen, but he felt a sudden fierce pride in both his regiment and his division.

"Well done," he said. "Let's get out of here. I don't like how fast these fires are spreading. I want to get up to the castle wall, find out who's in command since it doesn't look to me like anybody is and get some bloody orders before we all burn to death. Keep together, keep alert and fight if you have to, but we don't go looking for them. I think they'll all be holed up in that castle by now and how to get them to surrender is going to be somebody else's damned problem."

They reached the foot of Mount Urgall, the steep hill which led up to the castle, without further incident. There was a scattering of officers and men along the line, exchanging an erratic fire with the first line of the French defenders. Michael surveyed the castle and wondered how many of the defenders had made it inside. Judging by the thin line in the first trenches, he suspected not many. A determined rush by a fresh division would probably have these men out of here within an hour, but looking around him at the filthy, exhausted remains of Graham's army, Michael did not think it was going to happen today. There were alarmingly few Allied troops present and, listening to the rising sounds in the town behind him, Michael suspected that the systematic sacking of San Sebastian had thoroughly begun.

He could see no sign of Leith so he settled his small band behind a broken wall opposite the convent of St Teresa with orders to shoot any Frenchman who raised his head. He also gave very specific warnings about what would happen to any man who left his post to join in the looting and destruction.

Michael did not bother to make threats of disciplinary proceedings. Instead he fixed his eyes on the four men from the 110th who remained with the group.

"Gallagher, how long have you been with the 110th?"

"Eight years, sir. Joined just before Copenhagen."

"Good man. While I go and find out who the bloody hell is in command around here, why don't you explain to these gentlemen all about Major-General van Daan and what he'll do to any one of them who deserts his post to go after the locals? It'll save me time."

Gallagher, who was from Dublin and an excellent raconteur gave a broad grin which Michael thought was frankly terrifying in his filthy, battered face. "Glad to, sir."

"I'll be back soon."

It took some time to work out who was in command of the depleted troops, but repeated enquiries finally led Michael to Major-General Andrew Hay who was apparently the only general officer unwounded. Hay looked fraught, his face beaded with sweat and his eyes sore and red from the acrid sting of gunpowder. He stared in some bewilderment as Michael saluted and gave a brief account of himself and requested orders. Hay had the air of a man who had given enough orders for one day and would prefer to be left alone but he rallied himself with a noble effort.

"Hunt down, is he? And did you say all of the other Light Division officers?"

"As far as I know, sir, though it's possible some of them went over at a different point. I don't know the condition of any of the wounded yet but I'm currently the most senior - and the only officer - from our group of volunteers. They're over there taking pot shots at the convent but I'm not sure it's doing much good. Are you intending an attack on the castle?"

There was an ominous rumble from the leaden sky. Both Michael and Hay looked up. The heavy clouds had grown black and threatening. Hay made a sound in his throat which sounded suspiciously like a growl.

"All we need is a storm at this point. Bloody weather."

"I think that's what we're about to get, sir."

"At least if it rains it might douse some of these fires. If it doesn't, the entire town is going to go up in smoke. As for an assault, I don't have enough men for it and the ones I have are exhausted. We'll blockade the place and wait for orders from Sir Thomas Graham."

"Very good, sir."

A few heavy raindrops splashed onto Michael's hand. He looked up again, welcoming them on his heated face although they were not really the cool water he desperately wanted; they felt as warm as the hot air around him. Hay sighed.

"Van Daan's brigade, did you say? 110th?"

"112th, sir, under Colonel Wheeler."

"Bloody good man, Wheeler. Look, there's no point you hanging around here away from your battalion. I've sent several other parties of volunteers to escort prisoners over the breaches. You can wait for the next batch, get them up to the lines and get some food and rest. I imagine tomorrow they'll send you back to your battalion, though I don't know exactly where they'll be. There's been some action out towards Irun I believe, not sure if the Light Bobs are involved."

Michael felt a lurch in his stomach. He wondered, not for the first time today, what had made him think it was a good idea to volunteer for a battle away from his own battalion. He felt suddenly very isolated and very lonely. He thought of Brat and had to blink back unexpected and embarrassing tears but the rain was falling more heavily now and Hay's blackened face was also streaked.

"Sir, if you really have no need of us just now I'd like permission to take them back through the town. You've got plenty of escorts for prisoners here but I'm worried about the townspeople."

"So am I," Hay said grimly. "A lot of them got out before the storming. Graham allowed women and children and obvious civilians through on a regular basis. But some won't leave their homes or their business and some are just too stubborn to admit they're at risk."

"Well these fires are about to deal with the first of those problems and the Fifth Division on a drunken rampage through the town is going to convince them of the second. In a couple of hours they'll be drunk enough to shoot my men if we stand between them and a barrel of wine or a householder's daughter. I'm not risking their lives, not after what they've done today. But I might be able to get a few of the locals out."

Hay regarded him with sympathetic eyes. "Were you at Badajoz?"

"No, I was wounded. But I was at Seringapatam, Ciudad Rodrigo and a little place called Castro Urdiales. I've seen enough slaughtered civilians and raped women to last me two lifetimes. Permission to try, sir."

"Granted," Hay said quietly. "We've not met before, O'Reilly, but I know who you are now and be assured your name will feature in my report of today. Bloody good work, Captain."

Michael saluted again. As he went to collect his filthy, exhausted band of men he reflected that was exactly the reason he had volunteered for this hell hole in the first place. He wondered why it brought him so little satisfaction now.

After two hours, he decided that his men had done enough and led them, along with around twenty terrified refugees, over the hornwork and back towards the Allied lines. As Hay had predicted, it had been impossible to organise an attack on the castle with so few troops. Fires had flared up all through the town and with the thunderstorm came a fierce wind which drove the flames on, faster than the deluge of rain could douse them. Sand from the dunes blew in a thick cloud through the streets blinding the drunken men of Graham's army as they staggered through the streets. Thunder crashed in an echo of the now silenced guns and lightning ripped the dark sky apart with dazzling brilliance.

The rain made any use of muskets or rifles impossible on both sides. It was a deluge which drenched both civilians and soldiers as Michael's men trudged back to the Allied camp, bayonets ready to defend the half dozen women who huddled together in miserable, terrified silence. Michael thought that these women seemed to have been the lucky ones, although he had found two girls in one of the empty houses who had not been so. The fire was close by and they were both clearly dead, so he had covered them, said a furious prayer for their souls and moved on.

The hillside slopes were denuded now of their spectators. Michael wondered if they had all gone home to find their dinner and get dry and tried hard to rein in his anger because he knew how pointless it was. He delivered his refugees to a weary officer of the quartermaster's department who had set up two marquee tents which were being buffeted about in the wind. Other refugees huddled miserably within, accepting rations and watching from a safe distance as their town burned.

With his official duties done, Michael made enquiries and went in search of the hospital provision. He found it in an abbey set up on the hillside. Vegetable gardens and well-tended fields stretched down to the river and the buildings had a prosperous air which suggested that the French invaders had left this small community of monks alone apart from periodic raids on their livestock, produce and fish ponds.

Michael settled his men in a dry feed store on the edge of the estate and walked up to the abbey church to make enquiries about his wounded. He was met in a cool stone hallway by a harried surgeon in a bloody apron who barely listened to his question.

"I've no idea where they are. Or who they are. We're treating them as they come in; it's too soon to make up returns yet. You'll get to know in time…"

"These men are my responsibility and my friends," Michael snapped. "There must be some kind of list of names."

"There are hundreds of them coming in. They're maimed. They're dying. They're…"

"Michael."

He looked up startled. She was standing on the opposite side of the hallway, a stained apron over her plain dark gown. Her hair was pinned up from her face in a riot of auburn curls and she was pale and grave but her heart was in her eyes. Michael had no idea how she was there or why. He only knew that suddenly he felt calm again as though just being in the room with her brought him peace.

"Ariana."

She walked forwards into his arms and he kissed her hard, completely ignoring the bewildered surgeon. After a while he heard the man mutter something and then a door closed. Michael did not care. He was conscious of his soaked filthy clothing, his dirty face and the blood of some of his men on his coat but it did not seem to matter. He was in her arms and he was home and he realised at that moment that nothing else would ever matter.

Eventually they broke apart purely to breathe. "I'm sorry," Michael said on a gasp. "Dear God, I'm sorry, love. I'm so sorry I ever did this, but I swear to God the only battles I'll ever fight in the future are those I'm honour bound to. Are you all right? What are you doing here? Where's the brigade: is there fighting over there? I heard…and Brat, do you know anything about Giles? He was hit when he came to warn us about the artillery bombardment and…"

"Michael, if you do not stop speaking I will have to slap you," Brat said firmly. "I wish you to take a big breath and then another. Then you shall follow me. Mrs van Daan and Dr Hanson are here; we have set up a temporary hospital in one of the hay barns. Giles is here and he is alive, though not well. Come this way."

She took his hand and led him through a side door and across a yard. A young novice was feeding a flock of chickens by a wooden coop and a brown-robed brother was harvesting the neat rows of a herb garden, his hood pulled up against the relentless rain. Michael and Brat ran hand in hand between several buildings and down a narrow track to a big wooden barn. She pushed open the door and drew him inside.

It was warm and dry, redolent with the smell of fresh hay overlaid by an unpleasant but familiar smell of blood and pus and unwashed human bodies. At the far end, neat rows of patients were laid out on thin straw mattresses covered with army blankets. Closer at hand there were several tables set up, screened from the ward by makeshift wooden barriers cobbled together. Two surgeons were hard at work and there was a long row of men laid out waiting for attention.

At a third table a woman bent over a patient with an injured leg. She was setting stitches, slowly and carefully while a girl stood holding the man's leg steady. Michael paused for a moment to view the scene, his heart full. He had watched Anne van Daan work so many times over the years but her total concentration in the middle of the bloody horror of an army hospital never failed to amaze him.

She did not look up until she had placed the final stitch. Michael saw her expression change as she saw him and knew she had been worrying. He gave her a very faint smile and she returned it.

Alison Macdonald released the patient's leg and brought a basin of water and Anne carefully cleaned the blood and pus from around the wound then surveyed her work with satisfaction.

"That will do, I think. Will you dress it for me, Alison and then find Private Seddon a bed?"

"Yes, ma'am."

Anne washed her hands then came towards Michael. She embraced him and he held her for a long moment feeling some of the tension of battle drain out of him. She stepped back and surveyed him carefully.

"No injuries?"

"Not really, ma'am."

In response she reached up to touch a graze on his temple. "Sit down and I'll clean it, just to make sure there's no gravel in there. You look as though you could do with a rest. I'm told you've been commanding our volunteers."

"What was left of them," Michael said bitterly. "Did Colonel Hunt tell you that, ma'am? Have you seen him? Is he all right? I…"

"He's doing very well, Captain," Anne said soothingly, pushing him firmly onto a wooden chair. "He was in here earlier and Colin Hanson removed a ball from just below his knee, but we don't think he'll need amputation. We've sent him over to the convent because they've facilities to accommodate officers over there and I think he'll be more comfortable, but I'm going to keep an eye on him personally. He had very good things to say of you, Captain O'Reilly."

"I don't even know who made it through," Michael said. She was cleaning the graze carefully, washing away blood and powder. It made him feel like a small child having his face washed. Brat was beside him, holding his hand. "We lost a lot. I think we lost too many. Ma'am, what of Giles Fenwick? He exposed himself to French fire to warn us about the artillery; I saw him go down. I sent Coates back to help him which I shouldn't have done but…"

"Thank God you did or he'd have bled to death out there," Anne said flatly. "Michael, will you stop fidgeting or I'm going to call two hospital assistants to hold you still. Giles is here and you can see him once I've finished with you, but I thought you might like to know what else has been going on first?"

Michael realised he had been moving restlessly. He was always this way in the immediate aftermath of battle, as though the heightened tension took time to leave his body. He took Brat's hand in both of his and forced himself to sit still.

"I'm sorry," he said. "I'm desperate for news, ma'am, I've been hearing all kinds of rumours out there. And you…how are you here?"

"It was Johnny's idea," Anne said, dropping the cloth back into the bowl. "That's better, I can see your face properly now. Come through this way and have some tea. There's no milk or sugar of course, but it's hot and strong which is probably all you need just now and I could do with a break; I've been working for four hours straight."

The tea was being brewed by a lanky infantryman with a bandage around his head working in a big round tent in the yard at the back of the barn. A number of officers, all with minor wounds, were scattered about the tent drinking from mess cups, and a box of tack biscuits lay open on a folding table. Anne collected cups and Brat settled Michael on a damp blanket then brought three biscuits. Dipped in the hot tea they were easier to eat and steadied Michael's churning stomach. He watched as Anne seated herself elegantly on the canvas and blew on the scalding tea. Something in her manner told him that not all the news she had for him was good.

"Who have we lost?" he asked, wanting it over with quickly.

"You know about Sir Richard Fletcher, I presume? Generals Leith, Oswald and Robinson are all wounded but I'm told they should all recover. I'm dreading telling Paul; he and Fletcher have been friends for years."

227

"I had the same thought," Michael said. He realised he was speaking too loudly, still partly deaf from the endless sound of the guns and lowered his voice deliberately. "What of our men?"

"It isn't good, Michael. I still don't know all the numbers and we probably won't for a few days but of the Light Division officers who went out there, only two of you made it out in one piece."

Michael felt very sick. "Who did we lose, ma'am?" he asked again. "Please."

"Ensign Hardy was killed in the breach," Anne said in level tones. "Lieutenant Jackman was shot through the arm. We've decided not to do an immediate amputation though I think Hanson would have done it if I hadn't been here. You know…"

"Bowlby," Michael said. He could hear the panic in his own voice. "Jim Bowlby. He was with Hardy, they were climbing together behind me. He was keeping an eye on Hardy for me, we both thought he was too young to have volunteered for this but he was the most senior subaltern who did in the 115th. Do you…?"

"He's dead, Michael. I'm so sorry. They brought him in with his left leg shot away. We did what we could but he died on the operating table."

"Mary, mother of God, no. Poor Hannah. And the boys. They lost the baby last year too. What in Christ's name is she going to do now?"

"We'll make sure they're all right, Michael, you know we will."

"It's not that. They were devoted to each other, Hannah and Jim. Standing joke of the battalion that she'd follow him into hell if he was posted there. How is she going to get through this?" Another thought struck him and he stared at her for a long moment in dawning horror. "Giles. Does Giles know? Bowlby was his sergeant since before he even joined the rest of the battalion, they were in Walcheren together."

"I've told Giles," Anne said and her tone told Michael it had been bad. "He was all for getting out of his bed and trying to ride back to camp to see Hannah but I have dealt with that nonsense. As far as I can tell we have four dead and nine wounded from our brigade. Plus poor Lieutenant Ronaldo and his Portuguese contingent."

"He's dead, isn't he?"

"Not yet, but it's only a matter of time. He asked for a priest so the Abbot sent his chaplain to minister to him and the other Portuguese wounded."

"How many of his men did we lose?"

"Four of them are dead, the other six are all wounded. A terrible loss."

"I'd like to see them. All of our wounded."

"Finish your tea and then Ariana can show you where they are."

Michael dipped a second tack biscuit in his cup and forced himself to eat. "You still haven't explained why you're here, ma'am."

"I'm sorry, I got distracted. The brigade marched out along with Kempt's brigade. Soult launched an attack along the lines to try to get through to relieve San Sebastian. Paul was in his usual panic about where I would be

228

safest given we had so little information and Johnny suggested that since the Light Division had no medical staff at San Sebastian, it might be a good idea to send at least one of our surgeons over to assist, with me to accompany him. Captain White provided an escort with some of his Staff Cavalry Corps."

"Do you have any news about what's happening?"

"Not yet, though I've been told that the Spanish bore the brunt of the attack at Irun and San Marcial. Paul will send a message as soon as he can but I have a feeling we've not seen much action. I'm surprised anybody can see to fight at all in this weather; is it never going to stop raining?"

Michael sat in silence for a while listening to the rain pounding against the canvas. Brat moved closer to him and he put his arm about her. She rested her head on his shoulder and he felt her curls brushing against his unshaven chin, catching on the bristles. He wondered how it was possible to feel such happiness and such grief and pain simultaneously.

Anne uncurled her long legs with a sigh and got to her feet. "I should get back to work," she said. "When you're ready, Michael, Ariana can take you to see our wounded. I've put them together at the far end of the barn. There's a general hospital in Pasajes and I believe it's the intention to transfer the wounded over to there but I'd like to keep ours local if at all possible."

"Well there won't be provision in San Sebastian, ma'am, that's for sure. The way that fire spread I'd be amazed if there's much left standing."

"Was it bad, Michael? The townspeople, I mean. I heard that the Fifth Division ran wild in there."

"They did, the drunken bastards," Michael said grimly. "It wasn't as bad as Badajoz or Castro Urdiales but that's probably only because there weren't that many civilians left in there. I think most of them either left before the siege began or were evacuated during the past week or so. There's been a lot of looting and the usual misbehaviour but most of the property damage will be due to the fires, and they were caused by artillery not deliberate arson. Though that's not going to be any consolation to the families who have lost their homes."

"No. I've spoken to the Abbot and he's happy for you and your men to sleep in the church providing you'll answer for their good behaviour. The brothers will provide hot food later and I'll join you for that. In the meantime…"

There was a rustle then a mad flapping of canvas as a man ducked into the tent. A few more officers had wandered in to dry off while Michael, Anne and Ariana had been talking but this was a private of the 52nd, soaked to the skin with one arm resting in a sling. He looked around then approached quickly, saluting awkwardly with his left hand.

"Begging your pardon, ma'am, but I've been asked to find Mrs van Daan?"

"That's me. What is it, Private?"

"Dr Hanson wants you, ma'am. Something to do with the Portuguese officer."

"Lieutenant Ronaldo?"

"Don't know, ma'am."

"All right. Thank you, Private. Just wait there by the tent flap and Ariana will bring you some tea and biscuit."

As they ducked out into the wind and rain, Michael offered Anne his arm. They fought their way back to the door of the barn.

"The officers aren't going to like the rank and file invading their tent, ma'am."

"The fire, the tea and the biscuit were provided by the 110th, Captain. Specifically me. If they want to argue about it, they can speak to me. They won't though. Your fiancée has mastered the art of silencing debate with one look. I admire her very much."

"So do I, ma'am, though I've a feeling it's going to make married life an interesting affair at times."

They arrived back in the barn wet, windswept and laughing. Dr Hanson met them inside. His clothing was soaked in blood and he looked tired and harassed. Anne stopped laughing immediately.

"I'm sorry, Doctor, I went to get some tea and take a break. I also wanted to bring Captain O'Reilly up to date with what news we have. Is it poor Mr Ronaldo? Has he gone?"

"Not at all, ma'am. He's rallied slightly as a matter of fact; he's conscious and talking. It's not going to last, poor chap. He's drowning in his own blood, it's only a matter of time. But he's very agitated, trying to say something to that priest. The man can't understand a word, I don't think he speaks any more Portuguese than I do. I tried to ask him in English, but he's very distressed. I wondered if you might try."

"Of course," Anne said quickly. "He might be trying to send a message to his wife. I know her. Michael…"

"I'll come with you, ma'am."

Lieutenant Ronaldo was at the far end of the barn on a mattress. They had found a milking stool for the priest to sit beside him. The man rose to make way as Anne and Michael approached. Ronaldo was visibly restless, shifting about on the mattress and trying to sit up. His breathing was quick and shallow and Michael could hear an ominous gurgle every time he tried to take in air. His chest was swathed in bloodstained bandages and his good-looking young face was grey and sheened with sweat. He looked like a dying man.

Anne spoke quickly to the priest in low tones. Eventually she put her hand on his arm and thanked him. The man moved away looking relieved to go and Anne turned to Michael.

"He speaks very little Portuguese but he was happy to administer the sacrament and hear confession. He's done so but it seems Lieutenant Ronaldo became very upset afterwards. He tried to speak to the priest in English but he doesn't speak any so Hanson sent for me. You can stay if you want to, Michael, but let me talk to him first in case it's a personal message for Tasia."

"Of course, ma'am. I'll have a word with Barforth over there. Where's Giles?"

"He's in the main house in a private room. I'll take you over afterwards, I won't be long."

***

Anne seated herself on the low stool and reached for Ronaldo's hand. It was cold and flecked with dried blood. He turned his head to look at her and she could see that the attractive dark eyes were unfocused. She was not sure at first if he could see her at all. It was not unusual for a dying patient to rally a little at the end and Anne always dreaded the false hope it could give to friends and family if they were present.

She could tell that he recognised her when his grip on her hand tightened painfully. "Senhora, thank God. Thank God," he said in his own language. His voice was so faint she had to lean forward to hear him against the noise of the ward. "I need to speak. I need to tell somebody, for my soul's sake."

Anne reached out and gently brushed the matted dark hair back from his face. "It's all right, Lieutenant, you may tell me anything you wish," she said soothingly in Portuguese. "Father Juan tells me that he has heard your confession and granted absolution and he will come back to you as soon as you wish. I'm guessing you want to send a message to Tasia? To your wife and son?"

"No," Ronaldo said, his voice rising. The effort made him cough and foamy pink blood spattered the blanket. Anne took out her handkerchief and wiped his mouth, wondering if this was the end and if he had left it too late to say whatever he was trying to say. "Yes. Yes, of course. Tell them I love them. Tell them I'm sorry. Tell them I died with the flag of Portugal in my hand, at the top of the breach."

"I will, Alfredo, I promise you. They'll be very proud of you."

"They will not," Ronaldo said, and the bitterness in his tone startled Anne. "But maybe the manner of my death might atone for the disgrace I bring to my family."

"Alfredo, what on earth are you talking about? I've known your family for years and you've brought them nothing but joy and pride." Anne stopped herself speaking with an effort. Whatever was bothering this man on his deathbed was clearly important to him. He needed her attention not vague reassurances. "I'm sorry, I'm interrupting you. I will tell Tasia what you have said. What else do you want me to know?"

He looked relieved and seemed suddenly calmer, lying still on the grubby mattress, trying to find the words – and the remaining breath – to speak his truth. Anne waited with a combination of painful sympathy and pure curiosity. She could not imagine what an apparently blameless young husband and father might need to confess.

Eventually he spoke again, this time taking care to enunciate every syllable as though fearing he would never have the chance to repeat his words if she failed to understand him.

"I killed him," he said. "I need to confess. I killed him and another man suffered and almost died for my sin. I killed him."

Anne sat in silence, biting back a rush of bewildered questions. She did not think Ronaldo was speaking of some battlefield encounter. He was young but he had been with the army for several years, had fought bravely and well at Vitoria and in three minor battles and if his men were to be believed had taken this final wound in an act of conspicuous though possibly foolish heroism. Alfredo Ronaldo was unlikely to be fretting about killing Frenchmen in his final hours. She wondered if this was some early misdemeanour that had plagued him for years and for which he sought absolution but that did not make sense either. The priest had already granted him that.

Eventually, when he did not speak further, Anne said:

"Who did you kill, Alfredo? Do you want to tell me?"

Ronaldo turned his head to look up at her. There were tears on his cheeks. "No," he whispered. "I do not wish to, but I must, for the sake of my soul. He must not go on taking the blame for what I did."

"Who?"

"The Scottish sergeant," Ronaldo said. "The one they tried for the murder. The one they flogged. They might have hanged him. They would have hanged him, Tasia told me, if you had not persuaded her and the others to speak at the trial. I did not know. I was not there, I was away with my regiment and she did not tell me until afterwards in case I was angry with her. As if I could blame her for what that evil man tried to do."

Anne sat frozen in shock. He did not seem to expect her to speak which was just as well because she could not possibly have done so. Suddenly his words made perfect sense and she was appalled at the thought that he might have died without telling anybody his secret and terrified that he would still do so before she could ensure that his words would be believed.

"Michael," she hissed as loudly as she could. "Over here, now."

His shadow loomed over her in the dimly lit barn. She could still hear the thunder of heavy rain on the roof and wondered irrelevantly if it had finally doused the fires that were consuming San Sebastian.

"What is it, ma'am?"

"Captain White is over in the marquee guzzling tea," Anne whispered. Ronaldo's eyes were closed and she was afraid that with his story told he would slip peacefully away. "At least he was. Find him and get him over here, I need him to witness this. Tell him it's urgent."

"Won't I do?"

"No, you're his friend. Just do it, Michael."

He moved with blessed speed and Anne went for a cloth and some water and bathed the Lieutenant's face. As she had hoped, it revived him a little and the dark eyes met hers.

"Did I tell you?" he asked confusedly.

"Yes, you did. Alfredo, I think that's the bravest thing I've ever seen. To think of another man now, when you should be resting tells me the kind of man you are. Can you talk a little more?"

She could see Michael and White approaching, spraying raindrops from their wet clothing. White gave a bewildered bow.

"At your service, ma'am. Captain O'Reilly tells me…"

"We've no time," Anne said quickly. "Kneel down to make sure you hear this properly, his voice is growing fainter."

White obligingly dropped to his knees on the packed earth floor and Anne squeezed Ronaldo's cold hand reassuringly and spoke in English.

"Alfredo, Captain White is going to listen to what you have to say and he'll make sure that your courage isn't wasted. I know this is hard but can you tell him about the death of Major Leonard Vane? How did you find out that he'd been behaving badly towards your wife? Did she write to you or did she tell you during one of your spells of leave? I know it is difficult, but can you say it in English? I know you speak it well."

"I will try. She did not tell me at all, she was too ashamed," Ronaldo said, this time in heavily accented English. His voice was barely audible. "My father-in-law told his son who served with me and he told me that your husband had sent Vane away because of his behaviour towards the women of the household. I was so angry. He tried to dishonour my wife. I decided that when I could, I would challenge him and kill him."

"And did you?"

"I did, though it was not as I meant. I was on my way back to camp after visiting my wife and my horse was lamed. I walked to a farmhouse. On the way I came across Vane. He was beating the Scottish sergeant who was very drunk. I thought he would kill him."

"That would be Sergeant Rory Stewart, Lieutenant?" White said clearly.

"Yes. He – the Scotsman – was unconscious. He did not see me."

"Did you challenge Vane?"

"I asked him to meet me, to fight with swords. He laughed at me. He called me a boy and said things of Tasia…of my wife…that I could not bear to hear. It was very dark out on that road with just a little moon. Not the right way to fight honourably…"

Ronaldo coughed again and this time a gush of blood came with it, soaking his chest. Anne moved forward to bathe his face, wondering if this was the end. It was a horrible way to die and it seemed brutal to be forcing this confession at such a moment but she remembered the bloody mess of Rory Stewart's back after his flogging and how near he had come to being hanged and did not tell Ronaldo to rest.

After a moment the dark eyes opened again and fixed on White's face. White's expression was full of compassion. "Give yourself some time, Lieutenant."

"I have no more time, Captain." Ronaldo's voice was more faint than ever but he seemed to gather himself for a final effort. "I drew my sword. He drew his. We fought a little but I could not see and he disarmed me. I was ready to die but he just laughed at me. He threw my sword into a thorn bush and said if I came after him again he would slit my throat then go to Tasia and finish what he had begun. He turned away and walked towards his horse. I had a knife in my belt. It is there with my kit, I always carry it. I ran after him and I cut his throat.

"He did not die immediately. He crawled a little, towards the Scotsman, tried to shake him. I suppose to ask for help. The man did not awaken. Afterwards I worried that they might blame the man so I rolled Vane's body down into a ditch away from him. I found my sword and took my knife and went on to the farm. The next day I went back to my regiment. I did not regret his death. It made Tasia safe."

Anne realised that she was crying. She lifted Ronaldo's hand to her lips and kissed it. "Yes, you did," she said. "You don't have anything to regret, Alfredo – how could you? I don't suppose you knew anything about the trial until it was over, did you?"

"No. But still the man was beaten for my deed. He should know that. The General should know that."

Anne looked at White. The Staff Cavalry Corps officer looked slightly stunned but he rallied himself at her glare.

"Lieutenant Ronaldo, I give you my word as an officer that I'll make sure that Sergeant Stewart's reputation is restored. I'll also make sure they all know that you did what you did in defence of your wife. You're a brave man. Rest now."

Ronaldo gave a sigh which came out as a gurgling rattle. A steady stream of blood trickled from the corner of his mouth. Anne wiped it again but it reappeared immediately. She looked round at Michael and saw that his face was streaked with tears as well.

"Will you get the priest back, Michael?"

"I will, ma'am. Thank you. Rory Stewart owes you a great debt."

"Rory Stewart owes Lieutenant Ronaldo a great debt. Go and find Giles, I'll join you when I can."

Anne watched him go, accompanied by Captain White, then turned back to Lieutenant Ronaldo. He lay still, his eyes closed and his breath rattling in his throat. When the priest returned Anne gave up the stool but knelt on the other side, still holding his hand as the priest murmured a final prayer. Anne did not understand all the Latin words but she sensed that they comforted Ronaldo. Eventually the priest made the sign of the cross and fell silent. Time stretched out and darkness began to fall outside the barn, barely noticed above the relentless heavy rainfall.

Lamps were lit around the barn and the surgeons continued to operate in their uneven light as more casualties were brought in from San Sebastian. Anne wondered if the fires were out; wondered if Sir Thomas Graham would order the storming of the castle tomorrow and wondered where Paul was and if he was safe. She said her own silent prayer, both for Lieutenant Ronaldo and for the people she loved.

As her prayer came to an end she realised that the cold hand in hers had gone limp. She leaned forward to feel for a pulse in his neck then very gently closed his long-lashed eyes.

"He is gone, Father."

"I know. He died bravely. Did he manage to tell you what troubled him so sorely at the end, Señora?"

"Yes."

"I hope it was nothing to his detriment?"

"No," Anne said. "It was a matter of righting a past wrong. I think it took courage to do so."

"He was a brave young man," the priest said, and drifted away leaving Anne to summon an orderly to prepare the body for burial.

***

Giles cried when he tried to talk about Sergeant Jim Bowlby. Michael sat helplessly, feeling a horrible sense of familiarity. Earlier in the year, during the bloody storming of Castro Urdiales, Giles had lost Antonio, his Spanish guide and closest friend. He had mourned privately for the most part, sharing his grief only occasionally with his friends. Bowlby was not exactly a friend but he had served with Giles for a long time. His attractive wife Hannah took care of Giles' laundry and mending, often without payment when Giles was low on funds though Michael knew his friend always paid her back in full when he had the money.

"I shouldn't be here," Giles said for the third time. "I need to get back to camp, to tell Hannah what's happened. She should hear it from me, I'm his company officer. What if they send the news in some dispatch and she hears it from somebody who didn't know him and doesn't give a damn? I don't understand why I can't go."

"You can't go because you've a hole the size of a cricket ball in your side and it's a miracle it didn't damage any major organs," Michael said. "According to Mrs van Daan you'd lost so much blood by the time Coates found you and brought you in that she wasn't sure if you'd make it. I know how that feels. It happened to me in the trench outside Badajoz. You need complete rest, good food and time to heal. And she isn't going to let you out of her sight in case some over-enthusiastic junior surgeon bleeds you until you expire. She doesn't trust them."

It drew the shadow of a smile from Giles. "I don't trust them either. Any news at all from the brigade?"

"They marched out in support of Kempt's men, bloody little happened and by now they're bivouacked on the banks of the Bidassoa in the pouring rain listening to Major-General van Daan swearing in his sleep. He sent a note to his wife to reassure her."

235

"Thank God. Although if he's writing notes, he's probably not sleeping."

"He'll definitely be swearing though."

"Definitely." Giles managed another ghost of a smile. "Go and find your girl, Michael, get some dinner and then some sleep yourself. You don't have to keep sentry duty over me, I'm not going anywhere."

"Taken your clothing has she?"

"How did you guess?"

"She did it to me once."

"Of course she did." Giles shook his head. "I couldn't make it to the end of the cloisters, Michael, I'm so weak. You can safely leave me."

"I believe you. I'll go and eat but I'm coming back; they're going to put a mattress in here for me. Ariana is staying with Mrs van Daan tonight, a matter of propriety. And I…"

He stopped, suddenly unable to find the words. Giles studied him, waiting. Eventually Michael said:

"You saved my life out there today, Giles, and those of my men. And you took a bullet in the process. Just now I feel as though I'd like to stay close to you. That's twice you've brought me through utter shit and out the other side. I think you're my good luck charm."

Giles gave a genuine splutter of laughter which made Michael happy. "You sentimental Irish bastard. Well if you're coming back, see if you can find out what she's done with my kit. There's a pack of cards in there and I'm not sure I'll be sleeping much. This fucking hurts."

"I'm not letting you fleece me, Giles. I'm saving to be married."

"Imaginary money only, I promise you. It'll take my mind off this."

Michael got up to leave. "I miss Carl for the cards," he said wistfully. "He loved to play, was happy with low stakes and paid up like a gentleman."

There was a brief silence then Giles said:

"I can play for low stakes too, Michael. Or none at all if it suits you. I'd value your company."

Michael felt a warmth which had nothing to do with the fact that his soaked clothing was finally drying out.

"I'll be back with the cards later," he said. "Try to get some sleep, Giles. Oh…Christ, I'd forgotten to ask. What happened to the boy that was with you? The bugler?"

Giles laughed again. "Young Hutchins? He was from the 47th, I kidnapped him. You'd have cried laughing if you'd heard me trying to teach him our bugle call but thank God he's a bright lad and picked it up fast. He's completely fine. The shot hit his bugle and knocked it out of his hands straight into his head. He has a lump like an egg on his temple and he's furious at the damage to his instrument but I've promised I'll ask Major-General van Daan if he'll pay for a replacement."

"I think it was a safe promise," Michael said. "Get some rest, I'll be back later."

"I'll try. Any news about Soult's advance yet? If he didn't make a serious assault on the Light Division…"

Michael grinned, glad to be able to deliver some good news. "I forgot to tell you. I went in to see Colonel Hunt before I came here and he's sharing a billet with poor Oswald. It looks as though the advance on the Light Division might have been a feint, they're not sure. What we do know is that Soult threw his main attack at Freire's Spanish troops at San Marcial."

"And?"

"And our Spanish allies kicked their arses all the way back to the Bidassoa. Twice. Soult's in full retreat again, though how he's going to cross that river in the dark I've no idea. With this rain storm the fords are completely impassable."

Giles considered. "The bridge at Vera?"

"He's not getting over that, Captain. Skerrett's brigade was left behind on the heights behind Vera. One whiff of the French and that bridge will be crawling with the 52nd and the 95th. They're ugly buggers; Soult's men are going to run a mile."

"It'll be interesting to see which direction they run in, then," Giles said. "Not that I'm going to be doing much reconnaissance for a while. Perhaps this Spanish officer they're foisting onto me will be useful after all."

"That's not what you said when the General first told you. I'll be back after supper with the cards and any more news I can glean, but I doubt we'll hear much more tonight. Even Lord Wellington isn't going to expect a courier to get through in this weather."

"I think you underestimate our Commander-in-Chief, Michael," Giles said seriously. He settled back against his pillow with a resigned air and closed his eyes. Michael watched him for a moment with a little smile then went in search of Brat and supper.

Chapter Sixteen

The second French attack came at noon. Ángel watched them beginning the climb. There were a lot more of them this time, as the French commander had brought up his reserves to make the assault at the western end of the heights. It was the highest point of San Marcial and was topped by a small hermitage chapel which had been built to commemorate a victory over the French in some previous century.

Freire had used the intervening hours to consult with his officers and had redeployed several battalions, including the Mallorcan regiment, to give support to the troops occupying the hermitage. It appeared that this time the French had learned something from the rout of the first attack. They made no attempt to throw out a skirmish line over the broken, uneven ground. Instead they marched forward in solid lines; an intimidating swarm of blue-coated men scrambling up the steep slope.

Once again Freire had positioned his men high up the slope, with the Hermitage hill defended by the young General Porlier's Fifth Spanish Division. Anaya's men were stationed further back out of sight of the advancing French but ready to come to Porlier's aid should the French reserves, presumably fresher than the men who had been driven back that morning, manage to gain a foothold on the hill.

Ángel could not resist clambering up to the white rectangular chapel to watch the French advance. Around him, Porlier's men stood ready. The General had placed most of them on the front slope of the hill with half a battalion left to guard the chapel itself. Ángel watched Porlier as he moved among his men in the minutes before the attack. He wondered how it felt to command at this level at such a young age. Porlier was at least five years younger than Ángel. He had risen to prominence as a guerilla leader and Ángel supposed that years of operating independently outside the formal structure of the Spanish army had given him experience of leading men. It was difficult not to resent the contrast with Ángel's own career, which looked likely to hit a new low point after the recent duels, but as far as he could tell, Porlier knew his business and his men seemed to idolise him.

Ángel observed with satisfaction that despite their early attempt to keep the line intact, the French were once again breaking apart as they climbed the steep slope. There were too many obstacles and the officers did not seem able to keep their men together. Gaps were appearing in the line and several sections were surging ahead while others hung back, seeming almost reluctant to engage with the waiting Spaniards.

"It is good to see them falter," a voice said beside him. Ángel was surprised to realise that Porlier had come to stand next to him at the stone wall.

"Do you think they will fall back again, General?" he asked, because he could think of nothing else to say.

Porlier shot him a slight smile. "Don't you, Captain? What has changed since this morning other than their numbers? They could have held back a reserve in the hope of attacking us once we have committed to the charge, but they have not. I have spent my life hiding behind trees waiting to make a surprise attack on these men. It feels good to face them like this, with the belief that we can win."

Ángel felt a tug of fellow feeling. "It does," he said. "I was at Tarragona two years ago and we spent too much time running for our lives. I think you are right today. Unless they have reserves very well hidden, we can drive them back."

Porlier clapped him on the shoulder and moved away and Ángel went back to his men, waiting silently in the woodland behind the chapel. He could no longer see over the crest of the ridge but he could hear the French drums beating out their monotonous rhythm and hear the Spanish officers shouting the order to fire.

The crash of muskets echoed down the valley. It was quickly followed by a second volley and then the Spanish charged. Ángel fidgeted, wishing he could see what was happening on the hillside, but the only thing visible was a cloud of smoke above the trees, drifting up to the summit of Hermitage Hill. It was the smell of battle: a sharp stinging in his nose and throat. He coughed a little, listening to the roar of the Spanish troops as they launched themselves down the hill to meet the oncoming French.

For a while there was nothing but the sounds of fighting, a sporadic firing of muskets, the clash of steel on steel as bayonets met, and cries of pain, of rage and perhaps of fear. They seemed to be getting further away. Ángel longed to lead his men forward into the charge and looking over at Colonel Anaya he suspected he was not the only one feeling frustrated. Anaya had drawn his sword even though there was no enemy in sight. Further across the line, García almost seemed to vibrate with tension as though silently begging for the order to release them. Ángel did not think it was going to come. The French troops had been tired and demoralised from the rout of that morning and they must be experiencing heavy losses. He did not think they would make a third attack.

A yell of warning coming from the western edge of the ridge startled him so much that he physically jumped. There was a panicked neighing of horses. Freire had established a transport park for the officers' horses in an area of meadow beyond the woods and had set sentries. Ángel suspected that the warning had come from the first line of pickets, quickly cut off by a surprise French attack on the Spanish flank.

They surged up the steep slope to the top of the hill, at least a battalion, wearing blue coats and distinctive yellow trousers. Ángel did not recognise them from earlier in the day and presumed these were fresh troops from the reserve. They had either broken through Porlier's line or somehow managed to outflank him and were charging forward to attack the men left to defend the chapel.

Anaya bellowed the order to charge and his men raced into the fray. Porlier's men had been driven back by the sheer force of the French advance and were fighting a desperate hand to hand combat on the hill around the chapel. The enemy were getting the best of it and several of the Spaniards were on the ground. Ángel could hear cheering as the French took possession of the summit. He wondered briefly if the sound would rally their fleeing comrades to turn and make another attempt.

Anaya did not give them time to enjoy their triumph. He surged forward, bellowing orders to Porlier's battered troops to fall in behind the Mallorcan regiment. The Spanish officers grasped his intention quickly and began to rally their men, turning back towards the Hermitage with fresh determination.

Some of Ángel's men roared defiance as they charged up the slope. The French battalions at the top had been waving a flag to signal their possession of the summit but they fell quickly into a defensive line at the sight of the approaching Spaniards. Anaya called an order and his front line halted, their front rank forming quickly into a firing line while those behind them stood poised impatiently.

The volley blew the first row of the French apart. Some of them managed to maintain their position long enough to return fire and several of Ángel's men fell but the Spanish troops did not falter. They did not bother to reload for another volley but launched themselves up the hill with bayonets at the ready. The chapel was wreathed in dark smoke both from Anaya's muskets and from the combat which continued at the bottom of the long slope.

Ángel reached the first Frenchmen and swung his sword, slashing a man across the chest then cutting into his arm on the return pass. A French officer advanced, sword raised and Ángel kicked aside his falling opponent and parried quickly. The man was strong and he heard the clang as the blades crossed and felt it jar through his arm and shoulder. For a moment they remained immobile, swords locked together, waiting for the other to move.

Ángel moved first, trusting his own speed and skill. He swept his sword low to thrust under the Frenchman's guard at the same time weaving backwards to avoid his opponent's desperate slash. The blade almost reached him as he twisted his body sideways but the French officer was off balance. Ángel drove his blade deep into the man's torso. As he withdrew it, the officer toppled forward. Ángel jumped back to let him fall and turned quickly to check for further attacks.

There were none. It had taken minutes only for the French brigade commander to realise that the rest of the army was in full flight and that his battalions were alone and cut off at the summit of Hermitage Hill. He bellowed an order to retreat and his men turned and ran for their lives.

Anaya's men followed, ruthlessly hunting them down the slopes of San Marcial. They were met by the rest of Porlier's men who raced to block the French retreat, cutting them down as they veered off to try to avoid being trapped between the two Spanish forces. Ángel could see bodies littering the slopes and wondered how costly that brief victory would prove for the French brigade.

He could hear bugles sounding across the line, calling the Spaniards in. Ángel slowed his run and came to a halt, holding up his hand to his men. He was sweating, breathless and spattered with another man's blood. Most of his company had come to a halt behind him but half a dozen raced on, carried away by their triumph and by the kind of bloodlust which could get a man killed in a battle like this. Ángel raised his voice, bellowing to them to stop.

His throat was sore, raw from the billowing musket smoke and from shouting orders, but the men heard him and came to a stumbling halt. They looked around them, seeming bewildered to find themselves here, so far out from the rest of their comrades. It would have been funny if it had not been so dangerous. Most of the French were far ahead but there were still small pockets of resistance from men unwilling to accept defeat who were fighting a desperate rear guard action. Ángel gestured to his men to fall back and they did so quickly as though they had just realised their vulnerability. They were welcomed by the rest of their company with laughter and ribald remarks. Ángel considered ordering them to silence but he could see Anaya grinning and he decided to let it go. They had fought so well that he could not bring himself to quash their high spirits.

Anaya walked over to join him. "Well done, Captain Cortez. Your men are a credit to you. You should be very proud of them. They took the brunt of that first attack and they did not hesitate. You may be sure that your name will be mentioned in my report."

Ángel gave a faint smile. "Thank you, Colonel. I do not think it will help my cause but I am proud to have fought under you today."

"It cannot hurt your cause. In the short term I am afraid you must resign yourself to a period of exile. In the long term I hope we will serve together again. You are a brave man."

It was not enough, but Ángel decided to enjoy the moment anyway. He thought he was getting better at learning to set his resentment aside. He felt a hand on his shoulder and turned to see Óscar García beside him. The younger man's face was blackened with smoke and he was splashed with mud.

"Your face is dirty, Captain García."

"At least I am not covered in blood. Is it yours?"

"No. A French officer who was impertinent enough to believe he could best me in a sword fight." Ángel bent to clean his sword on the grass before returning it to its scabbard. As he did so, he felt the first drops of rain and heard a rumbling which was not from the distant guns of Irun and San Sebastian. He straightened, realising suddenly how tired and how hungry he was. He wondered how his men had fought so valiantly on so little food.

"It seems that there will be a storm."

"General Freire sent a message to Lord Wellington to ask for support part way through the battle, but it was not needed," Anaya said.

"Good. I am glad it did not arrive. This victory was ours alone. We have relied on others to fight for our country too often."

Ángel lifted his face towards the lowering sky. The rain was warm, big heavy drops which fell so hard they almost hurt. He did not mind. It was a cleansing rain, washing away the filth and blood of battle. He closed his eyes and scrubbed at his face with his hands to clear it of blood.

"Let's get them back up to the top, Captain. We should remain prepared just in case they have the stomach for a third attempt."

Ángel opened his eyes and turned to look back down the slope. He could see the winding shape of the Bidassoa over the top of the stunted trees. The fleeing French troops had reached the banks in complete disorder and many of them were trying to make their way across the bridge of boats that Soult's men had so carefully constructed that morning. It was not designed to take that many men at once and already some of them were in the water. Ángel could not be sure but he thought the centre of the bridge might have broken and be drifting with the current. He hoped that it was deep and that at least some of the French could not swim. Further away he could still hear the guns of San Sebastian, blasting defiance into the storm. He wondered how much longer they would be able to continue to fire in this weather.

"They are not coming back," he said, his eyes on the Frenchmen floundering in the water. "I hope Marshal Soult has his excuses ready for his Imperial master. He is going to need them."

***

News of Soult's advance reached the Light Division in the early morning. The bugles sounded the alarm and Paul's brigade scrambled to strike the camp, bundling tents into the baggage wagons and loading luggage onto pack mules in the early darkness. News came in dribs and drabs but it was clear that the Marshal had decided to make one final attempt to relieve San Sebastian before the town fell. Paul, who had been receiving regular updates from Giles Fenwick at the front, suspected that he had left it too late but that did not mean he could not inflict considerable damage on Wellington's stretched line.

As the Light Division formed up for the march, Sir James Kempt, who was temporarily in command during Alten's absence, convened a hasty meeting in the kitchen of the farmhouse where he had been staying.

"I've orders from his Lordship," he said briefly. "Van Daan, is there any chance you've got Fenwick's map with you? The sketch I've been sent looks like a deformed elephant, I can't make head or tail of it."

Paul retrieved the map from his pack and spread it on the wooden table. Kempt pointed.

"They're moving troops against the Spanish at Irun and San Marcial. There's a considerable force heading towards us and they're close. His Lordship has ordered the Seventh Division towards Lesaca. He's ordered me to use my discretion whether to remain here to defend Vera or to cross the river at the Lesaca bridge to maintain contact with Lord Dalhousie and the Seventh. He doesn't want us to engage the French heavily unless we have absolutely no choice."

Paul swore under his breath and then realised both Skerrett and Kempt had heard. He met Kempt's eyes and the older man raised his brows. Paul sighed.

"Sorry. For some reason I'm reminded of Robert Craufurd and that debacle on the Coa. What are we going to do?"

"I'd welcome your advice, Van Daan. Both of you of course, but you know Lord Wellington better than either of us. Or was that the reason for that particularly vulgar oath?"

"Yes," Paul said honestly. "He has no idea what he wants us to do, General because he can't predict what the French are going to do. What he'd really like is to be in six places at once but even Wellington hasn't managed to work out how to do that yet. Thank God."

"What would you do?"

Paul thought fast. "I'd leave a brigade here to keep an eye on the bridge. There's no need to hold the whole village; we can pull back up to the hills above and leave a strong picket on the bridge which can easily be withdrawn if necessary. Keep the men at arms and see what the French do. The other two brigades should cross the river in support of the Seventh."

"Why is that your choice?"

"Because the very fact that he's mentioned that as an option means that he's afraid it might be necessary. I think one brigade can keep out of trouble in Vera and might even be able to give them something to worry about. I don't think they'll launch a major attack there though, not if their aim is to relieve San Sebastian."

Kempt studied the map for a long time. "All right," he said finally. "Baggage to leave immediately to cross at Lesaca. I'll send an escort of the Staff Cavalry Corps with them. Van Daan, what about your wife?"

"She can travel with the baggage wagons and the other women," Paul said. He had already discussed it with Anne in a hasty conversation as they were packing. "As a matter of fact, Johnny Wheeler has suggested that she and the medical staff of the 112th make their way over to the lines outside San Sebastian. They'll be short of surgeons as usual and they'll be able to take care of any wounded from our volunteers."

"Are you all right with that?"

"I'd rather that than have her with us, given that we've no idea what's going to happen today. Graham will take care of her."

Kempt nodded. "Very well, let's get moving. Skerrett, you'll remain here. I'll leave you a small contingent of the 9th Dragoon Guards to act as couriers if need be. Don't engage unless you have to. Van Daan, you'll bring your brigade up to Lesaca. I'm going to send a detachment on ahead – half of the 43rd and three companies of the 95th. The rest of us will follow up. Once we're in touch with Dalhousie and Inglis I'll have a better idea of where we're likely to be needed."

They marched out under cover of darkness. Already Paul could hear the sounds of French troop movements. This felt like a hasty retreat and he kept Anne close beside him until the last possible moment. Once they had crossed the bridge at Lesaca she would ride on to join the baggage train. Paul hated being parted from her with the French this close but he was slightly reassured that the cavalry escort was commanded by Captain White. Paul had formed a very good opinion of White who was quick-witted and could think on his feet.

It was a warm, cloudy morning with the threat of rain. By the time Kempt's men reached Lesaca the mist had fully cleared and the sun could occasionally be seen between the thick clouds. All the same, Paul suspected it would rain before the end of the day.

He could smell gun smoke drifting on the breeze and the air was filled with the stuttering sound of musket fire and the occasional boom of artillery. It was impossible to judge exactly where it was coming from. Some of it must be from the fighting at San Sebastian over to the north-west but Paul thought there was also some action closer at hand. He felt tense and uneasy, simultaneously worrying about Anne's journey to San Sebastian, Michael and his men who would probably be fighting in the breaches by now and Skerrett's brigade playing a waiting game on the heights above Vera.

"I'm getting as bad as Wellington," he said to Johnny as they watched Anne's little party set off. "I keep running over everything in my head as though worrying about it can fix a damned thing."

His friend gave a smile. "Giving yourself a bollocking about it isn't going to help either, sir. Your wife will be fine and I'm glad she'll be on hand if any of our men need her. I wonder how Michael is?"

"I'm wondering that too," Paul admitted. Anne had reached a bend in the road and she turned her horse to look back at him and wave. Paul blew a kiss and she did the same before joining White at the front of the group. Paul watched until she was out of sight then trotted back to the head of his men. Johnny fell in beside him.

"Michael will be all right, sir. He's like a cat with nine lives, you know he is."

"I used to say that about Carl until those bastards blew his hand off. I'm far less sanguine about my friends' invincibility these days."

"Well don't worry about me, I have every intention of surviving this war. I promised Mary I would and I'd never break a promise to her."

Paul grinned. "Thank God I can cross you off my list then. It's a relief."

"So what else?"

Paul hesitated, thinking about it. Suddenly he knew what was bothering him. "It's Skerrett. I don't know him that well, Johnny. If it was you left back there in command, or Kempt or Andrew Barnard I wouldn't be fretting. He seems like a good enough man, if a bit awkward, but he's not that experienced. Harry Smith has spent a lot of time around him as brigade-major and he's not impressed."

"Sometimes Smith will put down a senior officer just to show off how clever he is.

"I know he does, but that doesn't mean that he's wrong."

"Are you worried Skerrett will do a Craufurd and take on a fight he can't win, sir?"

"Either that or he'll sit up on that hillside and not take action when he ought to. I actually can't decide which worries me more. I wish…I think I should have asked Kempt if I could stay. I think if one brigade was left back there alone, it should have been this one."

"Kempt is in command today, sir and he gave very clear orders. He wanted you with him."

"I know. And I didn't want to argue with him. I didn't want him to think I was trying to undermine him. Or that I didn't trust Skerrett. Only now I realise that if it had been Alten I'd have spoken up and he'd have agreed with me."

"Sir, you can't do anything about it now. Stop fretting."

Paul gave a tight smile. "Excellent advice, Colonel Wheeler. Let me know when you work out how to achieve it, will you?"

"I'll send you a memorandum, sir. You can save it for your memoirs."

"Oh fuck off, Wheeler. You're not funny." Paul stopped speaking and listened for a moment. "Am I imagining things or is that firing suddenly much closer at hand?"

Johnny was listening as well. "It sounds as though it's coming from directly ahead of us, over those next hills."

"Christ, do you think Kempt's advance guard is engaged?"

"Either that or it's the Seventh Division."

"Whichever it is, we need to speed up. You have command, Colonel, I'm riding up to speak to Kempt."

"Yes, sir."

Paul was just setting Rufus into a canter when his friend raised his voice again. "Piece of advice, sir. Don't go climbing any hills on your own to reconnoitre the enemy. Carter's not back yet and I'm not coming after you."

Paul heard a roar of laughter from the front ranks of the 110th. He wheeled his horse round and made a vulgar gesture which was entirely unsuitable for an officer and a gentleman. Johnny was laughing, leaning forward over his horse's neck. Behind him the laughter turned to cheers. Paul cupped his hands around his mouth like a speaking horn and bellowed back.

"You're not funny, Colonel Wheeler."

245

Johnny uncurled himself and raised his own hands to his mouth in response.

"They think I am," he yelled and the cheers redoubled. Unexpectedly they were taken up by the men at the back of the column and then further back among the 112th, 115th and the Portuguese battalion. Ahead of Paul the men of Kempt's brigade were looking around in bewilderment trying to work out the reason for the cheering. One or two of them showed willing and began to cheer and it spread rapidly until both brigades were cheering and clapping.

Paul was laughing uncontrollably. He could see Kempt cantering back along the column to meet him and he sent up a brief prayer that there was no particular need for silence. Kempt looked slightly stunned.

"Van Daan, what in God's name is going on back here? It sounds like…actually I've no idea what it sounds like. It's bloody noisy."

"I am sorry, sir. It began as a joke but it got a bit out of control. Do we know…?"

"There's a large French force over that rise. They've exchanged casual fire with our advanced party but they're showing no sign of attacking. The cavalry scout I sent out just galloped back to inform me that your impromptu display of cheering appears to have sent them into something of a panic. It's possible they think Lord Wellington is approaching with the rest of the army."

Paul gave a splutter of laughter. "Well that can't hurt," he said. "Orders, sir?"

"The same as before, Paul. We exchange fire, stay back and wait to see what they're going to do."

"Yes, sir. We'll try to be a bit quieter about it as well."

"Oh I don't know," Kempt said with a slight smile. "I think you may have just scared the life out of them. Quick time, General, to the top of the next rise. Then we wait."

**

Bonnet had joined Soult's latest advance across the Spanish border with a combination of exasperation and curiosity. Once again the Marshal had led his men forward with no more than two days rations in their packs and no possibility of supply wagons reaching them when the food ran out. Once again the army was reorganised, with the regiments who had suffered most at Maya, Roncesvalles and Sorauren being sent back to Bayonne in reserve. Once again Soult made rousing speeches designed to raise the battered morale of his army. Once again, it seemed to Bonnet, he did all of this while looking over his shoulder towards Paris and the reaction of the Emperor.

Bonnet was genuinely curious to see whether Soult really thought he could dislodge Wellington from the gates of San Sebastian and push him back down the foothills of the Pyrenees or whether this advance was one enormous feint to make Bonaparte believe he was still trying. Sometimes Bonnet thought that, since the debacle in Russia the previous winter, all Bonaparte's marshals must be playing the same dangerous game, using the lives of their men as chess pieces to hold on to their jobs and bolster the Emperor's delusional sense that he was still master of Europe. Bonnet would have loved to spend fifteen minutes alone in a room with Bonaparte to explain why he was wrong using the pointed end of a regulation bayonet. He was sick of this war.

Bonnet had hoped that the 30th légère would be among the regiments to be effectively stood down after its losses but he had reckoned without Chassé's dogged determination to rebuild his brigade. Bonnet could not help admiring the Dutch General's energy as he negotiated for reinforcements and new recruits which should probably have gone to other battalions. By the time they crossed the River Bidassoa in the early morning mist on the last day of August, the 30th was not actually up to strength but was two thirds of the way there and had a full complement of officers once more, thanks to two transfers and several field promotions. Bonnet had no idea if he had done the paperwork right on those; he had grown bored with the detail and eventually given it to Cavel. Hopefully the new sous-lieutenants would at least receive the correct pay.

Soult was fortunate with the weather. A dense mist hung over the river as the French columns marched down to their intended crossing points. In addition to his infantry, Soult had brought artillery to cover the various fords and temporary bridges but it was not needed; the fog was cover enough. Bonnet sat on his horse which was up to its knees in the river, watching his men crossing the ford. It was a ghostly scene. The troops had been ordered to keep silent during the crossing so nothing could be heard apart from the splashing of boots through the water and a faint jingling of horse tack. Even those sounds seemed muffled by the heavy mist. No guns fired although Bonnet knew their crews were standing by in case the fog should suddenly lift, exposing them to fire from the Allied army.

While Reille's men made their way to the foot of San Marcial, General D'Armagnac led his division across the river by a ford to the north. His men made their way cautiously up the slopes from the fords. Chassé's brigade was towards the rear of the column and the hillside was still mired in heavy fog when Bonnet heard shots fired towards the front. He presumed the advanced scouts had run across Allied pickets, though given how poor the visibility was, he hoped they were not accidentally shooting at the men of General Taupin's division who had crossed via another ford further south.

The fog began to lift some time after seven o clock and for the first time the Allied and French troops could see each other clearly. Looking through his telescope, Bonnet thought the closest battalions seemed to be Portuguese troops, though further away he could see a mass of men on the hillside of Santa Barbara above the little town of Vera. Bonnet studied them for a while as the bickering fire of muskets intensified, now that both armies could see what they were shooting at.

"If I'm not mistaken, that's the fucking Light Division up there," he said eventually, turning to hand the telescope to Cavel. "Have a look."

247

Cavel peered at the troops then handed back the glass. "I think so," he said. "Certainly there are green jackets among them. They do not appear to be preparing to advance though; just a few pickets in the village."

"Not for long there won't be," Bonnet said with satisfaction, putting the telescope back in his pocket. "Now that this fog has cleared they'll have the guns trained on them and they'll either be running like rabbits or blown to bits."

His prediction proved accurate. The French guns opened up almost immediately with one battery concentrated on the village. Bonnet, who had developed a dislike for the green-jacketed riflemen during the long and bloody battle at Vitoria, enjoyed the sight of the Light Division pickets withdrawing at speed from the bridge and the village. He presumed that Clausel, who was in overall command of this wing of the army, would send his own pickets down to take control of the bridge. Bonnet did not know this section of the Bidassoa at all well but it seemed to him that the French were very dependent on fords and temporary bridges, none of which were particularly reliable. He liked the idea of being in possession of the one undamaged bridge that he had so far seen.

Of more immediate importance was the French advance against the Portuguese. There was an attempt at long-range shelling which was quickly halted when several shells crashed into the front line of Taupin's skirmishers. With full visibility and considerable numerical superiority the French were ready to advance.

The initial frontal attack was made by Taupin's men while D'Armagnac's division marched in from the right in a flanking movement. Bonnet could not see much of the action which was hidden by a series of rolling hills, but he could hear a furious fire fight going on as Taupin deployed his men to push the Allied troops back.

From time to time as they advanced, Bonnet caught glimpses of the fighting. Some red-coated British troops had joined the Portuguese as they ascended a second ridge and seemed ready to make a determined stand. The crash of muskets echoed loudly through the warm morning air and the hill was wreathed in black smoke. Battle was thoroughly joined and D'Armagnac gave the order to speed up. Chassé led his men up a steep slope and into a thickly wooded area.

It was unbearably hot under the trees and Bonnet was sweating freely, having sent his horse to the rear to join the baggage train. The most senior officers were required to remain on horseback to give them a good view across the battlefield. Bonnet also wondered if it was to enable them to make a swift escape if a retreat was necessary but he knew better than to say so. At battalion level in this kind of action, Bonnet preferred to be on foot. An officer on horseback made a very tempting target, particularly for the riflemen. He was also reluctant to risk losing his horse. The exigencies of the past year meant that Bonnet only had one spare horse and one baggage mule and without a victory he could see no prospect of acquiring another.

At the top of the hill the trees thinned out and the Allied troops were directly ahead of them. D'Armagnac gave the order to charge immediately.

Bonnet drew his sword, silently approving the decision not to wait around to form up. By the time they were ready the element of surprise would have been lost. Chassé led his men forward with a roar which even Bonnet found faintly terrifying and the somewhat ragged column crashed into the enemy's right flank.

The encounter was brief and bloody, fought hand to hand with bayonets and swords. The redcoats did not seem inclined to pull back as quickly as Bonnet had expected. They were taking heavy losses but so were the French. The grassy hillside was littered with dead and wounded from both sides and Bonnet, cutting his way through the British lines ruthlessly, was beginning to wonder if Clausel had got this wrong and if there were in fact large numbers of Allied reinforcements just over the next hill which was why these men fought with such confidence.

For a time it seemed that the French were being pushed back, but the Allied commanders seemed to realise that they were losing too many men. The smell of gun smoke still lingered in the air up here, though they were well out of range of the artillery and it was no longer possible to use muskets without risking hitting their own troops. Even stronger was the smell of blood and sweat. The air was so heavy and humid that Bonnet thought it was like fighting under the weight of some thick blanket. The clouds were growing darker and darker with the threat of imminent rain.

Abruptly the bugles sang out and the Allied troops began to fall back, leaving their dead and wounded on the field. Bonnet expected a rout but these men knew their business and those few officers still on their feet pulled their men together magnificently. Several times, Clausel's men were hit by well-executed counter-attacks from small groups of redcoats. The cost was high in terms of lives but it kept the French busy while the rest of the Allied troops made a swift retreat down the slope then up again to a third ridge about a mile to the south. To Bonnet's surprise and admiration they rallied again and stood ready to fight.

"Who the hell are this lot?" he demanded of Chassé as the General halted to call his men into line before making the ascent. "They're making a fight of it, that's for damned sure."

"I don't know, but Clausel is getting nervous, I've just had instructions to wait. He's got scouts out in all directions and it seems there's movement over from Lesaca, above Vandermaesen's position. Not much action yet, just some long-range firing but I think he wants to wait for more information."

Bonnet reached for his water bottle and gulped down a long drink. His throat was dry and scratchy from breathing in gun smoke as well as from shouting orders and encouragement during the skirmish. He ran his eye over his battalion and decided that he had lost maybe a dozen men though he had no idea if they were dead, wounded or hiding back in the trees in the hope of being taken prisoner. He was under no illusion that all his missing men were casualties. At this point of a campaign, with a string of defeats and withdrawals behind them and no prospect of women, plunder or even regular rations, some men were bound to desert. Bonnet had no intention of either reporting them or trying to find them. Morale was already bad enough in Clausel's army and if a man was so demoralised that he was ready to desert, Bonnet did not want him stirring up trouble among the rest of the battalion.

"If he doesn't order the advance soon, sir, they're going to be reinforced and we'll be the ones scuttling away," he said shortly. "I don't give a damn about being ordered back across the river and into France but if he's going to do it, he should do it now and stop playacting for the Emperor's sake. I've left about a dozen men up on that hillside. I don't particularly want to lose a dozen more for no good reason."

Chassé gave a short barking laugh. "Strong words, Colonel Bonnet. Spoken a bit loudly as well."

"I don't think any of my officers or men are going to report me to the Imperial police, sir. They've heard it all before. As I said, I'll fight when I need to but I'm not keen on sitting here with a target painted on my back while General Clausel puts on a good show to convince the Emperor that he tried hard. Christ, it's like a schoolboy pretending he did his Latin instead of bunking off to fish in the river. You can lie as much as you want but with a blank slate, wet feet and three dead trout you're not going to convince anybody. He should stop trying and get us out of here before this storm breaks. Look at the sky."

Chassé looked upwards. "Won't be long," he said, somewhat cryptically. "I didn't hear any of that, by the way."

"Obviously not, sir, or you'd have bawled me out for showing disrespect to the Emperor and his marshals."

Chassé grinned and made his way back along the column. Bonnet settled himself to wait as patiently as possible. When no orders came after half an hour he abandoned his post and went to enquire about the missing men. He found that four were definitely dead and five were wounded, though none of them that seriously. All had managed to get themselves off the field and back to the surgeons. Nobody knew anything about the three missing men. Hearing their names, Bonnet would have placed a wager that two of them had deserted and was glad they were gone. He was not sure about the third.

After a short interval, Clausel moved his troops up to a wooded ridge directly in front of the Allied position. Bonnet wondered if the General had decided to risk an attack after all. He had heard a low voiced conversation among some of his younger officers who appeared to be betting on the likelihood of advance or retreat. Bonnet was considering where he would place his money if he was invited to join the book when he heard the crackle of musket fire towards the flank of Taupin's division. Bonnet immediately revised the odds. The battalions on the hill ahead of them had not moved from their defensive position and the firing did not come from the troops above Lesaca. Bonnet deduced that Wellington was moving yet more troops against Clausel and he had a lot more men to play with than Soult.

It was clearly time to retreat. Another hour passed. Horsemen could be seen riding up to the copse of trees where Clausel had based his headquarters party then riding out again presumably with further messages. Ahead of them, the Allied troops remained watchful on their hilltop. They were grossly outnumbered and Bonnet thought that a determined rush would dislodge them and probably drive them back a mile or two, but what could that achieve given that it sounded as though other Allied divisions were beginning to surround the beleaguered French? Soult's stated aim had been to relieve the garrison of San Sebastian and it was clear that was no longer an option. Bonnet waited, composing a vulgar rhyme about dithering generals in his head until Chassé rode back, summoning his battalion commanders to join him. As Bonnet made his way forward it began to rain heavily. Chassé dismounted and beckoned them under some trees, leading his skittish horse.

"We're going to retreat," Chassé said without preamble. "Clausel has received orders from Marshal Soult. The Spanish have driven our men back at San Marcial with heavy losses and D'Erlon's other brigade are now being attacked on their flank. We'll be next. They're going to take San Sebastian no matter what we do. It's time to get them out of here."

The rain had turned into a deluge. It was so noisy as it bounced off Bonnet's hat that he had to strain to hear properly.

"What does Clausel say?"

"Apparently he shook his fist in the air and complained that the Marshal has got this wrong and that we're half way to victory."

Bonnet gave a contemptuous snort. "Posturing," he said. "He's hoping his officers will write home to their loved ones who will tell the newspapers that while Soult ordered the retreat, Clausel was willing to fight on to the death. He bloody wasn't by the way or we'd have been kicking those bastards off that hill two hours ago. Look at them sitting there like a flock of wet ducks. If we had any dry powder I'd be happy to delay the retreat by half an hour just to give them something to think about before we go."

"I'd just as soon miss that, if it's all the same to you, Colonel," Chassé said dryly. "With this weather it'll be slow going and the chances are it'll be dark before we get to the fords. Form them up and let's get moving. Once we're back in France we'll get drunk together and you can rip up the character of our noble Emperor and his marshals as much as you like. Where's that wife of yours?"

"Back with the surgeons and the pack animals," Bonnet said. He was already aware of a nagging anxiety about Bianca. She had marched with the army for more than two years now and her hardy practicality meant that she was almost never at a loss, but in this crisis he wanted her with him. He trusted her survival skills over many of his new recruits but he did not trust any party of soldiers, French or Allied to behave themselves with a lone woman should she find herself cut off with only his seventeen year old Spanish groom to defend her. Bonnet would regret the loss of his meagre baggage and his spare horse but he could not bring himself to imagine life without Bianca and he wanted to find her urgently so that they could make the miserable crossing together.

"We'll pick them up on the way, they're not that far back," Chassé said. "Get them moving, Colonel."

It seemed to take forever for D'Armagnac's division to form up for the march back and by the time they set off there had been a brief, spectacular thunderstorm. Bonnet could still hear it rumbling in the distance and there was an occasional flicker of lightning over the far hills. The rain did not let up for a moment though. It soaked through every garment, right down to Bonnet's underclothes, and the pounding on his hat gave him a headache. Visibility was appalling and the track was steep and slippery with rivulets of water running down it which turned the ground to thick mud. Clausel's troops squelched through it, slowed down by heavy clay clinging to their boots. Some of the new recruits only wore shoes and several lost one or both in the mud and marched on in their stockinged feet with no time to search for the missing footwear in the rapidly approaching darkness. Bonnet winced at the thought of how badly their feet would be bruised and cut by stones and branches which had been blown down in the driving wind.

General Clausel gave orders for both his fighting divisions to retire to the fords, leaving Vandermaesen's unbloodied division to cover their retreat before following them over the river. The orders sounded simple but it became immediately obvious that there was nothing simple about finding the right path in unfamiliar terrain during a deluge. At least once, the leading battalions went the wrong way at a fork and found themselves looping back up the hillside again. The second time it happened, their commanding officer made the decision to turn back and retrace their steps. They were soon hopelessly lost. In addition, a gap had opened up between the first and second brigade and the division was split into two sections. This lasted for almost an hour until Chassé gave a yell of sheer exasperation at the sight of the first brigade marching directly towards them down the track. There was no way of knowing which route to take next and Bonnet stood shivering and worrying about Bianca while his seniors consulted in low tones as though it was even possible to make some kind of plan in these conditions.

Bonnet did not know how long they had been there when there was a shout from below, then a flurry of activity. Suddenly the long straggly column was on the move again, this time taking a narrow track which cut across the slope at an angle, going gradually downwards. Bonnet wondered who was leading them this time and why they thought this would be any more successful than their previous wanderings through the darkness but as he slithered along the track he realised he could hear a new sound. It filled him with both hope and dread. It was the sound of rushing water as the Bidassoa, swollen by rainfall overflowed its banks.

Eventually he stood looking out over the racing water, grey and foam-flecked in the fading light. He was not sure where they were. Taupin's men had been aiming for the northern ford at Enderlaza while D'Armagnac's division had been ordered to the little hamlet of Salain. Peering through the sheets of rain which showed no sign of letting up, Bonnet could see the shapes of several buildings but he could recognise nothing in such poor light and he doubted anybody else could either. He looked around him, trying to locate his brigade commander because he thought that Chassé would have a better chance of finding out what was going on than he would. Instead he found Cavel at his shoulder, yelling something. Bonnet leaned towards him, thinking that he was sick of the sound of water whether it was falling from the sky or rushing between swollen banks.

"What did you say, Cavel?"

"Sir, look. Over there."

Bonnet followed his pointing finger. A cloaked figure had emerged from one of the buildings and was running towards the troops lining the river bank. He stared for a moment as the figure paused beside the first rank of men to ask a question. A man replied, turned and pointed up towards Bonnet's battalion. Bonnet understood. He began to run, clumsy in the darkness, his boots slipping in the mud. She was moving too, far more sure-footed over the rough, churned-up track. They met in an enormous puddle which splashed water over the top of his boots, but Bonnet did not care. He wrapped her in his arms and kissed her, tasting rainwater on her lips.

"Maybe there is a God after all, little bird, because I can't think of anything but a miracle that you found me in this bloody chaos. Are you all right? Where's Manuel, is he safe? What about...?"

"We are quite safe, Gabriel, and exactly where we are supposed to be. It is you who have been lost for many hours. We came back here with some of the wounded and have been waiting."

"Our men?"

"They are here but most of them cannot travel. There is a man – a carpenter – who gave us shelter in his workshop. He will keep the wounded men until the British come."

"Or he'll cut their throats the minute we're out of here," Bonnet muttered.

"If he was going to do that, Gabriel, he would have done it already and mine with them. I think we may trust him."

"If he's been looking after you, cherie, he's an angel in human form. Did you hear us blundering down the slope?"

"We heard you a long way off. It was the carpenter's son who came up to show your General the path down, it is difficult to find in the dark. Did you not see him?"

"No." Bonnet was peering at the pale oval of her face framed by soaked dark hair under the hood. He wished he could see her better but the light was too bad. "Did you send him up to find us, Bianca?"

"Yes, for the carpenter said that men had become lost and blundered into the river and drowned sometimes when it was flooded. I was afraid for you."

Bonnet held her close. "You're a wonderful woman and a perfect wife, Bianca Bonnet. What's going on?"

Cavel was striding down the path towards them. He paused to execute a little bow to Bianca which made Bonnet want to laugh. Only Cavel would have taken the time for a show of good manners in these conditions.

253

"Sir, they are going to try to cross. We should not do it. I have swum in a river in full flood before and survived it but then I swim very well. This water is rising fast. We're going to lose men to drowning. Even the horses may not manage it in this."

"We're not even going to try," Bonnet said savagely. "I've not survived the past few days just to drown myself. Where are the horses, cherie?"

"Behind the workshop; there is a store. Gabriel, I do not think I can do this."

She was staring past him at the water as it swept past them, surging further and further up the banks. The fear in her voice decided Bonnet.

"You're not going to do it, sweetheart. None of us are."

"I will find General Chassé, sir. Perhaps you can reason with him."

"No." Bonnet caught hold of Cavel's cloak. "No, Cavel, not this time. Chassé will follow orders. No point in arguing. We're going to go through the battalion quickly and quietly and tell them to fall back on the far side of the path out of sight behind the buildings. Everybody is scrabbling to make the crossing before the enemy catches up with us. Let them. We'll step back a bit to find some shelter from this bloody wind and see how the crossing goes. I'm not suggesting desertion, merely caution. No need to be first to try it."

He had wondered if Cavel was exaggerating, but as the men of the 30th melted silently back from the pathway to the back of the division, Bonnet took up a position at the edge of the carpenter's barn. His two horses, his bad-tempered pack mule and his sunny-tempered servant waited within, ready to move out when necessary. The other houses in the little hamlet were occupied by medical staff, officers' servants and whatever horses and pack animals had managed to find their way through the storm. None seemed keen to leave their shelters.

It was obvious as the first men began the crossing that Cavel had been right. The ford was barely passable, already up to the waist and rising fast. Half a battalion made it across and some of the officers' horses managed to cross, though one of them was almost swept away. His rider managed to slide from the saddle and dragged on the reins, guiding the terrified horse to swim diagonally to the opposite bank. Bonnet admired the man's courage and dedication to his animal. He was not sure he could have done the same thing.

By the time one battalion was across, it was becoming dangerous. An attempt to take two wagons pulled by bullocks with supplies and ammunition across was a dismal failure and all the Spanish drivers could do was cut the traces and swim for their lives, leaving the animals to blunder their way to shore. The next line of men was swept over almost immediately by the raging torrent. Most of them managed to hang on to each other and drag themselves up and back to shore. Two did not make it. Their cries of terror tore at Bonnet's heart as their bodies tumbled over and over in the dark, white-flecked water until they disappeared and could be heard no more.

Bonnet turned away, not wanting to watch any more. He could not believe that the officers would continue to send men to their deaths, but he

254

decided that if he was ordered into the flood he was going to give a flat refusal and recommend that his men do the same. There might be consequences later but nobody was going to be able to shoot them on the spot. There could not possibly be a dry powder horn in the entire army tonight.

In the event, with the senior officers and more than half the men over, the order to call a halt came from General Vandermaesen, whose men had been left to cover the crossing. Bonnet could not imagine how D'Armagnac's men had missed them in the dark. He also wondered, given that there had been four thousand French soldiers shivering on the river bank less than two miles away, why it had been left to a Spanish carpenter's son to clamber up the treacherous path to guide them in. He decided not to ask any difficult questions however. General Vandermaesen had enough to worry about.

It was clear that the ford had become impassable. It must be six feet deep by now, a raging torrent sweeping along fallen trees and drowned livestock in its thundering passage towards the sea. Bonnet stood, his arm about his wife, watching as Vandermaesen consulted with some of his officers then issued his orders. He was trapped, with his own division plus one brigade from Taupin's division and a jumble of men from D'Armagnac's including the 30ᵗʰ légère. Nobody questioned why Bonnet's men had not made the crossing. As he had suspected, his strategic withdrawal had not been noticed in the chaos. Bonnet received his orders and went back to his officers.

"We're marching along the river to the bridge at Vera. General Vandermaesen believes it's being held by Maransin's division. We should be able to get across and get ourselves back over the French border before the bloody Light Division realises we're there. We've no idea what enemy troops are out there but we're probably safe to assume that in this weather, they won't be able to manage an organised attack. Keep quiet, keep together and keep moving. And watch your footing, it's bloody dark and very slippery and any man who falls into that river is gone."

Bonnet lost track of time during the stumbling march along the river bank. He chose to lead his horses rather than to ride them. They were less likely to slip and injure themselves that way and given his wife's heroic efforts to preserve them in difficult circumstances, he had no intention of allowing them to lame themselves now. Bianca trudged beside him, leading his second horse, while Manuel followed behind with the pack mule. There was not much of value in Bonnet's baggage these days. He had lost most of it during the previous campaign and only replaced the essentials. Still, the mule had survived several years in his service and he was surprised to realise that he valued the grumpy animal more than the items it carried. He decided he must be getting old and sentimental and thought that was probably a sign that he should retire from soldiering and set up as a tradesman or a shopkeeper of some kind. The thought was surprisingly appealing and Bonnet spent the remainder of the miserable march coming up with entertaining ways to earn a living.

They stumbled upon the bridge in the early hours of the morning purely by accident. Bonnet's men were in the centre of the column, if such a ragged body of soaked, exhausted men could be called a column at all. He heard a cry of alarm from the front followed by a flurry of shots. The French column straggled to a halt and waited for further orders. Bonnet was almost too tired to think but he could remember seeing the bridge and the village of Vera earlier in the day. He did not understand for a long moment but then his brain groaned its way into action again.

"He didn't take the bridge did he?" he said to Cavel. "That dopey bastard Maransin didn't leave pickets in the town and on the bridge. It's the one reliable way across this fucking river before Wellington drops half his army on our heads at dawn and it didn't occur to anybody to secure it. Who's holding it?"

"I don't want to tell you, sir."

"Oh fuck it," Bonnet said. He felt a rising sense of indignation which was made worse because it had no legitimate target that he could reach. He could hardly shout at poor Cavel, who looked as though he could barely stand. "It's the fucking Light Division, isn't it?"

"Yes, sir. Riflemen. Our advanced party caught their pickets out on the bridge and bayonetted them, but it looks like a couple of companies are occupying the buildings on the far side."

"With rifles."

"Yes, sir."

"Inside."

"Yes, sir."

"So they have dry powder?"

"Yes, sir."

"Oh for fuck's sake," Bonnet said with feeling. "This day can't get any worse. I don't care how I die, Cavel. As long as it's not at the hands of one of those bastard green jackets. I hate them."

"What do we do now, Gabriel?" Bianca asked quietly. Bonnet turned to her quickly. She sounded as though she had reached the end of her tether.

"We wait for the order, little bird. When it comes, I want you and Manuel well back out of range."

"Do you think the General will attack?"

"He has to," Bonnet said grimly. "It's the only way we're getting out of here. Either we force this bridge or the rest of the Light Division is going to come down from those hills like the plague that they are and we're all dead or prisoners. I'm amazed they're not already on their way. Come with me. I want to find you somewhere safe to wait until it's possible to cross."

Chapter Seventeen

It was a frustrating day of marching and counter-marching, enlivened by an occasional brief skirmish with enemy troops. Paul hated this kind of fighting. He would have felt better if he had been in command although he liked Sir James Kempt and respected his leadership. There was nothing he would have done differently from Kempt apart from his decision to leave Skerrett in command back in Vera. Since there was nothing Paul could do to change that, he tried hard not to fret about it.

He also tried not to worry about Michael and his other men at San Sebastian. By mid-afternoon the news had reached them that the breach was stormed and the town on its way to being taken. Paul was relieved at the news, simply because it meant there would not need to be another attempt, but he dreaded the cost in lives. At least Anne was there and he knew she would send a message as soon as it was safe to do so. He scribbled a note to her and managed to slip it to one of the cavalrymen acting as messengers between the various wings of Wellington's army, along with a generous bribe.

It was clear by early evening that the French were in full retreat. Paul had taken shelter in a partly ruined farmhouse with some of his officers while his men huddled under the trees in a nearby wooded area. The rain fell in a continuous stream and Paul wondered how easy it would be for Soult's men to cross the Bidassoa by the fords. Every mountain stream was at full capacity, tumbling down steep slopes into the river which was already swollen by the heavy rain.

It began to ease a little during the evening though it did not stop and Kempt rode over from his own brigade to find Paul.

"I'm in search of a messenger and we seem to have mislaid every one of the Staff Cavalry Corps. I think they're lost in the rain. Any chance you've got any of the 9th Dragoon Guards holed up in here with you?"

"No. I wouldn't have let them in; I've got better taste, sir."

Kempt grinned. "I've heard your views on the cavalry before."

"I don't mind White's men, they're fairly well behaved, but there are one or two of the 9th that I wouldn't trust to use a chamber pot safely. I've not seen any of them for hours. They're either lost or they're holed up in some farmhouse with a jug of looted wine."

"I envy them. I'll have to send one of my junior officers then. I want to make sure General Skerrett received Lord Wellington's message warning them that the French are in full flight and might make their way to the bridge before morning. The original orders were not to engage unless attacked, but if there's an opportunity to cut them off so that we can get to them, I want to take it."

Paul felt a rush of relief. "I think you're right," he said warmly. "Some of them will have made it over earlier in the day but if they were delayed in the hills, that river rose into a torrent within a couple of hours. Look, don't worry about getting back to your men. Write the orders here and I'll send one of my officers."

"Thank you," Kempt said gratefully. He seated himself on a piece of broken wall with his note tablets and a cup of brandy produced by Jenson while Paul considered his options, then went in search of Captain Simon Carlyon.

"I'm sorry to send you out in this."

"I'm out in it anyway," Simon said ruefully, peering up into the canopy of trees which was dripping steadily. "Might as well be on the move. I'll get Reynolds to saddle up…"

"Sir – permission to accompany Captain Carlyon?"

Paul turned in astonishment to see Ensign Fox, his face pale in the darkness. He looked very serious.

"What on earth for? It's easing off but it's still a foul night out there, Ensign. No reason…"

"It was Captain Cadoux's night for picket duty, sir. He'll be at the bridge."

"How on earth do you know that?" Simon asked curiously.

"He told me so yesterday, sir. He was…we ate our rations together and he shared some wine."

Paul was surprised and a little touched. "I'd no idea you and Dan Cadoux were friends, Ensign."

"Not exactly friends, sir. We've an acquaintance in common back home and when he heard I was out here he sought me out. We had dinner one evening in camp and we went riding once or twice. He gave me some advice. Good advice, I think."

Paul studied him. "Is Daniel Cadoux the reason you've been less of an arsehole recently, Fox?"

He regretted the words as soon as he had spoken them but he was cold and wet and tired. He thought Fox flushed a little though it was hard to tell in such poor light, but to his surprise the boy said:

"Maybe, sir. He's a good officer and he seemed to understand. He said he had some difficult times when he first joined."

"He did," Paul said, remembering. "They used to say he was as pretty as a girl with his good looks and elegant manners. But he shut them up very quickly once they'd been in a fight or two with him. I appreciate his intervention,

Fox and you could do a lot worse than listen to Daniel Cadoux. All right, if Captain Carlyon is willing to have you, you can go with him. You're not likely to get much sleep out here anyway. Get your horse saddled up. Simon, once you've delivered the orders don't even try to ride back tonight. Stay with Skerrett's brigade and try to get some sleep. Unless we get different orders, we'll be back in the morning anyway."

"Yes, sir. Glad to be out and doing something useful to be honest."

Paul looked after Fox who had retreated into the trees in search of his horse. "I think that's the first time I've ever known him to volunteer for anything apart from a hand of cards and a drink. Keep an eye on him."

"I will, sir. Don't worry. Whatever his other shortcomings, Fox can ride well and he's not going to go haring off on his own in the dark in this weather. I wonder if he's still intending to stay in the army? If he does, he might want to think about a transfer. It might do him good to make a fresh start."

"I'm not sure I see Fox as an officer of the Rifles, Captain, but I take your point. If we ever get a chance to dry out and have a drink, I'll have a chat with Cadoux. If he knows the family he might be able to give me a clue about what's gone so badly wrong for Fox."

"No news from San Sebastian, sir?"

Paul shook his head. "No. I don't suppose there will be tonight. Unless we have new orders, they're not going to send anybody out in this. I'm hoping we'll hear early tomorrow. I just want to know that Michael and the others are safe, but Nan will realise that and she'll get a note to me as soon as she can. Get going, Simon and ride safely. Don't take any chances."

"I won't, sir. I'll see you tomorrow, I expect."

Paul stood in the broken doorway of his makeshift shelter watching the two men ride out. The rain had eased to a fine misty drizzle which quickly swallowed up the horsemen. He felt a little pang of anxiety which had nothing to do with his faith in Simon Carlyon's horsemanship and common sense. It was just that his brigade and even his regiment felt suddenly fractured and separate in a way that unsettled him. He had led his men into dangers far worse than a night ride through difficult conditions but it felt different when they were all together. This campaigning season seemed to have torn his brigade apart and Paul would never have admitted to anybody other than Anne how much it bothered him.

He went back into the cottage out of the rain and looked around at his officers. Johnny was wedged into a corner, wrapped in his shabby dark cloak, playing cards with Ross Mackenzie and Gervase Clevedon by the flickering light of a small camp fire. Paul smiled at their ability to make the best of appalling conditions but was aware of how much he missed Carl, Leo, Michael and even Giles Fenwick who should have been huddled with them. He also missed his Regimental Sergeant-Major with an ache of loss and was having to force himself not to persecute Carter with regular letters asking about his return.

"Are you all right, sir?"

Paul turned and smiled at his orderly who was holding out a pewter cup of brandy. He took it and drank gratefully.

"Yes. Jenson, am I getting old?"

"I don't think thirty-three counts as old, sir. Though a few years with this army can age you fast."

"I wasn't really thinking of that, though. Just that I'm standing here missing people. And I'm beginning to hate it."

Jenson did not reply immediately. Paul watched him sip from a matching cup. They were part of a set of four which Paul had bought for his first campaign to India eleven years ago. One of them had got lost somewhere along the way but Jenson kept careful charge of the other three and it was seldom that he could not produce brandy or wine on a cold night in camp, even if the quality was variable. There was an engraved flower design on each cup. Paul ran his fingers over the worn pattern.

"Grace used to play with these back in India and on the voyage home," he said inconsequentially. "I remember showing her how to stack them. We were a bit short on children's toys back then. I wasn't really expecting to sail home half-lame with a toddler in tow."

Jenson grinned. "It wasn't part of my plan to leave half my leg buried on the field of Assaye, sir, but we've both done all right since. I miss them too, but I keep telling myself that most of them will be back soon."

"Christ, I hope so. I wish I knew about Michael and Giles. And bloody Nick Coates. He's only been back for five minutes and you can never trust him not to do something mad in a fight."

"You can talk."

Paul laughed aloud. Suddenly he felt unaccountably better. "I miss my wife."

"I know, sir. You're getting worse for that as well; you can't go twenty-four hours these days. If she ever decides she's had enough and is going back to England, I'm going with her."

"No, you're bloody not. You wouldn't anyway. You don't trust me to manage without both of you."

Jenson laughed as well. "I don't trust you to manage without either of us. Have some more brandy, sir. Might as well finish it, we should be back in camp tomorrow and I'll be able to get some more."

Paul held out his cup. "Freddie, I'm fairly sure I don't tell you often enough how grateful I am that you decided to stay on with me after Assaye. I have no idea how you've put up with me for all these years."

"Nor have I, sir. Though I can cope with you yelling at me a lot better than when you get maudlin on me. Go and sit down, have a drink and help Captain Kuhn to criticise Mr Sousa's chess game. You'll enjoy that and it will annoy him, which you'll enjoy even more."

Paul decided he was right. "Good idea, Jenson. Bring the rest of the brandy over then. Sousa is going to need it. He plays the worst chess I've seen since Lieutenant-Colonel Swanson left us. Tomorrow I'll hear from Nan and I'll feel better again. At least, I bloody hope so."

He took the brandy bottle, went over to the fire and seated himself beside Kuhn, who smiled at him. Paul handed him the bottle.

"How's it going, Mr Sousa?" he asked cordially.

***

It was past midnight when Simon arrived at the small bridge over the Bidassoa. He approached carefully, making his presence and identity very clear. There was no sign yet of the French but the churned up condition of some of the paths and roads he had crossed suggested large scale troop movements very recently. It was possible that all the French troops had made it over the swollen fords but Simon, having observed the raging torrent of the Bidassoa did not believe it.

Makeshift barricades had been erected across the bridge using barrels filled with stones and what looked like cottage doors. A small picket of riflemen called out a challenge in response to his shouted greeting and the corporal in charge came to meet Simon and Fox. He was as soaked to the skin as they were, with rain dripping off the brim of his hat. Simon identified himself and his companion and was waved forward.

At the far end of the bridge were several houses which had been loopholed so that the defenders could fire easily on any troops crossing the bridge. A rifleman came forward to take their horses and another escorted Simon into the largest house. It was surprisingly warm, with a small fire burning in the hearth and groups of riflemen were scattered throughout the building. Some were trying to sleep, wrapped in cloaks if they had them. Others had their hands wrapped around mess cups and Simon was delighted to see a camp kettle with tea brewing on the hearth.

Captain Daniel Cadoux came forward to greet them with a broad smile. "What ho, Captain Carlyon. Mr Fox. You've chosen the devil of a night for a leisurely ride. Briggs, get them some tea man, they're half frozen. If this is summer in Vera, they can keep it. I'd rather have a gentle sea breeze on the front at Brighton."

Simon laughed and accepted the cup gladly. "Is that where you'd rather be just now, Cadoux? Personally I'd quite like to be in my parents drawing room after a long day's hunting in front of a roaring fire with a glass of fine wine."

"Pah! You'd be asleep in five minutes. This is much livelier. Have you a message for General Skerrett?"

"Yes, from Major-General Kempt. You're about to be visited by a large French force who were unable to cross by the fords apparently. The General wanted to be sure the bridge was well guarded. I'm glad your men are taking the front line, Cadoux. Where's General Skerrett based, is he in one of the other houses here or further back in the town?"

261

"He's in neither place," Cadoux said evenly. "Take a seat, Fox. You look worn out; was it a difficult ride?"

"Like riding through a swamp," Simon said. He was studying Cadoux thoughtfully. Something about the other man's tone informed him that Cadoux was not happy but unwilling to say much in front of his men. Simon drank his tea and gave Cadoux an account of the other two brigades of the Light Division and asked in turn what news had been received from San Sebastian.

"I can't tell you much, old boy, apart from that the town has fallen and is almost burned to the ground and the French garrison are still holding out in the castle. I think it was bloody. We've not had news of our volunteers yet but I can tell you that Leith and Oswald were both wounded and poor Sir Richard Fletcher was killed."

"Oh no. That will come hard to the General. He and Fletcher were close."

"It's a loss to the army." Cadoux stood up and stretched. "Just going over to the other house to check on the men there, make sure they're not all asleep. I've told them to keep their rifles loaded and to take it in turns. Stay there, Fox and have some more tea. You look all-in."

Ensign Fox subsided back onto the wooden crate he was sitting on. Cadoux caught Simon's eye and made a small motion of his head and Simon followed him outside. The rain had finally stopped though there was a fine mist which was almost as bad. Cadoux crossed the path towards the other blockaded house and stepped into a small covered porch. It was empty, though Simon could hear the voices of the riflemen beyond the inner door.

"What's going on, Cadoux?"

"Bloody Skerrett," Cadoux said shortly. "We've all had our doubts about him but it's obvious he's not fit to be in command of a dog kennel."

"What's happened? And where is he?"

"He's up there, on the heights above the town." Cadoux made a contemptuous gesture. "After your brigade marched out this morning, a French column came through the town. Skerrett made no attempt to stop them or even to hold the bridge. He pulled us all back. It was completely disorganised. Hart and I lost several men from our companies: dead and wounded, while poor Sergeant Hamilton from the 43rd was cut off with his far picket further along the river. Not sure if they were all killed or just captured but it should never have bloody happened."

"Christ," Simon breathed. Suddenly, his commander's anxiety about Skerrett's command seemed alarmingly justified. "What happened?"

"Fortunately, whoever was in charge of the French was just as incompetent as Skerrett and failed to leave a proper guard on the town and the bridge. Colonel Colborne from the 52nd took command on his own initiative and cleared out the remaining French with his men and the Portuguese. It was my turn on picket duty anyway, but normally I'd have left it to one of my subalterns. Given that we were so depleted after that fiasco this morning I thought I'd take charge myself. Smith has been nagging him for hours to send the rest of the battalion down to hold this position but he refused to do it. They're safely up there, probably sleeping off dinner and I'm stuck down here waiting for the French to hit."

"Aren't some of these Hart's men though?" Simon asked.

"Yes, he's here with half a company. About all he had left. We thought we could make a full company between us, though he's going against orders by doing it. What orders do you have for Skerrett? He's gone back to the farmhouse up in the hills that he's been using as his headquarters. I suppose one of my men can show you the way..."

"I don't need a guide, Cadoux, I've been here as long as you have. General Kempt's orders are that he should be ready to hold this damned bridge. I need to get up there."

"I wouldn't hurry, old chap," Cadoux said with heavy irony. "General Alten has already sent a very similar order, but Skerrett considers he's done enough. Harry Smith is beside himself with rage. He's taken to writing down every order Skerrett gives him and then reading it back to him to make sure he can't get the blame."

Simon realised his mouth had fallen open. He closed it. "Are you telling me he's already had orders to hold this position and he's ignoring them?"

"I think he's placing a very wide interpretation on the meaning of the phrase 'show caution'. He's ordered me to withdraw if I'm attacked but I'm going to pretend I didn't get the orders. I'm hoping Kempt's are a bit more unequivocal."

"They're pretty damned clear but very brief," Simon said. He was aware of a sense of urgency. "Look, I want to get up there, Cadoux but I'm going to go to Colborne's camp first. If I tell him Kempt has given the order to support you, he'll get his men on the move, I know it. I'll keep the orders verbal and that way I can embroider them as much as I like."

"Jesus, Carlyon, you can't make up orders," Cadoux said, startled. "If Kempt gave you written orders you need to..."

"I intend to tell them that I have verbal orders from Major-General van Daan, which very specifically state that they should all get their arses down here in support," Simon said flatly. "Kempt might be in overall command but Van Daan is senior to Skerrett and he knows it. And Colborne will definitely take orders from him."

"But he hasn't given any orders," Cadoux said.

"Well he would have if he'd known about this almighty fuck-up," Simon said recklessly. "He'll back me up, I know he will."

"He's a bloody major-general, Captain. They put their careers first."

"Not this one. He'll back me up," Simon said again. He had never been more certain of anything in his life. "Either way, I'm doing it."

There was a flurry of shots from one of the other fortified houses. Both Simon and Cadoux froze. For a moment, nothing more was heard and Simon began to breathe again. It was probably a false alarm; not surprising on such a wild night with nerves stretched to breaking point. However as he opened his mouth to finish his sentence, a rifleman burst through the door of the opposite house and at the same time a bugle sang out a frantic call to arms.

"They're here," Cadoux said. He spun around and sprinted back to his headquarters. "Pickford, Morgan, what the bloody hell is happening. Why didn't the pickets...?"

"They're dead, sir. Probably couldn't fire off a warning shot in this weather. Briggs saw it from upstairs, they bayonetted them. They're coming."

Cadoux ran to the stairs and Simon followed, taking them two at a time. From the windows overlooking the bridge the enemy could be seen very clearly, a huge mass of men on the far bank. Simon could not even begin to guess how many of them were forming up ready to storm the bridge. He could hear their voices now, a low rumbling sound. A block of men was beginning to advance. Their officers were shouting orders, urging them on. Simon's French was not especially good, but even he could understand them as they promised honour and glory and the gratitude of an Emperor to those men who made the first advance. Simon looked around him at Cadoux and the grim faces of his riflemen, ready at the windows and loopholes, and thought that the first men across the bridge would not survive to receive Bonaparte's promised gratitude.

"Where do you want me, Cadoux?"

Cadoux looked around at him. Simon could see him considering options. Given the damage done to his company earlier in the day, he was short of officers and NCOs and he had known Simon for long enough to value him. On the other hand they both knew that what Cadoux really needed was reinforcements.

"Send Fox," Simon said quietly. "He's a capable rider and he knows the way. We've all been up and down those hills enough over the past month. You need me here."

"It's as black as Hades out there."

"They're less than two miles away. He might not be much of a soldier yet, but he can ride. Even the General admits he's useful as a courier. Stop protecting him, Cadoux. He's a man grown."

"He's a frightened boy," Cadoux said. Even in the stress of this moment, his voice was curiously gentle. "He shouldn't be here."

"I know. But he is and he'll be a lot safer taking messages than getting cut to pieces when these bastards break through. Which they will do without reinforcements. Give him a job to do."

Abruptly, Cadoux nodded and sprinted to the stairs yelling for Fox. He paused halfway and looked up.

"Take command up there. Hart's in the other house. If I go down, you have command."

"Don't go down, Cadoux."

The other man flashed him a blinding smile. "Try not to, old boy," he said and vanished in search of Fox.

Simon went back to the front window. The riflemen were spread out across the wide room, out into the hallway and into another room. They stood at

264

windows and loopholes, still and watchful and they gave Simon considerable confidence. He wondered briefly about ammunition but decided not to ask. There was an open box in the corner of the room and he presumed Cadoux was very well aware of what supplies he had. Simon thought of Fox trying to make his way up to Colborne and Skerrett. He thought the ride was probably unnecessary but was glad to have the boy out of the way. Once the noise of battle reached the General he would have to send reinforcements and Simon thought that an unexpected attack from Colborne's 52nd would give the French something new to worry about. They just had to hold on.

***

Colonel Bonnet had often found reason to be grateful when his battalion was not at the front of the column but he had never been as glad as he was now. The passage over the bridge was narrow at best, but with the makeshift but very effective barricades set up by the riflemen, it was only wide enough for one person or possibly two at a push. Before any concerted rush could be made on the fortified houses on the far side of the bridge, those barricades would have to come down.

Bonnet had dealt with similar obstacles before, during the storming of Tarragona two years earlier, and he knew how heavy they were and how difficult to move. This was made worse because instead of a company of terrified Spaniards with bayonets and no space to use muskets if they had tried, the French were faced with an unknown number of well-trained, well-armed riflemen. Very few of Vandermaesen's men had managed to keep their powder dry although Bonnet had been told that two supply wagons were following up the column to rectify this. He hoped they were driven by reliable army transport staff instead of the usual locally drafted waggoneers who were likely to run at the first sign of trouble, leaving the powder to be picked up at leisure by Wellington's advancing troops once it was daylight.

There were enough muskets to make a showing though and Vandermaesen brought them to the front of the advance. The riflemen watched them come from windows and loopholes across the two houses. These were experienced men who knew the range of their weapons well and Bonnet realised he was already flinching in anticipation of the first shots.

The volley still took him by surprise. It was so clean he heard only one sound, terrifyingly loud. It blew the first row of French troops apart and was followed almost immediately by a second volley. The bridge was blocked by bodies.

It was quickly obvious that this was to be a battle of attrition. With few muskets ready to fire and no chance of aiming accurately at the riflemen who were under cover, Vandermaesen had no choice but to throw men at the bridge, relying on sheer numbers to get the barricades shifted. If that could be done it might be possible to rush the houses, though even then it would be costly.

Bonnet peered through the darkness as men advanced and died on the bridge. Eventually it was becoming clogged with dead and wounded men and Bonnet was appalled to see the front line of troops heaving bodies over the bridge into the river. They could not possibly know if the men were dead or wounded and did not seem to care.

Reluctantly, Bonnet pulled his battalion forward and gave his officers and NCOs their orders. Clearing the bridge was a useful exercise and he was hoping that, as dawn approached and visibility improved, the riflemen would not choose to target men who were trying to carry the wounded to the rear, though he would not have bet good money on it. He set his men up in two long lines, passing the bodies backwards without bothering to check their condition. It kept the bridge at least partly clear and although a few of his men were shot down, Bonnet quickly realised that the riflemen preferred to target the men who were trying to overturn the barricades. The 30th were getting off fairly lightly.

His involvement brought a heavy slap on the shoulder from General Vandermaesen. Bonnet had not seen him coming and physically jumped. The General gave a snort of amusement.

"Sorry. Saw what your men were doing. Good work. Who the hell are you?"

"Colonel Gabriel Bonnet, sir. Chassé's brigade. We didn't make it over the fords."

Vandermaesen grunted. "Christ knows if we're going to make it over this bridge before daylight, but if we don't, we might as well surrender. They're going to hit us from both directions. At least one of the ammunition wagons has arrived."

"I can't believe they've not sent reinforcements already," Bonnet said. He had been straining his eyes for the past hour trying to make out any activity from the heights of Santa Barbara above the town. There was the flicker of a few camp fires now that the rain had stopped but he presumed that somewhere the British officers were forming up their men ready to march to the assistance of the riflemen. Bonnet could not imagine why they were so slow. If he had been one of the officers in the fortified houses, he would have been furious.

Another rush of French infantry was cut down at the barricades and Vandermaesen swore loudly. "How the fuck are we going to shift those things?"

"Stop charging at them," Bonnet said without thinking. "They can see us coming."

The General turned to stare at him and Bonnet wished he had not spoken but it was too late now. He sighed.

"I've seen them before, at Tarragona. This is worse but to tip them over you need to get enough men in low. I'd set up a wall of musket fire, now that we've got more powder. We won't hit them but it will distract them. Then send in your biggest men. They need to crawl low until they're right behind the barrels and can get their shoulders against them. The rifles can't hit them behind the barrels and they won't know what's happening until it's done."

"Bloody hell," Vandermaesen said softly. "Did it work...?"

266

"Yes, sir. Though we didn't have riflemen shooting at us back then."

"Organise it," the General said shortly. "You're in command; pick your men. I'll get the muskets set up."

Bonnet obeyed, remembering all the reasons why he never volunteered for anything. He selected his men at random, based entirely on size and strength and put Sergeant-Major Belmas in charge of organising them into three groups. The rest of his battalion concentrated on trying to clear bodies out of the way, though when Bonnet was ready to go he ordered them to stop. He was hoping that the riflemen might mistake his small party for dead and wounded as they made their way forward on their stomachs to the foot of the barricades.

As the French muskets crashed defiance out through the early morning mist, Bonnet led his men forward. They went initially at an awkward run, bent double, then threw themselves flat the moment they came within range of the rifles. It was easy enough by now to know what that range was, by the position of dead men on the bridge.

Bonnet reached the centre barrel uninjured, though two of his men had been hit. The rest squirmed into position and as Belmas gave the order they set their backs and shoulders to the barrels and heaved.

It seemed to take forever and Bonnet was horribly conscious of the rain of rifle fire around them and of the gradually lightening sky overhead. He could only assume that for some reason darkness had prevented the rest of the Light Division from coming to the aid of their beleaguered men, but once dawn came they would appear and Vandermaesen's men would face a solid wall of rifle and musket fire from the far side of the river bank as well as over the bridge. Bonnet worried about his men but he worried more about Bianca. Privately he had decided that once defeat became inevitable, he was going to desert his post and go back to get her. A prison camp with her beside him might not be such a dreadful prospect and he was not leaving her to the mercy of troops from either side.

Abruptly the barrel began to shift. Bonnet redoubled his efforts and Belmas, seeing that the centre was about to give, flung himself over to add his considerable weight to the attempt. It made the difference and after a long time of heaving and grunting, so that Bonnet began to think he was about to give himself a stroke, the barrel toppled with an enormous crash. The door which was nailed across it splintered noisily and at the same time a second barrel went over. The bridge was partially blocked by shattered wood and heaps of rocks and stones but beyond that the way was clear.

Bonnet, his cover gone, scrambled clumsily to his feet and raced back over the bridge yelling to his men to do the same. He made it into cover with bullets kicking up stones and mud on either side of him. Belmas thundered up beside him and the other men scrabbled to safety. Only one of them did not make it. When Bonnet looked back he was sprawled face down on the stone bridge. Two more bullets struck him in the back with sickening thuds but Bonnet did not think he could have felt them.

He could hear Vandermaesen screaming orders to his men to form up and rush the bridge. They were running out of time and this was probably going to be their last chance to make it over in one piece. Bonnet stood watching, unexpectedly paralysed. He knew his duty to his men, his battalion and his brigade. He was even willing to acknowledge a vague sense of obligation to his country. He felt no loyalty whatsoever to his Emperor and he decided, quite suddenly, that he had risked everything he was willing to risk today.

"Cavel! Get them formed up and get them over. Don't go in the front line," he bellowed. His friend turned to stare at him and Bonnet could see his surprised expression very clearly. It made him realise that dawn was close. He pointed. "Get them out of here and don't look back. I'll join you as soon as I can. I'm going back for Bianca."

"But sir…"

"I'm not leaving her for the entertainment of the fucking Light Division," Bonnet yelled. "Get them out of here."

He made his way backwards against the press of men who were forming up ready for the final charge. Vaguely he realised that there were fewer shots coming from the houses and it occurred to him that the riflemen might well be running out of ammunition and making their shots count. If that was the case all he needed to do was wait until the firing stopped and he and Bianca could make a dash for it.

He found her ready, mounted on Fredrico, the fine Spanish gelding he had acquired after Tarragona. Manuel was behind her on Marisa, his sturdy mare, and the pack mule was roped behind. Bonnet mounted behind his wife, put his arms about her to take the reins and kissed the back of her neck where her hair was coming down.

"I was so afraid for you," she whispered.

"We're going to make it. They're running out of ammunition and there is still no sign of reinforcements though I have no fucking idea why. Manuel, stay close and keep that bloody mule under control."

"His name is Blanco, Colonel. I decided he should have a name."

It was so irrelevant that Bonnet almost laughed aloud. "Well I hope he's grateful enough not to get us all killed, but if he digs his heels in, loose that rope and let him go. I've got all I need here, we're not risking your neck for a bad-tempered mule called Blanco."

They waited at the edge of the tree line and watched as Vandermaesen led the charge across the bridge. Firing from the houses suggested that the defenders had indeed been trying to conserve ammunition. Bonnet watched as men were cut down by accurate fire. It was the first time he had ever deliberately stood back and let his men advance without him and he was surprised at how much it hurt but he still felt no inclination to dismount and run forward. If he was killed or wounded, his wife would be alone. She had no family to go to, very little money and although men of Wellington's army had been kind to her once before, Bonnet was not naïve enough to believe that the Allied army did not have its share of brutes. He had heard what they had done at Badajoz and Ciudad

Rodrigo the previous year. Bianca had marched beside him every step for the past two years. This once, he was putting her first.

Initially he thought that the riflemen were going to drive them back once again, but without the added hindrance of the barricade there were too many of them and the impetus was too great. Bonnet realised suddenly that the first men were across and racing up towards the houses. Others followed. Some were shot down but far more were making it over. Bonnet pulled his wife against him in a quick, fierce embrace.

"Be ready," he said. "Once they're up and into the houses, those bastards won't have time to be shooting us down on the bridge and we're going to ride for our lives. They won't like having to jump over the bodies, Manuel and that's when that mule might kick off, so be ready. Any minute now."

**

It had lasted for more than two hours and Simon could not believe they had held out for so long. He also could not believe that General Skerrett had not sent reinforcements. He was exhausted after the long ride and his ears were ringing as rifle shots echoed around the bare rooms of their makeshift fortress. His arms and shoulders ached with the unaccustomed effort of firing a rifle.

It was not the job of an officer to shoot alongside his men, but Simon had been taught informally during winter quarters by Sergeant-Major Daniel Carter who had made the wholly unauthorised transition from the 95th to the 110th years ago, thanks to Paul van Daan's genius for manipulating the paperwork. Carter was an expert marksman and during the long break the previous winter he had cheerfully agreed to teach a few of the young officers of Paul's brigade how to shoot a Baker rifle. Simon had been astonished at how difficult it was but he enjoyed shooting on his father's estate in Yorkshire and had found it a challenge to master the technique. When Rifleman Ingleby fell back from the window he was covering due to a fluke shot from a French musket, Simon hesitated, looking around the room. The rest of the loopholes were occupied.

He went forward to Ingleby and checked his wound and then his pulse. He was unconscious, with a bloody wound high up on his right shoulder. Simon felt along it and suspected a broken collar bone but he did not think any vital organs had been hit. He eased the man into the centre of the room and fashioned a makeshift dressing using his silver-grey sash and the man's own belt. The Corporal who had been in command of the room looked approvingly over his shoulder.

"He all right, sir?"

"So far."

"Don't suppose you feel like covering his window as well?"

It was said cheerfully, with an NCO's understanding of what an officer could and could not do. Simon thought about it for a moment and realised that within his own regiment, he would not have hesitated. He got to his feet, went

269

to the window and picked up the rifle. For a moment he was horribly self-conscious as the eyes of every rifleman in the room turned towards him briefly. He checked the rifle, went back to Ingleby and collected his ammunition then returned to the window and settled himself. His heart was beating faster than usual and he could feel himself flushing a little.

"Sir, I was joking."

Simon turned his head to look at Corporal Masters. "I'm not," he said calmly and began to load the rifle.

He was too busy for the first fifteen minutes for further conversation. As the French fell back finally to regroup, Simon put down the rifle and rotated his arm, feeling bruised and sore from both holding the heavy weapon and from the recoil. Across the room, Masters said:

"Begging your pardon, sir, but where the hell did you learn how to do that?"

"I'm in Van Daan's brigade, Corporal. Don't you know that we all have to be able to do everything?"

"You're bloody good, sir. Want some advice? If you shift your position a bit, the recoil will be easier. Show him, Mapstone, while we've got a minute."

The brief lesson eased the tension and as the French came again, Simon resumed his position feeling as though he had crossed an unseen barrier. He had wielded a sword in battle alongside a bayonet charge often enough but this use of a learned skill alongside experts was something new and he felt ridiculously proud that they thought him useful enough to share their tips with.

Charge after charge came across the bridge and was beaten back. Men ran into the room to the case of ammunition and returned to their windows. Simon did not ask and did not look. When his own shot ran out he went for more and realised they were in the lower half of the box.

Ensign Fox returned in one piece and Simon left his post for a while and went to hear the news. Cadoux was speaking so loudly that he could probably have heard it from upstairs.

"He's not coming? What the fuck is he thinking?"

"Sir, I'm sorry." Fox sounded close to tears. He was soaked to the skin again and splattered with mud. "I tried to tell him and Captain Smith was still shouting at him when I left to come back here. He says he has no authorisation to risk his brigade against such overwhelming numbers and advises you to withdraw."

"I can't bloody withdraw. If I pull them out now, we'll be cut to pieces. He has to understand." Cadoux took a deep breath. "I'm going to write him a note. Stand down, Mr Fox, you're exhausted. I'll send one of my…"

"I can go again, sir. I'm all right."

"What about your horse?"

"He's fine, sir. It's not far, just a bit slippery but I know the path." Fox straightened and unexpectedly saluted. "Sir, I'm no use for anything else here. Perhaps if you put it in writing, he'll listen."

270

Simon came forward. "Do it, Cadoux and I'm going to scribble my wholly imaginary orders from Major-General van Daan as well. Get a drink while you're waiting, Fox. They'll be back any minute."

"I don't suppose you can forge Lord Wellington's signature, can you?" Cadoux murmured. Simon thought he was probably joking, although upon reflection, he might have been that desperate.

As Fox left, the French came again. Simon went back to his post and fired his rifle, again and again into the mass of advancing blue coats. It was becoming lighter outside, with the faintest hint of dawn. Simon's aim was not particularly accurate but it did not need to be. The French formed a solid phalanx of desperate men and it was hard to miss.

The sun was not yet up but the sky was becoming brighter when the French made their final charge. The ammunition chest was empty and Simon's men ran downstairs and brought up the last shot from the remaining box. They waited as the French advanced, a mass charge with what was clearly a high ranking officer at their head. The barricades were gone, broken and dragged aside after a massive effort, and Simon felt sick and rather light-headed. He had no idea how this was going to go but he doubted that the French would be inclined to take prisoners. They were desperate men, knowing that this was their final opportunity to escape.

Simon thought briefly of his parents, who had already lost one son in Portugal. His brain shied away from the memory and instead he thought about his friends in the regiment and the brigade. He hoped that Paul van Daan did not berate himself for sending him on what should have been a simple courier assignment and sent a brief, affectionate prayer for Anne, his former sister-in-law who would know how to comfort his grieving friends.

His last thought before the charge began was of Colonel Johnny Wheeler, whom he had once seen as an enemy but who had become his mentor and one of his closest friends. He knew that Wheeler would mourn him if he did not manage to survive this, but he also knew that he would be proud of him. The thought pleased Simon as he laid aside his empty rifle just as Cadoux burst into the room.

"Get to horse, Carlyon. We're going to have to pull out, they're over the bridge. I've told my men to pull back. We can't stand."

"Sir, there are men running down from the town. Our men, sir. Rifles."

Cadoux wheeled and stared at the Corporal in sudden blazing hope. "Reinforcements?"

"Only a company or so, sir. And some Portuguese."

Cadoux raced to the window and peered out. Simon went to join him. The reinforcements were pitifully few, but Simon was astonished to see Laurence Fox in the middle of them. He was so muddy that it would have been impossible even to guess his regiment but he was there and had brought help, however limited.

"Christ, we need to stop them occupying these houses, they'll be trapped," Cadoux yelled. "It's too late for that."

He raced out of the room and Simon waved for the riflemen to follow him. They went, bayonets at the ready, clattering down the wooden stairs and out into the grey early light after their elegant young Captain.

The horses had been left at the rear of the house and by the time Simon rounded the corner of the building, Cadoux was already in the saddle, his sword drawn. He set his horse to a canter towards the approaching troops, yelling at them to halt.

"Over there! Form them up over there! They're over the bridge but we can fire on them as they're retreating. It's too late to stop them, they're over…"

The musket shots echoed through the still air, clearly audible over the low roar of the French infantry as they thundered over the bridge. Cadoux's body jerked once, twice and then a third time. Simon screamed his name. It was utterly pointless, as he could not possibly have heard. The rifleman's horse reared up, terrified. Cadoux tumbled from the saddle, crashed to the ground heavily and lay still. There was a wide, spreading stain across his green jacket.

Cadoux's horse took off, racing towards the town in sheer panic. The other, tethered horses shied nervously, panicked by its distress and by the smell of blood in their nostrils. Simon ran towards his own mount then stopped, changing his mind. Any mounted British officer would present a similar target.

The French were coming, racing up the path from the bridge. There was no time to think or plan. Simon ran to the head of the riflemen, yelling orders. Behind him, thankfully, the officer in charge of the reinforcements had understood what Cadoux was saying and pulled his men into a defensive position. They had rifles and ammunition and as the French charged towards Simon, several of them fell.

He had been in desperate situations before, but never like this. Even at Salamanca he had been part of an entire army, fighting alongside thousands. It had been brutal and bloody but he had never before felt this isolated. Around him the riflemen wielded bayonets and defended their lives. Men fell and died and Simon backed up, slashing savagely at any blue coat that came close enough. There were too many of them. He knew that there must be thousands of them and that he was going to die.

There were bodies on the ground, green jackets but also some blue. Simon felt a savage pain across his lower arm and thrust forward, bringing down the man who had cut him. He was backing up towards the reinforcements, his sword arm bloody and aching and his breath coming in quick gasps. His chest hurt so much, with a burning agony, that he could barely take in air. It could not be more than a few more steps but he was not sure he could take them.

Abruptly hands grasped him and dragged him back and suddenly he was behind a solid phalanx of men and lying on the ground. He heard the crash of rifle fire and a voice calmly giving orders, again and again. There were no more blue-coated men trying to spit him on their bayonets and Simon closed his eyes. He wished he had not, because he could immediately visualise Cadoux's body jerking twice then falling from the saddle.

272

The firing was dying away and Simon lay still and realised that so far he was neither dead nor a prisoner. He supposed that he should open his eyes and try to speak although he resented the effort.

"Sir. Captain Carlyon, can you hear me?"

Fox's voice was muffled. Simon was not sure if that was his hearing or if Fox was not sounding clear for other reasons. He forced himself to open his eyes.

"Mr Fox, are you all right?"

"Yes, sir. They're going. The French are marching on. But there are so many dead. Captain Cadoux…"

Fox's face was filthy and streaked with tears. He looked so young that it broke Simon's heart. It also goaded him into action. He eased himself slowly into a sitting position, wincing as he took the weight on his injured arm. He lifted it up to look at it, then wished he had not. The slash was so deep that he suspected it must be close to the bone. It made him feel sick again. He closed his eyes for a long moment then opened them again.

"They've gone? Why have they gone? They could have slaughtered us."

"Their officers called them away, sir. It's dawn, the sun is up and the reinforcements say the rest of the brigade are on their way down." Fox wiped his streaming eyes on his sleeve, making the mess worse. "There are so many French dead. The bridge is blocked by them and they're in the river…they're everywhere."

"Where's Cadoux? Get me up, Fox. I want to see him."

The riflemen had laid out their Captain in the main room of the house. He was covered with a sheet. Other bodies were being carried in, while outside, Simon could hear somebody giving orders about the treatment of the wounded.

Gently he knelt by the body and drew back the sheet. He stared down at the handsome face, the delicate features looking almost feminine with the pale cast of death. Somebody must have washed that face very carefully. Simon looked over at Fox, who was standing beside the body looking down.

"I'm sorry, Fox. I liked Cadoux, but I didn't know him all that well. He said you were friends."

"Not really, sir. He knew…we had some mutual friends back in England. We talked a bit about how hard I was finding this. He's the first person I'd spoken to who seemed to understand."

"What did he say to you?" Simon asked. He was genuinely curious.

"He recommended that I sell out, go home and speak to my brother. He said that the army wasn't the place to hide. That nobody could really hide here, unless it was where they were always meant to be. He said that's what happened to him."

"Is that what you want to do?"

"I can't, sir. I don't think my brother wants me back and there's not much else I'm good for. I don't know. I can't think about it just now."

273

"Don't try. I'm an arsehole to be asking you stupid questions at a time like this. You did bloody well last night, Fox. You made it up into those hills twice and managed to bring back some reinforcements. It's not your bloody fault that they came too late. Though I think if you'd not managed it, we'd all be dead."

Fox's fair skin had flushed bright red. He mumbled something incoherent and Simon wondered suddenly when was the last time somebody had paid Fox a genuine compliment. He heaved himself to his feet and put his hand awkwardly on the younger man's shoulder.

"Why don't you stay with him for a bit?" he said gently. "I need to go and find somebody to report to. I wonder when General van Daan will get back? And whether there is anywhere safe enough to hide Major-General John Byrne Skerrett once he finds out what happened here?"

Chapter Eighteen

Captain Leo Manson was determined not to spend all his time in Oporto wondering if this was the last time he would be with Diana like this. Mostly he succeeded. Diana had planned well for this trip and they travelled in comfort and were welcomed graciously into the faded elegance of Senhor Miranda's hotel and given the best suite. Diana seemed on excellent terms with their host who took it upon himself to introduce his guests into the trading and mercantile society of the city.

The suite had two bedrooms, a dressing room with a bath and a sitting room. Senhor Miranda asked no questions about Diana's relationship with the young English officer. Manson was included in all invitations as a matter of course and once his rank and experience had been established, he found himself a popular guest at a number of army and navy functions as well. For a man accustomed to life on campaign there was something slightly unreal about this leisurely round of social activities. Wellington's army was social enough during winter quarters but they were never so far from the front that they could forget about the war entirely.

Oporto had last seen French occupation four years ago and there were still signs of rebuilding in some areas, but the town had a surprisingly prosperous air. Manson spoke limited Portuguese but most of the wealthy gentlemen who welcomed the newcomers into their homes spoke good English. Diana chattered easily in both languages, talking freely about her plans for the hotel. She had obviously made up her mind and her new acquaintances seemed to welcome the initiative. After Bonaparte's Russian disaster and Wellington's triumph at Vitoria, many of them seemed to be looking towards the end of hostilities and a resumption of free trading again, with a need for good quality accommodation for visiting merchants and businessmen.

Manson inspected Diana's proposed purchase thoroughly with her and thought she had made a good choice. The hotel had been built during the previous century and its elegance had faded but the design and structure was good and Diana was full of ideas for its restoration. She too was looking ahead

275

to the end of the war when trade would flow freely again throughout Europe and Oporto would be a thriving centre for merchant shipping.

Surprisingly, seeing Diana like this made it easier for Manson to understand the reasons for her decision not to formalise their relationship in the future, though he still did not feel the same way. Diana was a born businesswoman and blossomed when she was busy and active and engaged. She reminded Manson a little of his commanding officer's clever, energetic wife and he thought that if Diana ever did agree to marry him she would never settle as an officer's wife. She was used to managing her own life and he believed she would make a success of this, and any other ventures, because of her vision and her capacity for sheer hard work.

Manson thought they had that in common and the idea of joining her in this venture was not unappealing. He went with her to visit suppliers and bankers and attended dinners with local businessmen who clearly assumed that Diana was in some way being supported or financed by him. Diana made no attempt to disabuse them of this idea and Manson quickly realised that although she had invited him to accompany her for the pleasure of his company, she had probably also recognised the advantages of a respectable male escort as she made her first forays into the very masculine world of business in Oporto. He had no doubt that within a week of his departure she would have found one or two other gentlemen friends to lend her respectability so that she could continue to build a network of useful contacts.

Manson was not jealous. He did not think Diana was ready to take another lover. She was determined to leave her former profession behind her and portrayed herself as the owner of a successful tavern without ever mentioning exactly how that tavern had done so well. Oporto society pretended to believe her though Manson was sure that there was speculation. As long as she kept up the fiction, she would do well in this mercantile community. Manson felt less comfortable and was pleased when he was introduced to one or two of the local army officers. He thought he could have made it work if Diana had been willing to try, but he also admitted how good it felt to sit at dinner with men of his own profession who spoke the same language and knew the same people.

For several weeks they attended parties or dinners every night, spent their days exploring the town or wandering through the rooms of the hotel, sharing ideas for its future. They made love into the early hours and had breakfast on the balcony of their suite. It was a happy time and Manson refused to spoil it with renewed pleas and recriminations. He decided to give himself up to the enjoyment of the moment so that he could treasure the memories of this time in the future.

The sense of time passing nagged at him all the same. He wrote to Paul with his new address and received a cheerful response telling him to enjoy himself and not to rush his convalescence. Manson, who was riding and walking further and further each morning to strengthen the injured muscles, was not deceived. He read the faint sense of depression behind the letter and knew his commander was dying to hear news of his return. Manson could do nothing about the loss of Colonel Swanson but without conceit he knew that his own presence would fill at least some of that gap. It was more than time to go back.

Diana was immediately understanding and threw herself into helping to plan his journey. She took over the task of supplying him for the campaign and Manson was slightly bemused to find himself in possession of a new baggage mule and a well-designed campaign chest which doubled as a storage box, a wash stand and a writing desk. He accepted both gifts graciously but intervened firmly in matters of clothing and boots. He was all too aware of her generosity over the past months but he had no desire to be sent off like a boy in his first week at school, loaded with gifts from a doting mother.

Diana clung to him on the morning of his departure, her face damp with tears. Manson kissed her for a long time.

"I'm going to miss you."

"You're going to be too busy to miss me, Diana. You've definitely decided then?"

"Yes, I've spoken to the lawyer and he will make the arrangements for the sale. I am going to return to Elvas to pack up and will probably return here after Christmas. There will be so much to do. Leo…thank you for this time. I don't think I have ever been happier."

"Nor have I," Manson said. "Look, Diana, we've not really talked about this. Deliberately on my part, because I didn't want to spoil this time with sadness. It's up to you. Do you want to carry on as we have done, or…"

"Yes," she said quickly and he detected something like panic in her voice. "Yes, of course. I know what I said about the future and I meant it. But we have always said that until the end of the war…unless you've changed your mind? Unless you want to end it…"

"Love, I don't want to end it at all. Nothing has changed for me. I'll write to you at Elvas then."

"No, write to me here. I want to be back as soon as I can to supervise the renovations. I hope to spend more time here than there, but if I'm delayed in Elvas they can send any letters on. Take care of yourself, Leo. I hope…I would like you to visit me again if you can. But not if it means you being wounded. Please be careful."

"I will. I'm not going to say the same to you because I don't need to. You'll do very well here. I will see you again, Diana, I promise. In the meantime, write often. I want to know every detail of how this is going."

"You will quickly become bored with it."

"No, I won't. I must go or Captain Winterton will sail without me. I love you."

"You too."

He kissed her again and left quickly because he did not want her to see him cry.

**

277

The journey from Oporto to Santander was accomplished quickly. From there, Manson made his way by easy stages to the city of Vitoria where he had an important duty to perform before he could return to his regiment. He remembered the city well from the weeks of his convalescence but it felt different now. There were still British officers in red coats strolling through the fashionable squares, but there were far more Spanish uniforms on display. This was a Spanish city once again and Manson approved the change.

He was welcomed at the convent which housed the General Hospital by Major Sean O'Connor, the district superintendent who worked with Dr Adam Norris. O'Connor was a cheerfully competent administrator who showed Manson to a room and then to the stables where his spare horse and pack mule had remained throughout his absence. Manson fussed Winter, his grey gelding, who whickered in pleased recognition.

"I don't know who has been looking after him for me, Major, but I'm very grateful."

"We've plenty of grooms here and Dr Norris and I have kept him exercised. It's been a pleasure, I'll miss him. I understand you're fully fit for duty again?"

"The surgeon in Elvas was happy to sign me off as fit, but I suspect I'll have to pass muster with Dr Norris before General van Daan will allow me back. And the same goes for RSM Carter. What's your opinion, sir?"

"Carter? Oh I don't think it will be long, though as you say the final approval will have to come from Adam Norris. He's made a remarkable recovery. Adam thought it would be months longer. I'd be happy for him to stay to be honest, he's been a great help in the office. Somebody taught him well."

Manson grinned, thinking of Anne van Daan's meticulous administration. "Yes, they're like that in the General's brigade. Can I see him?"

"I'll take you over. I'll be honest, Adam has been trying to persuade him to stay until his wife's child is born, but they both seem adamant that they'd like to return before then. Are you in a particular hurry?"

"Not really, though I do want to get back. If Carter isn't quite ready yet, I won't wait, he can follow when Dr Norris gives him permission. I wanted to come this way though. Partly to collect my horse and the rest of my baggage but mostly so that I can tell General van Daan that I've seen Carter in person and that he's doing well. I know how worried he's been."

"Yes, he seems to put a very high value on Carter. I've been surprised, to be honest, it's not that common in an officer, but Adam informs me that Van Daan is a little different. Come over and see him, it's not far."

Manson found Regimental-Sergeant-Major Daniel Carter and his wife in a small, four-roomed cottage which was part of a row of tied-cottages built to house labourers and servants who worked for the convent but were not part of the religious community. It was simply furnished but Manson thought it must have seemed like luxury to Carter and Teresa who were accustomed to the over-crowded conditions of an army camp.

Carter greeted his company officer with unfeigned pleasure and Teresa went to bring wine. The first half hour was spent catching up on news. Both Carter and Manson had received regular letters from the regiment, but often from different people which meant that they had stories to tell of the recent French invasion and of Wellington's frantic scramble to repel them. Major-General van Daan was not a discreet correspondent and Carter yelled with laughter as Manson read a letter from his pack which described several of the Light Division's night marches in colourful detail. In return, Carter described Sergeant Hammond's account of his commanding officer's foul temper at some of the antics of the 9th Dragoon Guards who seemed to be taking a lax view of their duties.

Manson noticed with interest that both he and Carter had chosen to share light-hearted anecdotes, with no mention of the losses of Maya, Roncesvalles and Sorauren and no speculation about what might have happened at San Sebastian by now. They talked of neutral topics for a while; transport and supplies and some of the changes to the brigade. Manson had a sudden thought.

"I wonder how Hammond's love life is coming along? Has he mentioned her?"

Carter grinned. "Not in detail but then he wouldn't. He's a gentleman at heart. They're doing nicely, Captain. In fact there are rumours of a wedding when Lord Wellington's chaplain finally arrives back."

"According to an officer I met in Oporto, he's already arrived in Lisbon. I think he's preparing himself for the next stage of the journey."

"What the bloody hell is he doing in Lisbon?" Carter said in surprise. "Much quicker to sail to Santander these days."

"I don't know if it's true, Sergeant-Major, but I've been told he's been in Lisbon for so long he could have walked it by now."

Carter gave a splutter of laughter. "Maybe he's hoping the war will be over soon and he won't have to travel up to the lines at all."

"He'll be lucky. We're doing well, but not that well and his Lordship wants his chaplain back. As, presumably, do Hammond and Alison Macdonald."

They fell silent for a while. Manson glanced around the small cottage. On a rag rug before the fireplace, little Ana was stretched out on her tummy playing with a collection of smooth pebbles, arranging and rearranging them contentedly. Manson was astonished at how much she had grown. Teresa was seated in a plain wooden armchair mending a shirt. She was humming softly but Manson did not think she intended it to be heard. She just sounded happy. He looked back at Carter.

The Sergeant-Major looked older, Manson thought. He had always been slim, with long rangy limbs but his face was still gaunt from his illness and there were shadows under his eyes. The eyes were the same though and as Manson studied him, he saw them light up with the familiar imp of mischief.

"Do you know, sir, I always used to think you were hard to read. The General now, is like an open book. With really big printing and a lot of pictures. But you were such a contained little bugger when I first knew you, I didn't get

279

you at all. I don't know if you've changed over the past few years or if I've got to know you better but just now, I can read your bloody mind."

Manson could not help smiling. "Go on then, Sergeant-Major. What am I thinking?"

"You're looking round this place and wondering if you can talk me into extending my sick leave and staying here where it's safe and comfortable. Preferably to the end of the war. Aren't you?"

Manson laughed aloud. "I just think you've got to know me better, Carter. But I am worried you're trying to rush back too soon."

"Says the man who was gritting his teeth when he got down off his horse earlier. Don't deny it, I was watching you. Have you tested how fast you are at swordplay yet?"

"The closest I've been to a fight involved my girl and two feather pillows, Carter."

"Christ, I don't want to know how that one ended. Come on."

Carter got up, reaching for his jacket. He smiled at Teresa and she smiled back, her face lighting up. Manson followed him out of the cottage, reflecting that whatever the couple had been through over these past difficult months, their marriage seemed stronger than ever. It made him happy, although a little envious, but he brushed the thought firmly aside. He had made a promise to Diana only to dwell on the happiness of their love affair and he had left her this time with so many joyous memories.

Carter led him to a wooden barn beside the convent stables. It was used for storing hay and various farm and gardening implements but a big space had been cleared in the centre. On the far side was an array of weapons, including several rifles left neatly standing against the wall. Carter went to collect one and scooped up his shot belt then turned, slinging the weapon over his shoulder. Manson thought he immediately looked taller and more solid. The rifle was like an extension of his long body. He flashed a grin at Manson and led the way out of the opposite door to a broad expanse of sandy ground.

It was obvious that both the barn and the area outside had been set up for training. There were a number of straw dummies for bayonet training and several targets. These were clearly not for musket training. A musket was not accurate enough to aim at a specific target; it was a weapon designed to be fired quickly and steadily at a mass of bodies.

Carter unslung the rifle and began to load it methodically. Even from here, Manson could see that it was immaculately clean and wondered how many hours Carter had spent bringing it to this level of perfection.

When the rifle was loaded, Carter turned and held it out to Manson. Manson blinked in surprise then took it. It was months since he had handled one and it felt heavier than he remembered. Something of that must have shown in his face because he saw the flicker of a smile on Carter's countenance.

"It'll come back with practice, sir."

Memory flooded back and Manson froze. Three years ago he had been a green young officer trying to recover from an appalling start in the army when

Carter and Corporal Hammond had offered to teach him to shoot a rifle. It was not necessary for officers to learn, although in the 110th Paul van Daan expected every one of them to know the basics of the weapons their men fought with. Manson had been a fair shot with a pistol when he was younger but he had found the rifle heavy and unwieldy and had felt like an idiot beside Carter and Hammond's calm competence. He had allowed his frustration to show as his first shots went wide and the recoil almost took him off his feet. Carter had steadied him and held out more shot.

"It'll come with practice, sir."

Manson glanced at Carter, wondering if he remembered and knew by his smiling expression that he did. He smiled back, hoisted the rifle and stood for a moment, regaining his balance and getting used to the feel of the weapon in his hands. Carter waited with no sign of impatience.

When Manson was ready he stepped forward, his eyes on the target. Carter watched as he lifted the weapon and settled it into his shoulder. Finally it felt natural again and Manson became very still, the world around him receding as he fixed his eyes on the target. Very gently he squeezed the trigger.

The recoil still caught him off balance but he knew it was a good shot. He recovered himself and looked at the wooden target. It was a clear hit, slightly off centre but very good for a man out of practice. Manson turned to Carter who was applauding. He handed the Sergeant-Major the rifle, not even attempting to hide how delighted he was.

"Your turn, Sergeant-Major."

"Smug bastard." Carter took the weapon and began to load. This time he did it quickly, as though in battle. Manson watched, admiring the other man's skill. The moment it was done, Carter turned and swung the rifle up to his shoulder. He seemed to take aim and fire in one smooth movement absorbing the recoil easily.

For a moment, Manson thought he had missed and was appalled. Then he saw Carter's grim smile and looked again. There was another target, well behind the first. When he had been taking aim, Manson had not even noticed it. It would have been an incredible shot even for a man as experienced as Carter. Manson set off towards the targets at a jog, ignoring the twinge in his leg muscles. He noted with pleasure his own clean shot as he passed the first target then pulled up at the sight of Carter's. It had struck the centre of the target, blowing it away. Manson flinched internally at the thought of what that would have done to a man. He turned as Carter arrived beside him at a more leisurely pace.

"Smug bastard," Manson said. Carter grinned but his expression was immediately serious. He reached out and touched the shattered wood with the tips of his fingers.

"I can still remember how it felt," he said quietly. "Lying in that church after they blew it apart. There was something sticking through my chest, though I couldn't work out what it was at first. I thought somehow they'd bayonetted me, but then I tried to move and I realised I was pinned. It was agony."

281

Manson tried to speak but realised that his throat was closed up with tears. He could see tears in Carter's brown eyes as well.

"It's the closest I've ever come to dying and I thought I wasn't going to make it. I'd pull round then something would go wrong again. All I could think about was that I had everything to live for – Teresa, Ana and the new baby – and I might not make it. I've never felt that bad in my life."

Manson finally found his voice. "You made it, Carter."

Carter turned. His voice was suddenly hard. "Yes, I fucking did. But we're not done yet, me and Bonaparte. There's been a few times through the years that I've thought I need to see this through to the end. But that day, in that church, his bastards killed some of my mates, took the hand off my commanding officer and half-killed me. I'm coming back. When he goes down, I intend to be there to watch in person."

Manson saluted although he had no idea why. "Fair enough, Sergeant-Major Carter. I'll be coming with you."

"Not just yet you bloody won't. I reckon I passed my return-to-duty medical examination there. Yours is still to come. Get yourself in that barn, Captain Manson and find your sword."

Manson looked at him in astonishment for a moment then began to laugh. "Carter, I am going to disarm you in ten seconds. You know this."

"Well if you do, sir, I'm declaring you fit for duty. Then we'll see what Dr Norris has to say about both of us. Come on."

***

Simon had been invited to dine with Captain Harry Smith and his young Spanish wife Juana along with Ensign Fox and one or two of Smith's friends in the Rifles. Smith was unusually quiet and the men around him seemed on edge, their good-humour a little forced as though to disguise their companion's gloom. Simon understood. The officers and men of Skerrett's brigade were still in shock, as though unable to grasp the enormity of what had happened. Sixteen men, including Captain Daniel Cadoux, had died during the defence of the bridge along with several men from the reinforcements belatedly sent down. They had died while Skerrett remained in his billet in a farmhouse arguing with his young brigade-major about the wisdom of sending men to help Cadoux.

Over the past twenty-four hours, Simon had heard various rumours spreading through Skerrett's brigade. Some men said that Cadoux had asked for help and been refused. Some said that arrogantly he had believed he could hold the bridge against the French alone. Simon knew that was not true; Fox had carried Cadoux's desperate requests for reinforcements. There was another story that Skerrett had twice sent orders for Cadoux to withdraw and Cadoux had refused. Simon did not think that was likely. He had been with Cadoux and his riflemen for several hours and nobody had mentioned any such order arriving.

Simon questioned Fox about it as they rode back down to their former campsite after the meal and the younger man shook his head emphatically.

"No," he said. "None of them said a word about that; it was all about Cadoux asking for reinforcements. He honestly thought they'd be sent eventually, sir. If he hadn't, he would have retreated, no matter how angry he was. He'd already lost men unnecessarily that morning. He wouldn't have put more of their lives at risk if no help was coming. He thought General Skerrett was just dithering. He had that reputation."

"Perhaps he was," Simon said. "Perhaps this time he just dithered too long."

"They're not speaking to him, sir," Fox said.

"Who?"

"The other officers of the 95th and the 52nd. They took a vote this morning at an informal mess meeting that they would only speak to him when duty obliged them to do so. I wonder if the rest of the division will do the same?"

Something in Fox's voice made Simon turn to study him. The younger man was still very pale, though they had been well fed and had managed a decent night's sleep in the Casa Martinez. They had been the only occupants. Simon wondered when the rest of the brigade would return.

"I'd have thought it would be difficult to send a Major-General to Coventry," he said mildly.

"A lot easier with an ensign," Fox said.

Simon felt himself freeze. He bit back on any immediate response though he was dying to ask. Fox had never been this forthcoming before and Simon suspected that a combination of exhaustion and grief had loosened his tongue. He was desperate not to ruin the moment. He counted in his head, waiting to see if the boy would say more. He did not. Eventually Simon decided he would have to take the risk.

"Is that what they've done to you, Fox?"

Fox did not reply. Simon almost bit his tongue in his effort not to press him. Another long silence ensued. Then Fox said:

"There was a rumour that I'd absented myself deliberately during the battle, sir. These things get around. Nobody wants to be associated with a coward."

Simon did not respond. He wanted to think carefully about his reply. It was not the first time he had come across a situation where a new officer had struggled to cope in his first battle. There were always a few loud-mouthed idiots who were quick to criticise but Simon had found that most officers were tolerant, assuming that the youngster would learn. A captain or major accused of cowardice might have a harder time but an ensign was usually given the benefit of the doubt in his first engagement.

"Is that what happened, Fox?" Simon said eventually.

"That was their excuse, anyway. The real reason is that I don't fit in. That I'm strange. A freak. Doesn't matter how hard I try to man up and behave like the other young gentlemen, it always follows me. The only way I'm ever going to escape it is on the other end of a French bullet. I thought I might do it today but I couldn't even get that right. Instead they shot him."

Fox was crying. Simon could think of nothing to say that might help him or comfort him in his bitter, tearing grief. He had only the vaguest idea of what Fox was trying to say and was not sure that he ought to enquire further for both their sakes but he desperately wanted to offer some kind of reassurance.

He was still weighing up his words as they approached the Casa Martinez and rode into a blaze of lantern-light, noise and what looked like utter chaos. Baggage wagons were lined up along the driveway and were backed up down the path. NCOs were calling orders for the men to unload tents and baggage while Quartermaster-Sergeant Stewart stood in the first field with a slate marked out in blocks for the various locations of the battalion tents. Forage parties were already assembled to go in search of firewood and in front of the house itself, Major-General Paul van Daan was lifting his wife down from her mare while Sergeant Jenson stood waiting to lead the horses to the field marked out for grazing.

The sudden onslaught of noise and people and light was almost too much for Simon and it gave him an unexpected insight about how it might be for Ensign Fox, whose face was still streaked with tears. He felt an unexpected need to protect the younger man, at least until the chaos had died down, and he looked around, searching for a way out. He was forestalled by a familiar bellow which raised itself easily above the general noise of an army brigade arriving in camp.

"Captain Carlyon, Ensign Fox. I'm glad to see you both. Over here, if you please."

Simon shot an agonised glance at his companion who was scrubbing frantically at his face with his sleeve. "I'm sorry. The timing of this is shit. Tell him whatever you like. I won't repeat what you just said unless you want me to."

Fox shot him an astonished, grateful glance. They arrived before the house and grooms came to take their horses. Simon went forward. His former sister-in-law was holding out her arms.

"We heard the news, Simon. I'm so sorry, it must have been awful. Thank God you're both safe."

Simon embraced her warmly. "Thank you, ma'am. Look, we camped out in one of the rooms last night. We'll collect our kit and…"

"What nonsense. I was going to suggest you share a room with Captain Witham and Mr Fox. We raided the sutlers in Lesaca on our way through and Sergeant Kelly is unloading the wine. I'm guessing you've both dined but please join us for a drink while the orderlies sort out the rooms. Mr Fox, how are you?"

"Captain Carlyon, Mr Fox."

Simon turned to his commanding officer and saluted. He did not look at Fox, hoping that if he ignored the younger man, Paul would do the same. Paul returned the salute, his eyes on Simon's face.

"I've been receiving reports throughout the march back," he said briefly. "Are you both all right? Clearly not, because your arm is bandaged up and should probably be in a sling. What happened?

"A nasty gash, sir, but the surgeon doesn't seem too worried. It will slow me down for a bit, that's all."

"It will certainly slow you down while my wife is organising your treatment plan. Listen to her, Simon, she knows what she's doing and you're family. I don't want to lose you to an incompetent surgeon. Ensign Fox, step forward if you please."

Fox did so, saluting. Simon, with his new understanding of the younger man's misery, ached for him but could do nothing to help. He waited, hovering protectively, looking for an opportunity to step in.

"I've received a full report of your conduct this week, Ensign. I know you were friendly with Captain Cadoux. He was an excellent officer and a good man. I'm so sorry for your loss. With regard to you, I'm hearing news of a young officer who rode through the night in appalling conditions to try to bring reinforcements in the face of impossible difficulties. Well done, Fox. You and I have not always seen eye to eye. I've still not the least idea what's going on with you, but before you get some well-earned rest, I'd like you to know that as far as I'm concerned, the slate is wiped clean. I'm proud of you and you may be sure that the rest of the officers of this brigade are about to hear that loud and clear. Later on we'll work out what you want to do next. Get yourself cleaned up and join us for a drink."

Simon turned to look at Fox. The expression on the younger man's face was painful; a mix of shock and confusion along with something like happiness. He managed a salute and turned towards the house. Simon watched him go then looked back at Paul in some bewilderment. His commanding officer studied him for a moment then shrugged.

"I don't know, Simon and if you have any more idea than I do, I'll welcome your insights when we get a fucking moment to breathe. You've clearly had more success with the boy than any of the rest of us so just keep on with what you're doing. Just now, I've got other things on my mind. Where the fuck is Skerrett?"

Simon's stomach lurched. He was not surprised. Ever since the full import of Skerrett's errors had sunk in, he had been praying that Lieutenant-General Alten would get back before Paul did. Not only did he outrank Paul, he also had a famously calming effect on him. Unfortunately there was currently no sign of the Hanoverian commander. Sir James Kempt was busy setting up his own brigade headquarters back at his former camp site and as far as Simon was aware, had made no attempt to approach Skerrett. If there were to be consequences for what had happened on the bridge at Vera they should come from Lord Wellington, who had appointed Skerrett in the first place, but looking at the expression on his commanding officer's face, Simon thought it unlikely that there would be much left for his Lordship to deal with. Simon tried.

"Sir, wouldn't it be better to wait until…"

"Until we get another call to arms and he gets the other half of his brigade slaughtered? No it fucking wouldn't. Where is he?"

"I've no idea, sir."

"You wouldn't tell me if you did, would you? I'm going to make a guess that he's hiding in his billet with a blanket over his head. Am I right?"

Simon hesitated then gave in. "I've no idea about the blanket, sir."

"A good effort, but nothing is going to make me laugh today until I've had the satisfaction of explaining to that pointless sack of shit that he's in the wrong job. Get them settled, girl of my heart. I'll be back for supper. This won't take long."

"Unless you get arrested, in which case I think you will very likely miss supper," Anne said acerbically. Simon shot her a glance and decided that she had recently lost an argument for restraint. He watched as Paul took Rufus' reins from Jenson and swung himself easily into the saddle. If Anne had been unable to dissuade him, nobody else stood a chance.

"Are you all right, Simon?" Anne said gently as Paul cantered away.

"Yes, ma'am. It's painful though. The surgeon said it looks worse than it is."

"That does not reassure me. I once heard Cradock say that about poor General Craufurd's broken spine. Would you mind coming through to the office and allowing me to have a look? I just want to reassure myself."

"It would reassure me too, ma'am." Simon looked after the retreating figure of his commanding officer. "Will he be all right?"

"I'm sure he will be perfectly fine, Simon. I am a little worried about Major-General John Byrne Skerrett but I'm afraid I cannot help him. When Paul starts threatening to send me home if I persist in interfering in army business I know I can't reach him. The only person who might be able to is probably at evening prayer in a Leicestershire church just now. Come inside and let me do something useful. And you can tell me all about Ensign Fox. Paul thinks you're some kind of miracle worker."

***

Major-General Skerrett occupied two rooms in a small farmhouse perched on a hillside above the Bidassoa. The last time Paul had visited there had been chickens running free in the front yard and two milk cows in a fenced pasture at the back. The cows were still there, their solid shapes outlined against the last of the evening light. There was no sign of the poultry. Either they had been bought or looted by the army or the farmer had seen the wisdom of keeping them out of sight while Skerrett's brigade occupied these hills.

Paul tied Rufus to an iron ring outside the house and went through the open door, knocking to announce his presence. His curiosity about the chickens was immediately answered. They were pecking at the earth floor of a lean-to shack off the kitchen, penned in by a rough plank of wood. The farmer's wife, a thin woman of around thirty, was seated at a spinning wheel. A girl of around ten was showing a younger boy some weaving on a simple hand loom. All three looked up in surprise at Paul's entrance. Paul spoke slowly in Spanish, knowing that most of the local farming community were most comfortable in the Basque language. Paul had no intention of attempting to learn that.

"Your pardon, Señora. I am looking for General Skerrett. Is he here?"

286

The woman said nothing for a moment, keeping her attention on her spinning. Paul waited as patiently as he could, suspecting that the delay had more to do with needing to pay attention to her work than because she was ignoring him. He was proved right within two minutes when she carefully slowed the wheel, eased the thread into a basket at her feet and looked up.

"He is upstairs, but does not wish to see anyone."

Her accent was difficult to understand but the words were simple. Paul gave a little bow. "Thank you, Señora. My apologies, but I must go up. It is important."

She shrugged and waved her hand towards the narrow wooden stairs which were so steep they were almost like a ladder. Paul took it for permission and went up carefully. He reflected that if Skerrett wanted to hide, he would have done better to station a sentry below. It would have made no difference to Paul however; he outranked Skerrett's entire brigade and was perfectly willing to tell them so.

Skerrett was sitting at a small table writing a letter by lamplight. Paul entered the room without knocking and closed the door behind him. Skerrett got up. Even in the dim light, his face looked pale and his jaw was clenched in what might have been defiance.

"Major-General Skerrett. Glad to find you at home."

"It is customary to knock, Van Daan."

"Why the fuck would I knock when you're only going to tell me to piss off? Which I would then ignore. It's a lot quicker this way. I've just arrived back from Lesaca and while my brigade is setting up camp, I thought I'd call to ask you what the fuck you thought you were doing? Sixteen men dead and that's without taking into account those who got killed, wounded or captured earlier in the day the first time you failed to do your duty. I hope you've got your excuses ready for Lord Wellington when he sends for you. Feel free to start practising them on me. Right now."

Skerrett straightened, as though he was trying to make himself taller. "Lord Wellington has already sent his report to London, sir and I think you will find he makes no criticism of my actions. Indeed I am reliably informed…"

"He didn't fucking know what had happened when he wrote that report," Paul interrupted ruthlessly. "He made the assumption – mistakenly as it turned out – that your entire brigade was involved in the defence of that bridge. I must say it was an impressive defence by the way; I can see how he could have made that mistake. Two hundred or more French dead and wounded I'm told, though we don't really know as they're still hauling them ou,t of the river to stop them polluting the drinking water. The French commander, General Vandermaesen is among the deceased. It made your brigade look bloody impressive, Skerrett, holding off four thousand Frenchmen for as long as you did. Except that you fucking didn't, did you? Because you were sitting up here shivering in your shoes leaving it to Cadoux and his men to do your job for you."

"Are you calling me a coward, sir?"

287

"No. I'm told you're a brave man on a battlefield. Reckless even. I'm calling you a fucking idiot. If you'd taken your men down there with every scrap of ammunition in your possession you could have held them there until the rest of the army caught up with them and we'd be facing four thousand fewer Frenchmen at the next engagement. What the fuck were you thinking, Skerrett? Can you even think?"

"I was following orders!" Skerrett burst out. "My orders were to avoid engaging the enemy unless attacked. I followed orders and if Cadoux had…"

"Don't you fucking dare blame Cadoux," Paul yelled. "He paid for your mistake with his life and half his company with him. Two of my officers were there. I know exactly what happened, Skerrett. Yes, you had orders. We all did, if you can use the word orders to describe the endless stream of guesses and vague suggestions that came out of headquarters this week. But you're a fucking major-general. They don't hand over that insignia and then expect you to hide behind out-of-date orders when the French are advancing and yours is the only brigade close enough to stop them. At that point it's your job to use your initiative and your brain, if you have one, get your men down the hill and support your pickets. And if you genuinely don't understand that, you have no place in command, no place in the Light Division and no right to wear that fucking uniform."

"He hates officers using their initiative," Skerrett blurted out. "Everybody knows that. It's the first thing they told me when I transferred over here from the east. He doesn't like…"

"Why in God's name would you sit there worrying about his Lordship's temper tantrums when men are dying?" Paul roared. "Stop making fucking excuses before I lose what little is left of my self-control and kick you into the dung heap. You made a mistake. A huge, lethal mistake. Men died because of it. It happens all the bloody time in this army, including to me. Admittedly if I make a mistake it's more likely to be due to too much initiative rather than too little but that's not the point. The least you can do, is admit your error to Alten and to Lord Wellington, even if you can't say it to your officers. After that it's up to them."

Skerrett did not speak for a long time. He turned and walked back to the table, looking down at the letter he was writing and some other paperwork scattered there. After a long time he walked over to a small window and looked out over the darkening hills.

It was so quiet in the room that Paul could hear his own breathing. He used the pause to breathe more evenly, trying desperately to bring his rage under control. He had been on his way back when he had received Simon Carlyon's letter about the events at Vera and he had been wanting to punch Skerrett for the past seven miles plus an extended pause at headquarters where Lord Wellington had given him the news of Sir Richard Fletcher's death. Since then he had been so angry that he had shouted at everybody who had tried to tell him not to approach Skerrett, including Anne. He was suddenly aware that he owed a number of apologies.

The fact that he realised it, told Paul that he was beginning to calm down. Skerrett had still not spoken. For the first time, it occurred to Paul that something else was going on.

"Are you all right?" he asked abruptly.

Skerrett walked to a brass bound trunk. There was a silver tray on it, set out with glasses and a wine bottle. He picked up the bottle and attempted to unstopper it but his hands were shaking so much that he could not do so. Paul watched him for a moment then moved forward and took it from his hands.

"I'll do it. Sit down, for God's sake, you look as though you're going to vomit."

He hooked his foot around the leg of a chair, pulled it towards him and pushed Skerrett into it then poured two glasses of wine, handed one to Skerrett and perched on a second chair rather gingerly, not sure that it would take his weight.

"What's going on?"

"Apart from a probable court martial?" Skerrett said, somewhat waspishly.

"Wellington won't send you for court martial. He'd never do that to an officer at your level unless he absolutely had to."

"My father is dead."

Paul almost spat out the wine he had just drunk. He managed to gulp it down with an effort and put down his glass on the chest, staring at Skerrett.

"You mean just now? Recently? When did you find out?"

To his immense surprise, Skerrett gave a weary smile. "Are you wondering if the news arrived just before the French army, Van Daan? I'm afraid not. The letters came this morning. One from my mother and one from his...my...man of business."

"I'm sorry, Skerrett. I wish I'd known. I can't promise I wouldn't have yelled at you but I'd probably have postponed it. He was an army man as well, wasn't he?"

Skerrett reached over and picked up one of the letters from the table. "Lieutenant-General John Nicholas Skerrett. He gave good service in Ireland and in Newfoundland. Commanded in Jamaica briefly. A very distinguished career. Thank God he won't have to hear about this."

Paul closed his eyes briefly, considering his words. He was wishing heartily that he had listened to his wife and his officers and waited until Alten's return before speaking to Skerrett. He was still furious and heartsick at the loss of Cadoux and his men. He also knew, now that he was calmer, that he had been grief-stricken at the death of Sir Richard Fletcher, Sergeant Bowlby and Alfredo Ronaldo and had been looking for a target for his anger. Paul had not changed his opinion of Skerrett's actions but he could not carry on berating him. The man looked broken.

"Wellington won't court martial you," he said again, more gently. "Earlier on, I was bloody furious about it. He's done this before. He did tell me that he'd find a way of moving you on from the Light Division. You can't command them now. You probably know that."

"It would be difficult for me to do so given that the officers will barely speak to me," Skerrett said flatly. "That does not worry me as much as the thought of having the 95th behind me with loaded rifles during the next engagement, however. And please do not tell me they would not consider it, General van Daan."

"I suspect they're already talking about it," Paul said. "To be honest, it's one of the reasons I came here to tell you that you need to go. I wasn't going to be quite so blunt about it, mind."

"Oh I think that given how blunt you have already been, we can speak as men. My mother wants me at home and my lawyer informs me there are business matters which will require my attention. Apparently there is an inheritance, which I did not know about. I would have needed to ask his Lordship for furlough even if this had not happened."

"I'm sorry about your father, Skerrett. Truly. But I'm not going to tell you I'm sorry about anything I've said to you and I'm certainly not going to tell you to forget I said it. You fucked up badly. You're fortunate to have a good excuse to leave and Lord Wellington will be so pleased with you for solving a delicate problem for him and getting me off his back that he won't even reprimand you. That's why you need to remember what I've said, work out why you did what you did and, if you stay in the army, make sure you never fucking do it again. Next time it might be a battalion rather than half a company and it might be an officer who has no problem nailing your arse to the wall. If I had the commanding of you, I'd do it in a heartbeat."

Skerrett did not reply. Paul finished his wine and stood up. "I'm going back to see if my wife is still speaking to me," he said. "Get yourself over to Wellington in the morning, make your arrangements and go home. I know you probably can't think about much at all at the moment, but when your head finally clears, think about what I've said. Good luck."

Skerrett remained seated, staring into his wine glass. He did not speak again so Paul closed the door quietly and went in search of the man's orderly to instruct him to keep an eye on his master. Then he went to collect Rufus and set the horse down the narrow pathway at a careful walk, wondering if Anne had given his supper to Craufurd.

Chapter Nineteen

Giles Fenwick had attempted to insist that he was capable of riding the twenty miles from the army hospital near San Sebastian when the doctor agreed to discharge him into the care of his regimental surgeons. He was thwarted by the discovery that Anne had sent her carriage to collect him, with Michael O'Reilly as escort. She had also removed his horse from the stables and had him taken back to Vera. Giles called her a variety of rude names and settled himself in the carriage beside his friend. Michael studied him thoughtfully.

"How are you doing, Captain Fenwick? You still look a bit peaky to me. Are you sure they said you could travel?"

"Peaky?" Giles said indignantly. "What the hell does that mean?"

"Pale. Wan. Lacking colour. Jesus, Giles, where on earth were you brought up?"

"In aristocratic poverty, my dear Michael. It clearly had a detrimental effect on my vocabulary. You are not precisely glowing either. Did you knock yourself out?"

Michael touched the fading bruise on his temple. "Not that I'm aware of, though the whole assault is something of a blur to be honest."

"I'm told you were a hero."

"Then you're listening to idiots."

"You shouldn't speak of Sir James Leith that way, it's disrespectful. I heard what happened to the 95th at the bridge. Is Carlyon all right?"

"He's under medical supervision with a slashed arm and he's bloody upset but he's fine. Young Fox was there as well."

"Hiding under a table?"

"Don't, Giles. It's not fair. He's having a shit time according to Carlyon and he rode up that path in pitch darkness twice that night to try to get bloody Skerrett to send reinforcements. He'd got friendly with Cadoux and he's cut up about it."

Giles realised that he was thoroughly behind on the news. He studied Michael's expression and decided to rein in his sarcasm.

"Sorry. I don't know any of the details. I liked Cadoux as well. Played a good hand of cards and paid his gaming debts like a gentleman."

291

"That's an epitaph of a kind, I suppose." Michael took out a silver flask and passed it to Giles. It was a good French brandy and Giles drank and leaned his head back on the comfortable upholstery of Anne's carriage.

"I have no idea how I'd have done this on horseback," he said honestly.

"Nor had anybody else, but she has more sense than to argue with you. We're stopping for the night at the St Anton hermitage; they have a guest hut there and I've arranged for a meal. Don't look at me like that, Captain Fenwick. I know we can do it in a day but you'll be exhausted and you're still not well."

"Christ, Michael, if she'd seen the conditions I lived in on the road at times she'd have had a fit."

"No she wouldn't, she already knows. Or have you forgotten the retreat from Madrid? She's not stupid; she knows what you can endure if you have to, but you've recently left a few pints of blood in the dust outside San Sebastian, your wound hasn't properly healed and she takes the view that when you have time to convalesce, you should take it. And I agree with her."

"You always bloody agree with her."

"She's generally right."

The exchange had inexplicably cheered Giles. He grinned. "All right, I'll stop complaining. You can while away the journey by bringing me up to date with all the news. Is it true that Skerrett is going home? That's got to be the shortest brigade command in history. Who takes over?"

"Colborne is taking temporary charge, though it's been stressed that it's temporary. The official story is that Skerrett has taken furlough because of the death of his father, to sort out his affairs."

"Surely Wellington won't bring him back?"

"I hope not, for Skerrett's sake. If Major-General van Daan doesn't drown him in the Bidassoa, some friend of Rifleman Mapstone and the others is going to blow the back of his head off in the next fight they get into. Better all round if he stays away."

"What about Barnard?"

"You mean Sir Andrew Barnard?" Michael said innocently. Giles choked on another slug of brandy.

"They've knighted Andrew Barnard?"

"Apparently so. The General tells me Barnard has known for a month but didn't tell him because he couldn't be doing with the roasting. It's out now though and believe me, that bastard is making the most of it."

"I'll just bet he is," Giles said appreciatively. "On reflection, Michael, I'm glad she sent you with the carriage. You're the best gossip in the army and I hope to be very well-informed by the time we reach Vera. Carry on."

They reached the bridge at Vera in the early afternoon on the following day and Giles felt nothing but relief. He was more tired than he had expected and the wound was so painful that he was beginning to wonder if it had opened up again although he did not dare to check with Michael's eagle eyes upon him. As they drove down the bumpy track past the bridge, Giles leaned out of the window on impulse and shouted up to the driver.

292

"Can you stop here?"

It was an effort to climb down from the carriage. Giles was briefly amused at Michael visibly forcing himself not to offer help. They walked down to the two houses defended by Cadoux and his men. Giles could see the damage done to the outside walls by musket balls and possibly some kind of small field gun. Inside the furniture was broken and scattered about. There were marks on the floor which might well have been blood.

Outside, he stood looking over the bridge, wondering about the men who had died. He had known Cadoux and his officers casually but his men had been just anonymous riflemen, quick with a joke and a laugh. Giles knew he must have seen them often but could not remember a single face. It bothered him, though he knew it was ridiculous to expect an officer to remember every passing soldier he exchanged a word with.

"How is young Fox?" he asked.

"Not so good. Simon Carlyon and Nick Witham seem to have taken him under their wing a bit, which I think has helped. More to the point, after his surprising heroics that night, Major-General van Daan is keen to have a chat with the officers of the 112th to find out exactly what Fox is supposed to have done to get ostracised. I can't wait for the next chapter, I must say. Come on, Giles, get back in the carriage. Mrs van Daan has a room for you in the house and I want her to have a look at you. You're clearly in pain, you can barely stand up straight."

Giles laughed despite himself. "I thought I was hiding that quite well."

"Don't be a bloody idiot. Come and get comfortable."

The room was a cosy box on the second floor of the Casa Martinez and instead of the usual camp bed or mattress on the floor, Anne had found him a proper wooden bed frame with a straw mattress. She accompanied him to the room and insisted on inspecting the wound before he was allowed even to wash his face. To his dismay the dressing was soaked in blood which had leaked through onto his shirt. Giles swore under his breath then looked up guiltily. Anne was laughing.

"It's all right, Captain, I've heard worse. Lie back and let me look at that."

Giles obeyed. She was very gentle as she washed the wound thoroughly and examined it in silence. Giles hated being in the hands of doctors but it was impossible not to be soothed by Anne van Daan's quiet competence.

"Have I made a mess of it, ma'am?"

"Goodness no, it's healing very well. Still needs a few weeks, but it's looking very healthy with no sign of infection. It's opened up a little during the journey, but nothing to worry about. It's up to you, Captain. I can dress it and bind it up again properly. I think it will heal perfectly well if you give it a chance. If not, I'll have to stitch it again and then you'll be confined to your bed."

Giles heard the gentle threat behind her words and laughed aloud. "I'll be good, ma'am, I promise. Do I have to remain in bed today?"

"No. You may join us for dinner providing you come back and rest again afterwards. And since I know it is going to drive you mad, I am going to give permission for you to speak to Hannah Bowlby. You won't have to go far, she has a job helping George Kelly in the kitchen."

Giles felt sheer relief wash over him. "Was that your idea, ma'am?"

"It was Paul's actually, but I would have found her something. We're not pushing her to make any kind of decision yet, Captain, but Paul has told her that he will pay for and arrange a passage home for her and the boys if that's what she wants. She has also been told that under no circumstances should she feel obliged to find a new husband in order to draw rations. We'll take care of her for a bit until she's over the worst."

"They were devoted," Giles said. "I remember when I first joined. She was such a pretty girl, all us young officers used to spend half our time hanging around trying to find an excuse to talk to her. She was always friendly, but she and Jim were like two halves of a whole."

"I know, Captain. It's painful to watch. She'll want to see you, though. She's been asking about you. Go and find her and then come through to the dining room for a drink. Welcome back. Oh and Giles…"

"Ma'am?"

"I have been informed by several of our men that you saved their lives at considerable risk to your own that day. I know the General will have something to say about it, but this is from me. Thank you for Michael's life. He's one of my oldest friends and I can't imagine what it would have done to Ariana."

Giles felt his face grow warm. "He's my friend too, ma'am."

"I know he is. Which is why you should make sure that you keep Thursday morning free. I believe that both of us have an appointment at San Esteban Church at eleven o'clock. Ariana tells me you made her a promise."

Giles broke into a smile. "Yes. Oh God, yes. I'll be on my feet for that, ma'am, even if I have to take to my bed for a week afterwards."

"You'll be fine, Captain. Go and speak to Hannah. I think it will help – both her and you."

Giles found Hannah Bowlby in the kitchen. At a nod from Sergeant Kelly she abandoned the roasting spit and followed him out into the farmyard. She looked white and heavy-eyed, her dark hair pulled back into a knot.

"Hannah, I'm so sorry. I wish I could have come sooner, they've had me laid up with this wound."

"It's all right, sir. I heard about it. I'm so sorry that you were hurt, but I'm thankful you're back. I've been fretting about you."

Giles was touched. "I'm fine," he said quickly. "How are you coping? What about the boys?"

"We're managing. Young Charlie has them out the back, helping him muck out the officers' horses. I'm not sure how much use they are; Jem is only seven and Bertie is a year younger but they feel like they're doing something to help."

"That will be important to them."

"You weren't there, I hear. When my Jim was shot down?"

"No. Our volunteers were all over the place and I wasn't really supposed to be there at all. They'd got our lads spread out, trying to pick off the French in the breaches. When Colonel Hunt finally got the order to lead them in, Jim was climbing alongside Ensign Hardy. They were both shot down in the breach. I didn't see it. I'm sorry, Hannah."

She was crying, wiping her eyes on her sleeve. "Oh hush, it's not your fault. Nor Captain O'Reilly. Jim volunteered. I knew he would, the minute we heard. He always volunteered for anything. It's like he thought it was his duty to do more than anybody else. I liked that about him, I was proud of him. Sometimes I wished he wouldn't, but he always came back. Like he had a charmed life. He came back so many times, I forgot that one day he might not."

Giles stepped forward and took her into his arms. She sobbed against his shoulder and he held her in helpless misery, wishing there was something he could do or say that would ease her pain, but he knew there was not.

Eventually her crying eased out of sheer exhaustion. Giles sat her down on a rickety bench against the kitchen wall and went in search of a drink. He returned with two cups of wine and they sat drinking it, watching the sun beginning to move lower in the sky. They did not speak. There was nothing more to say.

Finally she stirred as though coming out of a trance. "I should go. Sergeant Kelly will need help with dinner. He's been very good. They all have."

"Do you think you'll want to go home?"

She raised warm brown eyes to his. "Home? I don't have a home, sir. Ma and Pa are dead, no idea what happened to my brother and sister. They could be anywhere. Or dead too. None of us could read or write. I learned off Jim and he was taught by his company sergeant so he could go for promotion. Never lived anywhere but in barracks or camps. When I couldn't be with him – like that time you went to Holland – I got jobs cleaning or tending bar to feed the boys 'til he came back. He always came back. We'd write then. I was glad I'd learned just for that."

She was crying again but scrubbed her face fiercely as if to push back the tears. Giles understood with painful clarity that for this woman there was no time to grieve. No matter how much she had loved her husband, survival came first.

"This is home," she said, when she had her voice under control again. "This. The army. Filthy camps and bad food and marching in all weathers. It's all I know. If I go back...I know they'll help me – the General and Mrs van Daan. They've been so good. But once I'm there I've got to manage and I can't rely on anyone but me now." She gave a little snort. "I've had an offer. Two of sorts. Corporal Duncan will marry me as soon as the chaplain gets back. Take on the boys and all. It's a good offer and he says I can think about it. The other one's a trooper from that new cavalry regiment. He reckons if I lay with him he'll keep me fed. Knows a couple of his mates who might give me a penny or two for a quick tumble as well."

295

Giles felt cold anger. He drank some wine. "Did you get his name, Hannah?"

She surprised him with a laugh. "There's a reason I didn't give it you, Captain, but don't worry. I told Gisele about it. She found me crying. Sergeant Cooper and Sergeant Dawson went over to have a word with him and I don't think he'll be back."

"Good," Giles said, satisfied. "If I went for a wander through their lines I could probably pick him out by the state of his face."

"I reckon so, sir." Hannah finished her wine and took his empty glass. "She's all right, Gisele. We weren't sure at first, what with her being French and all. But she's all right. She's told me I'm to pitch my tent with the NCOs just like I always have and the lads will help me with the heavy stuff. I'm going to stay for a bit. Think about Duncan's offer. There's nothing wrong with him, though he could wash a bit more. But I could fix that. It's just he's not Jim and right now I can't think about letting another man..."

She broke off, closing her eyes to squeeze back the tears. Giles leaned forward and kissed the top of her head.

"Don't think about it. Think about what it'll cost me to pay you to sort out my kit. I've a hole in everything I own right now."

She laughed then. "Oh you. I'll do yours for nothing, sir."

"No you bloody won't. Go on, get back to the kitchen. And if any other arsehole so much looks at you the wrong way, come straight to me and I'll make him wish he hadn't."

"Thank you, sir."

She bobbed him a little curtsey and was gone. He watched her trim form disappearing through the kitchen door and realised that his own cheeks were wet with tears for her loss and her gallant spirit.

***

Sergeant Rory Stewart brought his wife to the meeting in Paul's office at Anne's suggestion. The room had one long table in the centre and Anne had organised chairs around it for herself and Paul, the Stewarts, Ross Mackenzie and Michael O'Reilly. Paul had contemplated asking Captain White to be present but had decided against it. He suspected this would be a considerable shock to Stewart and he wanted him to hear the news with his friends around before having to deal with the authorities.

Stewart did not speak at all as Anne told the story of Alfredo Ronaldo's deathbed confession. Sally sat beside him and, half-way through, reached out to take his hand. Paul suspected that she was remembering her own ordeal at the hands of Leonard Vane as well as the nightmare of her husband's trial for murder. He wondered if it helped to hear how Vane had really died.

When Anne had finished, Stewart remained silent. He looked completely stunned. Paul did not blame him. When she and Michael had told him about Ronaldo's astonishing tale, he had wondered if the man had been

296

delirious or even if he had lied in some heroic attempt to restore Stewart's reputation. Neither of these made any sense. Ronaldo had not even known Stewart personally and had no reason to lie, especially on his deathbed. The story made sense in a way that Stewart's murder of Vane had not.

Stewart still seemed unable to speak. His wife squeezed his hand, her eyes on Paul's face. "Is it true, sir?"

"Yes, I think it is. The confession was witnessed by Captain White, who investigated the death at the time. Afterwards, he and my wife went through Lieutenant Ronaldo's kit and found the knife. White has since spoken to the doctor who gave evidence at your trial. Though it was a long time ago, he'd kept fairly detailed notes, given that it was a murder case. He can't be certain but he thinks that could well be the knife used on Vane. It makes sense, Sergeant."

Stewart raised Sally's hand to his lips and kissed it. "I don't know what to say. I thought I'd done it. I thought I'd killed him. And sir…though I couldn't remember a damned thing about it, there was a part of me that was glad I'd killed him. After what he'd done to Sal, and what he'd caused me to do to her, thinking she was unfaithful to me, it felt like justice."

"It was justice," Anne said. Her voice was hard and Paul glanced at her and then reached for her hand. It was cold in his. He never forgot that his wife's passionate championing of women who had suffered this kind of abuse came from painful personal experience. "Lieutenant Ronaldo had no idea what Vane had done to Sally but he knew what he'd been trying to do to Tasia. He killed him to protect her. From what he said, he also made some attempt to protect you from suspicion by rolling Vane out of sight. I think if he'd known about your trial he might have come forward. He seemed like an honourable man."

"Aye, he did. It hardly matters who killed the bastard as long as he's gone. Sorry ma'am."

"Don't worry about it, Sergeant, I've called him that myself."

"I've spoken briefly to Captain White," Paul said. "He's preparing a written statement for the Judge Advocate's department with a copy for Colonel Scovell and another for Lord Wellington. Nobody has any idea what the procedure is after that. Mr Larpent will probably have to spend some time with his books searching for any precedent. The important thing is that eventually, your conviction will be quashed and removed from your army record. His Lordship has also agreed that as the events of that night effectively caused your demotion, you'll be reinstated as Sergeant-Major, effective immediately. I'm going to get the back pay out of him but that might take a bit longer. Murray will help me with that."

"Can I stay working with Captain Mackenzie?" Stewart said, looking over at Ross. "Because I've no wish to go back to the company."

"If anybody tries to rob me of my Quartermaster-Sergeant, Stewart, there will be another murder," Ross said reassuringly. "No reason why you can't be a Quartermaster-Sergeant-Major."

"Sir, thank you," Sally said. "And you, ma'am. Captain O'Reilly. All of you, for believing in him and for finding this out. I'm that happy, I can't think straight or I'd say it better."

"The first thanks should go to Captain Mackenzie," Paul said. "Whether we'd have found out anyway from poor Mr Ronaldo, we were already making enquiries because he raised the matter of your lost bayonet. I thought he was being overly stubborn about it to be honest, but he wasn't going to let it go. This is a lot to take in, I know. We won't make a formal announcement until the paperwork is done, but your re-instatement starts now. Captain Mackenzie will give you your stripes."

"What about Mr Ronaldo?" Stewart asked. "Does his wife know of his passing?"

"Yes, I wrote to her as soon as I knew. She knows nothing of this yet, but I'll have to tell her before anything becomes public. I suppose Larpent will hand everything over to the Portuguese authorities. I've no idea what they'll do about it. They can hardly charge a dead man and in consideration of his excellent service and gallant death, I'm hoping they'll quietly close the book on it. His family will have to know. I don't know his parents but it will grieve the Riveros, he was like a son to them. Still..."

"Don't tell them."

The room was silent for a moment apart from the buzzing of a particularly irritating fly. Paul badly wanted to get up and reach for the improvised fly swat he had made out of a bunch of twigs from a cork oak, tied together with string. He resisted the temptation.

"I'll have to, Rory," he said gently. "If they're going to quash your conviction, they have to give a good reason and that will mean a formal report that an officer of the Portuguese army murdered a British officer on a dark road outside Freineda. Even if the Portuguese don't do much about it, his family is going to find out. Better that they hear it from me first. It will be a shock but I think that Tasia at least will realise that he did it for her and understand."

"It's a big jump from a heroic death in battle in the breaches of San Sebastian to knowing that if he'd lived, he'd have stood trial for murder and probably had his commission stripped from him," Stewart said.

"You might have been hanged, Sergeant."

"Aye, I know that. But it weren't his fault, poor little bugger. He was away with his regiment and knew nothing about it. And let's be honest, sir. If I'd not taken my usual recourse in times of trouble I wouldn't have been out there on that road so drunk I couldn't even defend myself against a charge of murder because I couldn't remember."

"I can't see any other way to put this right, Rory."

"Is the promotion linked to my innocence or could you give it anyway?"

Paul froze, suddenly understanding what the Scot was asking. "It doesn't have to be linked. Lord Wellington suggested it as some tangible acknowledgement that you'd been wrongly convicted but there's nothing to stop me promoting you anyway. Though you wouldn't get the back pay."

298

"It's his Lordship. I was probably never getting the back pay anyway. If I ask them to, would they leave it alone, d'you think, sir? Colonel Scovell, Captain White and Mr Larpent? Just close the book and pretend this didn't happen?"

Nobody spoke for a long time. Paul could feel a lump in his throat which had nothing to do with the dry, hot late-summer day. He reached for the water jug Anne had set out on the desk, poured a glass and drank. There was wine waiting on a side table but he was suddenly not sure if they were going to be celebrating.

Stewart turned to look at his wife who was staring at him in apparent bewilderment. "Won't make any difference to us, Sal. We're all right again. So are the children. It would be grand to stand up and tell everybody that I didn't do it. That I didn't deserve that flogging. But it won't really change anything. I know I didn't do it. So do my officers and we'll make sure the children know. I'm happy about that. But I was never ashamed of killing Vane. Just of what I did to you and my family and of the disgrace I brought to the regiment. I've paid for that. What good will it do to break the heart of that pretty young woman who was brave enough to come to court to speak up for me? If it weren't for her and her maid and Mrs Swanson, they'd have hanged me. Let me give her this."

"She'll never know about the gift, husband."

"I'll know. You'll know. That's all that matters."

She moved suddenly, into his arms, ignoring the rest of the room. She was crying but Paul did not think they were tears of anger or sadness. He stood up and went for the wine and glasses. He had decided that they were celebrating after all, though not in the way he had expected.

When the glasses were filled and Anne had mopped Sally's streaming eyes, Paul raised his glass to Stewart. Words were tumbling over themselves in his head but none of them were good enough to express what he was feeling. Eventually he cleared his choked throat.

"To Quartermaster Sergeant-Major Rory Stewart. I've never been more proud of you, Stewart. Well done."

The toast was drunk. Afterwards, Stewart carefully set the wine glass to one side and went back to drinking water. Paul let the conversation flow for a while but he could sense that Stewart wanted to be alone with his wife so he called the meeting to an end. He stood with Anne at the door of the house, watching the Stewarts making their way back to their tent, arms about one another.

"Did you expect that?"

"Not at all," Anne said. "It didn't occur to me. Do you think Mr Larpent and Lord Wellington will agree?"

"God, yes, they'll take my arm off. None of them had any idea how to manage this. They were only doing it because I wouldn't stop nagging. Wellington might even authorise that back pay out of sheer relief. I'm going to see if I can catch him while he's still delighted. Oh sod it."

"What is it, Paul?"

"Nothing. I was just considering sneaking off to our room for a couple of hours but I've remembered that Wellington is sending this blasted Spanish officer over this afternoon and I need to speak to him before I decide whether I'm landing him on Giles or sending him back for Alava to deal with."

Anne laughed and kissed him. "Make it a short interview, General."

"I will. He won't know what's hit him, I promise you. I'm going to grab Mackenzie while I'm waiting for him to arrive. There are a few administrative matters to deal with. Might as well get them out of the way.

***

Paul seated himself back at the long table, this time at the end he used as his desk. It was the usual jumble of papers and ledgers. His wife, was as organised with paperwork as she was untidy in domestic matters. Once a day she would go through his desk, file everything in sight, put ledgers back on shelves and leave a neat pile of matters needing attention beside his pen and ink pot. Paul sometimes wondered how quickly his brigade would fall apart if Anne went home. He was worried that it might be faster than he thought.

Ross Mackenzie joined him almost immediately. Since Ross had taken over as quartermaster of the 110th, Paul's attitude to his administrative duties had significantly improved. He had liked his previous quartermaster but Ross had become a friend and the tedious hours of paperwork were enlivened by the Scot's dry sense of humour.

Disciplinary matters were mainly dealt with at battalion level, but Paul insisted on going over the returns for his entire brigade. He believed that a commander could learn a lot about how his troops were functioning by keeping an eye on the number of regimental courts martial and how the officers in each battalion handled discipline. He disliked the formal court martial process and loathed flogging, believing that a good officer should be able to manage his men without beating them. When Ross had first joined the battalion, Paul knew he had considered this attitude highly eccentric but he could tell that the Scot had become interested in his ideas and the application of them.

There was a glaring omission in the most recent set of returns and Paul waited to see if Ross would comment on it. Ross did not, but Paul was sure he had noticed. As his quartermaster turned the last page, Paul said:

"I have a strong suspicion that these returns are incomplete, Captain Mackenzie."

Ross pulled a face. "If they are, sir, they won't be the only ones in the Light Division with a few items missing."

"Or in the rest of the army," Paul said grimly. "And yet three men from this brigade were on the sick list after San Sebastian as a result of flogging."

"Yes, sir."

Paul sat staring at the ledger for a while then slammed it shut abruptly, making Ross jump. Paul gave a bleak little smile.

"Sorry. Working with me will give you bad nerves. I hate flogging. But what I hate even more is flogging without a trial and a proper record. I saw too much of it in my early days in the army."

"Drum head courts martial, sir. No written records most of the time."

"No. Which means nobody is accountable. Don't get me wrong, I've administered some fairly harsh punishments myself in the field, where it isn't possible to convene a proper trial. But that is not the case here. We have enough officers to serve on as many juries as necessary and for most of the time we've all been sitting on our arses watching the French climb hills. He could have done this properly."

"Yes, sir."

"So why didn't he?"

"I've no idea, sir. To be fair, there was the panic of Soult crossing the mountains and the fighting up in the passes. Lord Wellington had a lot on his mind."

"Lord Wellington's mind can encompass more in one day than anybody else I know. Apart from my wife of course. Anyway, it's not as though he needed to do it himself. A brief note to the Provost-Marshal and the Judge-Advocate-General and it would have been done. And don't tell me he had no time to write an order, he can write them in his sleep. In fact I've often suspected he must do so given the volume of correspondence he manages."

Ross shook his head. "I don't know, sir. What's bothering you about it?"

"I think he did it this way deliberately. San Sebastian is in ruins and the Spanish are howling for compensation and claiming we burned it on purpose. He's furious about the breakdown in discipline, although it was nothing like Badajoz, and he wants the men to know he won't stand for it. But he doesn't want it neatly documented in these ledgers as evidence for the Spanish."

Ross raised surprised brows. "You think he'd do that, sir?"

"Of course he'd fucking do that, Captain, he's a devious Irish bastard. But I wish he hadn't."

Ross was silent for a while. Finally he said:

"Are you going to speak to him about it?"

"I don't know. It can't do any good now." Paul thought about it and gave a little grin. "But it will probably come up at some point. I'm not good at keeping my mouth shut. Though I'm better than I used to be. What is it, Jenson?"

"Sorry to disturb you sir, but there's a Spanish officer asking to speak to you. Captain Cortez. He says you're expecting him."

"To my sorrow, I am. Ship him in, Jenson."

"Yes, sir. He's just gone to the barn with his horse."

"Isn't Charlie there?"

"Yes, sir, he's gone with him. Captain Cortez didn't seem confident that young Bannan could manage to lead his horse a hundred and fifty yards without getting the urge to steal it."

301

Jenson's expression was deadpan. Paul gave a splutter of laughter. "You're not serious?"

"Yes, sir. Charlie's very indignant."

"I don't blame him; I'd trust his honesty over one or two Spanish officers I've met."

"Try not to tell Captain Cortez that, sir, it will get things off to a bad start."

"Look at me, Jenson and tell me how much you think I care."

Jenson rolled his eyes expressively and disappeared in search of the missing visitor, his wooden leg stomping ominously. Ross began to collect his papers together.

"I'll leave you to it, sir. I'll come back to you about transport for the men's greatcoats and winter clothing, although I don't know how quickly we'll be able to get them here. Have you spoken to Lord Wellington...?"

"No and I don't intend to. He will be furious that I've overridden his ridiculous order, even though by now he must be starting to realise he made a mistake. If he's having a really bad day he'll order me not to do it and then everybody is going to regret it. Far easier to ask for forgiveness than for permission. Thank you, Captain. Speak to my wife about the transport, she'll have some ideas about it."

"I will. Good luck with Captain Cortez. Don't shout at him."

"You sound like Fenwick. And Fenwick is beginning to sound more and more like my childhood governess. I miss Manson, he never bothers giving me pointless instructions."

"I expect that's a matter of experience, sir."

Paul laughed aloud and Ross saluted and left. As he waited, Paul rummaged on his untidy desk and found the letter he had received from General Alava about the Spanish Captain. He read it again, put it down then picked it up, wondering where on earth Cortez had got to.

It was several more minutes before the Spanish officer appeared. Paul heard Jenson's halting limp followed by another, more regular footstep. Jenson entered the room and saluted very smartly. He was having trouble with his expression. Paul, who knew his orderly's tendency to snort with laughter at inappropriate moments, longed to know what had set him off and deliberately avoided meeting his eyes.

"Captain Don Ángel Cortez, General."

"Thank you, Jenson. On your way out, will you stop by the kitchen to let Sergeant Kelly know we have a guest for dinner? And make sure my wife knows."

"Yes, sir."

"And Jenson. Where's Craufurd?"

Jenson's eyes gleamed with amusement.

"He's down at the river with Captain O'Reilly and Brat, sir. They've invented a new game. He'll be there for hours, don't worry."

Paul tried desperately to resist but could not. "A new game?"

"Yes, sir. He stands in the water under the bridge and they throw sticks for him to catch. Or chase. He loves it. He was so tired yesterday, Charlie had to wake him up for dinner."

"How much time does Captain O'Reilly spend away from his duties playing with the dog, Jenson?"

"I've not timed it, sir, but to be honest as long as we're not actually under attack from the French, I think it's worth it. Think about it."

Paul thought. "Good point. Carry on then. Come in, Captain Cortez."

Jenson left, closing the door. Paul indicated a chair on the opposite side of the table, studying the other man with interest. Ángel Cortez was tall, elegant and had a memorable face with pronounced cheekbones, one of which bore a faded scar. His striking blue-grey eyes made Paul think of very cold water. He kept his fair hair short and wore the uniform of a Spanish officer: a white jacket with red facings and white trousers. This was clearly his dress uniform because the cloth was remarkably stain free, given that this man had just distinguished himself on the bloody slopes of San Marcial. He wore no medals or clasps and surprisingly little gold braid for a Spanish officer, which interested Paul, because he was fairly sure those medals existed.

"It's good to meet you, Captain. I hope you found suitable stabling for your horse. We're fairly well supplied here."

Cortez looked surprised at the gentle sarcasm but did not hesitate. "I always prefer to supervise such matters myself, General. I have but one good horse and I cannot afford to lose him. Your boy is no doubt reliable, but I have no way of verifying that personally, and my judgement is the only one I trust."

Paul was momentarily speechless. He wondered if Cortez had any idea how rude he had sounded but then it occurred to him that perhaps his English was the problem rather than his manners. He decided to give the man the benefit of the doubt and switched to Spanish.

"I see. In the matter of a horse, we may have to do something about that if you decide to take Lord Wellington up on his offer. You'll be spending a lot of time in the saddle. I keep a number of spare horses in the brigade, most of them previously the property of the French and you'll be welcome to make use of them…"

"I prefer to ride my own horse and I dislike being indebted to anybody, General. Though your offer is most kind, of course. And I am perfectly able to converse in English."

Paul could feel his temper beginning to slip out of his grasp. He decided to give Cortez one more chance. "That's a useful skill," he said mildly, reverting to English again. "I believe your French is also fluent. Do you speak any Portuguese at all?"

"Very little, but that hardly matters as we are a long way from Portugal here."

"Nevertheless, you'll hear the language spoken a lot in this army."

Cortez lip visibly curled. "I am hardly likely to wish to converse with servants and muleteers and I can make myself understood by an idle groom in any language with the help of a riding crop."

Paul gave up his heroic struggle. "If you raise a riding crop to any man in my brigade, whether he be servant, groom or an itinerant lemonade seller, you're going to find yourself face down in the regimental dung heap with my boot on the back of your neck. And in case you're wondering, you arrogant arsehole, you've managed to get yourself very close to that point in less than five minutes which is impressive. I've commanded a Portuguese battalion for three years now and I've a lot more respect for them than I have for you, so if you want to maintain your dignity and keep that pretty jacket clean I'd get to your feet, salute a senior officer and apologise. Very quickly."

Cortez flushed to the roots of his hair but did not immediately move. Paul rose and took a step towards him and the Spaniard capitulated and jumped up, saluting smartly.

"My apologies, General. I had no intention of being rude to a man of your rank and reputation."

Paul stopped himself with an effort. He sat down again and looked Cortez over for a long time until the silence became painful even for him. Eventually he said:

"I accept your apology even if it was only given in self-defence. Sit down. Out of curiosity, are you always this much of an arrogant twat or are you having a bad day?"

Cortez did not respond, which was what Paul had intended. He allowed the other man to think about it, rose and went to collect the wine and two glasses. Cortez looked faintly surprised as Paul handed him a glass and even more surprised when he sipped it. Paul resumed his seat.

"Thank you. This is very good wine."

"One of the only positive aspects of this war is that I've discovered some very good local wines on my travels. Though how many of them will still be in business by the end, who knows? It's brutal."

"I know."

"Has Lord Wellington spoken to you?"

"My own commanding officer discussed it with me, and then I dined with Lord Wellington and some of his staff, including Colonel Waters."

"I bet the food was dreadful. How is Waters? I'm glad he's up and around again"

"He told me he had been wounded but is recovering well."

"Good. He was standing around talking to Wellington, which is never a good idea when there are French about. They never manage to get Hookey, he's like a cat with nine lives, but anybody else in the vicinity is a likely target. I'm curious, Captain. Was it Lord Wellington's shining eloquence that caused you to accept this post or something else?"

Cortez was silent for a long moment, staring into his wine glass as though lost in thought. When he looked up, he met Paul's gaze properly for the first time.

"I think you already know, General and that you are mocking me. I cannot complain of this, you are a senior officer, so I must endure."

Paul could not help smiling. "Christ, Cortez, are you always this serious? I'm not mocking you, for fuck's sake. Fighting illegal duels isn't something I find all that funny. But I was trying to find out if you'd lie to me."

"I do not lie," Cortez said sharply.

Paul grinned and sipped his wine. "Nor do I, but that's because I'm bloody terrible at it. There's no point. General Alava told me what happened. I have to say I was less than amused at the idea of being landed with you but Lord Wellington convinced me to at least meet you."

"Did he not order you to do so?"

"He thinks he did, which is the important part. You've served with the Mallorcan regiment for two years and before that you were ADC to General Contreras, I believe."

"I am sure you know my history, General. In case they have tactfully left it out, I fought for Bonaparte until 1808."

Paul studied him thoughtfully. "No, they didn't leave it out, but it hardly matters unless you intend to change sides again. That would be a problem."

Cortez looked furious. Paul waited with interest. He was beginning to understand how this man, who was undoubtedly a courageous soldier and a fierce patriot, had reached the point where he was about to be given a promotion and also to be kicked out of his regiment all in the same week.

"You have insulted me, General."

"Not as much as I'm going to if you don't calm down, get off your high horse and pay attention. The briefing was very thorough. Your commanding officers have nothing but praise for your courage, your work ethic and your patriotism. They also claim that you're arrogant, rude and difficult to work with. Your attitude to the men verges on bullying and your attitude to your seniors verges on insubordination. I can sympathise with one of those but not the other. I meant what I said about that riding crop, by the way. Wave it at any of my men and I'll shove it so far up your arse that you'll feel it catching the back of your throat. The incident that led you to my doorstep has me worried. You challenged a fellow officer to a duel."

"Yes, sir."

"You then actually fought the duel, which is monumentally stupid."

"It was a matter of honour."

"At twenty-one I might have sympathised with that a bit more. At your age...what are you now?"

"Thirty-three, sir."

"Close to my own age. At thirty-three, Cortez, you're old enough to know better. Fighting him was bad enough, but I'm told you're a very good

305

swordsman. Good enough to draw first blood, make your point and get the arsehole to apologise for whatever he did to upset you. In fact, you almost killed him."

"There was no agreement that honour would be satisfied..."

"Well there fucking should have been, you imbecile. And you didn't stop there, did you? You then accepted a challenge from the officer's brother, a stripling of nineteen, new to the regiment. He got away with a slash across the arm but only because another officer intervened at that point."

"He challenged me publicly," Cortez almost spat. "What would you have me do? Brand myself a coward?"

Paul rolled his eyes, took a long drink of wine and wondered if it was too early for a second glass. He decided he did not care and reached for the bottle.

"I read the letter from your commanding officer about your conduct at San Marcial, Cortez. You reinforced a failing section of the line and held those men without waving a riding crop in their faces or threatening to run them through if they looked at you the wrong way. What in God's name made you think you couldn't command the loyalty of your men? And knowing that you can do so in very good style, why the fuck did you throw it all away for the sake of an imaginary insult to your honour? Bloody idiot."

Cortez had flushed scarlet again. "That is not why I fought that duel. Well, the first one, anyway."

"Then why did you?"

"I refuse to say."

"Which is another reason they're kicking you out."

"I cannot help that."

"Yes you can, you twat. You can stop behaving like an understudy at Drury Lane and throwing your arms about and tell me. You're going to have to tell somebody if you want this posting and you need to believe me, you do want this posting. Give it a year of riding around drawing pretty sketch maps and listing troop movements for Wellington and they'll have forgiven you and will offer you another command. Until then, I'll take you on, but only if you tell me the truth."

"I cannot."

"Yes, you can."

"I cannot. It is a matter of honour."

"Whose honour? Yours or hers?"

Paul observed with satisfaction that the heightened colour drained from Cortez' face. He sat in silence for a long moment. Paul gave a faint smile.

"Tell me. I don't need to know her name or anything about her. I just need to know that there was some semblance of a reason why you threw your career away, other than your obsessive need to prove yourself."

"Do you consider that a woman is a good enough reason, General?"

Paul thought for a moment. "Yes," he said. "I almost did it myself once. These days, I would tell the arsehole to fuck off and if he persisted, I'd punch him. But I was younger then."

306

"Should I ask you the question you asked me? Whose honour was at stake, yours or hers?"

Paul considered his response and decided to tell the truth. "Her honour was never in question in the eyes of any man who ever knew her. What the fuck is that all about anyway – honour? Is a woman dishonoured because some arsehole says she is? It's ridiculous."

"Who was she?"

"She is my wife. You'll meet her at dinner. Be very polite. She has less tolerance of bad manners than I do and she will kick you out."

He had the satisfaction of seeing a look of complete astonishment on the Spaniard's face. He gave Cortez time to absorb what he had just learned. Eventually he said:

"I answered your question, Captain."

"I cannot, General. She is not, and never could be, my wife."

"A former lover."

"No." The response was quick and angry and gave Paul the information he had wanted. Cortez clamped his lips together as if trying to stop himself saying more. Paul refilled his glass.

"Anything you say remains in this room, between the two of us. You need to trust me, or you need to ride back to your commanding officer and ask where he's sending you next. Those are the only alternatives, Cortez. But it's not going to be a combat posting. They're always looking for administrators in Madrid. Is that what you want?"

"I want to kill the French."

"Well you can't do that from behind a desk in Madrid. What happened?"

Cortez took a deep, painful breath. "Captain Torres recently arrived from Mallorca. He was introduced to my fellow officer, Captain Óscar García, who was with me both at Tarragona and during our time in Mallorca. García married there."

"Ah, I see. The mysterious lady. What's her name?"

"Her name is Señora García."

Paul gave a splutter of appreciative laughter. "Well done, Cortez. I'm beginning to think perhaps we can make this work after all. What did Captain Torres – I man I already dislike by the way – have to say about Captain García's wife? I'm guessing he didn't say it to García?"

"No, but he was free with his opinions with some other officers. I warned him that I would not tolerate another disrespectful word. He disregarded my warning."

"So you challenged him and half killed him. I still think a good punch would have worked just as well."

"It would not, General, because then he would immediately have challenged me."

"Then you could have refused."

"I could not. My honour…"

307

"If we're ever going to get to the end of this story I think you need to stop talking about your honour. What did he say? Is there scandal about Señora García?"

"Dona Raquel is a charming girl with an unblemished reputation. However, she is a member of the Xuerta people, who suffer persecution and great prejudice on the island of Mallorca. Usually, her people are not allowed to marry outside their community. They are also not allowed to join the army, enter the church or take any form of public office. Captain García chose to ignore the prohibition. I was not sure, at first, that he was wise. I was mistaken. I will attempt to follow your rules, General van Daan, but I will not allow any man to say one word against Dona Raquel or her people."

Paul stared at him, utterly bewildered. "What on earth are you talking about, Cortez? I've never heard of such a thing in my life."

"Neither had I until I went to Mallorca. What I learned...shocked me."

Paul sat in silence for a while. He wanted to know more about the extraordinary story, but he had a feeling that Cortez might not be the best person to ask just now.

"All right," he said finally. "I'm going to leave it there, though at some point, I want the whole story. If you want this posting, you have it, subject to your very good behaviour. Lord Wellington has suggested that you act as one of his exploring officers. Nominally, those are often attached to headquarters in some capacity, usually to the adjutant's department. His Lordship doesn't really want you there, given your recent mishaps. He's probably worried you'll challenge the Prince of Orange to a duel."

"Why would I do that?"

"Have you met Slender Billy yet?"

"No, sir."

"Well when you have, you'll understand. At some point, the young idiot is probably going to drive me to challenging him to a duel myself. He's charming but infuriating. I did suggest you join General Alava's staff, but he already has more ADCs and hangers on than he knows what to do with. As always, when Wellington espies a problem that nobody else wants to touch with a six-foot pike, my name is the first he thinks of. You'll join my staff in some unstated capacity and I'm going to hand you over to my acting brigade-major who was one of Wellington's intelligence officers for two years. Depending on the needs of the job, you'll either be under my feet a lot or I'll hardly see you. We'll go over how it will work in more detail once you've formally arrived. You'll dine with us today and I'll introduce you to my wife who will sort out a billet for you. Tomorrow you can bring your kit over..."

"Your wife, General?"

"Yes. She is my informal assistant quartermaster and usually manages the officers' accommodation. My advice is to say please and thank you and for God's sake don't annoy her; she's had a busy month and she's a little tetchy right now."

"Tetchy?"

"You'll find out. Try not to find out too soon. Right, come along. I'll take you to find Captain Fenwick."

Chapter Twenty

The church of San Esteban in Vera was built precariously on the hillside overlooking the town square. It had a bell tower and the remains of an ancient cemetery, though Michael suspected that centuries of erosion meant many of the graves had been lost. Father Xavier had told him that the original church building had been a medieval tower house. The church had grown up around it over the centuries but it still managed to retain the look of a building intended to withstand attack.

Father Xavier had been delighted by Michael's interest and fluent Spanish and took him on a brief tour of the building and the square outside. Opposite was the town hall and beside it was an imposing mansion which was known locally as the Lanrube House. It had apparently been used briefly to accommodate both King Joseph Bonaparte and Lord Wellington when they were passing through.

The church bell tower was locked. It had previously been used to house Allied prisoners of war. Currently it was being used to house wounded French prisoners, until arrangements could be made to transport them to a hospital. Michael knew that Anne was keeping a careful eye on conditions in the temporary prison.

He was very conscious, on this bright, blustery September morning, of the raw graves at the foot of the bell tower. He was not sure who had arranged for the bodies of Cadoux and his men to be transported from the house on the bridge to this final resting place but he was glad that they had. It felt fitting somehow that they should be close by on the most important day of his life. He wished that Hardy, Bowlby and the others could have been buried here, instead of in hasty graves dug around the ruined city of San Sebastian. Giles had told him that some of the senior officers would be buried on the slopes of the castle, now that Graham's men had finally forced the surrender of the remains of the French garrison. Michael hoped that Sir Richard Fletcher, who had been an unassuming man, would appreciate the honour.

It was a small wedding and necessarily private. Officers of the King's army were not permitted to practise the Roman Catholic faith, but Michael had joined as a common soldier where nobody cared. Since being given a commission nobody had asked him to take any oaths or questioned his religious leanings and he knew he was not the only Irish officer who kept his head down and went to Mass in secret. His commanding officer was utterly uninterested in interfering in the beliefs of other men and he was here today as Michael's groomsman, while Anne would act as Ariana's attendant.

He was touched and surprised to see Rory Stewart and his wife seated in the small side chapel where the wedding was to be held. He had not asked them to attend and supposed that Paul must have arranged it. He and Stewart had been friends since Michael joined the army, long before his unexpected promotion to lieutenant, and it felt right that he should be here.

He was talking to Stewart when Paul touched his shoulder. "Stand to, Captain O'Reilly. Too late to back out now."

"I wouldn't want to, sir."

"I know. She's here."

Ariana came into the church on Giles Fenwick's arm, with Anne a few steps behind her. There had been no time for elaborate wedding clothes and the men wore their dress uniforms, some of which were notably shabby. Anne was dressed in a charming yellow muslin which Michael knew had been made for her by Keren Swanson the previous year. It was not her finest gown though she was very fond of it, but Michael suspected she had deliberately chosen not to outshine the bride.

Ariana wore something white, threaded through with gold. Michael thought it had belonged to Anne though it was a ball gown and he had not seen her wear it for a long time. Somebody had added a lace fichu to make the gown more modest but few other alterations had been needed; Anne and Ariana were of a similar height and build. She wore her auburn curls loose with a wreath of late wildflowers which reminded Michael of the May celebrations in Sligo, when the prettiest girl in the village would have been crowned as May queen. She carried a small posy of roses, lavender and some kind of sweet smelling herbs, though she looked as though she had no idea what to do with it. Michael could not take his eyes from her. Giles was smiling as he took her hand and gave it to Michael. Ariana met his gaze, her expression unusually serious, then they turned as one towards the priest while Anne and Giles retreated to the pew.

Sunlight streamed through the windows, some of which had managed to retain their stained glass through the ravages of these wartime years. They made jewelled patterns on the stone flagged floor. Michael watched the dancing colours as his love spoke her vows clearly beside him. The ring looked old, a single emerald in a traditional setting. Michael had bought it from a Portuguese caçadore from Bradford's brigade. Paul had discovered it was for sale, though Michael had absolutely no idea how. Knowing nothing about jewellery, he had left the bargaining to his commanding officer and suspected he got a better price because of it. He wondered if the man had looted it from San Sebastian or earlier on, during the Vitoria campaign.

He could feel the ring on her slim finger as he took her hand to lead her out of the church. There were no bells ringing and there would be no crowd of well-wishers throwing rice and calling out congratulations. Michael did not care. He was happy.

He had ridden down to the church, but Anne had brought Ariana in her carriage and told Michael he should take his wife back to the Casa Mendoza in it, leaving Anne to ride his horse back to camp. He walked down the steep path from the church, still holding her hand. They had barely spoken since accepting congratulations from their small group of friends. Michael looked round at her and her smile dazzled him. He knew that, like him, she was silent from joy; still lost in the wonder of it.

"Company to attention!"

The voice was so loud that it made him jump. He whirled around, temporarily alarmed and was dazzled once again, by sunlight glinting off gold braid and buckles and a long arch of raised bayonets. A row of men holding muskets stood ready to fire a salute. Officers stood grouped around the square. Somebody cheered and then they were all yelling; causing the townspeople of Vera to come to their windows and doors to see what the noise was about.

Colonel Johnny Wheeler stood at the closest end of the arch, laughing. He beckoned and Michael drew Ariana forward. She looked startled and suddenly a little shy at being the centre of so much attention. Johnny took her hand and bowed over it formally.

"Congratulations, Mrs O'Reilly. Captain O'Reilly. I'm sorry, I couldn't stop them. And I didn't really want to. Go on, get it over with and then we'll get you out of here before Lord Wellington arrives from Lesaca thinking that Soult has invaded all over again."

Michael saluted. He was grinning widely and could not stop. He took Ariana's hand again and led her under the arch of shining bayonets. As he passed his men called out to him, offering congratulations and the occasional ribald piece of advice. Michael's heart was so full that he could not find replies, though he made a mental note to deal with the worst of them at a later date.

He was not surprised to find Paul awaiting him at the far end of the arch. Michael had been keeping his head low, just in case any of the newer recruits dropped the angle of their bayonet and took his ear off. He straightened and eyed his commanding officer balefully.

"This was your doing, wasn't it, sir? I thought we agreed we should keep this quiet?"

"That was your idea Michael, not mine. Not that it matters at all since, if anybody asks stupid questions, I've come up with a perfectly valid reason for the celebrations."

"I can't wait to hear it."

Paul stepped forward. His expression was suddenly more serious. "I wasn't sure I'd be able to do this today, Michael, but confirmation came through with the last batch of post yesterday. Congratulations, Major O'Reilly. Horse Guards have approved your promotion without purchase, after receiving testimonials from Generals Leith and Oswald, Sir Thomas Graham and myself.

I believe even Lord Wellington wrote a few lines. It's probably the most impressive array of recommendations they've ever received in one go."

Michael took the insignia. He stared down at it for a long time then looked up at Paul. "I didn't expect this."

"Don't be ridiculous, Major. You wanted this. It was the only reason you volunteered for San Sebastian."

"But I didn't think it would work like this. I wanted to get noticed. They've handed me this on a plate. It was your doing, wasn't it? How the bloody hell did you manage it this time?"

Paul was laughing. "Don't be so bloody ungrateful, Michael. Yes, I admit I hurried them along a bit, but they were all very willing to do it. The person who is actually responsible, however, is Nick Barry. He's requested a transfer to a regiment stationed in London to be close to his father, who is very ill. You know how Wellington is about Colonel Barry and Kate. The transfer was approved so fast I don't think Nick has had time to catch his breath. That left me with a vacancy in the 110th. There's only one man I'm willing to offer it to."

"Oh dear Christ."

"Don't you dare cry at me. Not now. Get to attention and salute your regimental colonel, Major."

Michael did so. Paul returned the salute. Michael's vision was slightly blurred but he noted with satisfaction that there was a slight sheen to Paul's eyes as well.

"Right, that's done. You've got five days leave, Major, though if Soult makes a third try I'll be calling you back. You're not free tonight though. We're having a party if this weather holds. Tomorrow I am summoned to headquarters where I'm hoping to find out what his Lordship has planned for us next. I'll need a few drinks tonight."

***

Sergeant Kelly had surpassed himself with the wedding breakfast. After the meal the officers dispersed about their own affairs. Paul saw nothing of Michael through the long afternoon. He suspected that he had taken Brat to their newly allocated room and closed the door on the world. Paul did not blame him at all.

As evening approached, officers and men began to gather in the broad meadow beyond the tents of the 110th. Paul walked outside with Anne, wandering across the meadow to look up at the green slopes of the foothills with the bluish outline of the mountains soaring above them. After a long, quiet interlude, Paul said:

"There are French outposts up there. Want to put money on who has to climb up and dislodge them?"

"You're such a romantic, General."

313

He gave a splutter of laughter, put his arm about her and kissed her soundly. "I'm sorry, love. Pretend I didn't say that and let's enjoy the evening. It's very lovely and we have a party to attend. Do you think I'm going to have to break down the door to collect the bride and groom?"

"No, they came down earlier. Why don't we walk over and join them? I can hear what sounds like Private Flanagan's fiddle."

"Good idea. I hope the rest of the wine was delivered."

"It was. Sergeant Hammond is supervising the drinks tables."

There was an awning set up and several women of the 110th were helping to serve drinks. Paul, knowing their tendency to serve the worst kind of home-made spirit, went to test their wares but found nothing stronger than army grog and wine punch. The men were dancing in the centre of a field, with their wives and girlfriends and a few local women who had come to join the party. There was a mellow feeling of late summer or early autumn and it reminded Paul of harvest dances at Southwinds when he was a boy.

The officers had settled themselves in a corner of the field with several crates of wine and a variety of camp chairs and stools. Some had brought blankets and were sprawled on the grass. Gradually some of the men came to join them. Anne and Brat quickly fell into conversation with Alison Macdonald and Gisele, Sergeant Cooper's companion who seemed keen to show off her much improved English. Michael was talking to Giles Fenwick. His expression was serene. Paul noticed that at least part of Brat's afternoon had been well spent. The new insignia had been stitched firmly on to Michael's worn red jacket.

Paul danced with his wife and with Brat and then made the rounds of several of the men's wives. He noticed Sally Stewart dancing with her husband and watched them for a moment, thinking of the past year and of how differently their particular story might have ended.

When he returned to the group he found that Hannah Bowlby had joined them. She looked a little embarrassed to be sitting in the company of the officers, with her sons playing with the other children close by. Giles Fenwick was sprawled on the grass beside her, talking to her, and Paul watched for a moment and reminded himself to ask Giles how Hannah was managing without her husband's pay and rations.

He had just sat down when there was a shout from up the track towards the house, and he saw Charlie Bannan racing towards him. He stood up as the boy pulled up, saluting and gasping for breath.

"Sir. There's a...a..."

"Halt, Private Bannan. Stop trying to speak until you catch your breath. Soult is a long way off and unless Lord Wellington has arrived, there's no emergency."

Charlie managed to contain himself with a visible effort until he could speak properly again. He gave a relieved sigh.

"Sorry, sir. There's a carriage arrived and another on the way up, with some wagons. It's Lord Wellington's chaplain, sir. He says he was on his way to headquarters but one of the horses has cast a shoe."

Paul swore and then remembered he was speaking about a clergyman and caught himself before he said anything worse. "Is he looking for a bed for the night, Charlie?"

"I think so, sir."

"Bugger. We'll have to oblige, but I want that shoe replaced early tomorrow. We'll get Private Clegg on the job first thing. I'm not having the place crawling with clergymen. I'm enjoying the break."

"I'll come with you, Paul," Anne said. "Poor Mr Briscall."

"Don't you dare, girl of my heart. You'll be far too gracious to him and I want you here, celebrating with our friends. He won't expect more than basic civility from me. I won't be long."

Two carriages were drawn up outside the house, along with four wagons loaded with chests and canvas wrapped bundles. Paul presumed these were intended for headquarters. He approached the first carriage. A gentleman had already alighted and was gazing around him with a slightly bewildered air. He caught sight of Paul and gave a pleasant smile.

"Major-General van Daan, it is very good to see you. I apologise for this intrusion, but one of the carriage horses is lame and..."

"Don't apologise at all, Mr Briscall, I perfectly understand," Paul said heartily. "Do come inside. I'm going to get Sergeant Kelly, who runs my mess, to organise a room for you and we'll get that horse shoed so you can head off to his Lordship in the morning. I hope you'll excuse me, I'm busy down in barracks right now, but..."

"That is very good of you, sir," Briscall said warmly. "It has been an appalling journey and just as I was beginning to believe I had reached safety, we were challenged by a number of Spaniards who were wholly unable to understand me and treated me with so little respect..."

"I'm sorry you've had such a difficult time, Mr Briscall, but you're safe now," Paul said briskly. "Allow me to speak to the gentleman in the other carriage and I'll arrange for an escort up to headquarters tomorrow, I promise. I just want to find out about these wagons, since I wasn't aware..."

"The wagons are nothing to do with me, sir. For that, you must ask my compatriot, since he appears to know all about them."

"Your compatriot?" Paul asked blankly.

"Yes. The new chaplain for the 110th light infantry. He joined me in Lisbon and seems to have taken control of my entire journey ever since."

Briscall's voice held a mixture of irritation and awe. Paul stared at him in astonishment.

"Chaplain for the 110th? We don't have a chaplain."

"I understand it is a new appointment, sir."

"What do you mean a new appointment? It's my bloody regiment. Nobody gets appointed to it without my prior agreement."

Briscall was looking extremely nervous. "I'm sorry I cannot help you, General. Like you, I knew nothing of this until Lisbon. Of course I recognised the gentleman but I was extremely surprised, though I understand the

315

appointment was approved by Horse Guards on the recommendation of Lord Wellington himself."

Paul lost his temper. "Oh of course it was. It was bound to be bloody Wellington's doing. He's on a campaign to stamp out the Methodist preachers in the ranks and he's nagged and bullied London to find him more chaplains willing to come out here without a bloody thought as to what he's going to do with them when they get here. No training, no experience and no idea of what they're walking into and when he suddenly realises what he's done, what is the first name that comes into his head? Mine. Well if he thinks I've got time to act as nursemaid to some wet-behind-the-ears parson, come to spread the word among the ungodly, I am going to shove a prayer book where the sun doesn't shine. My apologies, Mr Briscall. None of this is your fault. I'll make sure you're settled and find out where these wagons are going, then in the morning I'll…"

"The wagons are for the 110th."

The voice came from the second carriage. Paul turned and strode towards it in intense irritation. He had almost reached it when his brain caught up with his anger and he stopped, utterly frozen to the spot.

The carriage door opened and a man jumped down without bothering to let down the steps. He was above average height, wearing a shabby army great coat and no hat. The brown hair was shorter than Paul was used to and amused green eyes surveyed him. One arm was tucked neatly into the front of his coat.

"That was shockingly rude to Mr Briscall, sir. It's not his fault."

Paul could neither move nor speak. He stood staring at the former commander of the 110th first battalion, who had suddenly and inexplicably appeared before him. Carl Swanson merely gazed back tranquilly for a while. He looked as though he was enjoying himself. Paul opened his mouth to speak but nothing came out. He was appalled to feel tears starting in his eyes.

The spell was broken by a young woman in a warm green pelisse who jumped agilely from the carriage and looked from Paul to Carl.

"Oh for goodness sake, Carl, speak to him. You've shocked the life out of him."

Her voice broke the spell and Paul walked forward. He picked her up and kissed her on the cheek, squeezing her until she yelped in protest. Eventually he set her down and turned to his boyhood friend.

"You're here. I can't believe you're here. What the fuck are you doing here?"

Carl laughed and held out both arms. One of them was unnaturally shortened by the loss of his left hand. Paul walked into his embrace and stood there for a long time. Eventually he felt Keren's arms about him and he reached out and scooped her into a three-way embrace.

"I can't believe you're here," he said again. He was crying, tears flowing uncontrollably down his cheeks. "How are you here?"

"Oh hush," Keren said in motherly tones. "You can't imagine we would have left you to do all this without us? It took some time to arrange the appointment, but Lord Wellington was very helpful. As for the supply wagons,

Nan wrote and told us how worried you were about the lack of the men's great coats this winter. As we were coming anyway, we arranged it through Sir Matthew Howard. He knows all the army suppliers."

Paul could not speak for a long time. Eventually he broke away, wiping his face with both hands. "Does Nan know?"

"She hasn't a clue. Where is she?"

"Down with the men. We're celebrating...no, I'll let him tell you himself. Stay there. Don't move a muscle. I'll get Briscall settled then I'm taking you down there myself. I want to see their faces."

It took less than twenty minutes to arrange accommodation for the bewildered chaplain. Paul walked between Carl and Keren down towards the camp with a sense of unreality. He could see Anne laughing with Sally and Rory Stewart. When she saw his approach, she stood up, peering through the dim light, trying to identify his companions.

He knew the moment she recognised them, because she began to run. He kept his eyes on her face as she raced towards them, her skirts caught up inelegantly to stop her tripping up. She reached Keren first and threw herself into the other woman's arms, crying and exclaiming, with questions bubbling over. Carl joined the embrace and Paul stood looking at them, waiting for the initial joy to subside.

Eventually they parted and Anne turned to him, her face alight with happiness.

"Did you know?"

"Not an earthly clue, girl of my heart. I'm told you were equally ignorant."

"I had no idea. Carl, why didn't you write to us?"

Carl was laughing. "Sorry, ma'am. It's just that you know how argumentative he is, and also how over-protective. Once we'd decided to come back it seemed easier just to do it and surprise you. I hope you're pleased."

Anne reached for his hand. "I can't begin to describe how happy I am. Come and see the others and then I want you to dance with me, Carl. I've missed you so much. Keren I've so much to tell you."

Carl was looking around him. "I'm glad I arrived in time for the party. What's the occasion?"

Paul laughed. "My turn to shock the life out of you, Swanson. I can't tell you how satisfying that is. Come over here and make your bow to Major Michael O'Reilly of the 110th and his lovely bride. They were married earlier today."

***

The 30th légère camped where they finally came to rest, in the little Basque village of Sara. The villagers regarded Bonnet with wary curiosity as he ventured out in search of supplies. The men had no rations and were exhausted, battered and hungry. Bonnet had sent Cavel and several of his men out in search

317

of some orders but he refused to march his men any further without food and rest.

He had discovered that taking Bianca with him when he went to speak to householders about supplying his men opened doors more readily. Even here, on French soil, men were wary about the depredations of starving troops and preferred to keep their food, wine and womenfolk hidden. A French colonel with his Spanish wife in tow was less threatening and Bianca was good with people. Bonnet watched as she admired babies, patted dogs and explained that receipts would be provided for any food given and that Colonel Gabriel Bonnet was a man of his word and would make sure they were paid. Bonnet hoped that he would be able to do so.

Once they were reassured, the people of Sara were generous with both food and shelter. The priest came to find Bonnet with the offer of his church for the men who were shivering in the mountain drizzle. A local farmer offered a dry barn and fodder for the officers' horses and the few baggage mules that had made it over the bridge intact.

Bonnet was passionately grateful and threatened appalling retribution to any one of his men who so much as scratched a wooden pew in the church. He and Bianca were offered a room in one of the larger houses but Bonnet decided to remain with his men to keep them honest. His officers knew the rules but without Cavel there to act as his informal second-in-command, he preferred to keep an eye on them personally.

He and Bianca took possession of a tiny alcove dedicated to the Virgin Mary. The church was beautiful with three floors of wooden galleries and intricately carved pews and balustrades. Bonnet was not even faintly interested in religion but he could see why the priest might be protective of this place. He banned the lighting of fires in the church but the priest managed to find several small braziers which provided a surprising amount of heat. Once they were fed, his men stretched out on the stone floors or along the pews and slept.

Cavel returned in the early hours and Bonnet pulled on his boots and went outside into the little graveyard. There was a gate with a wooden arched roof and they huddled beneath it while Cavel ate the food Bonnet had saved for him.

"We've orders to march to the muster point as soon as possible. I don't think Marsal Soult even knows if Vandermaesen's division made it over so I'm hoping they get the message to him as soon as possible."

"Vandermaesen didn't make it," Bonnet said. "He went down on the bridge. I saw him as we crossed."

"Yes, Delain told me. He thought he was dead."

"That or badly wounded. I wonder where Chassé is?"

"We'll find out once we join the rest of the army. I spoke to a Colonel Paquin. He thinks we'll be sent back to our former posts along the border while Soult plans his next move."

"The next move is going to be Wellington's army invading France, Captain. Might be next week or next month or he might decide to take Christmas off and give us all a break, though I doubt it. But he's coming."

Cavel studied him with troubled eyes. "Can we defend it with the troops we have?"

"Clearly not, given that we've just been handed our arses by a pack of Spaniards and about a hundred riflemen on a bridge. Somebody needs to get hold of Bonaparte, smack his face a few times and tell him to wake up to what's happening on his borders. While he's still pretending to be master of Europe the fucking English are going to be marching on Paris."

Cavel gave a jaw-cracking yawn which recalled Bonnet to his duty. He clapped his hand on his friend's shoulder. "Well there's nothing you and I can do about it. Inside and get some sleep. No need to be up with the dawn either. The priest reckons if we behave they can supply us here for at least another day or two and I want them to rest. We'll join Marshal Soult in our own sweet time, Captain and I don't think France is going to fall because of it. In you come."

***

Ángel Cortez had not intended to go anywhere near the wedding party, but the noise of music and raucous laughter kept him awake. Eventually he got up, dressed and walked down to the meadow, following the light from the camp fires and the sound of a fiddle playing country dances. He stood at the edge of the field watching for a while. Some of the men were very drunk but the atmosphere was amiable. Junior officers and NCOs seemed to be keeping an eye on the drinks tables and were quick to step in at any sign of trouble.

Ángel was slightly shocked to see some of the officers dancing with the camp women and he wondered if this was normal in the British lines. He was even more horrified at the sight of the General's wife, dressed in yellow muslin, in the centre of one of the country dances. She was hand in hand with a dark-haired sergeant with a scarred face and a boy who did not look old enough to be wearing the uniform. Her face was alight with happiness.

Ángel, who had arrived determined not to be impressed with anything in this English brigade, had been unwillingly impressed by Anne van Daan. She had seated him beside her at dinner on the day of his arrival and had conversed easily with him in both English and Spanish. She was very lovely with exactly the kind of slender beauty which Ángel admired. He had been hoping for a decorous flirtation and discovered to his astonishment that his hostess had a knowledge and understanding of military affairs which would have shamed most regimental officers.

He could not believe that a married woman of her quality was here, dancing with common soldiers, and he looked around, wondering where her husband was. Before he managed to locate the General, a voice beside him said:

"There you are. I'm glad you decided to join us after all. Come and have a drink. Don't go near the tables, it's mostly army grog laced with home-

319

made gut-rot spirits. The General has provided some decent wine for the officers and Lieutenant Powell is guarding it."

Ángel turned to survey Captain Giles Fenwick. He had not yet decided what to make of his new mentor. Fenwick was supposedly on light duties after being wounded at San Sebastian but he seemed determined not to take to his bed.

"I find this very strange," Ángel said, indicating the dancers. "Surely the General cannot approve of his wife dancing in such company? And the drinking. I would never allow my men to behave this way."

Fenwick shrugged. "Then they'll do it behind your back."

"Then they should be disciplined."

"Then they'll do it even further behind your back and call you an arsehole." Fenwick smiled as if to rob the words of any offence. "Look, it takes some getting used to. When I first came out here from a spell with the second battalion I thought he was bloody mad and the rest of his officers with him. But I've seen how well this works. It's not your job to command these men but while you're here it will make you look good if you muck in and show willing. That includes being social with the other officers. Plaster a smile on your face even if you don't mean it yet and come and have a drink. And if Mrs van Daan asks you to dance, which she probably will, I'd take her up on the offer. She's a very good dancer."

Ángel looked back across the field with a sense of bewilderment. "How can men like this win battles?" he asked.

"I'll show you on the training field tomorrow," Fenwick said.

***

As darkness fell, Paul stood watching them dance, the firelight flickering over beloved faces. He thought briefly of other times and other places and faces missing from this moment and felt a sharp pang of grief. He supposed that, in this strange life, where sadness and joy met so regularly, mourning and loving would always run side by side. Silently, watching the dancers, he raised his glass to Sir Richard Fletcher, to Sergeant Jim Bowlby and to Lieutenant Ronaldo, who in his last breath had given Rory Stewart back his self-respect.

He sensed them come to join him, one on either side. Paul did not look round; he did not need to. He was choked with emotion, remembering other times when they had stood like this, feeling their solid support. He had thought this feeling lost and he savoured it for a long moment.

"Do you think we'll have long?" Carl asked.

"No. A few weeks maybe, while he reorganises the troops and plans his next move. I've been standing here thinking how happy I am and how wonderful this is. It should be the end of the play, with everybody dancing their way to a grand finale. But it's not."

"I think the final act is in sight though," Johnny said.

"In the distance, maybe. I'm getting a glimpse of it. Somehow, just at this moment, it feels possible. Anything feels possible."

"We need Carter and Manson back."

"They'll be with us soon. I'm not worried about them." Paul turned his head to study Carl's familiar features in the firelight. "Now that you're here, Swanson, I've been meaning to ask. What the fuck does a regimental chaplain do anyway?"

"Well it definitely involves a prayer or two, so I'll expect you to get your arse out of bed on a Sunday to set a good example. As for the rest, I have no bloody idea. It turns out there's not a manual."

"Is there even a salary?"

"Oh yes, and you're paying it. I'm not expensive though and I'll be worth every penny. I suspect I'll just make up the rest of my duties as I go along."

"Sounds about right. It's what we've all been doing from the start," Johnny commented.

Paul laughed, his mood suddenly soaring. "Yes, we have and we turned out to be fucking good at it. Race you to the drinks table, gentlemen."

They were off in an instant, charging across the field. Dancers sprang out of their way and turned to stare. Somebody set up a shout of encouragement, then half the field were clapping and cheering. They arrived at the drinks tables all together, catching at each other in order to stop. Johnny was scarlet faced with effort and with laughter and Carl was almost choking as he caught his breath. Paul stood with a hand on each of their shoulders, looking around the field.

"You can piss off tonight, Marshal Soult," he said softly. "But just give me a week or two and you can bring Bonaparte himself if you like. I'm ready for you now."

Author's Note

When I began this book I realised that in terms of research and organisation, this was the one I'd been dreading. The battles of the Pyrenees are confusing and until I started writing I still hadn't really decided how I would split everything up. I now have a plan for the next few books but I can't promise that won't change. Army life is unpredictable.

The addition of both French and Spanish characters has enabled me to show battles in which the Light Division weren't involved. I particularly enjoyed Colonel Bonnet's increasing exasperation with the French campaign. I'm fairly sure he wasn't the only one.

There are many accounts of the various battles and a lot of them are contradictory. For the assault on San Sebastian, I've combined a number of sources and tried to slot Michael O'Reilly's story into the overall attack in a way that might have made some sense. Please refer to the bibliography on my website at www.lynnbryant.co.uk for details of the sources I've used. As always, I apologise if at any stage I've stolen the thunder of men who fought and died at the time in order to give my fictional heroes something to do. I try to do that as little as possible.

The aftermath of San Sebastian is an interesting conundrum. Before I began researching this book I thought I was going to be in for another painful account of army misbehaviour similar to Badajoz and Castro Urdiales. Once I began to read about it, I realised it was not that simple. It's clear that there was a level of looting, violence and rape in San Sebastian after the storming on 31st August 1813. However the degree of it is uncertain. The Spanish claimed an appalling level of misbehaviour, but it seems clear they were hoping for compensation. Some British sources written after the event seem to back up their claims but many others, though agreeing there were some incidents, seem to suggest that many of the civilians and most of the women and children had already left and that the worst damage that night was caused by fire. This was the result of the battle rather than arson.

Given the differing opinions of the night in question I've chosen to leave my account deliberately vague. While acknowledging that some Allied troops definitely behaved badly, I've concentrated on other aspects of this

322

campaign. I've already written detailed accounts in other books of what happened to civilians in Spain and Portugal during wartime. This time I've left the matter open.

There are also many accounts of the combat on the Bridge at Vera on the night of the 31st August. Once again I've looked at all of them and written my fictional account in a way that fits in with the story I want to tell. Whichever way you interpret the various accounts of that night, it's fairly clear that Major-General Skerrett blundered badly. What Wellington thought of the matter we don't know. If there was a rebuke it was never made public. Skerrett went home to deal with his family affairs and never returned to the Peninsula, which was the way Wellington preferred to deal with a problematic senior officer.

I love to weave my favourite anecdotes of any campaign into the narrative to bring a human touch to real historical characters. Andrew Barnard is the gift that keeps on giving. The story of him disguising himself as a rifleman so that he could volunteer at San Sebastian is entirely true. It's also true that the officers of the 95th Rifles held a dinner on the banks of the Bidassoa to celebrate the founding of their regiment. The French must have wondered what on earth was going on.

At the beginning of the Peninsular War Saga I had a very clear view of how I would divide up the books and the various campaigns right up until I reached the Pyrenees. This part of the war isn't as well covered in fiction as the earlier campaigns and I now know why. Writing a clear narrative through such a fractured campaign isn't easy. I didn't realise until I did my first edit of the book that it's no coincidence that Paul van Daan is unhappy about the fact that his brigade is all over the place. I know how he feels.

I'm glad we've got the Pyrenees out of the way and pleased with the way it's turned out. Book nine will pick up the story from the Battle of the Bidassoa and will probably take us through to the battle of the Nive in December 1813. The next Manxman book, meanwhile picks up the story of Hugh Kelly and Alfred Durrell as they join the squadron commanded by Sir Home Riggs Popham off the northern coast of Spain in 1812. I absolutely can't wait.

Once again I've included one of my free short stories as a bonus at the end of this book. *The Recruit* was written for St Patrick's Day last year and I've chosen it to accompany this book because *An Unattainable Stronghold* is very much about Michael O'Reilly and in it, he finally gives away a little more about the story of his early years. *The Recruit* is part of that story. I hope you enjoy it.

The Recruit

Ten Guineas Bounty

And a Crown to drink His Majesty's Health

Wanted, to complete the Companies of His Majesty's

One Hundred and Tenth Line Infantry

Commanded by Colonel Charles Dixon

A few high-spirited, handsome Young Men who wish to enter into high
pay, free quarters, good clothing and a number of other advantages to be
found in serving His Majesty, should make themselves known to
Lieutenant Longford or Lieutenant Wheeler at the Castle and Falcon on
Watergate Row North, in Chester

*Where they will meet with every attention and encouragement a soldier can
require*

N.B. The bringer of a good handsome recruit shall be liberally rewarded.

God Save the King

Ireland, June 1798

It was barely mid-morning, but the sun was already hot and a shimmering haze lay over the rebel camp at Carrigburn. The men took their ease, recovering from the fighting and marching of the past week. Many of them were also nursing hangovers from wine, ale and cider which they had either looted or been freely given by enthusiastic supporters.

Ciaran Donnelly had not been drunk on the previous evening, although after a restless night under the stars he wished he had. He was finding sleep difficult, and not just because he was not accustomed to resting on the hard ground with nothing but his cloak to cover him. Every night as darkness fell and the camp settled to sleep around him, Ciaran found himself lying awake with the events of the day, and the week, and the month, running riot through his exhausted brain. In daylight hours the need for action stilled his racing mind, but when he was quiet, the memories flooded back robbing him of much needed rest. Around him his fellow rebels slept peacefully and Ciaran envied them and wondered what was wrong with him.

He had no duties that morning. On the previous day, the new commander-in-chief of the rebel forces in Wexford had arrived in camp and was presumably taking time to get to know his officers and plan his next move. Ciaran did not know Bagenal Harvey personally, although he knew his reputation. Harvey had been imprisoned in Wexford Gaol before the armed rebellion by the United Irishmen had even begun and had only been released when the rebels triumphantly took Wexford Town. Listening to the men around him, Ciaran had learned that Harvey was a barrister, educated at Trinity College. He was said to be an honest, compassionate man, but had no military experience. Ciaran wondered how far honesty and compassion could take a man in this bloody conflict.

"Donnelly, are you sleeping or dead over there?"

Ciaran sat up, looking around him, and located the speaker. He was mounted on a bay mare; a stocky, square-featured man in his early twenties, his appearance unremarkable apart from long-lashed, luminous blue eyes. He was grinning.

"Get your horse. There's been an attack over at Old Ross, a troop of yeoman cavalry. One man dead, the other just rode into camp to bring the news. I'm away to speak to General Harvey about it. Come with me, you should meet him."

Ciaran got up and made his way between the lounging men to where his horse was tied up along with several others. Denis was a black gelding, a gift from Ciaran's parents when he had left home eighteen months earlier, to study

325

at Trinity in Dublin. Taking the horse with him had been a ridiculous thing to do, given the cost of stabling in the city and Ciaran often thought he had spent more on feeding the horse than on feeding himself, but he had never regretted it.

It had been the name of the horse which had brought him to the attention of Colonel Thomas Cloney. When Ciaran first joined the Wexford insurgents, Cloney had heard him speaking to his horse and hooted with laughter.

"Denis? Is that what you call him? Jesus, I was looking round for my old man there, it's his name as well." Cloney had come forward, running an experienced hand down the horse's smooth coat. "Not that my father is as good-looking as this beauty. Is he yours? How old? Does he ride as well as he looks?"

A shared passion for horses had proved a blessing for Ciaran, who knew nobody in camp. He had ridden from Dublin in the wake of a flurry of arrests, as the government at Dublin Castle decided it was time to deal with the rebellion in their midst. Informants had provided the names of the chief members of the United Irishmen in the capital and they had swept down in a series of raids, beginning with most of the leaders while they were gathered together at a meeting. From there, they moved through the city, collecting lesser individuals who were significant enough to make it onto the lists compiled by government informers.

Ciaran knew he was going to be on one of those lists. Raised a good Catholic, the son of a respectable schoolmaster, he had set his faith to one side at the suggestion of his patron, a Protestant landowner who had offered him a scholarship to study at Trinity. Ciaran had been dazzled by the prospect and tried to ignore his parents' sadness at his choice. He had reasoned that religion was something to be considered when he was older and that if he could obtain a degree and good connections in Dublin, he would be in a far better position to help his family and his people than if he took some low-paid position in Sligo.

Ciaran had not realised how much the necessary compromise would rankle. It made him an ideal candidate for a political movement which sought to free Catholics from the necessity of leaving their religion behind in order to make their way in the world. It also sought to set aside the differences between the two religions, numbering both eminent Protestants and Catholics among its leaders. Ciaran was easily drawn in and quickly found himself much in demand as a courier to take messages beyond Dublin. He spent weekends in muddy fields outside the city, drilling and training with muskets and pikes under the tuition of disaffected militia officers, and found to his surprise that he was very good at it. Weapons were in short supply, and so were qualified officers. Ciaran was quickly promoted to lead a company of men and enjoyed both the responsibility and the distant dream of overthrowing the restrictions of English rule and living under an Irish republic, even if that must be achieved with the help of a French invasion.

The movement in Dublin came crashing down with the first arrests in March, and Ciaran knew his time was running out fast. Several of his fellow students, known for their sympathy with the movement, slipped away quietly and went back to their families, hoping they would be seen as too insignificant to pursue. Ciaran had no such hopes; he was heavily involved. There would be letters and documents with his name on and, at some point, the authorities would get round to him. He had no intention of waiting for the knock on the door and even less intention of leading the authorities back to his family home in Sligo. His parents and his younger sister had no inkling of his involvement with the rebellion and Ciaran intended it to stay that way.

He had left Dublin under cover of darkness and rode through a land under martial law, where districts refusing to give up their arms might be given over to the reprisals of the troops. Ciaran knew that the severity of these reprisals would depend very much on the temper of the officer in charge of the district. Men like Sir Charles Asgill in Queen's County and Sir John Moore in the south, seemed able to restrain their troops from the worst excesses. Others would not try.

Ciaran found shelter with a rebel family in North Wexford and held his patience as best he could, hearing news of murder and torture and the burning of houses and farms on both sides of the conflict. The arrests of Harvey and the other Wexford leaders, and the massacre of captured rebels in the neighbouring county, finally pushed the people of Wexford into open rebellion. Ciaran joined the swelling ranks of the rebel army as it swept through the north of the county, attacking military and loyalist targets to steal arms. They lost ground at Ballyminaun Hill but gained victories at Oulart Hill, Enniscorthy, and finally Wexford Town. Ciaran was slightly shocked at their success, and sensed that he was not the only one.

Mounting up, Ciaran walked his horse over to join Cloney. "What happened with the yeomanry?" he asked, falling in beside the older man.

"Murdering bastards. I'm not sure if they were trying to reconnoitre our camp or if they were just on a looting spree, but they came across two unarmed locals on the road. They killed the man with the slower horse, the other rode straight here to warn us. Here, it's up this way."

"I didn't see you yesterday."

"No, I was away to see my father and my sisters. It's not far, and I thought I should see them, in case…"

Cloney broke off and Ciaran felt rush of guilt and misery at the thought of his own family. "I wish I could do the same."

"I'm sorry, Donnelly. Have you heard at all?"

"No, and I don't want to. As far as I know, it's peaceful there. They've a good relationship with their landlord, he'll take care of them if he can. As long as I'm a good way off, they should be safe."

Cloney did not answer, and they rode in silence for a few minutes. A farmhouse came into view, with two men apparently doing sentry duty outside. Cloney dismounted, motioning for Ciaran to join him. They tied the two horses to an iron ring set into the side of the house for the purpose and entered.

Bagenal Harvey was seated at the head of a long table in the farmhouse kitchen. The room was crowded with men, most of whom Ciaran recognised from his weeks with the rebel army. Several of them nodded to him. At a big fireplace on the outside wall, a woman, possibly the farmer's wife, was stirring something savoury in a pot over the fire. The room was far too hot.

Harvey was a pleasantly spoken man in his thirties with a worried expression. Cloney had confided that he was not convinced that Harvey had really wanted this command, but he had accepted it when offered and seemed to be doing his best to bring the wilder elements under control and to extend at least some protection to local loyalist families who lived in terror of rebel reprisals. He listened to Cloney's story without interruption, then looked around the room at his officers.

"I think we're in agreement that we must take action, gentlemen."

"Of course, sir. It's shocking."

There was a murmur of indignant assent. Ciaran, with only an observer's part to play, thought there was also a sense of discomfort. As he thought it, Ciaran saw Cloney look over at him. To his surprise, Cloney gave an unmistakeable wink.

"Who will you send, sir?" Cloney asked.

"We will need a strong party of horse. They can intercept these scoundrels on their way back. Captain Keogh, will you take command? Or perhaps you, Mr Donoghue? You both have experience of..."

"I'd rather not, sir," Donoghue said quickly. "We've no reliable information as to the numbers of these yeomanry and our horsemen are not yet reliably trained. It's one thing to command as part of an army, but to go out alone without proper intelligence..."

"Well, I'm not going," Keogh said decidedly. "I'd not trust that rebel rabble not to take off and plunder the neighbourhood. Best keep them here, and busy with the drink while we finish reorganising, and decide..."

"It's going to be difficult to reorganise any of them if they're half-sprung all the time," Cloney said, echoing Ciaran's thought. "General Harvey, if you'll trust me..."

"I was just going to suggest it," Harvey said, apparently completely ignoring the outrageous disregard for military discipline displayed by two of his officers. "Select fifty of the best horsemen, Colonel Cloney. And perhaps another officer."

"With your leave, General, I'd like to take my good friend Mr Donnelly. May I introduce him? He's from Sligo but was a student in Dublin and had to make himself scarce when the arrests began. He fought beside me on the advance to Wexford and is an excellent horseman and a brave man in a fight."

Harvey gave his sweet, slightly abstracted smile. "I am happy to meet you, Mr Donnelly, and thankful for your courage and dedication. I hope you will continue to act as Colonel Cloney's lieutenant."

"Have I been promoted?" Ciaran enquired of his friend, as they left the farmhouse.

"I'm thinking you might have, if you want the job. I've become used to a reliable man beside me, but it's good to make it official. Come on, I want to catch these bastards before they get back to Ross."

It proved an exhilarating, but ultimately pointless, expedition. They rode fast, intent on their prey, but it was too easy for the yeomanry, returning with whatever plunder they had acquired, to see fifty horsemen descending from Carrigburn Hill. Both sides spotted each other at the same time and each troop paused in a moment of uncertainty.

Cloney broke the impasse, standing up in his stirrups with a triumphant yell which Ciaran suspected did not feature in any army training manual. He touched his heels to Denis' flanks and set him to a gallop, pulling up beside Cloney who was careering down the hill like a madman. Behind them, Ciaran could hear the thundering of fifty sets of hooves, the jangling of harness and the occasional whoop of excitement as the rebels began to pull closer to their quarry.

The yeomanry galloped ahead, racing over the crossroads of Old Ross towards the town of New Ross, and sanctuary. Ciaran found himself caught up in the thrill of the chase but, as the town walls came into view, common sense reasserted itself. He had never been to New Ross and did not know anything about the strength of its defences, but he could see several towers and an imposing wall joining them. He glanced over towards Cloney, who had pulled a little ahead of him. Cloney's eyes were fixed on the retreating cavalry and his expression told Ciaran that he had no intention of pulling back. Ciaran looked at the walls and found himself mentally placing musket men along the ramparts. There was room for a good few. He had no idea if they had artillery. He took a deep breath and yelled.

"Colonel Cloney, we need to pull back. We can't get within musket range of the town."

Cloney did not pull up or look around. Ciaran could not decide if the man had not heard him or was ignoring him. They were getting closer and the yeomanry had almost reached one of the town gates. Ciaran glanced behind him. Not one of the horsemen appeared to have realised that they were charging into potential disaster and Ciaran felt suddenly cold with fear. He had only moments to make his decision.

Ciaran tightened his hands and pulled back on the reins. Denis pulled up immediately, without rearing or making any kind of fuss. Two of the following horsemen had to veer sharply to one side to avoid crashing into him. Ciaran stood up in the saddle, snatched off his hat and waved it in huge circles in the air, yelling like a madman.

"Halt! Pull back. Cavalry halt and turn about!"

He thought for a long agonising minute that nobody was hearing him, then he realised that the men behind him were slowing and stopping, dragging back their sweating horses into a rough line. Those few who had passed him continued their headlong rush towards the town. Ciaran said something vulgar, took a deep breath and yelled again.

"Thomas! For the love of Christ, get yourself back here!"

Cloney looked around, realising for the first time that most of his men had pulled up. He looked over his shoulder then bellowed an order, turned his horse in a wide arc, and began to gallop back towards Ciaran. The rest of his men followed, thundering out of range of the town walls. As they drew closer to Ciaran, a musket crashed from the defenders, the shot falling harmlessly short. Cloney pulled up in front of Ciaran, the blue eyes steady on his. Ciaran took a deep breath and waited.

"Mother of God, Donnelly, I'm glad I'd the wit to bring you with me. I got bit carried away there, don't you think?"

Ciaran let out his breath. "I think so, sir," he said.

Cloney studied him for a long moment. "We're both fairly new at this," he said in conversational tones. "Myself, I'm beginning to wonder if you're going to be better at it than I am. Come on, let's get them back. General Harvey is holding a meeting to discuss our next move and I'm hoping to be there."

***

General Harvey, after lengthy and often noisy discussion with his officers, decided on a dawn attack on the town of New Ross. Ciaran awoke with a hangover. It had probably been unwise to stay up so late eating and drinking, but the food was good, the wine plentiful and Ciaran was flattered to be included in the feasting as Cloney's lieutenant. Eighteen months as a student in Dublin had given him a good head for drinking, but as he attempted to rouse his men in the pre-dawn darkness and get them into some kind of order, he had a thumping headache and a dry mouth. He had a useful water bottle on a strap which he had looted from the army stores at Enniscorthy, and he drank it dry and refilled it several times over before the army was ready to march.

Ciaran wondered if the garrison lined up to defend New Ross had been able to hear the laughter and the music, and to smell the roasted meat from the camp on Carrigburn Hill. If they had, would they have been intimidated by the sheer numbers they must face the following day? Or would they be contemptuous of an army so ill-disciplined that it spent the night before battle in an orgy of feasting, drinking and dancing? Ciaran had a suspicion it might be the latter.

He had spent much of the evening with a young gentleman farmer by the name of Matthew Furlong, who acted as one of General Harvey's aides. Ciaran had not met Furlong properly before and found the man very likeable. He was from much the same background as Ciaran and they talked of crops and horses, alongside philosophy and the revolution in France. They also spoke, more candidly than Ciaran had managed with anybody else, about their experience so far of war.

"I'd never fought before this. I'd certainly never killed. Never really thought I would. All those meetings in Dublin, where they spoke of rising up and crushing the government troops, and I was thumping the table with the best of them. It's different somehow when you're at the safer end of a pike or a musket and the man you've just killed looks no older than you are."

Furlong gave a little smile. "How old are you, Donnelly?"

"Nineteen. Almost twenty. You?"

330

"Twenty-three. It's the same for most of us. We weren't soldiers before this. Some had joined the militia or the yeomanry, but the rest are just farmers or farriers or over-educated students of classics…"

Ciaran aimed a mock punch at him, and Furlong ducked, laughing. "Sorry. I'm not laughing at what you feel, Donnelly. It's good that you feel it. I do myself. It's men like us – and like Cloney and Harvey – who can make something out of this mess if we win. The rest of them would just slaughter the Protestants – or the Catholics – and get drunk to celebrate."

"That's something else I'm struggling with," Ciaran admitted. "The reprisals. Christ aid me, I know what they've done to our people over the years. But I watched them shoot twenty unarmed loyalist prisoners last month, with the bodies thrown into the river. It sickened me."

"And the unarmed United Irishmen they slaughtered at Dunlavin Green and Carnew?"

"That sickened me too."

"I feel the same way," Furlong said. "There are some of us that will have none of it, Donnelly."

"Are there enough of us to stop these men going mad if they get into New Ross tomorrow morning? It's well known what they did in Wexford."

"I hope so, lad. Though from what I've been told, you'd be hard put to know if it's Protestants or Catholics you're more worried about."

"I'm Catholic," Ciaran said. He realised it was a long time since he had said the words. "But if they're saying I'm the man who abandoned his religion for gain, and the chance of a scholarship to Trinity, they'd be right. Though it wasn't just for that."

There was a long silence, then Furlong said:

"What's her name?"

Ciaran looked up sharply, but he could see only sympathy in the other man's eyes. "Her name is Sinead, and it's over. It should never have begun. Stupid to think I could turn myself into something I'm not. Her parents would never have agreed, no matter how well I did and what I made of myself."

"That's hard. Is she back in Sligo?"

"It's where her home is, but the last I saw her she was in Dublin, staying with her uncle's family while they look for a good Protestant gentleman for her to marry. I went to see her before I left. She hates me."

"She probably doesn't, Donnelly."

"Oh, I think she does. Her father was my patron. He'd no son of his own, and he's known me since childhood. He offered to pay for my education and help me find a position afterwards. He's a generous man. A good man."

"But your religion was the price?"

"He didn't insist on it, but it made no sense to go unless I started attending Anglican services. They'll let us study there now, but we can't be elected Scholars or Fellows or be made a professor. More to the point, most of the positions I could apply for afterwards are open only to Anglicans. I was ambitious. And I thought if I did what he clearly wanted, if I pleased him enough,

331

he might consider a marriage with Sinead in a few years. She wanted it too, we talked it through many times. She said she'd wait for me, refuse any other offers. She argued that one church was much the same as another and that God didn't care. But it turned out that I cared. I hated myself for it. I disappointed my parents by turning away from the church in search of personal gain and now I've betrayed my patron in turning my coat again. I'm ashamed of it."

"No wonder you were ripe for rebellion, boy. Here, have another drink. General Harvey is coming this way."

Harvey appeared to be completely sober. "Furlong, Donnelly. I'm looking for a volunteer for the morning. I've written a note to General Johnson asking for an early surrender to avoid the town being sacked."

"Do you think he'll listen, sir?" Furlong asked. He sounded surprised.

"I have no idea, Matthew. But I feel that I should try. I need a reliable man to ride in under a flag of truce tomorrow, before we attack."

"I'll do it," Ciaran said quickly, then realised Furlong had spoken at the same time. He looked at the other man and Furlong laughed.

"It'll only take one of us. Do you have a coin on you? I'll toss you for it."

***

As the first pale light of dawn showed over the waiting walls of New Ross, Ciaran heard a rustle of sound behind him, and then a hand clapped him on the shoulder. "Good morning to you, Donnelly. How's your head?"

Ciaran grinned. "Sore. How's yours, Furlong?"

"Hammering like the gods of thunder. No hard feelings, I hope?"

"None at all," Ciaran said cheerfully. "Last night, with the drink in me, it felt like a good idea to be riding out under a flag of truce to ask General Johnson to surrender. This morning, I have to tell you, it feels an awful lot safer to be hiding here amongst my men."

Matthew Furlong chuckled. "I can't tell if you're speaking the truth or just a gracious loser, Donnelly, but whichever it is, you're a good lad. Keep an eye on Cloney in the battle today, will you? He told me about the charge on the town yesterday, and how well you kept your head. We need a few men of sense among us today."

Ciaran watched him mount up and ride downhill towards the gates of New Ross. The flag was made from a white handkerchief tied to a sturdy stick, and it was reassuringly visible in the rapidly improving light. All the same, Ciaran wished his new friend had not chosen to approach the town at a gallop. The past few weeks trying to train and lead inexperienced men had taught Ciaran the value of allowing them time to react, and he supposed it was true for regular units as well. In Furlong's place, Ciaran would have walked his horse forward, giving the men of the garrison a chance to see him properly and plenty of time to wait for orders.

It was still only half light as Furlong approached the gate. Ciaran could see the white flag very clearly and there was no possibility that the guards on the gate could miss it. He found that he was holding his breath, waiting for the sound of a shouted challenge which would cause Furlong to slow down or stop, but none came, or if it did Ciaran did not hear it. What he heard, shockingly loud, was gunfire, not just one shot but the thundering of half a dozen muskets.

The horse reared up in terror and Furlong's body hit the ground. Ciaran was surprised that the horse was not injured too, but if it was it was not serious because the animal wheeled around and came galloping back up Corbet's Hill to the rebel lines, where half a dozen men ran forward to catch it. Ciaran did not move. His eyes were on Furlong's body, as two redcoats ran out from their post by the gate, bending over him. After a moment they straightened and walked away, back to their line. From here, Ciaran could not see the blood on Furlong's dark coat, but he knew it must be there. It had been minutes only since Furlong had put his hand on Ciaran's shoulder, and Ciaran could almost still feel it there, warm and steady with the promise of future friendship. He wanted very badly to be sick.

"The murdering bastards," Cloney breathed beside him. "Under a flag of truce. Poor Matthew."

"That could have been me," Ciaran said. He could hear the tremor in his voice. "I volunteered. We threw a coin for it, and he won. On the toss of a coin, I could be lying there dead."

Around him, he was suddenly aware of a rising sound, and he looked about him. The shocked silence which had followed Furlong's brutal death was rapidly turning into a clamour of angry voices. Ciaran glanced at Cloney.

"What do we do now?" he asked.

"We fight, laddie. They're not bloody surrendering, are they? But I'm not sure the General's plan is going to count for much now. This lot are going in whether we like it or not. We can choose to go with them or stay here and watch."

Ciaran knew he was right. Already the men were moving forward, the angry clamour rising to a roar of fury and no order was going to pull them back. Ciaran took a deep breath and tightened his grip on his looted musket, instinctively checking that the bayonet was properly fixed.

"Best lead from the front then, sir," he said, hoping that his voice was steady. Cloney gave a small, tight smile and clapped him on the shoulder, very much as Furlong had recently done.

"Good lad. Let's get moving."

***

Superficially New Ross seemed well defended, with high walls, nine towers and several strong gates, but local intelligence pointed to weaknesses. Some of the fortifications had been taken apart during the previous century and the walls were old and not built to withstand modern artillery. The gates had been widened to improve the flow of traffic, and the town was overshadowed by the high ground of Corbet's Hill. A modern, well-equipped army could probably have stormed New Ross relatively quickly, but Harvey did not command such an army.

What his army did have was reckless courage, fuelled by anger, and they swept down from the heights of Corbet's Hill roaring like wild animals and firing muskets and ancient blunderbusses towards the line of redcoats guarding the Three Bullet Gate. Harvey's original plan had been to attack the town from three sides at once. Eight hundred men under Captain John Kelly were ordered to concentrate on capturing Johnson's scattered outposts rather than attack the town itself.

Either Kelly had forgotten his orders or he was unable to control his men, because Ciaran could see him at the front of the attack on the Three Bullet Gate. Harvey had attempted to send a herd of panicking cattle ahead of the main advance, a tactic which had worked brilliantly at Enniscorthy. Here, the cows swerved away long before they reached the gate and took off into the countryside leaving the rebels, headed by Kelly and his men, to make a desperate assault on the gate.

It was terrifying. The attackers were under fire on both sides from flanking companies placed there for the purpose. Ahead, artillery fire raked the disordered ranks, cutting down men in swathes. Ciaran, who was in the second rank along with Cloney and his men, had never experienced an assault like this. Around him, those men who had accompanied Kelly in the first rush were seriously depleted, and Ciaran found himself scrambling over dead and dying men to reach the redcoats in the defensive trenches.

Ciaran wanted to run, but it was impossible, and he would probably have been cut down as he fled. Most of his men had discharged their firearms, if they had them, and it was too close for the defenders to use either muskets or artillery without risking their own men. He fought with the bayonet, while around him most of his men used pikes. Here, there was no organisation and no plan, only the desperate cut and thrust at each man ahead of him, dodging their bayonets, stabbing down ruthlessly, killing and maiming in order to avoid being killed or maimed. It was exhausting. Ciaran's arms and shoulders ached; there was blood on his clothing and the sickly metallic smell of it in his nostrils. He could almost taste it.

Close to the gate the smoke of musket and artillery fire still lingered in the air, choking him and making his eyes water. Ciaran stood during a brief respite in the action, blinking and trying to catch his breath. Around him his men were still pushing forward, driving on despite cruel losses. Suddenly and unexpectedly, Ciaran was proud of them. They had everything to lose, these men, and he knew very well that it was blind rage over a lifetime of oppression that was driving them, but they were brave, and they endured, and their courage revived him.

The rebels did not break. They pressed on, foot by agonising foot. The two defending flanking companies fell back, shocked at their inability to hold this disorganised rabble. Cloney's men captured the trenches and then drove

334

forward right up to the gate. The fighting was bloody, and nearby some of the buildings were already on fire, the air thick with eye-watering smoke.

Kelly's men were the first into the town, although Kelly himself had been shot in the thigh and had to be carried to the rear. His men surged on to storm the barracks near the gate. The building was poorly defended and, as Cloney and Ciaran led their men into the barrack yard, the last of the guards fled before them. Cloney made no attempt to give chase.

"We need arms. Muskets and ammunition. Spread out and start breaking down doors, there'll be a storeroom somewhere. Donnelly, take that side."

Ciaran obeyed. As he led his men along a row of doors, kicking or battering them down, he was aware that the yard was rapidly filling with smoke. Houses on both sides had been set alight, the thatched roofs burning fiercely. Ciaran shouted at the men to move faster. He had no wish to be caught anywhere near the barracks if the fire spread to a gunpowder store.

"Here. Over here," Cloney yelled. The men raced to the open stores, and four men stripped the shelves, handing out muskets and ammunition. Once armed, the men were off, running back out into the streets. Ciaran turned to follow them.

"Donnelly, here."

Ciaran turned to see Cloney holding out a pistol. He took it and turned it over in his hands.

"Do you know what you're doing with it?"

"Yes," Ciaran said, taking the ammunition. He had learned to shoot as a boy on the estate, following Sir James Howarth through the coverts for long hours. They were some of the happiest times of his childhood, along with the time spent in Howarth's excellent stables. Ciaran could remember wishing with a passion that he had been born the son of this kindly, intelligent man and then had immediately felt disloyal to his own parents.

He loaded the pistol quickly, putting the spare ammunition into his pocket, then shoved the weapon into his belt and took up his bayonet again. Outside, he and Cloney separated, searching through the smoky streets to find their men. Ciaran caught up with them on the approach to the town gaol, following Kelly's leaderless men towards the building. Keeping them in sight, Ciaran began to check some of the side streets for ambush.

There was an enormous crash from the gaol, startling his men into precipitate retreat. Ciaran went with them, making no attempt to stop their flight. He was under no illusion about how much control he had over these men today, and he was not prepared to stand firm against the enemy with nobody beside him. Turning to look at the end of the street, he realised that Kelly's men had been cut to pieces by grapeshot blasts as they approached the gaol. The survivors were fleeing back to the gate, pushing their way through Ciaran's men in their haste.

The abrupt retreat set off a panic in those still storming down from the hill. Looking back up to the remainder of the army who had waited for orders,

Ciaran could see some of them were breaking and he felt the beginnings of despair wash over him. They had already lost so many men. He looked around him, wondering if it was time to cut their losses and call a general retreat, and wondering also if any one of the rebel leaders had enough control over their men to make it happen. He could not see Harvey, but Cloney was there, trying to direct a chaotic group of musket men into a firing line. Ciaran thought, with sudden anger, that if they had been given proper weapons and training, these men had enough courage to defeat a whole army of redcoats. Then, unexpectedly through the noise of battle, he heard horses, the clink of bridles and the clattering of hooves over the cobbled road out of town.

Ciaran spun around and stared in horror. He could not be sure of numbers but there looked to be between thirty and forty cavalrymen riding out through the Three Bullet Gate and forming up in the open space as if preparing for a charge. Around Ciaran was a confused melée as some men continued their flight back up the hill, while others tried to find their companies and their leaders amidst the chaos. He could no longer see Cloney anywhere and wondered in sudden panic if he had been hit.

Ciaran had trained on the fields outside Dublin with three former militia officers who had joined the United Irishmen. They drilled with broom handles and tree branches, and at times Ciaran had thought it a waste of time. Instead, he had talked to the men, asking questions about battles and tactics and weapons. They had talked of cavalry attacks and the best way to stop them, and Ciaran knew that in this conflict so far, pikes had proved remarkably successful.

"To me!" he roared. "Pikemen, to me, they've cavalry. We can take them if we stand!"

To his astonishment, the men around him turned. Ciaran dropped his bayonet and stooped, snatching up a pike from a fallen man. He whirled to face the approaching horsemen, and felt a solid wall of men surround him, pikes pointing upwards ready to impale the cavalry.

"Come on, you bastards!" he yelled. "Let's see how you do against Irish pikemen!"

The first horseman died with a high-pitched scream, and the sound echoed round and round in Ciaran's head. The line of cavalry crashed into the pikemen and Ciaran thrust upwards and was astonished at how easy it was, with this weapon, to unseat a horseman. Some of the horses were wounded, though none fatally, and with no rider to urge them on, they turned and galloped back through the gate, or out into the countryside, causing further chaos among the rest of the charging cavalry. Ciaran's men were yelling in triumph and several of them broke ranks, ran forward and finished off those dragoons still alive on the ground. One of them was the commanding officer, and his loss broke the nerve of the remaining troopers. They wheeled and galloped back through the gate, and with an inhuman roar, Ciaran's men raced after them, all thought of retreat forgotten.

Ciaran paused to catch his breath. He surveyed the fallen horsemen, counting them in his head. There were twenty-eight. He realised he was crying, tears pouring down his face and tried to wipe them away with his sleeve. He felt his eyes sting as black dirt from the smoke and powder mingled with salt tears.

"Donnelly. Ciaran. Jesus Christ, are you all right?"

Ciaran found Thomas Cloney beside him, his face full of concern and he nodded, because he could not speak. Cloney grabbed a handful of Ciaran's filthy sleeve.

"I thought you were about to get yourself killed there, you stupid bastard," he said. "That was unbelievable. I could never have rallied them like that."

"I think you could, sir. They're brave men." The words steadied Ciaran. He took another deep breath. "They've gone back to the attack. We need to join them. Where's General Harvey?"

"He's over there, I'm not sure he's made it into the town yet. It's down to us, Donnelly. Can you do it?"

"Yes," Ciaran said. Suddenly he felt very calm and very sure. "Yes, I can do this."

Within the town walls it was chaos as, for the second time that day, the garrison were pushed back through the streets in a confused melée of cavalry, infantry and artillery. After them fled the townspeople, terrified of reprisals from the enraged rebels. They ran towards the quay and the bridge with Harvey's musketeers and pikemen chasing them down. Ciaran pushed himself to run faster, overtaking his men, shouting to them to leave the civilians alone. He was not sure whether they heard, understood or even cared.

Many of the houses had been set on fire and it spread quickly, sending billows of black smoke through the narrow lanes. Ciaran prayed that the houses were empty. In most of the town the garrison had fled leaving just a stubborn group of officers and men with artillery which protected the crossroads leading to the bridge.

Ciaran found himself abruptly with nobody to fight. He took the opportunity to rest for a moment, drinking from his water bottle. It was almost empty. Around him, the rebel soldiers seemed confused, as though they had no idea what to do next. The crash of guns suggested that General Johnson's men were continuing to guard their retreat, but there seemed to be no fighting at all within the town. Ciaran found a water pump and drank gratefully, tipping cold water over his head, then refilling his bottle.

"Donnelly? Jesus, I'm glad to see you're still alive."

Ciaran turned in relief at the sound of Cloney's voice to see him making his way across the small square. He was filthy and there was blood on his coat. Ciaran held out the water bottle and Cloney gulped it down.

"You too, sir. I'm not sure what's happening though. Have they retreated?"

"Most of them are across the river, and our lads don't seem so keen to charge those guns. I'm going back to find Harvey, we need orders. The men are exhausted, and a lot of them are breaking into the houses and looking for food and wine."

337

"If they don't get orders soon, they'll get drunk and fall asleep," Ciaran said.

"If I don't get orders soon, I'll be doing the same thing. Look, stay here. Find some food if you can and see if you can keep an eye on our men. I'll be back as quick as I can."

Ciaran waited. Eventually, he made his way to the stone steps leading up to what looked like a public building and sat down. Nearby, small groups of men wandered aimlessly, some of them with bottles in their hands. One of them, a man Ciaran knew from his own company, approached him and held out a piece of bread. Ciaran took it and thanked him. It seemed ridiculous to be sitting alone on the steps in the middle of a battle eating rye bread, but he was very hungry.

Somewhere, he could hear men singing. He wondered if they were drunk, and if it was really the right time to celebrate their victory, with no information about whether the garrison had wholly abandoned the town or if they were regrouping for another attack. He finished the bread, drank more water and was just getting to his feet with the intention of going to find Cloney, when he heard his name called, and the tone chilled him.

"Donnelly! Get moving, we need to get the men together. They're attacking. They're coming back over the bridge. We need to fight, man!"

Ciaran snatched up an abandoned bayonet and began to run in the direction of the singing. Men were beginning to appear from houses and cottages, many of them unsteady on their feet, though whether it was from exhaustion or drink he had no idea. He tried desperately to pull them together into a defensive line, yelling himself hoarse, but he could already hear the approaching troops, the hooves of the cavalry and the disciplined marching of infantry, as General Johnson mobilised his tired troops and drove them back into the town.

The rebels had nothing left to give. Cloney and Ciaran held those they could, and through the streets of New Ross other leaders did the same, but it was impossible. Some attempts were made to use the captured guns against Johnson's men, but there were no trained artillerymen among the rebels, and attempts to force prisoners to operate the guns proved a failure. Ciaran's pikemen fought on, making repeated charges back through the streets, but there were too few of them and they were too exhausted. Ciaran continued to exhort them, to urge them to stand, and then realised that he must either call a retreat or watch them die in front of him. He called it and stood watching as they poured back through the Three Bullet Gate. Some of them could barely stand, but they staggered on, back up the slope towards the camp on Corbet's Hill. Ciaran prayed that Johnson would not order an immediate attack, but he doubted the garrison had either the men or the ammunition to do so.

Well away from any stray musket ball fired from the walls, Ciaran retrieved his horse, thankful that the makeshift stable nearby had survived the fires, and watched the last of the rebels stagger away from New Ross. Beyond the last ditch, General Harvey, Thomas Cloney and a few other officers sat

338

mounted, watching the flames which were beginning to die down now. Ciaran walked his horse to join them.

"General Harvey. I'm glad you're safe, sir."

"You too, Donnelly." Harvey's voice was muffled, and Ciaran suspected he had been crying. "A terrible day. A terrible loss."

They rode in silence back towards the camp, the gentle light of early evening settling over the town and the hill. Part way there, Cloney's horse stumbled then stopped and began to graze. Ciaran reined in, worried that his friend had a concealed injury, then realised to his surprise that Cloney had fallen asleep in the saddle. As Harvey and the others plodded on, Ciaran reached for the bridle and gently shook Cloney awake.

"Come on, Thomas. Just a bit further and you can sleep."

"Not for long," Cloney said. "We'll need to get out of here early, before they have time to regroup, or get reinforced."

"Where to?"

"Back to Carrigburn to start with. After that, I don't know."

Cloney sounded depressed as well as exhausted and Ciaran knew how he felt. "Is it over, Thomas?"

"The day or the struggle?"

"I'm pretty sure the day is over," Ciaran said.

"Not for me, it isn't," Cloney said, and suddenly Ciaran realised that something more than the slaughter of the battle was troubling his friend.

"What's happened?"

"I have to speak to General Harvey. To tell him what's been done. I took the message, just before the final assault, and I couldn't tell him then. There wasn't the time, and I hadn't the stomach for it."

Ciaran felt an icy chill settling around his already bruised heart. "What's happened?" he asked again.

Cloney picked up his reins and began to walk his horse towards the camp and Ciaran drew Denis alongside.

"There's been murder done," Cloney said flatly. "Murder of innocents and done in our name. In Harvey's name. You know him, Ciaran. You've seen what he's like. This news, on top of what he's been through today…it's going to break him."

"Tell me." Ciaran felt sick but he needed to know. "You need to speak of it, Thomas."

Cloney said nothing for a moment. Ahead, there were flickering lights, which suggested that some of the exhausted men had managed to get fires lit around the camp. Ciaran waited, his heart beating fast.

"You'll know that before the battle, there were prisoners taken. Loyalists from the surrounding countryside. Protestants mostly, people who might have taken information to the garrison. A few Catholics as well, those loyal to the government. Around two hundred people, mostly men but some women. And children. They were being held in a barn at Scullabogue.

Harvey...General Harvey told me yesterday he'd hold them only until the day was won, then would send a message for their release."

"Go on."

"At some point during the day, messengers arrived from the battle. I've no idea who they were, they might even have been deserters. God knows we had enough of those today. They claimed that the garrison were butchering our wounded men and that the prisoners in the barn should be killed in retaliation. The Captain in charge said no at first, but eventually they convinced him it was an order. They took out thirty-five men and shot them on a lawn. The rest of them - the families - were locked in and the barn was set alight. They're all dead."

Ciaran pulled up and slid from Denis' back. He dropped the reins, not caring if the horse ran, and fell to his knees, vomiting by the side of the track. He was shivering violently though the evening air was mild. There was little food in him, but he continued to retch distressingly for some time.

Eventually it stopped. Ciaran got to his feet, wiping his mouth on his sleeve. He turned and realised that Cloney had dismounted and was standing looking at him, his face streaked with tears.

Ciaran stepped forward and Cloney hugged him hard. They remained together for a long time, finding friendship a comfort, in the midst of death and injustice and misery. Eventually, Cloney stirred and stepped back. He looked around. Both horses were grazing peacefully beside the ditch.

"They're too knackered to run away," Ciaran said.

"Are you joking me? The idle bastards have done nothing but eat looted hay in a cosy barn all day. Jesus, I wish I'd had the wit to stay with them."

"So do I, Thomas."

Cloney managed a smile. "My friends call me Tom, Ciaran, and I'd think by now you qualify."

They mounted up and continued up the path to the camp. "I'll come with you," Ciaran offered. "When you tell him."

"Thank you, I'd be glad of it. I don't think he'll continue in command, Ciaran, he never wanted it in the first place."

"Good."

Cloney shot him a surprised glance. "I thought you liked him."

"I do like him. But he shouldn't be doing this. He hasn't the stomach for it."

"Do you?"

"I think my stomach made its point very well just now, Tom. But I'm in it now. I'll stick with it, until it's over. Which might not be very long. Unless Wolfe Tone really has managed to convince the French to lend a hand. King George has an awful lot more men than we do, and they've trained for this. So far, we're fighting the militia and whatever troops they've got to hand, but a battalion of experienced soldiers is going to slaughter us where we stand. They're good at this."

"So are you."

Ciaran gave a tired smile. "I was lucky today."

Cloney shook his head. "That wasn't luck, boy; I know the difference. When it comes to organising the resistance and writing political speeches, I reckon I've got you beat. But when you stood out there, pulling those men together today...didn't you realise I was leaving it to you?"

Ciaran had not, and the idea shook him a little. "I'm not old enough," he said. "And I think the responsibility would scare the shit out of me."

"It might do thinking of it now, lad, but once you're in a fight, it's a different matter. I'm telling you, if you need to run and have nowhere to hide, you should join the army. You'd look all right in a red coat. Come on, let's pick up the pace. I want to get up to headquarters and break the news, get it over with. And there might be food. My heart is broken into twenty pieces right now, but I'm still bloody hungry."

**

The magistrate was late to arrive in the private parlour at the back of the Castle and Falcon, but made an impressive entrance. Lieutenant Johnny Wheeler, who had rushed his breakfast, decided it was easy for a man of Sir Thomas Woodbridge's girth to look impressive. Woodbridge was almost as wide as he was high, and Johnny managed not to laugh as he surveyed the chair which had been set out for him, which had wooden arms and was clearly not up to the job. Woodbridge said nothing, merely looked, and there was a further awkward delay as Sergeant Stewart sent a man out into the tap room to find a chair wide enough for the magistrate. That done, Woodbridge seated himself, looked over at Sergeant Stewart and nodded to indicate that he was ready to begin.

The swearing in of new recruits was not a lengthy process, but Johnny had seen it often enough during the past month to be heartily bored with it. The 110th infantry had been under orders to embark for India when it was discovered to be significantly under strength. Johnny had no idea why this had come as a surprise to Colonel Dixon, since most of the company officers had been grumbling about it for a year or more, but the matter was rapidly turning into a crisis as the date of departure approached.

Johnny had not wanted to join the recruiting party, and there was an enthusiastic volunteer in the person of Lieutenant Vincent Longford of the seventh company. Johnny thought that his enthusiasm had probably aroused the suspicions of his seniors. Longford was a lazy officer, notorious for finding ways to avoid hard work. Touring the local area staying in inns and public houses accompanied by a sergeant, a drummer and four enlisted men was far easier than the long hours of training and drilling in barracks which were being supervised by Major Johnstone, but Johnny was in no doubt which he would have preferred.

Captain Mason called Johnny into the mess room to inform him that he was to join Longford's party. He grinned sympathetically at Johnny's expression and placed a glass of wine in front of him.

"Cheer up, Mr Wheeler. It will only be for a few weeks."

"Yes, sir. But may I ask why? It isn't usual to send two officers. And even if they wanted to, can't Longford take one of his ensigns? Two lieutenants seems excessive."

"One of his ensigns can hardly be expected to keep an eye on him. Longford loves doing this, but some of his recruitment practices are a little unscrupulous and we've no wish to find half our new recruits released from their oaths because it can be proved that Longford tricked them into it."

Johnny thought privately that the wording of the recruitment poster could be considered a piece of trickery in itself, given what he knew of the pay and conditions of the men under his command, but he decided not to mention it. He sipped the wine and asked gloomily:

"Why me?"

"Major Johnstone asked for you specifically," Mason said. "I was annoyed, to be honest, I could do with you on the training ground this week. But it's a compliment, Wheeler. He trusts you to see it's done right. If we leave it up to Longford, he'll find himself a comfortable inn and stay there an extra week at the army's expense."

Johnny thought that Mason probably had a point. "Then why send Longford at all?"

"Longford can be unscrupulous. You, on the other hand, are at risk of being over-scrupulous; you'd never recruit anybody. Between the two of you, I think we'll reach our quota before we have to sail."

Johnny was not sure if he had just been complimented or reprimanded. "Thank you, sir. Where are we…?"

"You're going to Chester."

"Chester?" Johnny said in surprise. "Isn't that rather out of the way for us? We could try Leicester and possibly Nottingham, with the towns and villages in between. I'm sure…"

"You're going to Chester on the Colonel's orders, Mr Wheeler, because he wants to speed up the process, and as it happens, he has a friend in Chester who is a magistrate," Mason said grimly. Johnny's heart sank.

"Oh no."

"Oh yes."

"Do we know how many, sir?"

"About twenty, I believe."

"Oh sir, that's too many. Even if we split them between the companies, they're going to cause trouble. It's one thing to take one or two at a time from the courts, but that sounds as though they're emptying out their gaol into our ranks."

"I suspect they are. There is nothing we can do about it, however. I'm sorry, Wheeler, I know you'd rather be doing anything other than this. You have my sympathy, I loathe the process. Longford is rather good at it though. He enjoys the spectacle of parading through town with a drummer. Let him have his way and only intervene if he's doing something obviously illegal, or if he's spending the army's money on himself. Oh, and don't let him snaffle all the best

342

men for the seventh company. They're only about ten men short, we need at least fifteen or so. If you two are doing the work, you'll get first pick. You know what we're looking for in the light company. Fast, agile and with a modicum of intelligence. And try not to allow half the pickpockets and highwaymen of Cheshire into my company, will you?"

"I'll do my best, sir."

The journey was not as bad as Johnny had feared. Despite his reservations, Johnny had to admit that Captain Mason was right about Vincent Longford. The man would do almost anything to avoid drill or training with his men, but given the opportunity to strut through a market town or a country fair to the sound of a beating drum, Longford was in his element. He could be surprisingly gracious to even the humblest of the potential recruits although once they joined, Johnny knew he was more likely to order a flogging than a offer a kind word. Longford was a harsh and unpredictable disciplinarian.

They had picked up eighteen men by the time they reached Chester, and Johnny only needed to intervene once, to remind Sergeant Stewart that while some magistrates would turn a blind eye to the common practice of making a man so drunk that he would swear to anything, others would call a halt to proceedings if the recruit appeared to be inebriated and wait for him to sober up before taking the oath. Longford did not attempt to intervene or contradict him, although Johnny was sure that if he had not been present, Longford would have happily signed up two men who could barely stand and taken a chance with the magistrate.

The weather remained fair into September, with some days as hot as midsummer. Johnny realised he was quite enjoying the break from routine. Longford was happy to take on the job of advertising their presence in the towns and villages, leaving it to Johnny to organise the paperwork, arrange the necessary medical examination that each recruit must pass and approach the local magistrate to oversee the taking of the oath. They stayed at inns and taverns along the way and although Johnny did not particularly like Longford, they got on well enough to enjoy a meal and a drink together. They were the same age and having managed to raise or borrow the funds for promotion to lieutenant, both found themselves looking at the faintly depressing prospect of not being able to progress further without money or a great deal of luck.

Johnny understood Longford's feelings, but after a week in his company was bored with his litany of complaints. Though he could not imagine how or when he would be able to obtain his captaincy, he preferred not to dwell on it. The army had been his life since he was seventeen and, at twenty-five, he had no desire to pursue any other profession. While Longford dreamed of finding a wealthy or influential patron to smooth his path, Johnny preferred to work hard and hope that at some point, somebody would recognise that intelligence and steady competence had as much value as noble connections.

Longford and Johnny called on Sir Thomas Woodbridge and accepted an invitation to dine. Woodbridge was clearly delighted with the prospect of a solution to the overcrowded city gaol and proudly informed his guests that he

343

had no less than twenty-five men from Chester and the surrounding area, who had declared themselves willing to don a red coat rather than face prison or transportation. Longford was at his most obsequious and Johnny cringed inwardly and hoped that at least some of the men would be pronounced unfit to serve by Dr Howland when he examined them. The custom of encouraging convicted felons to join the army was considerably less popular with serving officers than with serving magistrates.

Johnny studied the men who assembled in the parlour the following day, as Longford administered the oath which bound them to serve at his Majesty's pleasure. They ranged between a thin-faced cutpurse in his forties to a terrified boy who did not look older than fifteen, though he gave his age as seventeen. Only one of the prison recruits had been refused by the doctor on the grounds of a marked curvature of the spine. Most of these men looked skinny and underfed, but that was probably due to poor food in gaol and in many cases, the grinding poverty that had pushed them into criminality in the first place. Johnny had quizzed Dr Howland to ensure there were no signs of gaol fever. He had no wish to march back to barracks in Melton Mowbray with his new recruits dropping by the roadside.

With the swearing in completed, Johnny joined Longford and Dr Howland in the dining room, leaving Stewart and his men to get the new recruits settled in their temporary barracks. Over dinner, they discussed the time of their departure on the following day and the route to be taken on the way back. Longford suggested a slightly longer route, taking in the towns of Derby and Nottingham, and Johnny agreed. It was unusual for a recruiting party to fill its intended quota but if they were as successful as they had been in Leicester on the way out, Johnny thought they might do very well.

Johnny was awake early the following morning and, since they were not marching until noon and breakfast would not be for an hour or more, he dressed quietly so as not to wake Longford or Howland and went out into a world painted rosy by the first light of dawn. Strolling through quiet streets, he made his way down to the River Dee and stood watching the sun come up over the water. It was chilly this early, but with the promise of another lovely day, and Johnny lingered for a while. He knew he would miss days like this in the heat and dust of campaigning in India.

The inn had come to life by the time he returned, with a bustle of early departures in the stable yard and the clatter of pots and pans from the kitchen at the back of the building. Johnny stood for a moment watching a family party climbing into an elegant travelling carriage, piled high with luggage.

"Lieutenant Wheeler?"

Johnny turned to find the landlord calling him, framed in the open doorway of the kitchen.

"Sorry to disturb you, sir, it's just there's a man arrived asking about the recruiting officers. Mr Longford and the doctor aren't down yet, so I was going to direct him to the barn where the men are, but as you're here..."

"Another volunteer?"

"He didn't say, sir, but what else?"

Johnny sighed. "I'll speak to him. Where is he, Turner?"

"In the tap room, sir."

Johnny walked into the wood-panelled tap room. The man was seated at the bar with a tankard before him. Seen in profile, it was a face of considerable distinction. He was young, probably not much above twenty, with dark curly hair tied back neatly with a black ribbon. His clothing was dusty and travel stained, as though he had spent some time on the road, but Johnny observed that it was of far better quality than any of the other recruits. As Johnny studied him, the young man seemed to sense his regard and turned his head, revealing deep-set dark eyes. After a moment, he got up and bowed politely as Johnny approached.

"Lieutenant Wheeler of the 110th light company. I understand you're wishing to join the army."

"Aye, sir, I am. I'm hoping I'm not too late. The landlord said you're moving on today."

The voice was pleasant, with a musical lilt which was wholly and unmistakeably Irish. Johnny did not reply immediately. He looked again at the stained clothing, the stubble on the man's face and the dark, serious eyes and a warning bell clanged loudly in his head. Ireland was in turmoil, with the bloody uprising of the United Irishmen barely over. The army had its share of Irishmen, both officers and enlisted men, but Johnny was instinctively suspicious. This man was young, well-spoken and looked as though he had been sleeping rough on the road for days. Most of the Irish recruits in the 110th came either from the cities, where unemployment was high or from recruiting in Ireland itself, when a poor crop and a round of evictions made serving King George seem the only alternative to starvation. This man was cut from a different cloth.

Johnny studied him, troubled. It was his job to accept every willing recruit and he knew Longford would not hesitate. Johnny was already concerned about the collection of thieves, drunkards and vagrants they had signed up on the previous day and was trying to work out how best to divide them between the ten companies of the first battalion so that they could not easily influence each other. He had no wish to throw an Irish rebel fleeing for his life into such a dangerous mix.

"You've missed the swearing in, and we're marching out later today."

"I could go with you and be sworn in when it's possible."

"Which part of Ireland are you from?"

The Irishman was silent for a moment as if considering what it was safe to admit to. Then he seemed to make up his mind.

"I'm from Sligo sir, in the north-west, but I've been living in Dublin for a while."

"Why did you leave?"

This time the answer came more fluently as though the danger had passed. "Looking for work, sir."

345

Johnny felt a tug of sympathy. The younger man looked as though he had been on the road for a long time, probably with little to eat.

"Well we can give you breakfast. It's the least we can do, given that you've travelled to find us."

Unexpectedly the younger man smiled. "I didn't travel to find you, sir. As I said, I was travelling to find work, and I stumbled across you on the way. It seemed a good solution."

He reached into his pocket and drew out a crumpled sheet, which Johnny recognised as one of the posters or handbills they had distributed around taverns and ale houses in the district. It explained at least where the man had found out about the recruiting party.

"The army is a very hard life for a young man. Especially if you're not accustomed to hardship. You should give it some thought before taking that oath."

The Irishman laughed aloud and indicated the paper. "High pay, free quarters, good clothing and a number of other advantages. Are you telling me that's not true?"

Johnny could not help smiling. "It might be to a starving peasant, but I'm not convinced that's you."

The Irishman smoothed out the paper. "High-spirited, handsome young men. Don't I qualify, Lieutenant?"

Johnny did not speak for a long moment. Eventually, he said:

"Once you've eaten, get yourself over and speak to Sergeant Stewart. If you still want to, you can march with us until the next signing on. It may be a few days. You can change your mind at any time between now and then but if you're staying, you'll need to improve your attitude. If you speak to the other officers like this, you're going to end up at the wrong end of a flogging before the end of the month."

"I'm sorry, sir. I'll learn to do better."

"Good." Johnny studied him for a long moment. "Have you any experience of training or drilling? Or fighting?"

For the first time, the dark eyes did not meet his. The Irishman looked down at the paper which he still held. He crumpled it up again and put it back in his pocket, and Johnny was suddenly sure.

"Not really, sir. Apart from a few weeks when I thought I might join the militia. But I'm a quick learner."

"I'll just bet you are," Johnny said softly. "What's your name?"

The younger man looked up. There was just enough hesitation to convince Johnny that the name he was about to be given was not this man's real name and was possibly one he had thought up at a moment's notice.

"It's O'Reilly, sir. Michael O'Reilly."

By the Same Author

Printed in Great Britain
by Amazon

30622381R00195